W9-AWC-104

CHICKS UNRAVEL TIME

Women Journey Through Every Season of Doctor Who

Edited by Deborah Stanish & LM Myles

"Regeneration - Shaping the Road Ahead" © Barbara Hambly
"The Doctor's Balls" © Diana Gabaldon
"A Dance With Drashigs" © Emma Nichols
"No Competition" © Una McCormack
"Identity Crisis" © L.M. Myles
"The Still Point" © Anna Bratton
"For the Love of Tom" © Sarah Lotz
"Donna Noble Saves the Universe" © Martha Wells
"I'm From the TARDIS, and I'm Here to Help You: Barbara Wright and the Limits of Intervention" © Joan Frances Turner
"I Robot, You Sarah Jane: Sexual Politics in *Robot*" © Kaite Welsh
"Between Now and Now" © Juliet E. McKenna
"What Would Romana Do?" © Lara J. Scott
"The Women We Don't See" © K. Tempest Bradford
"The Ultimate Sixth" © Tansy Rayner Roberts
"Maids and Masters: The Distribution of Power in *Doctor Who* Series Three" © Courtney Stoker
"Robots, Orientalism and Yellowface: Minorities in the Fourteenth Season of *Doctor Who*" © Aliette de Bodard
"David Tennant's Bum" © Laura Mead
"Superficial Depth?: Spirituality in Season Eleven" © Caroline Symcox
"The Problem With Peri" © Jennifer Pelland
"All of Gallifrey's a Stage: The Doctor in Adolescence" © Teresa Jusino
"All the Way Out to the Stars" © Iona Sharma
"Build High for Happiness!" © Lynne M. Thomas
"Nimons are Forever" © Liz Barr
"Ace Through the Looking Glass" © Elisabeth Bolton-Gabrielsen
"Hey, You Got Science in My Fiction!" © Laura McCullough
"Seven to Doomsday: The Non-Domestication of Earthbound *Doctor Who* in Season Seven" © Mags L. Halliday
"The Sound's the Star" © Emily Kausalik
"Harking Back and Moving On" © Jenni Hughes
"Anything Goes" © Deborah Stanish
"How the Cold War Killed the Fifth Doctor" © Erica McGillivray
"Waiting for the Doctor: The Women of Series Five" © Seanan McGuire
"Timing Malfunction: Television Movie + the BBC Eighth Doctor Novels = A Respectable Series" © Kelly Hale
"Guten Tag, Hitler" © Rachel Swirsky
"Reversing Polarities: The Doctor, the Master and False Binaries in Season Eight" © Amal El-Mohtar

All rights reserved. No part of this book may be reproduced or transmitted in any form or by any means, electronic or mechanical, including photography, recording or any information storage and retrieval system, without express written permission from the publisher.

Published by Mad Norwegian Press (www.madnorwegian.com).
Edited by Deborah Stanish and L.M. Myles.
Editor-in-Chief: Lars Pearson.
Cover art by Katy Shuttleworth.
Design: Christa Dickson and Matt Dirkx.

ISBN: 978-1935234128. Printed in Illinois. First Printing: November 2012.

Also available from Mad Norwegian Press...

<u>The Geek Girl Chronicles</u>

Chicks Dig Time Lords: A Celebration of Doctor Who by the Women Who Love It, edited by Lynne M. Thomas and Tara O'Shea (Hugo Award winner, 2011)

Whedonistas: A Celebration of the Worlds of Joss Whedon by the Women Who Love Them, edited by Lynne M. Thomas and Deborah Stanish

Chicks Dig Comics: A Celebration of Comic Books by the Women Who Love Them, edited by Lynne M. Thomas and Sigrid Ellis

<u>Other Reference Guides / Essay Books / Critique Books</u>

Queers Dig Time Lords: A Celebration of Doctor Who by the LGBTQ Fans Who Love It, edited by Sigrid Ellis and Damian Taylor (forthcoming)

Space Helmet for a Cow: An Unlikely History of 50 Years of Doctor Who by Paul Kirkley (forthcoming)

Ahistory: An Unauthorized History of the Doctor Who Universe [3rd Edition] by Lance Parkin and Lars Pearson

Running Through Corridors: Rob and Toby's Marathon Watch of Doctor Who (Vol. 1: The 60s) by Robert Shearman and Toby Hadoke

Wanting to Believe: A Critical Guide to The X-Files, Millennium and The Lone Gunmen by Robert Shearman

Redeemed: The Unauthorized Guide to Angel (ebook only) by Lars Pearson and Christa Dickson

Dusted: The Unauthorized Guide to Buffy the Vampire Slayer by Lawrence Miles, Lars Pearson and Christa Dickson

<u>The About Time Series</u>

by Tat Wood and Lawrence Miles

About Time 1: The Unauthorized Guide to Doctor Who (Seasons 1 to 3)
About Time 2: The Unauthorized Guide to Doctor Who (Seasons 4 to 6)
About Time 3: The Unauthorized Guide to Doctor Who (Seasons 7 to 11) [2nd Edition now available]
About Time 4: The Unauthorized Guide to Doctor Who (Seasons 12 to 17)
About Time 5: The Unauthorized Guide to Doctor Who (Seasons 18 to 21)
About Time 6: The Unauthorized Guide to Doctor Who (Seasons 22 to 26, the TV Movie)
About Time 7: The Unauthorized Guide to Doctor Who (Series 1 to 2) (forthcoming)

This book is dedicated to Elisabeth Sladen, Caroline John, Mary Tamm and all the chicks who made (and make) Doctor Who fantastic.

Table of Contents

Introduction

Chicks Unravel Time takes it as a given that chicks dig Time Lords. We know women and girls watch and love *Doctor Who,* but in this volume, we set out to discover *why* and *how*. What delights, inspires, intrigues or even annoys us in *Doctor Who*? What ignites our enthusiasm, our love and our critical faculties? What is it about *Doctor Who* that *matters* to us? And, significantly, how do we filter *Doctor Who* through our female gaze?

To discuss this, we've gathered a diverse group of women from across the world to each take a fresh look at a season of *Doctor Who,* as filtered through their unique perspectives. We asked fans who first encountered the show post-2005 to talk about what aspects of the classic series appealed to them, we asked long-time fans to re-examine the stories of their youth, and we asked a global contributor list to bring their life experiences and world view to this very British show.

The result is an exciting and diverse collection of essays that reflect *Who* fandom in all its passion, creativity and complexity.

There are essays that delight in discussing favorite companions or Doctors; essays that wrap gender politics in witty commentary; essays that deliberate imperialism, Buddhist parables or the finer points of David Tennant's anatomy. We have scientists looking at fiction and fiction writers looking at science. We show why five, 20 or 50 years after they were first broadcast, the stories of *Doctor Who* can still engage us, and provoke reflection and discussion in a modern audience.

This volume journeys through *Doctor Who* in the most timey-wimey of fashions, foregoing a linear path and instead mirroring the viewing experiences of the vast majority of *Doctor Who* fans. This show has been around since 1963, but rare is the fan who can name *An Unearthly Child* as their first story. Most of us came to *Doctor Who,* whether as adults or children, somewhere in the middle of the classic series or much later with the 2005 reboot. Many of us in that latter group took a meandering road backwards, dipping into classic *Who* based on fellow fan recommendations, or perhaps finding an affinity with a particular Doctor or companion and following their story. This volume is very much like that experience: it is a proper wander through all of the seasons of *Doctor Who*. Although if you *are* a linear thinker, the essays are neatly labeled by season so you can begin with Season One and meet us at the end of Series Six. The choice is yours.

Chicks Unravel Time is *Doctor Who* through the eyes of female fans. Sometimes that path leads in the same direction as conventional fan wisdom, but more often there are fresh roads to follow and new ideas to explore. We hope you enjoy the journey as much as we have enjoyed gathering - and pulling apart - the threads of this amazing show.

Now let's go unravel time.

Regeneration - Shaping the Road Ahead

Barbara Hambly has been a fixture in the science fiction and mystery scenes for many years. Her newest vampire novel, *Blood Maidens* (Severn House), has recently appeared in the UK, and her historical whodunnit, *Ran Away*, continues the well-reviewed Benjamin January series. She also writes historical mysteries as Barbara Hamilton (*The Ninth Daughter* and its sequels). In addition - when she can - she writes short fiction about the further adventures of characters from her fantasy novels of the 80s and 90s, which can be purchased via download from barbarahambly.com.

If he was going to return from wherever he'd been, he had to come in swinging.

I've never been a great fan of reboots and sequels. I'd had a couple of stinging disappointments in shows that I'd lived for being "revived" years later, and books I'd waited years to see filmed turning out to be something I couldn't sit through (not to speak of films I'd loved being re-made into - let's just say films I *didn't* love).

If the Powers That Are are going to bollix up the original vision of something that badly, I'd rather they didn't do it at all. Let me keep it the way it is in my head. I had carefully stayed away from the 1996 *Doctor Who* TV movie and, having seen it much later, am glad that I did.

So it was with considerable trepidation that I rented that first disk of the 2005 *Doctor Who*, and settled down in front of the big-screen to see what "they" had done to it.

I watched all the episodes on the disk that night and ordered the season from Amazon - and advance-ordered the next season - before I went to bed.

The show was clearly in the hands of somebody who Got It.

All television, and pretty much all films, are a delicate balance of writing and chemistry, *Doctor Who* more than most. Rebooting the show meant understanding what it is that touches us about the exiled Time Lord. Understanding not only why we watch, but why we love as deeply as we do.

Getting the right person to be the Doctor was vital. To bring us back - to bring the story back - to bring *him* back - they had to get the right person for the Doctor. Without that, nothing would hold up.

But - as I think that 1996 TV movie clearly showed - without strong writing, they could cast even someone as wonderful as Paul McGann and still produce something that didn't work. The writing had to be spot-on. We have to see him doing what he does, and we have to believe, *Yes, this is him.*

To my mind, Christopher Eccleston is one of the best Doctors *ever,* a teeny-tiny nose (if such a phrase can be used in this context) behind my top favorite, Tom Baker. The writing of the character was perfect - Russell T Davies pegged that combination of wisdom, quiet courage and daffiness; the throwaway remarks about going down with the *Titanic* and shifting boxes at the Boston Tea Party; the calm willingness to let the Daleks kill him so that the human race might be saved. The quality of being an exiled god with a human soul who is also capable of blundering onto a night-club stage and asking innocently about stuff falling out of the sky during the London Blitz. ("Oh...")

Christopher Eccleston hit that characterization right on the money. For one thing, I absolutely had the sense that this person actually used to be Jon Pertwee and Tom Baker and the others - other than the superficial mannerisms, I could hear their voices delivering the lines just as well as his. His chemistry and physical presence, for me, carried the show. I was hooked. And I appreciated - and at the same time was hugely amused by - the about-face from the costume-y look of the previous couple of incarnations. The buzzed hair and the plain black non-outfit emphasized (at least to me) the return of the focus to story, character and relationships.

Not that the look of the show wasn't stunning. Yay for computer graphics! No more wobbly take-offs of interstellar vessels which had clearly begun their lives as studio microphones! No more planets that look like a rock quarry in Dorset! No more, "The world is being taken over by six guys in rubber suits with zippers up the back!" (My apologies to the noble race of the Zygons...) No more random dots of white light on a black paper background, or camera zoom-ins on giant clams to make the audience *think* the clams were attacking Our Heroes (using what for feet?).

Not that the production crews of previous seasons didn't do their level best with the funding that they had, and I've never had a problem with mentally editing in better-looking monsters. (Well, then again, there was the Peladon Monster...) Still...

But now! Galaxies, gas-clouds, suns burning up in holocausts of flame. Starships that took your breath away. Space vehicles crashing into Big Ben - and in a later episode somebody remembered to have Big Ben swathed in repair-scaffolding, which I considered a charming touch. Villains unzipping themselves from rubbery fat-people-suits, or existing as no more than - as Rose put it, uncharitably but accurately - a trampoline with lipstick.

But all the special effects in the world don't carry a weak story.

Rose. The beautiful Rose, the warrior child, whose relationship with the Doctor was the sheet-anchor not only of the season, but of the entire new direction of the show. (I won't even get into the marvelous casting of Billie Piper.)

The producers obviously no longer considered *Doctor Who* a children's show. They looked into grown-up themes, extrapolated the darker and more serious side of things that had been glossed over and taken for granted in earlier days, without losing the sense of wonder and silliness that is the good Doctor's magic.

The writing was faster-paced (thank God!), and the archaic serialized style of storytelling abandoned in favor of either single episodes or at most two-parters. The tighter, and far more intense, stories were for the most part beautifully written. A number of them that season - *Father's Day, The Unquiet Dead, The Empty Child* and *The End of the World* among them - work as independent science-fiction stories, completely apart from the series. (This was also something that re-appeared in later seasons.)

The writers dealt with the fact - from the beginning - that Rose is in love with the Doctor, and he with her. This theme was to return again and again in future seasons: what it actually means to be the Doctor's companion. (Well, we all knew Sarah Jane was in love with him, even back when they were running around dodging Daleks on Skaro.) And what it does to those who accept the invitation.

But, Rose had a life of her own, and that life wasn't lived in a vacuum. (We never saw Jo Grant's apartment, did we?) Rose already had a boyfriend, for one thing - the wonderful Mickey Smith, who loved her faithfully despite the fact that he knew jolly darn well that he was no competition for a Time Lord from Gallifrey. And who actually got pissed-off enough at the situation to take her to task about it. (Yay for Noel Clarke!)

Rose had a family. This was probably the most excellent innovation in the writing of the series, the thing that took it from serviceable adventures to resonances of deeper joy and a sense of genuine danger and loss. The Doctor had to get used to getting slapped by his companions' mums, and why not? His companions live in danger - something that he sometimes forgets. One of the things that I loved most about that season was the Doctor's relationship with Jackie Tyler, from the moment she came on to him at first sight ("There's a strange man in my bedroom... anything could happen..." "Uh - no."), to her plea to him, "Can you protect my daughter?" Jackie might be birdbrained, but she isn't stupid, and she and Mickey make up part of the stunning balance of that season, the alternation between delightfully comic and deadly serious. From the first time Jackie Tyler belts him, the Doctor is brought to the awareness that he's responsible *to* someone for the safety of these young ladies who he swans around the Universe with.

They don't always make it back home.

And when they do, they're not the same.

The writing that season was an introduction to the whole tone of the show from there on. Not just the stories, but how those stories were told. We were dealing with the whole spectrum: horror and tragedy, death and loss, time travel and ray-guns and the Doctor jitterbugging with Rose in the TARDIS console room. The Doctor is, after all, very much a Peter Pan character - and, as Wendy in the original Peter Pan learned to her sorrow, he sometimes forgets. Or the TARDIS goes wrong and a jaunt that was supposed to be for a couple of hours ends up with Rose's family not knowing where the hell she is or what happened to her when she disappears for nearly a year. (And poor Mickey gets tagged by the police as statistically the most likely suspect for murdering her. Talk about adding insult to injury!)

No wonder Jackie slapped him. I'd slap him, too.

For her part, Rose is a bit of a flirt. (Something she clearly gets from her Mum.) She's 19, she's traveling away from home for the first time, she loves the Doctor, but she has a soft spot for Adam Mitchell and she is dazzled - utterly swept off her feet - by Captain Jack Harkness. (Who wouldn't be?)

Captain Jack - and Mickey - come under the heading of something else I was very glad to see brought back: boy companions. William Hartnell and Patrick Troughton both had companion groups, male and female, like quasi-families. The guys were primarily along to do the rough-and-tumble stuff. (Can you really see Pat Troughton slugging it out with a Sontaran?) Troughton's primary companion - and one of the longest-running companions of them all - was one of my all-time favorites, the eighteenth century Scots Highlander Jamie McCrimmon. Jon

Pertwee - the most James Bondian Doctor in a very Bondian era - was competent (and delighted) to do his own rough-and-tumble, and not surprisingly on his watch there was no male companion, unless you count UNIT and the long-suffering Brigadier. Tom Baker had another of my favorite companions - the dim-wittedly engaging Harry Sullivan - and another of my favorite seasons was the one in which the TARDIS group was the Doctor, Harry and Sarah.

I never much liked Adric - through no fault of Matthew Waterhouse, who as far as I could tell was never given a lot to do - and circumstances prevented me from seeing a whole lot of Turlough. I suppose you could count Leela as an honorary boy in the testosterone department, but after Turlough, the Doctor seems to have stuck with the ladies for a long while.

And since Captain Jack is what is politely called tri-sexual - in that he'll try anything - the scenes of him flirting with the Doctor (and the Doctor flirting back) are pretty priceless. (To say nothing of the look on Rose's face when the Doctor mentions what humans do once they get out among the stars...)

But the rebooted series brought to the forefront the essential fact about the Doctor: that he's a loner. That he seeks companions because he craves companionship. He's a friendly soul who gets on with practically everybody (except Martha Jones' mother), but in truth, he is alone, and has been so for a long time.

In addition to what it actually means to be the Doctor's companion, the show explored - perhaps for the first time - what it means to the Doctor to have companions.

Eccleston played the Doctor as very alien. He isn't human. He works to save humanity, but forgets that Rose's boyfriend Mickey was probably killed by the Autons - forgets not once but twice. And that someone is going to have to tell Mickey's mother that her son is dead.

The key to the Doctor's relationship with his companions is the fact that he needs them to keep him human. To keep him from turning into what the Time Lords became - which was probably the reason that he ran away from Gallifrey in the first place.

Another theme surfaces in the second episode - the murder-mystery *The End of the World* - and recurs throughout the series thereafter: that somewhere between the time the Doctor kissed Grace Holloway goodby in San Francisco and the moment he grabbed Rose Tyler's hand in the basement of Hendrik's department store, Gallifrey was destroyed.

The Doctor is the last of the Time Lords. This is, in my opinion, a brilliant decision on the part of the show's producers, and lends a brooding and tragic quality to the Doctor that Eccleston - God bless him! - never overplayed. That he has lost everything - and it was, in some fashion, his doing that everyone he knew perished. He'd always had a curious relationship with the Time Lords - exile, fugitive, time agent, catspaw and President of the High Council - but Gallifrey was, after all, his home. In *The Empty Child*, Dr Constantine says to him, "Before the war, I was a father and a grandfather, and now I am neither," and the Doctor replies quietly, "I know the feeling." (Was Susan back on Gallifrey when it was destroyed? Were Leela and her children? Had Romana found her way back, and was she there?)

Another brilliant choice is a theme brought up in the opening episode - whenever the Doctor shows up on Earth, it's probably time to get under your desk and clasp your hands behind your neck. The Doctor as Protector is the flip-side of the coin of the Doctor as Stormcrow. He arrives just as trouble is about to start, and he generally gets little thanks for it after the carnage is done. This is something the original show occasionally dabbled in: that the Doctor is himself dangerous. The shadow of Gallifrey's destruction follows him. There is a sense that, in the intervening years, in addition to outrunning a *lot* of fireballs, he's learned things that he'd rather not know.

Maybe that's what Jackie sensed in him when she asked him, would he bring her daughter back safely?

As Clive (the charming nutter who has stalked the urban legend of "The Doctor - Blue Box" via Internet) says: "He has one constant companion... Death."

The mere fact that Clive has this massive collection of information about the Doctor, gleaned from the Internet, brings up the fact that Real World day-to-day technology has changed a lot since 1989. Our expectations as viewers are different. Things that were amazing in the 1960s (when Captain Kirk would glean *ooo's* and *aaah's* simply by calling the *Enterprise* on his cell phone) are very much, "Oh, that old thing," in 2005. So, of course the Internet is the first place Rose would go for information about the Doctor. Of course the Doctor uses a cell phone to communicate with his companions. The seamless way modern tech is incorporated into the stories was - and is - another mark of the show's good writing.

Not only does the Doctor give Rose a chip for her cell phone that allows her to talk to her mother from five billion AD - but Rose, in doing so, is brought to a screeching halt by the fact that from where she's standing, her mother has been dead for billions of years.

Time runs in strange, kinky pathways. One of the best episodes of the season - *Father's Day* - featured not a villain, but the inevitable phagocytes of the time-space continuum's immune system, set into motion by Rose's own desperate need to save the life of someone she loved. No villains, no heroes, but some of the most amazing writing I've seen on TV, about families and love and might-have-been's, and the stories we make up about the past.

That season also contains two on the short-list of my all-time favorite *Doctor Who* stories ever: the horrific, wonderful, zombies-in-the-Blitz tale *The Empty Child (and* Captain Jack!), and - because I'm a down-to-my-toes Dickens fan - *The Unquiet Dead*. Each of these tales, in turn, opened new avenues later pursued: Captain Jack and Torchwood, whose headquarters (140 years after *The Unquiet Dead*) ends up on the Cardiff Rift.

The Unquiet Dead likewise unpacked a sub-theme that I was delighted to see revisited in later seasons: the relationship of the Doctor with writers and artists. This happens roughly once per season: Shakespeare, Agatha Christie, Vincent van Gogh...

Other amazing things about that season:

• **New tech!** Yay for psychic paper, something the Doctor should have acquired a long time ago, if anybody had thought of it. Yay for Captain Jack's disintegrator gun, whose special features include a "rewind" function that will put the molecules from that square hole in the wall back the way they were, except that (as with a smartphone) those special features really eat up the battery. Yay for that little door Adam Mitchell got installed in his forehead. That was cool.

• **Old tech!** Love the new look of both the sonic screwdriver and the TARDIS, quirky and amazing as ever. The season continued the thread of the TARDIS' powers: powers of life, of energy, of regeneration and immortality.

• **New villains!** The obnoxious Slitheen hiding themselves in the rubbery bodies of fat people (note: one too many fart jokes, guys...), and an interesting opening to the recurring sub-theme of fatness, always treated with a combination of matter-of-factness and sensitivity that I find refreshing to say the least. The vile Cassandra and her pickety little mechanical spiders. The shadowy Gelth, demons masquerading as glowing angels, and the slug-like Jagrafess - who turns out to be just a sock-puppet for much older villains...

• **Old villains!** What a delight, to have the first would-be destroyer of the Earth be the third Doctor's old pal the Nestene Consciousness. Brought up-to-date with wonderful computer graphics, it was still for all intents and purposes a blob trapped in a fish tank and still trying to rule things through animate plastic dummies. The Daleks, spiffed up but still, thank goodness, resembling gigantic salt shakers with psychotic Nazis inside. Some things never change and never should.

• **A different sort of villain** was touched upon: the Doctor himself as villain, either by a well-meaning but ill-judged mistake (as in *The Long Game* and *Bad Wolf*, or driven by his own rage at the Daleks). This wasn't new. We'd seen it as far back, most notably, as Tom Baker's *The Face of Evil*, and a couple of times since, but the theme was darker and clearer now, and would be revisited to great effect in later seasons. And perhaps - and most wonderfully - the Doctor's oldest foe: human greed, human stupidity, human callousness. For every monster, there was the awareness that equal monstrousness lurks in the human head and human heart. Sometimes including his own.

• **New friends.** Besides the continuing characters of Rose's circle (including her wonderful Dad) and Captain Jack, the season introduced the Face of Boe - wise and nearly immortal - and Harriet Jones, future PM of the UK. I'm sorry they never did more with Harriet, who ended up being sort of thrown away in a later season. Not to mention one-shot guests, like the beautiful Jabe the Tree-Lady, and Simon Callow's amazing portrayal of Charles Dickens.

• **New places.** As I said before, yay for computer graphics! And because I love the *Doctor Who* historicals, I love the fact that the computer graphics weren't just to re-create space stations in orbit around the soon-to-be-destroyed ancient Earth. Beautiful recreations of Victorian Cardiff and London in the Blitz (did they borrow the background animation from the film *Mrs. Henderson Presents*, I wonder?). That first season never got very far away from Earth, and in fact dropped neatly back into the former story-pattern that alternated Outer Space/ Modern Earth/ Historical, but the production values gave promise of later settings in wonderful places to come.

• And the **excellence of the writing** pulled me along so swiftly that I barely noticed the background anyway until the second watching.

And I do re-watch episodes. For me they're mini-movies. Thus, one element introduced in this first season of the reboot bothered me at the time, and was later taken to much greater lengths. This was the season meta-arc. I understand that most television shows these days are structured around a meta-arc: everything directs the viewer to the season finale. I suppose it's a means of making sure you don't quit four episodes into the season. Continuity ties in many of the season's episodes pointed toward the two-part season finale: *Bad Wolf* and *The Parting of the Ways*. Personally, I find the presence of fragments of a greater story-arc distracting (and occasionally annoying).

Taken on the whole, however, that first season of the reboot - technically the show's twenty-seventh - was everything, and far beyond everything that I wanted or could have wanted it to be. It had to be seminal. My sense is that Russell T Davies knew that the Doctor had to come in swinging. That the show had to hook its audience from its opening moments, or it was in danger of fizzling, of being (like the eighth Doctor's brief tenure) a curiosity that didn't work.

The fact that it did work - through an astonishing combination of brilliant writing and Christopher Eccleston's portrayal of the character - puts Russell T Davies up there with Verity Lambert, Terry Nation, Robert Holmes, Philip Hinchcliffe and so many more who founded and shaped the original legend of this marvelous character. This manic and brooding, wonderful and dangerous, being whom we know as the Doctor.

The Doctor's Balls

Diana Gabaldon (it's pronounced "GAA-bull-dohn" - rhymes with "stone") is the author of the award-winning, #1 *NYT*-bestselling Outlander novels, described by *Salon* magazine as "the smartest historical sci-fi adventure-romance story ever written by a science Ph.D. with a background in scripting Scrooge McDuck comics." The adventure began in 1991 with the classic *Outlander* ("historical fiction with a Moebius twist"), and has continued through six more *New York Times*-bestselling novels (*Dragonfly in Amber, Voyager, Drums of Autumn, The Fiery Cross, A Breath of Snow and Ashes* and *An Echo in the Bone*), as well as *The Exile* (an *Outlander* graphic novel), several novels of a sub-series featuring Lord John Grey, and *The Scottish Prisoner* (half John and half Jamie). The series has twenty million copies in print worldwide. Gabaldon is presently working on the eighth novel in the main series. The title is *Written in My Own Heart's Blood*, and she thinks there should be an octopus on the cover.

I like men. Owing to my unorthodox choice of professions - starting with being the only female trombone-player in the high school marching band - all my close friends and most of my colleagues were men, until my early forties. Men are (usually) logical, direct and appealingly easy to deal with. They're also chemically insane. Under the influence of testosterone, they'll do things so jaw-droppingly idealistic, courageous and romantic that it's okay that this powerful substance also causes them to do things that are reckless, idiotic and terrifying.

It's no coincidence that "he's got balls" is the ultimate masculine compliment. (At least, I take it that way, when some man says it of me.) Neither is it a coincidence that testosterone-fueled behavior lies at the heart of the *Doctor Who* series. Men and women alike admire it; who can look away when some man risks his neck for something, especially something nominally noble?

I certainly couldn't.

I first encountered *Doctor Who* because our first baby wouldn't sleep - and the kid will be 30 any minute now. In fact, it was my husband who first made the Doctor's acquaintance. When he'd get up with the kid, he'd turn on the television and watch with her until she got sleepy. Back in the day, there wasn't much on at 4 am save screen-patterns, evangelists, and PBS re-runs - and what was re-running was often *Doctor Who.*

At the time, I was working two jobs and wasn't up for unseasonable television, but Doug had mentioned *Doctor Who* to me several times, and when we discovered that it was also televised on Sunday afternoons, we began watching it together as a family. It was the second Doctor's series, the Patrick Troughton years, and within a few shows, I'd discovered that the half-hour broadcast was exactly the right amount of time in which to do my nails.

A lot of the first stories I watched were understandably a blur, but when the multi-part *War Games* came on, I started to focus. This was in some part because of the presence of a particular character: a young Scotsman named Jamie McCrimmon, who appeared in his kilt. "Well, that's fetching," I thought, and began to pay closer attention.[1] Still, it wasn't until the young Scot said one word that I felt a sudden jolt.

I won't go into the rather convoluted plot, but in this particular scene, Jamie McCrimmon and Lady Jennifer, a WWI ambulance driver (hence demonstrably no one's delicate blossom) are somewhere with the TARDIS, but without the Doctor, who was presumably in considerable danger elsewhere/ when. Jamie declares that he must go rescue the Doctor, tells Lady Jennifer to wait there, and heads for the TARDIS - fol-

---

1 A very powerful and compelling image. A few years ago, one of my books won the Corine International Prize for Fiction, which was Very Cool, and I got to go to Germany to accept it - also Very Cool. While there, though, I was interviewed by everybody in the German press, from tabloids to the German equivalent of Vanity Fair. Toward the end of a very long week, I was talking to a nice gentleman from a literary journal, who told me he'd read my entire oeuvre. "Your narrative drive is tremendous!" he said. "Your images - just transcendental, and your characters are so three-D!"

"Yes, yes... go on," I thought.

But instead he paused and said, "There is just one thing - could you explain to me, what is the appeal of a man in a kilt?"

Well... I was Really Tired, or I might not have said it, but I looked at him for a moment and said, "Well, I suppose it's the idea that you could be up against a wall with him in a minute."

Three weeks later, at home, I got a packet of press-clippings from this junket, with that particular interview on top. The German publisher had put a sticky-note on it, reading: "I don't know what you told this man, but I think he is in love with you."

And really... a man who you know is running around with his dangly bits so immediately accessible is plainly a bold spirit, up for anything at the drop of a hat (or some more appropriate garment) and entirely willing to risk himself, body and soul. The English Government understood this very well; hence the DisKilting Act, passed after Culloden, which - as part of a program of cultural punishment and ethnic cleansing - forbade Highland men to wear the kilt or possess tartan.

lowed closely by Lady Jennifer. When he perceives that she plans to come, too, he insists that she must stay behind, ostensibly because someone needs to tell their other companions what's going on.

Lady Jennifer greets this piece of feeble persuasion with the scorn it deserves, demanding, "You just want me to stay behind because I'm a woman, isn't that right?"

To which our courageous young Scotsman (who is considerably shorter than Lady Jennifer) replies, "Well, no, I - that is... you... I... well... *yes*!"

Now, I found this demonstration of pig-headed male gallantry riveting. The entire philosophical background of the show has always assumed gender equality - much more remarkable 30 or 40 years ago than it is now. The Doctor routinely has/had both male and female companions, who care for and rescue each other - and the Doctor - with general disregard for physiology or twentieth-century gender roles. And Jamie McCrimmon, from the eighteenth century and a culture in which women were respected, but not considered men's physical equals (for the excellent reason that they aren't), appears for the most part to accept the notion that the women with whom he has to do on his travels through time are in fact his equals and treats them that way - until *now*.

When push comes to shove, and it's a matter of a woman taking on physical risk... he can't help it; he *has* to try to protect her, even though he accepts her as his intellectual and social equal.

While the kilt and culture of the Jamie McCrimmon character crystallize this attitude beautifully, it's one that pervades the entire show. While female companions do come to the rescue of the Doctor and/or the male companions, they don't usually do it in the neck-risking, jump-off-a-cliff, self-sacrificing manner that the men do. They tend to show up in the right place at the right time, or run to get help, whether of the physical or computer-based kind.

Conversely, the female companions not infrequently plead the cause of some helpless/hapless victim/civilization/etc. to the Doctor, urging him to abandon his immortal long-term perspective and *Help these people right now!* And he does. (Not much of a story if he didn't, mind.)

The show consequently walks a fine line between explicit acknowledgement of gender equality - and an unstated but obvious emphasis on that aspect of testosterone-fueled masculinity called "Protect and survive."[2]

---

2 One of my favorite Scottish bands is Runrig, who sometimes sing in Gaelic, and one

You see this particular type of... well, ballsy... behavior throughout the series, and while until quite recently the Doctor has been asexual toward his companions, that very male "protect and survive" (and do note the word order, there) instinct is and always has been at the heart of the show. Whether it's his companion, a hapless victim of intergalactic thuggery, the Queen, Earth or just possibly the whole universe (and a few parallel ones for good measure)... the Doctor is *there*, and willing to do what has to be done, regardless of the personal cost to himself.[3]

But it was that one-word speech by Frazer Hines (the actor playing Jamie McCrimmon)[4] that first focused my attention in a conscious way on this very instinctive visceral response (visceral to both sexes, but in different ways). It was in fact this one word - and the kilt - that led me to choose eighteenth century Scotland as the background to the historical novel I was planning to write for practice, and I gave the male protagonist of my story the name "Jamie" in compliment to the inspiration.

It's no wonder that the Doctor is universally popular. He's got balls.

---

of my favorite songs of theirs is "Protect and Survive." There are three (at least) versions of this available on YouTube. Highly recommended!

3 In the earlier seasons, you see it in the male companions, too (while the bad guys also have balls, they tend toward the idiotic/ reckless/ terrifying end of the spectrum). A few years ago, a fan made a video to Bonnie Tyler's "I Need a Hero," using a montage of the early Doctors and several of the male companions - including Jamie McCrimmon. Looking for it, I discovered a second video, this one with better production values - and featuring David Tennant's Doctor (he being the most highly sexualized of the Doctors, if you ask me) rather than the companions, though with a strong occasional backup from Mickey. www.youtube.com/ watch?v=2xxygjJn8qs

4 I wrote the book for practice, but Things Happened, and it was published. When it came out, I sent a copy to Frazer Hines, with a letter thanking him for the inspiration. Many years later, the BBC asked us to do a joint interview in Edinburgh for one of their radio segments, watching and responding to *The War Games* together. Terrific fun, and a great thrill to meet him!

A Dance with Drashigs

Emma Nichols managed to grow up an eager young nerd in the 1980s without ever seeing *Doctor Who*, an oversight she corrected with great enthusiasm once the new series arrived. After seven years in fandom, she's still terrible at picking favorites - name any Doctor or companion, and she'll explain at length why they're brilliant. These days, she's a science communicator at the University of Manchester, studying the science of wildfires. Her work has taken her to not-very-secret military bases and windswept moors and English villages with names like Devil's Causeway. She hasn't encountered an evil computer or hypnotic vicar yet, but she remains vigilant.

At any given moment in some corner of online *Doctor Who* fandom, two things are inevitably happening. Someone is wondering where they might find a Monoid knitting pattern or that epic Harry Sullivan/ River Song fanfic of their dreams, and a keen-as-mustard new series fan is posting "I want to give classic *Who* a try! Where should I start?"

The first of these, strange to say, is much easier to deal with. If it exists, fandom will find it. If it doesn't exist, someone will think "Monoids, you say? Now *that's* an idea..." and a month later the Eleven/ River shippers will be grumbling about how hard it is to find new stories among all this Harry stuff. Finding the perfect entry point for someone who's never seen pre-revival *Who* though, that's hard. This is because unless you take the endurance approach ("Start with *An Unearthly Child. No skipping.*"), there's no single right answer. Maybe our prospective new fan loves comedy and historicals, but can't stand Cybermen or unhappy endings; maybe she prefers multi-companion TARDIS teams but dislikes stories set on Earth. I've seen people argue at length that something continuity-heavy like *The Five Doctors* would put a newbie off forever, but I watched that story back in 2005, when Christopher Eccleston was the only Doctor I'd ever seen, and I loved it.

Let me quantify that: when Rose encountered an Auton in Henrick's basement, I had never seen an episode of *Doctor Who*. By the time she was crying on a Norwegian beach, I'd seen *every* episode of *Doctor Who*. And then there were the 70-ish eighth Doctor novels and dozens of Big

Finish audios... I suppose it's possible there could have been an even better gateway story for me than *The Five Doctors* - that if I'd seen *City of Death* or *The Mind Robber* first, I would have fallen even harder in love with *Doctor Who* - but that's an alarming prospect. As it is, my memories of 2005 / 2006 are a hazy mish-mash of Daleks and Autons and at least one talking cactus, all set to a glorious synthesiser soundtrack.

I can't speak for what's liable to make any other new fan love *Doctor Who,* but with 26 seasons worth of hindsight, I know exactly which stories would have hooked me and which ones would have driven me off forever - and I think you could do worse than to watch all of Season Ten in order. In terms of stories, that's *The Three Doctors, Carnival of Monsters, Frontier in Space, Planet of the Daleks* and *The Green Death.* That's 26 episodes, about the same length as a series of New *Who,* and they're all on DVD. You could (and I have) watch the whole thing over a wet weekend, curled on the sofa with plenty of tea and biscuits.

Tea and biscuits are mandatory when I watch the UNIT years. I'm sure this is exactly what puts some other fans off the era - my cosy and nice could very well be your smug and irritating - but I can pick any story from this period and be guaranteed it will feature at least one of the following: sinister goings-on in a picturesque village; epic use of science; extraordinary monsters; the Master being hypnotic and witty, possibly while in disguise; Jo Grant doing something brilliant (and, in the less delightful bit, usually getting no recognition for it); Benton just doing anything at all. If I'm very lucky, a Venusian martial art and a high-speed chase in an unlikely vehicle might show up too. Just typing that list makes me want to settle in and marathon every UNIT story *right now.*

If my squee sounds mocking, it really isn't. I unironically love these stories. They first aired a decade before I was born, but they still plug directly into the bit of my brain that's eight years old. And even though this era, with the Earth exile and the extended regular cast, is a bit different to *Doctor Who*'s usual fare (if there's such a thing as "usual" in a show spanning 50 years and 11-and-counting lead actors), the three things that most delight me in Season Ten are the things I love most about this show as a whole: science and scientists, the monsters, and the companions.

Science and Scientists ("E equals MC squared... yes, that's right")

On the subject of these stories making me emotionally eight, I'm childishly pleased by characters who are in some way like me. Back at the beginning of Season Eight, a man with a strong Northern Ireland accent (a regional accent in a UNIT story... you can already tell this doesn't end happily) got himself on the wrong side of the Master and was eaten by an inflatable chair. I've never been so proud of my country in my entire life.

That shining moment aside, my countrymen don't turn up much in *Doctor Who*. Luckily, I'm also a scientist, and if anything we're overrepresented in this show. There's the Doctor himself, for a start, and with his position as UNIT's scientific advisor we get to see him... well, he hangs around in his lab a lot. He drinks a lot of tea. Chats to Jo or the Brigadier. Occasionally investigates some mysterious happenstance. His lab has a bench and a sink and a few clunky pieces of kit, with no sign of the colored liquids bubbling in twisty glassware that usually indicate A Place Where Science Is Done. If you edited out the bits where a blob gets loose and starts transporting people to a parallel universe, you could show this on schools career days as a decent representation of the scientific working life.

And that's before you even get into the supporting characters. There are loads and loads of scientists on *Doctor Who*, running the spectrum from universe-saving heroes to "Nothing in ze world can stop me now!" supervillainy. Quite a few of these characters are women, which makes me simultaneously very happy indeed and disgruntled that I didn't see this show as a little girl; not to say that Donatello the ninja turtle wasn't a fine role model, but a woman scientist or two to look up to would have been nice.

One of my favorite incidental scientist characters in all *Who* turns up in *The Three Doctors*. Whether Dr Tyler is related to Rose and family is a question best left to fanfic; all we know about him is that he's a towering giant of science. I base this on two things: his moustache, which is full and magnificent and landed half a dozen screencaps of the man straight into my Great Facial Hair of Science picture folder; and his moment of profound wisdom when we find that he's survived being eaten by a special effect and is now in an antimatter universe. He muses out loud to himself - he may actually stroke his chin at the same time - "E equals M C squared... yes, that's right." If that isn't rock-solid proof of some real credentials, I don't know what is. I've taken to muttering it while looking wisely into the middle distance any time I want to look truly sciency.

The other important scientist in this season is Professor Cliff Jones, mushroom expert and future Mr Jo Grant. On paper, Cliff is a good chap: anti-pollution, pro-sustainable energy, and on my first viewing of *The*

Green Death, I assumed my antipathy towards him must be down to his high-handed treatment of Jo. It only dawned on me on a second watch that Stewart Bevan, who plays Cliff, was 25 years old when this was filmed. Cliff is younger than I am and he's not only a professor (when Dr Tyler is only a doctor! Jones doesn't even *have* a moustache!) but a Nobel Prize winner. For the record, the youngest Nobel laureate in history was 25. Cliff Jones is the Einstein of edible fungi. It's almost enough to make me grudgingly concede, once I've got over my professional sour grapes, that he's good enough for Jo, but more on that later.

For all *Doctor Who*'s great scientists, how the show deals with science itself is more of a mixed bag. Oh, there are obviously small mistakes, like the Doctor mispronouncing "chitinous," but if that sort of thing worked me up, I'd never watch TV or movies at all. What interests me is the difference between stories like *Carnival of Monsters*, where science is a handwave to get a fun story going (you could replace "aliens using technology outlawed by the Time Lords" with "wizards" and not change the plot), and the *Planet of the Daleks* types that try to do Hard Science. I don't know what it says about me that I was fine with invisible aliens and the lava-like "allotrope of ice," but harrumphed mightily at the slooow escape up the ventilation shaft. I was actually processing data on convection currents over hot plates when I watched this; I went so far as to grab a pen and paper to work out just how strong an updraft you'd need to lift four grown adults several hundred feet, then had to perform a nerd intervention on myself. It's possible I'm doing Terry Nation a great injustice and the science checks out, though I'd feel better if the Doctor's hair at least blew about a bit.

The point I was missing, of course, is that it's not just *for* me - *Doctor Who* has long been aware that its audience includes interested children as well as pedantic adults. Shouldn't I just be pleased that the Doctor saves the day with real science, even if it fudges the details? This was how I came to make my peace with *Planet*: it might be dull, it might be at least two episodes too long, it might be full of tedious Thals, but if even one kid saw this in 1972 and took away the lesson that they should damn well pay attention in science class because someday the knowledge that hot air rises might be the only thing that stands between them and an army of Daleks, then job well done, Mr Nation. Job well done.

Monsters

There's another reason I keep going back to the UNIT stories: they've got an excellent line in memorable monsters. I'm using "monsters" here as distinct from "villains," although the Daleks and the Cybermen arguably pull double duty on that most of the time. The Master is a villain (and I don't think he's ever more entertainingly villainous than in *Frontier in Space*, where he calls the Daleks "stupid tin pots" and brings a book in case his evil plans have a lull in the middle), but I wouldn't count him as a monster. Same thing with BOSS in *The Green Death*. As evil *Doctor Who* super-computers go, he's the best of an extensive bunch - affable, given to hypnotizing people, and prepared to hum his own dramatic background music - but if I can't imagine him advancing slowly on a doomed UNIT squadron while they futilely waste their bullets, then he's not a proper monster, and that's that.

Luckily, there are plenty of monsters that do meet my criteria in Season Ten, starting with Omega's gel guards. A tiny part of me wishes that one of the three Doctors of this story's title could be the tenth, because I'd like someone on screen to join me in exclaiming "oh, you are *beautiful*!" at the sight of them wobbling towards UNIT HQ like a terrible accident in a bubble-wrap factory. My notes for this scene read "bazooka-wielding soldiers face off against one-eyed monsters shooting fire from their stumpy claws." It's like someone went back in time and created this just to give me joy.

I've huffed about *Planet of the Daleks*, but I love the scene when the ice allotrope oozes over a mighty Dalek army, ten thousand strong, freezing them forever. It's clearly half a dozen toy Daleks and a bucket of water, but I admire an ambitious model shot. And anyway, that's part of the appeal of the classic monsters. I like the idea that, as a child, I could have played out these adventures at home with my action figures. "It looks like it's made from plasticine" makes no sense to me as a complaint - that's a selling point, surely?

I'm sure some intrepid 70s viewer recreated *The Green Death* at home with real maggots. That's the sort of childhood experience that would make an impression on me, and it might explain why this single-story monster seems to be so iconic. Before I'd seen an episode of *Doctor Who,* I knew of four monsters: Daleks, Cybermen, "those dummies who come alive and kill you" (thank goodness I didn't see that; hearing about it was enough to leave me nervously scuttling past shop windows for years) and the giant maggots. There's something about the sight of an underground cavern heaving with enormous larvae that seems to stick with people.

Most of the maggots don't get to do a lot beyond wiggle around, but they're oddly fun, especially when Benton is luring them to the car with a cry of "come and get some lovely din-dins." The maggots are definitely monsters, not villains. They aren't trying to take over the world. They were minding their own maggoty business when a chemical company controlled by an evil oscilloscope dropped a load of pollution on their heads. It's the B-movie trope of science going wrong and almost destroying us all, but I don't mind that when it's also science that saves the day, thanks to an implausibly youthful Nobel-prize-winning mushroom specialist. And how many TV shows can you say that about?

As great as the maggots and the Daleks and the gel guards are, the pinnacle of the season - in my humble opinion the pinnacle of *all Doctor Who ever*, monster-wise - comes, appropriately enough, in *Carnival of Monsters*. The Doctor and Jo are on a sailing ship, but it's in a time loop, and there's a sea monster, and they're really all on an alien planet in something called a miniscope, and the plot became irrelevant to me the moment the aforementioned sea monster turned up. For it is a drashig. It's a sort of snake/ dinosaur cross, with four little eyes that stick out of its head on stalks and a giant sock-puppet mouth filled with pointy teeth, and the cliffhanger to episode two features a whole swamp full of drashigs and nothing in this show has ever delighted me more. If Steven Moffat's looking to revive a classic monster... no, on second thoughts, the drashigs should be left alone. I don't care if it's silly to have an overwhelming nostalgia for something you'd never seen five years ago. They're my absolute favorite monster, in all their googly-eyed, razor-toothed, papier-mâché glory, and a CGI drashig would break my heart.

Josephine Grant, Space Adventurer

Before I watched a single Jo story, I'd heard plenty about her: "ditzy" if people had some affection for her, "stupid" if they didn't. It's even how she talks about herself in the otherwise lovely *Sarah Jane Adventures* story that reunites her with the Doctor. Most of the companions get this to some extent. Part of their job is to be the Watson to the Doctor's Sherlock Holmes, and never mind that Watson was a smart, brave war veteran; what people remember is that he wasn't as brilliant as the hero.[5]

Jo seems to get this more than the rest. I have to wonder whether people write her off because she's little and cute, all fluffy coats and Bambi eyes and *Play School*-presenter voice. Yes, she has moments of daftness that serve to set up a joke or explain part of the plot, but so do

5 Just to put this out there: Jo/ Watson is a crossover ship that needs to happen. I believe in you, fandom.

Benton and Yates and the Brig. Remember that scene where the Brigadier has to explain to Jo that "superluminal" means "faster than the speed of light"? No, because it was the other way around. That's in the first ten minutes of the first episode of this season, and Jo ratchets up the impressiveness from there. She's forever escaping from one cell or another (*Carnival of Monsters,* as with *Terror of the Autons* before it, reveals that she carries a skeleton key everywhere) to the point that by *Frontier in Space,* the Master's plans hinge on his belief that if left to her own devices in a prison cell, Jo can be relied upon to dig her way out with a spoon. *Which she does.* Later, he has a go at hypnotizing her. He fails, because after *Terror of the Autons,* Jo was determined he wouldn't manipulate her that way again and she learned how to stop it. A few mental blasts of "Mary Had a Little Lamb" from Jo and he backs off, defeated.

Frontier, incidentally, is a great story - world-building! Political intrigue! A drashig cameo! - but it's let down by a dull title. I hereby propose it be renamed *Josephine Grant, Space Adventurer* to better reflect its content.

Screaming and ankle-twisting get mentioned a lot in connection with classic companions. Jo does scream when a drashig bursts out of the swamp. But, who *wouldn't* scream? I'm firmly pro-drashig, and even I wouldn't like one to creep up on me. It makes it all the more impressive when Jo pulls herself together five minutes later and charges off to the sailing ship because "they must have rope somewhere." Plot intervenes before she can get very far, because the universe is simply not awesome enough to contain a scene of Jo Grant lassoing and riding a drashig, and she gets locked up. Naturally, she just rolls her eyes and escapes again.

Planet of the Daleks expands Jo's repertoire beyond mere escapology skills. In befriending Wester - the budget-saving invisible Spiridon - she comes close to winning the day through sheer force of niceness, but she also finds the time to blow up some Daleks with their own grenades. It's no wonder one of the Thals falls madly in love with her, leading to the single worst proposal any companion's ever had. "Let me take you away from all this" works as a romantic sentiment only if you're following it up with something, anything at all, that isn't "and we'll get a lovely little place together on Skaro." It's not obvious that this is the very last straw pushing Jo out of the TARDIS, but by the beginning of *The Green Death,* she's learned about a Welsh environmentalist commune and the writing's on the wall for her time as a companion.

In my year-long marathon of all of TV *Doctor Who,* I jumped all over the place: a Four story here, a bit of Seven there, and zooming back to the early 60s for some Sensorite action after that. When I came back to Season Ten and watched it in order, it surprised me to see what a cohesive arc builds throughout all 26 episodes towards Jo's decision to leave. As determined as the Doctor is to ignore subtle hints like "take me back to Earth *right now*," it's obvious the TARDIS life isn't for Jo. She adores the Doctor, so she'll humor him and let him show off, but it's not how she wants to spend her life. Her monologue in *Frontier* is a ruse to cover the Doctor's escape attempt, but she's being truthful when she says she's a dogsbody at UNIT with nothing to do but filing and tea-making. We saw that in her very first scene of the season - lugging files around, a peeved look on her face, while the men enjoy their tea and chat about alien invasions.

The Doctor really has no clue about any of this until she announces she's leaving. The news crushes him. "I'm offering you the universe" is his last try at getting her to stay; he says he can bring her back at the same moment she left. It's not only a promise he probably can't keep, it's one that misses the point by a mile. *Jo's* time would pass by just as quickly on the TARDIS as out of it, and she wants to spend that time making a difference on her own planet.

Jo tends to be grouped with the companions who left to get married, which doesn't seem quite right. By the middle of episode one, she's already left the Doctor for good without having met her future husband yet. Despite the knowing "oh ho, this is about a chap, is it?" look the Brigadier gives her when she announces she's resigning to join Cliff Jones' group, Jo has no inkling in that direction - possibly because she assumes it would be wildly unlikely for someone with Jones' credentials to be anywhere near her own age. When they do meet, and Cliff turns out to be a stroppy, long-haired 20-something, he and Jo fall for each other, despite or because of an awkward first meeting that has Jo stumbling around the lab wrecking his experiments. It's not her finest hour, but a few episodes down the line, it turns out to be a plot contrivance that defeats the maggots and saves the world, so I'm prepared to let it go.

It makes sense that Jo would end up with someone who reminds her of a younger, human version of the Doctor, especially if she's mentally comparing Cliff to the last man who tried to woo her. Patronising Cliff may be, but he doesn't want to whisk her away to his Dalek-infested homeworld, and that counts for something. Before Cliff even proposes, Jo quietly calls in a family favor to ensure grant funding for his expedition group. I don't know if this seems like a grand romantic gesture to non-scientists, or to anyone at all who isn't me, but I downright *swooned.*

I knew before I first saw it that Jo's final scene is held up as one of the great emotional moments of *Doctor Who.* Sure enough, the first time I saw it, I might have felt a bit of a lump in my throat as the Doctor slips out of the party and away into the dark. The second time, though... the second time, I found myself crying my eyes out, because Jo and the Doctor have been reunited on screen now, in *The Sarah Jane Adventures* story *Death of the Doctor,* so we know that Jo had children and grandchildren and a thousand passionate causes and an incredible life. But we also know that despite her "don't go too far away, will you?" comment to him, that one wistful backwards glance at her engagement party is the last time she ever saw *her* Doctor.

This is why classic *Doctor Who* is worth not only watching but rewatching - because this show can delight me and reduce me to a teary wreck and make me wish I was eight so I could have a go at making my own monsters, and it can often do these things all at the same time. And because as long as people are still making new stories, everything that came before can always be thrown into a new context, and everything new can be looked at in the light of what came before. Forty-nine years and counting, and if you haven't seen it yet, don't worry about where to start. Anywhere you pick will have the Doctor saving the universe and his companions being brilliant, and probably some scientists trying to save or destroy the world and some monsters being beautifully monstrous.

Meanwhile, my DVD shelves have been catching my eye. There's over a year to go till *Doctor Who* hits the half-century. That seems like enough time for a full rewatch, Hartnell to Smith, starting with *An Unearthly Child* and with no skipping.

I'm looking forward to the drashigs already.

No Competition

Una McCormack has written two *Doctor Who* novels featuring the eleventh Doctor for BBC Books: *The King's Dragon* and *The Way Through the Woods*. Her *Doctor Who* short fiction has appeared in *Doctor Who Magazine* and the Big Finish anthology *The Quality of Leadership*. She also writes *Star Trek* novels. She lives in Cambridge with her partner, Matthew, and their Dalek, Jefferson. She teaches creative writing and watches quite a lot of telly.

Really, I wanted to start this piece by asserting that Season Twenty-Six is far and away the best season of *Doctor Who*, old and new, no competition.

I'm aware that this sort of statement causes severe ructions on the Internet, the kind from which battlefield survivors emerge ashen-faced and traumatised, like the Ancient One shambling forth from his rotting world to face a dead future. I'm aware that even though this is a book and not the Internet, I'm easily found online. And even though I happen to think it's true - that Season Twenty-Six contains a magic combination of complex storytelling and satisfactory realization that, to my mind, is never *quite* matched before or since - such an assertion sadly runs entirely contrary to the theme of my piece. Because if there's one theme that holds these four stories together, it's the case for togetherness, even in the most hostile circumstances. The case for cooperation against competition.

If We Fight Like Animals, We'll Die Like Animals

The Doctor states it plainly enough in *Survival*: "If we fight like animals, we'll die like animals!" The logic of competition results in death. Morgaine will pursue Arthur across dimensions, and will sacrifice their son to kill him. Light will extinguish all life on Earth rather than have his work invalidated. The Master will fight the Doctor until one of them is dead. Fenric's age-long contest with the Doctor threatens to consume everything (although it is the corruption of Commander Millington that really interests me in this story; he's looking towards the next war before this one has ended, because war has become habit rather than reasoned response to threat). It seems we are to understand that bombing Dresden is the first step on a road that inevitably leads to the deployment of ultimate weapons: a toxin concealed in a machine that will poison Moscow; the Bomb (never far from one's mind during the 1980s, however much one tried not to think about it); the Destroyer of worlds. Even the Brigadier's stand against the Destroyer is seen as problematic - the war ends because the Doctor reasons with Morgaine and appeals to her sense of honor.

What drives the numerous conflicts in this season? What is the compulsion to compete? Why do the Doctor's "enemies" fight? Morgaine and Arthur represent the battle of the sexes that will end in the murder of their children. Light represents totalitarian ideology; the idea that will kill rather than be proven wrong. Fenric is malice taken to its ultimate limit, the all-consuming hatred that is the logic of Nazism and that corrupts Millington. And the Master represents the traditional enemy: the ones that we fight because we have always fought them, for so long that we have almost forgotten why. Until we decide to stop.

My Allegiance is to This Planet

There are powerful forces in the universe, then. Some will bring deadly lovers' tiffs across dimensions, deploying knights armed with techno-swords. Others will take humans apart to see how they work and become xenocidal when their ~~episode guides~~ catalogues become out of date. Others set fire to chess sets or send in the cats. So what protections do we have against them?

Not individualism, this season repeatedly suggests. This means isolation, and isolation means that you're easier to pick off. Those fugitives trapped on the planet of the Cheetah People who break away from the band and try to make it on their own are the ones that get quickly killed, and it's when Ace and Shou Yuing quarrel within their chalk circle that they come closest to being destroyed. It is connection with others that will save you. Solidarity, comrades.

The four stories present various potential sources of connection. Friendship helps in *Survival*. The pawns unite at the end of *The Curse of Fenric*, and Captain Sorin is saved from the Haemovores by clasping the symbol of the unity of the workers of the world (as Reverend Wainwright's sense of exile from the communion of his church contributes to his destruction). There is loyalty to the planet too, in its widest sense: not simply the Brigadier's protective impulse, but the Ancient

One's refusal to play his part in bringing about the environmental destruction of Earth, and Nimrod's rejection of his false god because of his allegiance to this planet. Even Morgaine is not prepared to use a weapon that will obliterate all life on Earth. But the season also shows the possibility of connection beyond species or locality, such as the sisterly bond between Ace and Karra, and of course the friendship between Doctor and companions. Mouthing the names of all the humans with whom he has travelled saves the Doctor from the Haemovores, and his charged but ultimately successful mentorship of Ace is one of the season's main narratives. We can contrast it with Sergeant Paterson's training-gone-wrong of his fight club in *Survival,* or Josiah's corruption of Gwendoline in *Ghost Light,* isolating her from her loving family, in a distorted version of Ace's complex, rocky, but ultimately productive studentship with her Professor.

The Dark Curse of the Dragon Ship

Because this is *Doctor Who,* there are connections, both destructive and productive, to be made across time. What is carried here from the past affects now; what happens now creates our future. Throughout the season, the dead weight of the past threatens many times to destroy both present and future - unless we can find ways to break free of the curse. We must choose what to pay forward - and choose carefully. Under the tyranny of the patriarch, Josiah, Victorian values have almost choked the life out of Gabriel Chase. Fear of the house has cast a long shadow over Ace's personal history. The babbling of Reverend Matthews, insisting on his quasi-divinity despite the evidence of his own eyes, is easily dismissed as ridiculous. More interesting is Light, a scientist whose sense of enquiry and curiosity has been lost in antiquarianism; he has become a record-keeper, not an explorer, and the record has become a purpose, not a tool. The war between Morgaine and Arthur has lasted aeons, but the much-heralded return of the king turns out to be nothing more than propaganda. The king is dead, and has been for a very long time - so much for traditional rulers coming to save us! Millington, a product of the first half of the twentieth century, cannot see anything but a future of permanent warfare, and, in concealing the toxin in the Ultima Machine, commits an act intended to ensure that future will happen. In clinging to old factions and old policies, we sow the seeds of our own destruction.

The Doctor faces long-standing enemies from his past (the Master, Fenric) or, in his guise as Merlin, long-standing enemies to come. But his solutions are different. He refuses to continue to compete with the Master, and has learned enough to be able, one day, to set up his own eventual victory against Morgaine. His associates learn from example. The Ancient One destroys Fenric, by that act refusing his own future and preventing that timeline from happening. Ace too, learns to put aside the hatred of her mother that has hitherto blighted her life and, in doing so, saves her mother and therefore herself. People change, and smile.

Are You Hungry, Sister?

Too often, in the stories that circulate amongst us, we see women competing with men; women competing with women (for men); women competing with their mothers; women permitted a little freedom from their father figures, but never truly allowed to grow beyond them and acquire the status of hero in their own stories. In trying to escape the pull of such entrenched narrative patterns and show new possibilities for connection between women, Season Twenty-Six starts problematically. At heart, the *Battlefield* is one between the sexes. The war between Morgaine and Arthur is replicated, humorously, between Brigadier Bambera and the knight Ancelyn; Bambera is shown to have a potentially civilizing effect upon her knight, lamenting the waste of war as he lovingly cleans his weapon. The story ends with a scene in which the thematic division between the "boys" and the "girls" is again played for humor - the girls taking a temporary freedom, the boys bewitched by these magical beings amongst them. Hardly a step forwards. *Ghost Light*, on first glance, seems to offer the mirror image of this relationship between men and women - the savage Control is transformed and made "ladylike" by the presence of the civilizing male Fenn-Cooper, in order to fulfil her destiny of controlling, in turn, the savagery of the patriarchal figure of Josiah. But *Ghost Light* concludes by asserting Control's agency and self-determination. No longer a tool of Light, she's the one in charge of that ship at the end.

Throughout this season, Ace makes a number of female friends who represent potential life courses that she could take. Her rejection of the most harmful of these is part of her long narrative of leaving behind her troubled past (a past characterized by impulsive, even destructive, behavior) and acquiring the capacity to make more considered, adult choices. The reckless rebellion of the young women Phyllis and Jean in *The Curse of Fenric* (caused by lack of sensible supervision) culminates in their destruction. Ace wisely resists the water. Karra and the Cheetah People seem to have found complete freedom in their hunt. Ace is certainly tempted, but abandoning oneself entirely to instinct is a freedom without responsibility. It is no freedom at all.

Throughout this season, we are shown the possibility of female friendship, how it can be among women, friendship that is vibrant and loving and tender and non-competitive, even when the choices you make are not the same choices. Chloe *liked* Olivia. Ace liked Karra (and Shou Yuing, and Kathleen, and even quite liked poor Gwendoline, until it becomes clear the extent to which patriarchy has got its claws into her). In Season Twenty-Six, Ace grows up, and *Doctor Who* grows up with her. Again and again, the season imagines women as heroes of their own narratives, as authors of their own stories. Ace's story in this season charts the painful growth from harmed child to happy adult, shows the difference that intelligent guidance can make - particularly when that guide understands that one of the most important rites of passage is coming to understand how your parents are flawed too. Ace moves on from her lifelong struggle with her mother and learns to love and, perhaps, forgive; she puts aside blind faith in the Doctor, forming a more accurate judgement of her father figure and moving to the sustainable friendship that can exist between adults who comprehend each other's flaws. Her statement to the Doctor in *The Curse of Fenric* is truer than she knows at the time she makes it: "I'm not a little girl any more." By the end of this season, Ace has released herself from her past, loved and lost, experimented with her sexuality, is happier and stronger than ever before - and is ready for more exploration of herself and the world around her. How often do you see this story told about a young woman? Believe me, I'm on the lookout for it most of the time, and I can tell you - not often enough.

Come On, We've Got Work to Do

Poor *Doctor Who*, singing the *Internationale* in the year that the Berlin Wall came down, arguing against the shibboleth of the survival of the fittest just as the internal market is about to hit the BBC with full force. In 1989, this sounded like the music of a bygone age.

But in our end is our beginning. Without this season (and, if I'm being honest, without the two that went before), there would have been no new show. It's all there. The companion-driven stories. The triumph of intellect and romance over brute force and cynicism. The shift from technocratic to mythic humanism (or humanistic myth-making, whichever you prefer) by which all of our grand narratives - legend, folklore, religion, communism, evolution - are understood to be the means by which we can enquire about the world and make sense of it in order to live, rather than accept the dead hand of authority or the compulsive repetition of the past.

So that's why I wanted to begin my essay by claiming that this is the best season of *Doctor Who*. Because it's got such a grip on how much it can do with the space and time and resources available, and because it's wiser and braver than ever before in asserting its principles. In 1989, nobody wanted to listen. But they will, eventually.

Come on, we've got work to do.

Identity Crisis

L. M. Myles lives in Scotland which, as you may know from *Doctor Who*, is a land of werewolves and ninjas. She's a writer and graphic designer, and her short fiction has been published in *Reflection's Edge, Every Day Fiction* and Big Finish's *Doctor Who* anthologies, amongst others. She can be found procrastinating at twitter.com/LMMyles

I've never met a *Doctor Who* fan who didn't think that Patrick Troughton was, at the very least, a rather good Doctor. By admitting this, I realize I've made it a virtual certainty that someone, somewhere, sometime is going to let me know that, actually, they think he's rubbish, the worst thing that ever happened to the program and by the way, it jumped the shark when Susan left anyway. Naturally, I'm prepared to counter such suggestions by shaking my head sadly, safe in the knowledge that they're being very, very wrong about *Doctor Who*. A bit like those fans who cruelly mock the wibble-wobble of the Gel Guards in *The Three Doctors*... or think that just because they're incapable of movement, Davros' Giant Clams in *Genesis of the Daleks* aren't a fantastic addition to the bestiary of the Whoniverse.

As far as I'm concerned though, Troughton's not merely good as the Doctor, he's the best. There's something magical about his screen presence. His performance combines humor, compassion, intelligence and mystery in a way that's still unmatched by any other actor to take on the role. By the end of Season Four, he is undeniably the Doctor; a Doctor who cares for his companions and saves the day just as much as his predecessor, but whose whimsy and apparent uncertainty in his own abilities makes him a very different sort of hero.

When Season Four begins, William Hartnell is still at the controls of the TARDIS and everything appears to be business as usual, albeit with a bit of a freshen up as there are two new companions onboard. Two stories later, the Doctor collapses to the floor of the console room, and with practically no warning unceremoniously transforms into Patrick Troughton. With the Doctor's new face comes a new personality and the question is asked: if the Doctor has changed so much, how can he possibly be the same person?

This Old Body of Mine's Wearing a Bit Thin

After the Doctor's regeneration, Polly is quick to accept his new incarnation as the same man. "It's the Doctor, I know it is," she insists, but Ben is not so sure. Much of the season plays with the idea of who the Doctor is, what his motives are and whether he is worthy of his companions' trust. In *The Power of the Daleks,* there's no time spent on any reassurances that this is indeed still the same person. In fact, the Doctor seems to go out of his way to suggest that he isn't: he refers to himself in the third person and doesn't directly answer his companions' questions about what's happened to him, refusing to ease their understandable concerns.

However, although the Doctor doesn't give his companions any satisfying answers, he doesn't try to stop them asking their questions either. "Life depends on change and renewal," he says, but although change is inevitable, that doesn't mean it should go unchallenged. Change is not necessarily progress. It should be questioned; it should be required to prove itself, which is exactly what the Doctor goes on to do, not with his words, but with his actions.

Highlighting his own change and doing nothing to allay his companions' misgivings, the first thing the new Doctor does when he steps out of the TARDIS is to take on another identity, one that is certainly a lie, that of the Examiner. It's only the first of the disguises he adopts over the next few stories. By the end of *The Underwater Menace,* he's pretended to be a German doctor (complete with an appallingly unconvincing accent), a washerwoman, a Red Coat and a sea captain with a highly suspect taste in eyewear. It's as though the Doctor shares some of his companions' uncertainty regarding his new persona - it's the first time he's regenerated, after all - and it takes a while for him to be comfortable with who he's become and settle into his new incarnation.

In the meantime, these early Troughton stories are happy to invite suspicion of the Doctor. He pretends to be a traitor in *The Highlanders,* convincing enough in the role that Ben appears uncertain over whether or not he really is willing to give up the Jacobites' secrets to the English. When Ben is converted to the colony's way of thinking in *The Macra Terror* and betrays the Doctor, it's an unsettling defection because Ben hasn't been turned into some sort of automaton: his personality hasn't changed at all, but his loyalties have. It's not much of a leap to make for one of the Doctor's companions to get to the point where they're sick of being told what to do and the Doctor always claiming he knows what's best and, actually, they'd quite like to stay and help the nice, friendly colony instead of overthrowing the leader. A few stories later, we (briefly; they make up, of course) reach that point: the Doctor appears eager enough to go along with the Daleks' plan in *The Evil of the Daleks,* and willing to manipulate his companion to such an extent that Jamie tells him their friendship is over. And when the Doctor switches from acting as though he's been infected with the Dalek Factor to acting like the Doctor again, Jamie is uncertain as to which persona is the lie.

The transformation that's the cause of all this doubt takes place in the Cybermen's first story, implicitly inviting comparisons between what happens to the Doctor and what's happened to the Cyber-race. In order to prevent the extinction of their species, the inhabitants of the planet Mondas began to replace their organic bodies with artificial components. At some point, they lost their ability to feel emotions and became beings who defined themselves by their logic. At what point did they cease to be Mondasians and become Cybermen? Mondas is Earth's sister planet and its continents are remarkably similar to Earth's; the planet casts a dark reflection of our own possible future. Replace an arm or a leg with an artificial limb and you're still human. But how much flesh and bone can be replaced before that's no longer true? If a human brain is put into a mechanical body that can no longer feel, is it still human? The Doctor's transformation lacks the body horror of the cyberization process, but he looks different, sounds different and behaves differently. How can he be the same person?

This new Doctor wouldn't answer that question. He refuses to be certain, refuses to give easy, comforting answers. He even doubts his own plans, appearing surprised at his success in *Power,* and flat out saying that his plans won't work in *The Highlanders* and *The Underwater Menace.* "Do you know what you're doing?" Ben asks him in the latter story. "Oh, what a question! Of course I don't!" the Doctor responds. "There's no rule against trying, is there?" He values flexibility over certainty, questions over answers, and encourages his companions never to make assumptions about what's impossible, and what's not.

His new personality is summed up nowhere better than in *The Macra Terror.* At the colony's futuristic spa, the Doctor finds himself in a "clothes reviver" that manages to clean and tidy his rumpled appearance. Polly's impressed with the effect but the Doctor is decidedly not and messes himself up again at the first opportunity. "Who wants to see their face in a pair of suede shoes?" he says, appalled at the very notion.

Bad Laws Were Made to Be Broken

"Bad laws were made to be broken," says the Doctor. In Season Four, he's not just a meddler but a champion of anarchism. Authority must be questioned. The state is not to be trusted. The people should be vigilant against lawful tyranny, because it's not just change that the Doctor wants questioned, but the status quo too.

In *The Macra Terror,* the TARDIS arrives in a bright, cheerful human colony. The inhabitants are happy, hard-working and welcome the TARDIS crew to their world; they also conform and they do not ask questions. We're told that the one man who does so is ill, dangerous and must be tortured (but it's for his own good; the leaders of the colony only want him to be happy). "He's an old friend, one of the best, cheerful as any of us," says one colonist about the dissenter, Medok. That's what matters here, being cheerful, fitting in. When Medok returns from his torture, "he'll be a changed man, he'll co-operate and obey orders. He'll be just like the rest of us." The horror here is that the colonists really believe it's being done for his own good. It's better not to ask questions, it's better just to follow orders and obey their leaders, they're happy this way, after all. But their happiness is a superficial, vapid sort of thing, one expressed through trite slogans and jingles. It's a soulless cheer being used to manipulate the colonists, and Medok is the only one who recognizes that.

Of course Medok is the man that the Doctor seeks out, the one loose thread that he tugs at until the whole wretched system is pulled apart. And how he delights in it. After the Doctor sabotages the colony's equipment, the Pilot asks of his crime, "You admit it?" "I'm proud of it," the Doctor gleefully tells him.

This isn't the only civilization whose state of affairs the Doctor challenges. He encourages the revolt of the Fish People in Atlantis. He warns the colonists on Vulcan that their useful new servants are not as docile as they seem and will end up killing them all. He infects Daleks with the Human Factor so that they will no longer simply accept whatever orders are given to them. "Question," the Doctor encourages. "Why?" the Human Daleks begin to ask their superiors, spelling the doom of their civilization.

"Don't just be obedient, always make up your own mind," the Doctor tells Polly. The irony is that despite his anti-authoritarianism, the Doctor himself is an authority figure. He's the one with the plans, he's the one who tells people what to do, and how to win through. He wants people to listen to him and they do. At last when authority is officially pressed upon him, he resists it; when he hears the colonists of *The Macra Terror* want him as their next leader, that's when he makes a run for it.

You're Not Turning Me Into a Fish

The Doctor's identity isn't the only one that's held up to scrutiny in Season Four. What does it mean to be a Dalek? A human? A Cyberman? In *The Faceless Ones,* the alien Chameleons have lost their own identities in a catastrophe on their planet and steal the appearances and memories of humans to survive. "A man is the sum of his memories," the fifth Doctor said once, "a Time Lord even more so," but the Chameleons do not become those humans whose identities they've copied. The Daleks kidnap the Doctor so they can use him to discover the Dalek Factor and infect humanity with it. It's scientific nonsense, sure, but the point isn't how we can change a Dalek into a human or vice-versa, but what those essential qualities that create an individual's sense of self are.

What defines humanity? This question is asked again and again through the season. In *The Tenth Planet,* the Cybermen are monstrous to the humans they encounter, but their advantages are clear enough: they are fearless, they feel no pain, they're physically stronger than humans, they don't age or succumb to disease. In *The Moonbase,* while the Doctor and his companions have to adapt to the lunar surface by wearing spacesuits, the Cybermen have no problems dealing with the absence of an atmosphere. "One tear in that spacesuit and you'll suffocate," the Doctor warns his companions. The Cybermen have no such vulnerability and they can attack the moon base en masse, impervious to the cold and unaffected by the low gravity.

The Cybermen want humanity to become like them, but despite the many advantages, the horror of the Cybermen is that once converted you are no longer a person, no longer yourself, but an unfeeling monster and a slave to logic. When Polly is about to be turned into a Fish Person in *The Underwater Menace,* it's a horrifying process to her, but while the Atlantean doctor may want to doom her to a life under the sea, changing the way her lungs operate wouldn't be enough for her to lose her sense of self.

What the Cybermen lack is neatly summed up with Jamie's medical treatment in *The Moonbase.* Everything needed to repair his body is provided by machines, but Polly wants to stay with him anyway. The machines "can't be nice to him" - they are creations without empathy, they lack a soul.

In both their appearances this season, the expectation of what

Daleks are is subverted. In *The Power of the Daleks,* the genocidal metal fascists have a new catchphrase: "I am your servant." Incongruous and unsettling, they're willing to put up with a lot of poking, prodding and patronising from Vulcan's human inhabitants in order to maintain their cover of subservient beings, biding their time before their true nature is unleashed. None of the humans in *Power* bother to ask why the Daleks accept their authority so easily; they do not question why the Daleks don't question. They assume it is their right to command the Daleks and that arrogance condemns the colony to destruction.

The appeal of authoritarianism isn't overlooked. Unlike the messy human societies we encounter, the Daleks are at peace with themselves. They have a single, united purpose. There's no uncertainty, no fear, no doubt. They don't kill each other and don't understand why humans do. It's only when given the Human Factor, when they become more human, that they turn on one another. They become playful, develop a sense of humor, and want to make friends; they also start to question. Their questions cause disagreement with other Daleks, and those disagreements escalate until their entire civilization is engulfed in war. They destroy themselves because they question. It's not an argument for authoritarianism, but an appeal to be open to dialogue and negotiation, to not accept absolutes. "If you want the Human Factor, a part of it must include mercy," says the Doctor, but there is none in either the Daleks, or the Human-Daleks.

When I Say Run, Run

So in Season Four, *Doctor Who* made the show's biggest, most daring change and didn't bother trying to make it an easy or comfortable one. Yet it succeeded so well that the Doctor's ability to regenerate is now a cornerstone of the show's mythology, and has been a fundamental part of what's allowed it to renew itself again and again over the decades.

No change is easy. Every new actor cast in the role of the Doctor will inevitably face criticism, accusations that they're the worst casting ever, and that the show will now be finished for good. "What have you done to BBC1's *Doctor Who?*" one disgruntled viewer wrote to the *Radio Times* in 1966. "Of all the stupid nonsense! Why turn a wonderful series into what looked like Coco the Clown?"[6] And quite right too. If Season Four is about anything, it's about how no change should be accepted on trust. It should be questioned, it should be made to justify itself, and it

6 David J. Howe and Stephen James Walker *Doctor Who: The Television Companion* (BBC Worldwide Ltd 1998) pg.110.

should not be rejected out of hand. Each time the Doctor regenerates, he's a new person, and each time he must win our trust, he must show his worth, and prove that he deserves to have us join him in his adventures.

Each time the Doctor succeeds - not completely, but it's been enough to keep him alive for 50 years. And no-one's success was more important than Patrick Troughton's.

The Still Point

As a Whovian raised on the lonely Dakota prairie, **Anna Bratton** was surprised to learn that PBS pledge drives are not actually part of *The Five Doctors*. She graduated from the Minneapolis College of Art and Design with a BFA in Comics and is scriptwriter for *Francis Sharp in the Grip of the Uncanny!*, the Xeric Award-winning comic illustrated by Brittney Sabo. Non-comic work includes the short story "Lares Domestici," published in Big Finish's *Short Trips: How the Doctor Changed My Life*. She lives in Minneapolis, sporadically updating her blog at sourbratton.wordpress.com.

By Season Twenty, the world of the fifth Doctor is starting to show signs of the darkness that would engulf the later seasons of *Doctor Who*; a vicious, unkind universe populated by venal and mercenary characters. Yet here, in its anniversary season, the show prefers to address "the dark places of the inside" in a more allegorical fashion, even as the Doctor faces old enemies and new with a subtle, quiet strength that is often mistaken for frailty and blandness.

In the play-within-a-play conceit featured in *Snakedance*, the possessed Lon takes on the role of his illustrious ancestor (and unfortunately, his ancestor's inane getup) and re-enacts the banishment of the Mara. The ceremony involves the challenger being confronted with three temptations that must be ritually denied: fear, despair and the greed for knowledge. The ritual Lon performs departs considerably from the actual script, as the real Mara doesn't find its papier-mâché counterpart terribly convincing; luckily, the Doctor manages to cut short its Becoming.

Anyone with a passing familiarity with Buddhist philosophy is aware that the Mara is named for a demon that attempted to distract the Buddha from achieving enlightenment, and the Abrahamic tradition has a thing or two to say about snakes bearing promises of knowledge as well. The Mara of *Kinda* and *Snakedance* is an amalgamation of hatred and fear whose incarnation invariably destroys whatever civilization is unfortunate enough to bear witness to it. Yet in Season Twenty, we also see evidence of the more traditional version of Mara: the entrapment found in an endless cycle of death and rebirth, constant change without hope.

The First Temptation: Fear

Doctor Who has a proud tradition of inducing night terrors in the unwary, and Season Twenty has more than its share of horrors. *Snakedance* is a subtle and consistently tense psychological thriller that shows us Tegan's mental barriers crumbling from the Mara's constant onslaught. Turlough suffers much the same under the Black Guardian's continual menacing abuse, while Nyssa comes face-to-face with her mortality (and an unconvincing monster) in *Terminus*. All three companions eventually prevail, thanks to either the intervention of the Doctor or a sharpening of resolve.

Apart from the usual dangers posed by the requisite Ergon or Garm, there is also a sense of almost Lovecraftian menace that hangs around this season, as if the dark old Universe is bleeding into the everyday world. We are introduced to the Eternals, a race of beings that do not exist in any sense of time, or possibly in any sense of the physical universe, characteristics which make them eerily unsettling pawns for the resurfaced Black Guardian, the personification of entropy and decay. The great old founders of Time Lord society, Omega and Rassilon, exude latent menace - the former is insane after years of isolation and is capable (and very willing) of destroying the Universe if he can't rejoin it, while the latter has immensely dangerous artifacts named for him and governs an entire region of Gallifrey which no Time Lord dares enter, in spite of being (supposedly) dead. Meanwhile, the Lazar colony Terminus rots in the middle of Creation - quite literally, as this dilapidated hulk of metal was once a time-ship responsible for Event One.

Season Twenty's rogue's gallery doesn't favor obvious favorites like Cybermen or Daleks (*The Five Doctors* hardly counts, as they are mostly cameos and do not dominate the plot), but instead features villains whose nature is shadowy, amorphous, terrible and ancient.[7] This is an interesting production choice, as Season Twenty is more psychologically and philosophically engaging than the seasons which bookend the fifth Doctor's tenure - it's not a stretch to say that it is the logical ancestor of the final year of classic *Who*, the criminally underrated Season Twenty-Six, with its Victorian metaphors, reflections on transience, and Evil (From the Dawn of Time).

7 Well, and the Master pretends to be French and has a robot propped up on chairs threatening Magna Carta, but whatever.

The Second Temptation: Despair

The second temptation logically stems from this awareness of the dangers and futility of existence, trapped as it is in a cycle of regeneration and decay. The aforementioned Terminus is mired in misery, full of the despondent sufferers of Lazar's Disease and staffed by the weakening Vanir, only one of whom realizes the danger that the ship poses to the Universe if it re-ignites its lost fuel. Mawdryn and his sickening fellows cycle though endless regenerations, incapable of death; meanwhile, the lifeless Eternals endure a similarly meaningless existence. Turlough's unwise pact with the Black Guardian is made in a fit of weakness as he contemplates his unhappiness at being stranded on backwater Earth, a decision he quickly regrets as he realizes that he can't force himself to kill the Doctor. Though Turlough may be an unwilling antagonist, the same can hardly be said of Lord President Borusa, who is painfully aware that his influence over Gallifreyan society must end with his final regeneration and is desperate enough to risk the Doctor's life to obtain an extension of his own.

The Time Lords themselves seem equally at a loss in moments of strife, unable to improvise any more intelligent strategy for the impending return of Omega than sacrificing the Doctor (this does not work, obviously). In fact, Gallifreyan society is shown here to be stagnant, its High Council riddled with intrigues and corruption, unable to solve internal affairs without the help of its wayward son, yet just as easily willing to destroy him. Both of Season Twenty's Gallifrey stories focus on heroes of its once epic past: Councillor Hedin attempts to bring Omega back to rule, while Borusa manipulates the Doctors to seize Rassilon's power for his own. But the hoary past of the Time Lords is far too wily and dangerous - Rassilon himself, manifesting briefly at the end of *The Five Doctors,* has more implied menace and unspoken powers in his "sleep" than any of his successors. The Death Zone is his, as are the tools of domination which Borusa wields, and Rassilon does not give gifts freely. Omega, seething in his Hadean half-life, seems far more potent than any guard, technician, or Council member in the Citadel, requiring only Hedin's misguided devotion to drive its occupants into giving him exactly what he needs.

The Third Temptation: Knowledge

As a result of the stellar experiment necessary in creating the Time Lord race, Omega was unwittingly banished to an anti-matter dimension; by attempting to make themselves Time Lords, the scientist

Mawdryn and his confederates got more than they bargained for and lost the ability to die. Unthinking technological growth inadvertently called the Mara into being and was responsible for Kamelion - a subtle war machine gifted with great intelligence, but amoral in the truest literal sense of the word. The former is primal fear which overrides all minds, the latter is sophisticated circuits with an easily-dominated will. The Eternals, equally without understanding of good or evil (somewhat debatable in the case of the pirate queen, Wrack) seek self-awareness, the means by which they will no longer be dependent on mortal minds for definition, yet it is heavily implied that the physical realm would suffer as a result of their unchecked power - they would re-enact the Fall, but without falling. Borusa, corrupt and deranged, hungers for the immortality promised by the legends of Rassilon's Tower so badly that he is willing to jeopardize his old friend, the Doctor, in order to obtain it, only to discover that the price of eternal life is never leaving Rassilon's tomb.

The greed for power almost certainly can be considered the impetus for virtually everything that happens within these stories, showing the dangers of overextending one's grasp. Many of Season Twenty's major players are either reduced to parasitism in order to survive or merely existing as shadows of themselves, hungry ghosts seeking either definition or dissolution.

Winner of Enlightenment

Much as the seventh Doctor's idiosyncratic appearance and manner initially makes him seem like an unlikely adversary of Elder Gods, so might Peter Davison's fifth Doctor appear thoroughly ill-suited to tackle this smorgasbord of cosmic darkness. He doesn't ever have all the answers, he is forced to raise his voice quite a bit, and the two things he's best known for wearing are a perpetually-pained expression and a celery stalk. He's often brusque in his dealings with Tegan (she reciprocates) and a running gag of this particular season is that he's never overly pleased to see her, a trend that starts as soon as Nyssa re-invites her onboard the TARDIS. His decision to induct the dubiously credentialed Turlough and the even less appealing Kamelion into the companion roster seems somewhat spur-of-the-moment and largely just to annoy Tegan. Nyssa herself is the brunt of a recurring joke where the Doctor frequently fails to notice her changes in wardrobe. (It seems she wants an opinion on Tegan's sartorial suggestions?)

However, the bickering and sniping between the Doctor and his crew is juxtaposed with a surprising amount of mutual trust and concern. Nyssa in particular becomes intensely protective of the Doctor in *Arc of Infinity*, shooting Citadel guards left and right and even threatening the High Council itself in order to save him from disintegration. The Doctor - who suspects that the execution is a ruse and that he isn't in real danger - gently but firmly instructs Nyssa to allow his sentence to be passed and asks the Council to pardon her actions. When she and Tegan suffer the contaminating effects of the retrovirus which afflicts Mawdryn, he prepares to give up his remaining incarnations to cure them - an act for which Tegan, not normally one to compliment the Doctor to his face (or at all), feels compelled to thank him. Embarrassed, he changes the subject.

The willingness to sacrifice himself for his friends is in many ways the defining characteristic of the fifth Doctor, as his very last story, *The Caves of Androzan*i, will attest. That purity of spirit also casts him as a sort of intergalactic exorcist in this season, banishing these nebulous evils back to the dark places of the inside. He cannot bring himself to hate Omega, a fact which he states to the disintegrating monster's face, but he nonetheless is responsible for returning him to his prison dimension. Granted, this involves shooting him with an anti-matter converter, but more conventional forms of spiritual warfare would follow. *Snakedance* has him seek out former historian Dojjen for aid in thwarting the Mara's return, and rather touchingly has him confessing his guilt for letting it possess Tegan so readily. Told that "fear is the only poison," he realizes that the key to defeating the Mara is to deny its power and thereby manages to disrupt its manifestation long enough to remove the crystal necessary for the process to stabilize. The minds of its thralls are freed and he comforts Tegan while the defeated snake rots gruesomely.

More literal instances of the Doctor granting independence occur when he frees the Garm (an unlikely monster with good intentions) from the control of Terminus' Vanir, allowing it free will. Similarly, the Doctor wrests control of Kamelion away from the Master, implying that despite appearances, his will is greater - impressive, considering that mind control is pretty much the Master's shtick. To the extent that his own mind is overrun by Borusa's in *The Five Doctors*, it is worth noting that the President has an unfair advantage in the Coronet of Rassilon, and even so, the Doctor manages to put up some resistance. More impressively and subtly, however, is the extent to which the Doctor defeats the Black Guardian by relying on nothing but his essential trust in Turlough, correctly surmising that his companion is sufficiently loyal not to betray him in favor of Enlightenment - and that Enlightenment was not the diamond, but the choice. Metaphorically and literally, light defeats the darkness, and Turlough's contract with the Guardian is terminated and freedom granted.

While those who seek power come to bad ends in Season Twenty - especially those seeking immortality (strange message in an anniversary season!) - the fifth Doctor is uniquely resistant of its charms. The same rigid ethical guidelines that won't let him alter the timeline to save Adric also demand his absolute commitment to thwarting whatever evil he encounters, and combined with his ravenous curiosity, this makes for lots of running up and down corridors. Presented with the mysteries of an abandoned cruise liner, a gap in the Brigadier's memory, archeological discrepancies or the fact that King John is in the wrong place at the right time, he throws himself into sleuthing with as much verve and gusto as any previous incarnation - more, considering that the more cautious first and second selves that Davison modeled his own Doctor's behavior upon would hardly have kept walking into a plague ship just to see what was there. He is dedicated to the pursuit of knowledge, but never for power or gain - his refusal of Enlightenment makes perfect sense in this light; if he knew everything, what would be the point of traveling in his rackety old TARDIS?

The fifth Doctor is a holy fool, a wise innocent who desires nothing more than his own personal idea of peace and quiet, which he defines as the safety of his friends and TARDIS, preferably very very very far away from Gallifrey. Whether he's dragged back home as a sacrificial lamb or handed the Presidency, it's evident that the Time Lords and their byzantine chicanery mean nothing to him, even if he has a healthy (and fearful) respect for the legacies of Omega and Rassilon. Granted, he obviously relies on his regenerative ability to allow him this freedom - witness his look of utter devastation when he realizes that he must forfeit his future lives to Mawdryn's company in order to save Nyssa and Tegan from the effects of their virus. The fact that he is willing to go through with this in order to give them their own freedom is further indication of his essential decency; he is the Doctor, after all.

Season Twenty is a teaching season, in that it shows how the fifth Doctor has begun to understand his limits. Despite being driven to frantic last-minute measures to save his friends/the world/the universe, despite being frayed around the edges, despite the victories never being quite effortless, despite lots and lots of running down corridors, he possessed an internal stillness to his character, and when he could remember to listen to this, he succeeded admirably.

In many ways, this very purity highlights the major difference between the fifth Doctor and his other incarnations - the thing that makes him so well-suited to fighting abstract demons makes him particularly poor at fighting named ones. The stories that pit him against Cybermen and Daleks (again, not counting *The Five Doctors*) have extremely high body counts and push him to the very limit of his abilities; while both are ultimately defeated, it isn't so much as a result of any direct action on his part than it is the actions of those he influences, and usually with fatal results. Davison's high-minded schoolboy Doctor may be true of heart, but that won't put a dent in a Dalekanium hull.

Season Twenty is obviously the show's celebratory season, but it is also the high water mark for the fifth Doctor. He is shown to be flighty but forgiving, capable of believing the best of anyone and everyone (everyone who isn't the Master, anyway), and utterly protective of his friends. To seek power is folly, to despair is folly, to fear is folly. The fifth Doctor ultimately defeats the three temptations of the Mara and walks away from his anniversary season a rejuvenated and contemplative hero.

For the Love of Tom

Sarah Lotz is a screenwriter with a fondness for the macabre and fake names. She writes urban horror novels under the name SL Grey with South African author Louis Greenberg (their first novel, *The Mall*, was published in 2011 by Corvus; their second, *The Ward,* is scheduled for release in late 2012), and a young adult zombie series, *Deadlands*, with her daughter Savannah under the name Lily Herne. When she's not hiding behind pseudonyms, she writes a comedic crime thriller series for Penguin SA. She lives in Cape Town with her family and other animals.

I'm sitting in my scruffy lounge in Cape Town, struggling with a post-New Year's Eve hangover. Primed to go in the DVD player is episode one of *Horror of Fang Rock*.

And I'm feeling nervous.

As the Whovian fan sites never tire of saying, "You never forget your first Doctor," and like countless other seventies children, since the reboot series aired in 2005, I have bored people senseless with lectures on why Tom Baker is the only *true* Doctor. Boggle-eyed, a voice like booming gravel, an insane halo of hair and that scarf, how can any other actor - even the fabulous lantern-jawed Matt Smith - compete with Tom? To my shame, all this proselytizing is based on nothing more than nostalgia, a hazy recollection of Davros-fuelled nightmares and a vague memory of the giant rat from *The Talons of Weng-Chiang*. I cannot, in all honesty, remember any of Tom's stories in detail, although I clearly recollect being scared shitless while watching them. Hence the nervousness: what if re-experiencing Tom in action is like meeting my first love decades later only to find he's become an obese serial killer with a comb-over and brown teeth?

But the Tom factor isn't the only issue. Back in the seventies, *Doctor Who's* oooooeeeeeeooooo title track had a Pavlovian effect on me and my brother. Whatever we were doing (usually beating the crap out of each other), we would stop, race to the telly and for 30 glorious minutes we'd be lost in TARDIS-land. Such was my obsession with the show that my friends and I would act out each episode at school the following week. (The feminist in me now winces that none of us wanted to "be"

Leela or even the Doctor, but rather fought over who would get to act out the role of the Doctor's robot dog, K9.) Along with the influences of the *Star Wars* trilogy, Lucio Fulci's video nasties and *Space: 1999*, I'm convinced that an early exposure to classic *Doctor Who* is the reason why I now scratch out a living writing horror and SF/F. So what happens if I re-watch it now and discover it's another nail in the nostalgia coffin - that same kind of sinking, childhood-ruining feeling I felt after watching the *Star Wars* prequels?

As if this isn't enough emotional baggage and over-reacting, there are other concerns. Classic *Doctor Who* has always been the most British of shows, so how will the fact that I've spent the last 20 years living in Africa - hypersensitive to issues of colonialism and post-colonial representations in fiction and film - affect this revisiting? Aware of the accusations of bigotry aimed at the Asian stereotypes in *Weng-Chiang*, am I going to cringe at "primitive" companion Leela's "noble savage" portrayal? Will the feminist in me rail against the Doctor acting as Professor Higgins to her "uncivilized" Eliza?

And will I still yearn to own my own K9 sidekick?

Geek neuroses now racked up to factor ten, I press play.

Season Fifteen has a nebulous place in Whovian classic history. It's where Leela comes into her own before abruptly leaving the series, K9 joins the Doctor on his travels, and the program starts slipping away from the Gothic era into the high camp, humor-orientated phase. Despite attracting record viewing figures for the era, the preceding season came under attack by the notorious Mary Whitehouse-led morality police, who accused the show of being too violent and disturbing. When producer Graham Williams took over the helm from the masterful Philip Hinchcliffe at the start of Season Fifteen, he was under strict instructions to tone down the horror element. Hampered by debilitating budget constraints, and plagued by a shifting production crew, the six stories that make up this season are startlingly diverse with no coherent theme or tone. *Horror of Fang Rock* is a Gothic, claustrophobic tale set in and around an Edwardian lighthouse which is under attack from the alien Rutans. *The Invisible Enemy* is basically a pastiche of *Fantastic Voyage*, where miniaturized Doctor and Leela clones invade the Doctor's body to kill the nucleus of the Swarm, an interstellar virus. *Image of the Fendahl* is set in a seventies research base located in a spooky priory, where a group of scientists are studying an ancient skull that's acting as the host for a life-absorbing alien. *The Sun Makers* is a thinly-veiled anti-taxation/corporation fable set on a futuristic Pluto.

Underworld is an overly-ambitious (and almost incomprehensible) mish-mash of various tales from the Jason and the Argonauts mythology. And slapped at the end of the season, *The Invasion of Time* is a sequel to Season Fourteen's *The Deadly Assassin*, set on Gallifrey and featuring a complex storyline that initially positions the Doctor as a power-hungry antagonist who is seemingly plotting against the Time Lords with the alien Vardans.

It's tempting to say that re-experiencing Season Fifteen was like "being my own Time Lord and travelling back to my childhood," but this would be vomit-inducing and untrue. Used to the slickness and CGI of the reboot episodes, I steeled myself for the notoriously tacky sets and rubbery monsters - issues that didn't bother me in the slightest as a child - but it was a challenge to ignore them completely. The one Rutan we actually see looks like the cross between an irradiated Brussels sprout and Skipper the Eyechild from *Garth Marenghi's Darkplace*. The Vardans from *The Invasion of Time* resemble teenagers wrapped in tin foil, and the phallic Fendahleens look like the unholy marriage between a plastic cobra and shredded Enron documents. The scenery wobbles in almost every story, and, as *Den of Geek* critic James Peaty points out, the Pluto setting in *The Sun Makers* is more reminiscent of "a factory roof in Bristol on a cloudy day" than a technologically advanced planet.[8] There are continuity errors galore: *Fang Rock*'s shipwrecked aristocrats emerge from the ocean complaining about being wet and cold, but their hair and costumes are notably dry and primped; the blurry red lasers in the climax of *The Invisible Enemy* appear to materialise from anywhere except a weapon. But as James Chapman sensibly states, "Doctor Who, the argument goes, is about ideas rather than action and its strength lies in its scripts rather than its special effects."[9] He's right, and it's a pointless exercise to harp on about the cheesy special effects (however much fun it is to do so) or imagine what a seventies *Doctor Who* production budget would make of say, *Let's Kill Hitler*. And once I ignored the trembling sets and erratic studio lighting, the series' strengths started to shine: the quality of the dialogue and humor (which is often deliciously dark and sharp); the atmosphere (the settings in *Fang Rock* and *Fendahl* evoke a creepy, brooding menace); and Tom Baker and Louise Jameson's scene-stealing performances.

---

8 Peaty, James. "*Doctor Who: The Sun Makers* DVD review." www.denofgeek.com/Reviews/987394/doctor_who_the_sun_makers_dvd_review.html 21/7/2011

9 Chapman, James. *Inside the Tardis: The Worlds of Doctor Who*. I B Tauris, London, New York. 2006

Most of the critics are in accordance that *Horror of Fang Rock* has the strongest, most coherent narrative, thanks to *Doctor Who* stalwart Terrance Dicks' excellent script. Paul Cornell nails it when he says that *Fang Rock* is a "perfect story" where all of the maguffins add up, and every element needed to destroy the Rutan has a purpose[10] (the ship-wrecked passengers' diamonds; the lighthouse lamp that's used as a laser; the alien technology). This is complimented by a genuinely chilling atmosphere: the claustrophobia-inducing mist, the lighthouse's confined interior and the constant mournful bellow of the foghorn in the background.

Despite the rather tragic Fendahleens, *Image of the Fendahl* runs a close second. Set in the seventies, almost entirely at night and within a creepy wood-paneled priory, it's reminiscent of a classic *Hammer House of Horror* episode. The strong supporting cast includes a standout performance from Daphne Heard as the witchy Ma Tyler - who, while playing somewhat of a country bumpkin stereotype, gives the role all she's got. It's perhaps best known for its notorious suicide scene, when the Doctor hands mad scientist Max Stael (Scott Fredericks) a gun to shoot himself rather than be Fendahleened. (The actual death, an oddly bloodless affair, presumably takes place off camera to avoid coming under attack from the Mary Whitehouse brigade.)

The Sun Makers, penned by celebrated script-editor Robert Holmes, has perhaps the most currently socially relevant storyline. Apparently written as a backlash against the Inland Revenue and the bureaucratic BBC, the story has the Doctor and Leela find themselves on Pluto, where, after encountering a suicidal over-taxed worker, they're drawn into stopping the cue-ball headed Gatherer from literally taxing the enslaved humans to death. In-jokes and sly references abound (such as a corridor named P45), and it also has some of the best kid-shocking cliff-hangers of the season (such as Leela about to be steamed alive, or the Doctor being gassed in a futuristic ATM). However, as critic Philip Sandifer rather brilliantly points out, the story isn't *just* about the evils of taxation: "It's not a story about unfair tax surprises that screw people over, it's a story about a world where no amount of work will ever make ends meet because the rich and powerful want more...[11] This is the most Occupy movement friendly story to date in *Doctor Who*."

---

10 "Terrance Dicks: Fact and Fiction" (supplementary material on *Horror of Fang Rock* DVD release), BBC Worldwide Ltd 2005

11 Sandifer, Philip. "Wrong With Authority (*The Sun Makers*)," *Tardis Eruditorum*. tardiseruditorum.blogspot.com/ 2011 / 12/ wrong-with-authority-sun-makers.html 5/ 2011

Underworld is easily the weakest story of the season (it understandably placed in the bottom five in The Mighty 200 episode poll in *Doctor Who Magazine* #413). I have no clue how my seven-year-old self managed to follow the story (probably by ignoring everything but K9's infrequent appearances), and the relentless reliance on blue screen is distracting and headache-inducing.

Many Whovians count *The Invisible Enemy* as one of the least successful stories, largely due to the poor production values. Undoubtedly, there are issues (the Nucleus - which resembles a giant hairy prawn that's been left out of the fridge to rot - is possibly the most unintentionally hilarious of the season's monsters, and the space shuttle crashes look like Lego thrown randomly at a couple of sparklers). On the upside, my seven-year-old self would have been entranced by the concept of teeny Leela and Doctor clones scrabbling around in the Doctor's cerebellum, and, of course, I would have been instantly hooked by the appearance of K9. (Embarrassingly, this time round, there was a tearful moment when K9 creaks his way into the TARDIS at the end of the last episode.)

The Invasion of Time has perhaps the most challenging opening episodes. Arriving on Gallifrey, the Doctor immediately seizes the presidency, and with little preamble or exposition, appears to have either lost his mind or been transformed into a power-hungry dictator, apparently set on allying himself with the tin-foil Vardans. Unfortunately, after the Doctor reveals that the alliance is a ruse to uncover the Vardans' puppet-masters (the Sontarans), the last episode slides into pure slapstick silliness. The Doctor, Leela and the supporting cast chase each other around the interior of the TARDIS (parts of which look like a disused school), hamming it up and embarking on some of the most inept fight scenes ever filmed (one of the Sontarans famously falls over a sun lounger).

On the whole, there were less obvious colonial/ imperialistic undertones than I expected (although my South African husband was quick to spot the Apartheid-era map of Africa on the wall of the office in *Fendahl*). Clearly, the very essence of *Doctor Who* often encompasses a more technologically advanced race oppressing a less powerful society, with the Doctor acting as mediator or saviour (sometimes unsuccessfully). The colonial aspects seen in Season Fourteen's *The Face of Evil* where, as anthropologist Fiona Moore points out, the "hero-colonialist" (ie the Doctor) demonstrates the "invalidity of the tribal belief system" (for which Leela's Sevateem tribe are "oddly grateful") aren't as overt in this season.[12] In fact, in *Fang Rock*, Terrance Dicks does a stellar job of contrasting Edwardian imperialistic mores with the Doctor's more tolerant, alien viewpoint; the toffs sneer at Leela's "savage" attributes, but it is they who are "punished" for their greed, racism and general stiff-upper lip Britishness.

In his analysis of *The Invasion of Time* (and citing Lawrence Miles and Tat Wood's *About Time* series as his source) Sandifer argues that the "... sorts of events that take place in this story would have been mostly associated with the rise of African dictators like Idi Amin or, a year or so after this story, Robert Mugabe."[13] In regard to Mugabe, save from a purely conservative Eurocentric viewpoint, the use of the term "dictator" is somewhat of a stretch (at least in the context of the time period in which the story was aired). *The Invasion of Time*, to me, represents an exterior alien force attempting to oppress from the inside, rather than reflect the transition of power from minority rule to the majority. That said, if considered from a purely contemporary viewpoint, the Doctor's seemingly power-hungry insanity in the opening episodes certainly reflects the mania associated with Mugabe's recent oligarchy, which resulted in Zimbabwe's economic collapse. However, Sandifer is spot on when he states that the ambiguity of the opening episodes mirrors the confusion of a military coup or change in power, where the seventies audience would be "... compellingly reminded that not only could it 'happen here,' they'd be hard-pressed to keep up with it and notice it was happening in time to stop it."

And, as pointed out above, *The Sun Makers*' anti-corporation message could apply just as easily to any contemporary society or culture beset with corruption and greed, where the masses are oppressed by a more powerful minority (the exploitation of the Rwandan Coltan mines comes to mind).

As several of the supporting female cast in this season come across as passive one-note stereotypes, Leela is a revelation. She's perhaps best and undeservedly remembered for her skimpy leather outfits, which seventies reviewers routinely termed as "something for the dads." Although this eye-candy aspect is impossible to ignore, Jameson's performance and Leela's strong personality and self-belief help neutralise this sexist element. While the season's writers clearly kept her "noble

12 Moore, Fiona. "Not as Primitive as They Look." www.kaldorcity.com/features/articles/primitives.html (first published in *Tides of Time*).

13 Sandifer, Philip. "Meanwhiles and Neverweres (*The Invasion of Time*)," *Tardis Eruditorum*. tardiseruditorum.blogspot.com/2011/12/meanwhiles-and-neverweres-invasion-of.html 12/2011

savage" stereotype as the base on which to build her character, it is by no means the defining aspect of Jameson's interpretation. Although tirelessly (and sometimes tiresomely) threatening to knife, fillet and kill any supporting character who disobeys the Doctor's instructions, it's a credit to Jameson that her often violent character is fully rounded and believable. For example, Leela makes an effort to bond with the other women she encounters - even Adelaide from *Fang Rock,* who is the epitome of a racist Edwardian simp; or the intellectual Time Lady Rodan, who starts off strong and refreshingly cerebral in *The Invasion of Time,* but who collapses into a hysterical mess when she and Leela flee Gallifrey's citadel.

Throughout the season, the Doctor's relationship with Leela is broadly based on a professor and pupil footing, with the Doctor seeking to "tame her savage heart" (in the opening episode of *The Invisible Enemy,* she is pictured carefully writing her name on the blackboard). This paternalistic aspect is made slightly more palatable by the fact that Leela is aware of the Doctor's attempts at "civilizing" her, and uses or loses what she deems valuable - she acknowledges the benefits of science, but balances this with her instinct. That said, there's a tetchiness to their relationship, replete with wince-inducing moments when he ridicules her for being "primitive," "savage" or just plain stupid.

The worst cases of this marginalization occur in the weaker stories. In *The Invisible Enemy,* the Swarm rejects Leela as a host, because the virus only attacks "intellectual activity," and the Doctor patronizingly rationalizes that Leela is all "instinct and intuition." Rather than crumple under the Doctor, Professor Marius and (to some extent) K9's condescension, Leela proudly proclaims that she is "not ashamed of who I am" (which is just as well, as her on-the-money instinct about the danger the virus poses is ignored for much of the story). Even worse, in *Underworld,* the second she steps onto the Minyans' ship, her "primitive" nature is pacified, disturbingly turning her into a weak-willed stereotype who immediately starts mooning after one of the blond-haired crew (one of the many reasons why this is the least successful story). Still, there's another side to the Doctor's relationship with Leela which goes some way to balance the negative aspects. In several instances, he places her in a position of trust (for example, when he entrusts her with the Great Key in *The Invasion of Time*) and he's happy to use her "savage" qualities when they benefit him (such as her skill as a huntress in *The Invisible Enemy*). Although she is constantly asking, in true classic companion style, "What's happening, Doctor?", she is the antithesis of the damsel-in-distress. In fact, she is more likely to take on the saviour role. In *Fendahl*, she saves the Doctor's life when the sinister glowing skull rejects his offer of jelly babies, choosing to eat his life instead; and she immediately takes the charge when she runs into the outcast Gallifreyans in *The Invasion of Time*. And when she's captured and almost steamed in *The Sun Makers*, she accepts her impending death with equanimity rather than screeching to be saved.

In fact, *The Sun Makers* is where she really comes into her own. Whether this is because - as some critics have suggested - that Louise Jameson's notoriously troubled relationship with Tom Baker was at its zenith, and she relished having so much screen time away from him, or because Holmes' script let her exhibit more character nuances (including some touching, child-delighting interactions with K9) is unclear.

I'll admit that this is a bit of a stretch, but Leela's character does seem to harbour some admirable non-Western traits (albeit contradictory to her penchant for violence) that echo the South African Ubuntu ethos (the notion that we are all connected and must respect each other), especially in regard to the respect she shows the elderly. "You should talk often with the old ones of your tribe. That is the only way to learn," she states to Vince, the hapless, soon-to-be annihilated lighthouse keeper assistant in *Fang Rock*. And in *Fendahl*, she treats Ma Tyler with kindness and deference. (I'm conveniently ignoring the fact that she almost decapitates the aged groundskeeper at the beginning of the story.) In this respect, her otherness is often portrayed as a positive attribute.

Sadly, her departure at the close of *The Invasion of Time* is a disaster. Jameson wanted her character to go out with a bang - preferably by suffering a violent death. Possibly mindful of the morality police and because he wanted to keep the option open for Leela to return to the show, Williams opted to marry her off to a dweebish guard with zero comic timing - in an ending that is so out of character and disappointing, I actually swore at the television.

Leela is such a compelling character, I'm struggling to figure out why I didn't want to "be" her as a child. (I certainly want to be her as an adult.) I can only suspect that my K9 obsession eclipsed her appeal.

Many Whovians associate K9's arrival with the show's slippage from tense Gothic serial into pure family show territory. Growing up with *Doctor Who*, for me it always *was* a children's show - or, at the very least, a program that worked on various levels for differing audiences. Even the obvious subtext of, say, *The Sun Makers* would have shot straight over my head at age seven, but I would have been glued to the screen when Leela rather cruelly asks K9 if he wants a biscuit and his tail droops. There's no doubt that K9 is a gimmick designed to appeal to younger viewers - complete with cute twisty ears, guard-zapping laser and wagging tail aerial - but thanks to John Leeson's voice characterization, he's elevated above this (and is there a single seventies child who didn't go around saying "affirmative master" in a faux robot voice?). K9's role as the Doctor's "second-best friend" also gave the writers the opportunity to contrast the irascible dog's logic with the Doctor's impulsiveness, which is played for laughs wherever possible (as in the chess scene in the first episode of *The Sun Makers*). He is also useful as a "dog ex machine" plot device - always handy with a laser when the Doctor and Leela need to escape an impossible situation, or on hand for unloading large chunks of exposition. I still find him charming, albeit much slower and noisier than I remember (he sounds like broken vacuum cleaner and moves at the speed of a slug).

The behind-the-scenes issues with K9 make amusing reading. In a compulsively readable, anarchic interview with Benjamin Cook, Tom Baker recalls that K9 was "...technically terribly difficult to work with, because it wasn't very powerful - it would topple if it ran over a cigarette end."[14] Hence K9's departure at the end of the season, albeit to be replaced with a more advanced model: K9 Mark II.

Enduring K9 affection and newfound Leela love aside, the biggest relief of all was that my childhood faith in Tom seemed to be sound. Along with Jameson's performance, Baker's wisecracks and pitch-perfect delivery are the only factors that make the weaker stories watchable at all. Thanks to his face-splitting grin and perfect comic-timing, Baker gleefully owns every second he's on screen, and it's a credit to Jameson that she held her own opposite him.

In fact, it's the glee he shows when he's uttering throw-away lines such as: "My dear old thing, all you need is a wily accountant" (in response to the overtaxed suicidal man in *The Sun Makers*) that makes his excesses - the tendency to allow his ego to dribble over in every shot - forgivable. He's also no slouch at playing it straight, as when he matter-of-factly delivers the devastating statement from *The Invisible Enemy*: "... some of my best friends are humans. When they get together in great numbers, other lifeforms sometimes suffer."

---

14 Cook, Benjamin. "Tom Baker." benjamincook.net/writing/doctor-who-magazine/interviews-and-articles/tom-baker/ (This article originally appeared in *Doctor Who Magazine* #429, December 2010.)

Part nutty professor spewing pseudo-science babble, part manic Harpo Marx-style loon and boomy-voiced bohemian eccentric, there's no doubt that Baker manages to capture the Doctor's essential "alienness" effectively, marrying contradictory facial expressions to portentous statements. In *Fang Rock,* he delivers the line: "This lighthouse is under attack and by morning we might all be dead," with a maniacal grin. He also relishes the Doctor's slightly alien morality (he shows no emotion when Skinsale is electrocuted by the Rutan). In *The Invasion of Time,* he hams it up to the hilt, playing the megalomaniac "evil" Doctor convincingly (right down to the tiniest facial tic and rolling eyes). And clearly, he's in his element in the sillier last episode, tripping over his scarf, skipping down corridors and - after saying farewell to his two best friends - breaking the fourth wall and grinning insanely into shot.

In the final analysis, despite the strength of *Fang Rock* and *Fendahl,* and despite Louise Jameson's superb performance as Leela, and despite child-pleaser K9, it's obvious that Season Fifteen is less about the stories, the supporting cast or the settings than it is about Tom Baker. It's tempting to blur the man with the character - in all of his interviews, Baker comes across as mercurial, playful and almost as loony as the Doctor. As he states to Cook, "The difference between Matt Smith and me is that he's an actor and I'm... well, I'm just Tom Baker. When I realized they liked Tom Baker, that's what they got. It was entirely me. Tom Baker in space."

He's right, and it's the force of his off-the-wall personality - the sense of fun that's apparent in every second he's on screen - that captivated me as a child (along with that trademark scarf). It's why I have never forgotten him, and why, after immersing myself in Season Fifteen, I'll concede that while he might not be the only *true* Doctor, he's certainly the most memorable.

Reboot fans, bring it on.

Additional sources consulted:

Lyon, Shaun, et al. "Image of the Fendahl," Outpost Gallifrey. 31/03/2007, tom-baker.co.uk

Miles, Lawrence and Wood, Tat. *About Time 4: The Unauthorized Guide to Doctor Who* (Seasons 12 to 17), Mad Norwegian Press. 2004

Preddle, Jon. "Affirmative, Master: All You Ever Wanted to Know About K9." nzdwfc.tetrap.com/archive/tsv41/affirmativemaster.html

Sullivan, Shannon. "Image of the Fendahl," *A Brief History of Time Travel.* shannonsullivan.com/drwho/serials/4x.html. 07/08/2007

Donna Noble Saves the Universe

Martha Wells is the author of eleven SF/F novels, including *The Element of Fire*, *City of Bones*, *Wheel of the Infinite*, *The Wizard Hunters* and the Nebula-nominated *The Death of the Necromancer*. Her most recent novels are *The Cloud Roads* and *The Serpent Sea* published by Night Shade Books. She has had short stories in *Realms of Fantasy*, *Black Gate*, *Lone Star Stories* and the anthologies *Elemental* and *Year's Best Fantasy 7*, and essays in the nonfiction anthologies *Farscape Forever* and *Mapping the World of Harry Potter*. She also has written two *Stargate Atlantis* media-tie-in novels: *Reliquary* and *Entanglement*. Her books have been published in seven languages, including French, Spanish, German, Russian and Dutch.

Donna Noble was always different.

While Rose Tyler and Martha Jones did show some marked differences to the companions of the earlier years of *Doctor Who*, in some ways they still fit the same mold. Donna not only broke that mold, she threw it down and stomped on it.

One of Donna's key characteristics is that she saw the Doctor's dark side from the beginning. She knew what he was capable of, and she saw the power and the violence under the charming exterior. But she also saw his vulnerability. She didn't expect the Doctor to be omniscient, and she wasn't afraid to tell him when she thought he had gone too far. From the beginning, she was willing to stop him.

But Donna was also different from many other TV heroines, especially those on American TV. She was a 40-something, not a 20-something. She was attractive in a normal woman way, not in a perfect fashion model beautiful way. And the biggest difference was that Donna Noble saved the universe by being her abrasive, forward, loud, in-your-face, aggressive self. By standing up for herself. Even with an injection of Time Lord metacrisis, not just any random human could have done what she did. A coward or a wimp combined with a Time Lord would still be a coward or a wimp. Donna combined with a Time Lord became something the universe had never seen before.

We saw in her first appearance (*The Runaway Bride*) that Donna had all the resilience of a strong personality that had been subjected to emotional abuse. The first sign of this is when her mother Sylvia reacts to Donna's disappearance from the wedding by insisting that Donna felt that being a bride on her wedding day was somehow inadequate, and had staged her own disappearance to get more attention. In most of their scenes together, the message that Donna got from Sylvia was that Donna was a useless disappointment. The Doctor even took Sylvia to task for it in *Journey's End*, saying that if she thought highly of her daughter, she should tell her so.

Because of this brainwashing by her mother, Donna still saw herself as just a temp from Chiswick, even after all her adventures. "You're special," the half-human version of the Doctor told her in *Journey's End*. But with his new knowledge of Donna's thoughts, he added, "But you really don't believe that, do you?"

The brains, imagination, courage and strong will that made Donna a good companion for the Doctor as an adult probably made her a difficult child, especially for a mother who was a very conventional person. Donna did have a close relationship with her grandfather, who showed many of the same qualities as she did. He encouraged her, and they were both shouted at by her mother.

Sylvia doesn't mean to wear Donna down (emotional abusers never do), but the constant criticism and the constant listing of Donna's failures and inadequacies made Donna used to having to fight to assert herself, bringing out the aggressive side of a naturally strong personality. It also made her search for an escape.

That urge for escape is partly what prompts Donna to push herself into a marriage with a man she had only known for six months. She focused on pursuing that marriage as if it was the ultimate goal of existence, and for Donna's mother and her friends it is the ultimate goal of existence.

On the outside, Lance was an attractive, attentive man with a good job. He was a way to please Sylvia and the rest of Donna's family, to show Donna's friends that she was a success. A marriage like that was an escape from Donna's life of temping and of being inadequate to her mother's expectations. We did see in *Forest of the Dead* - with its view into Donna's psyche - that she did want to be married, did want children, and that having a happy family was important to her at a very deep level. But pressure from her mother and her friends, and feelings of inadequacy, pushed Donna into pursuing the wrong man like a crazy person.

It was more than a bit suggestive that in *Turn Left*, it was Donna's surrender to Sylvia's badgering that sparks off the change in the timeline, the Doctor's death, the slow destruction of Earth and the eventual destruction of all the universes. Donna, and the rest of the universe, were better off when she stuck to her guns.

That kind of treatment from a parent made Donna abrasive, forward, in-your-face, aggressive and judgmental. But after Rose's love and faith, Martha's unrequited love and hero worship (and her disappointment as she became all too aware of the Doctor's less attractive qualities), this was exactly what the Doctor needed.

One of Donna's best qualities as a character was that she was always just as aggressive in her defense of those who needed defending as she was of herself. Donna always seemed irresistibly drawn to the underdog having been the underdog to her mother for so much of her life. Donna's reaction when the others poked fun at Miss Evangelista in *Silence in the Library* was to try to comfort her. It's a good example of how a female character can stand up for herself, be abrasive and aggressive, without being portrayed as a bad person.

Donna also made it clear she didn't expect anybody to save her. Nobody ever saved Donna before, so why should things be different now that she was best friends with a Time Lord? She never stood back and waited for the Doctor to rescue her; she always looked for her own way out and she often found it.

Donna's adamantine will was apparent from her first moment aboard the TARDIS in *The Runaway Bride*. She had been beamed onto an alien spaceship with a man who she first assumed was a serial kidnapper at best, and her reaction is anger, not fear. As soon as the Doctor characteristically started to fast-talk and take command, she slapped him hard enough to knock him back a step and took charge.

Donna was reeling from the sudden disruption of everything she knew to be solid and certain in her life, but when she took the chance and leapt from the robot-driven car into the TARDIS, it was a leap out of a conventional life of not-so-quiet desperation into extraordinary adventure.

And it was a life she was suited for. When she encountered her first alien, the dying Ood, she got through shock and disgust to compassion and sympathy within moments. In *Turn Left*, Donna showed her ability to survive, to take care of herself, her mother and her grandfather under increasingly adverse conditions. It was Donna and her grandfather who adapted and survived in the terrible landscape of the altered timeline, while Sylvia sank into despair. When Rose told Donna that she could stop the destruction of Earth if Donna came with her, she made it clear that Donna would die. Donna wanted very much to live, but in the end sacrificed herself, believing that she would not wake back in the real world.

Another element that set Donna apart as a companion is that she was never a worshipper, never a subordinate assistant. She was never starry-eyed with admiration of the Doctor, even from the beginning. Her first impression of him is that he was an evil guy who broke up her wedding, ruined her big day and that he may even be a murderer-rapist-kidnapper. Her next impression is that he seemed willing to help her return to the wedding but that he was completely crap at it, leaving her to take the initiative, begging a passer-by for the cab fare to get back on her own.

All the previous companions from the beginning of New *Who* argued with the Doctor and disagreed with him to some extent, but Donna never had an initial belief in the Doctor's omniscience or infallibility. The fact that the Doctor had to earn her trust, that she often found his abilities wanting and told him so in no uncertain terms, helped give the Doctor perspective and kept their relationship on an equal emotional footing.

She and the Doctor interacted with each other more as equals, talked to each other like a buddy team. The Doctor showed a healthy respect for Donna's ability to tell him exactly what she thought was wrong with him. Once they got the yelling and the hitting out of the way, the chemistry between the two of them in *The Runaway Bride* is obvious. When she faked tears to get out of trouble at the wedding reception, she winked at him, knowing he would understand. They both laughed at the incongruity of invading the secret Torchwood base aboard Segways, and shared a sense of humor and camaraderie immediately. That was what made the Doctor invite Donna to join him as a companion (though if he had phrased it that way, it might have earned him another punch-slap) but Donna wasn't quite ready to take that step yet.

When they first met, the Doctor and Donna were both in a dark place emotionally. The Doctor was still reeling from the consequences of his actions in the Time War, and still mourning Rose, apparently lost forever. Donna was still stunned by Lance's betrayal and his death, the sudden disruption of her plans for the rest of her life, and the knowledge of the danger that underlay ordinary life on Earth. She had seen the darkness inside the Doctor, the rage, the pain and the power he could wield. She told him he needed somebody to stop him and we knew that was exactly what he needed.

The key to their friendship was that Donna did see this, but grew to accept it. She could joke with him, insult him, sympathize with him, tell him off, hit him, push him around, all while being aware of the frightening extent of his power. And she cut the Doctor absolutely zero slack.

An important component of their relationship was that Donna was never physically attracted to the Doctor. She was never a lover, requited or unrequited. From the beginning, she saw him as a skinny alien and, while Donna had nothing against aliens, she was very clear about the fact that she didn't want to have sex with one. Donna was willing to be friends/ co-workers with him, but she stated unequivocally in *Partners in Crime* that she was repulsed by the idea of any physical relationship with him.

Even after a time of shared danger, of living together in the TARDIS and the establishment of a close and comfortable friendship and shared emotional confidences, Donna's lack of sexual attraction to the Doctor did not change one bit. It became a running joke that when someone mistook them for a couple, they both rushed to correct the misapprehension, even when they were being held at gunpoint. After arriving at the Library in *Silence in the Library* and beginning to realize the danger, the Doctor grabbed Donna to move her away from a shadow. "Hands!" she shouted, shoving him away. There won't be any funny business here.

When Donna and the Doctor met, he wasn't looking for a romantic relationship either. The Doctor didn't want to be alone, but when he encountered Martha Jones and lured her aboard the TARDIS, Martha fell in love. But the Doctor was still in love with Rose, and he couldn't return Martha's feelings, to the point where he seemed completely unaware of them. She eventually left the Doctor and, we later saw, this was the best decision she could have made as she found adventure, independence, success and love on her own. But the Doctor was left alone again. He still felt the loss of Rose and was missing Martha's company and, while keenly aware of the pain he had caused her, knew that she was far better off without him. The scene in *Partners in Crime* where he started to talk aloud in the TARDIS, then remembered that he was alone as the camera pulled back to show the empty and silent console room, is a very strong image of his loneliness.

The Doctor had at least learned one thing from the failure of his relationship with Martha: he was honest with Donna from the beginning. When Donna first came aboard the TARDIS, he told her that he was just looking for a friend, not love or a sexual relationship. But the

Doctor was also very clear about the fact that he didn't want to be alone. He needed a friend more than anything at that point.

It was lucky for the Doctor that he encountered Donna again and that Donna had decided to accept his invitation, to the point where she kept her bags packed in the trunk of her car, ready to go. Donna knew she needed something else but, after her tourist trip to Egypt, she realized that maybe that something else wasn't available on Earth.

Later, Donna told Martha that she never wanted to go back to normal life, that she wanted to travel with the Doctor forever. Considering that by that point, Donna had already been through danger to herself, her family, the entire Earth and had had another personal tour of the Doctor's dark side and the consequences he faced for his actions, this was saying something significant. Donna's first experience with the Doctor's world had included a terrible betrayal by her fiancé and a giant spider who was trying to colonize the Earth. She was never naive about what traveling with the Doctor would be like. She was daunted by the horror of the Ood's slavery but, in the end, didn't let it send her home and her resolve became stronger than ever.

In *Partners in Crime,* Donna comments dryly that not killing the Adipose children was a change for the Doctor. In *The Fires of Pompeii,* her first adventure as an official companion, the first thing Donna did was verbally pin the Doctor to the wall over saving the inhabitants of Pompeii. Donna came to understand where part of the Doctor's reluctance came from, that he was all too aware that his interference in these events could lead to death and destruction, that worse things could happen if he didn't keep his eye on the big picture. That saving one side in a conflict inevitably led to pain and suffering for the other, even if they had been the aggressor. When the Doctor had to destroy Pompeii to save the world, Donna saw the terrible responsibility of it and the effect it had on him. She put her hand on his so they pushed the control together. She gave him permission and included herself in the terrible weight of that decision.

But while Donna now realized that they couldn't save everyone, she reminded the Doctor that you save who you can. And that reminder kept the Doctor grounded.

Donna realized the complexities of the Doctor's situation, the power that he wielded and the responsibility and guilt that came from it. But it didn't change their relationship and she was still never afraid of him. She didn't stop pressing him for answers and explanations, she didn't stop pushing him. And she didn't hesitate to administer a verbal slap upside the head when she thought one was warranted.

Donna's good opinion was dependent on the Doctor quelling the more megalomaniac aspects of his personality. If he went too far, he knew he would hear about it immediately and in no uncertain terms, and Donna's regard (something he had to earn the hard way) was important to him. He had become used to the emotional support of someone who had no illusions about him.

It must be a powerful thing, to have a friend who sees you as you are, the good and the bad, and is still willing to hang out with you, travel with you, tease you, call you names, worry about you, save you, take care of you. The Doctor confided in Donna, telling her about his relationships with Rose and Martha, and the fact that he was a father and had had a family at one point, information which he later withheld even from Amy and Rory. Donna's forthright behavior, candor and plain-speaking engendered trust. She never hid anything from him, and he trusted her with his pain. ("Oh God, he's told you everything," Martha says in *The Sontaran Stratagem*.) The Doctor told Donna's grandfather, "She takes care of me," and he told Donna, "You've saved my life in so many ways." The Doctor didn't call Donna his best friend for nothing.

Donna's emotional relationship with the Doctor contrasted sharply with that of Rose and Martha, but less so with that of Amy Pond and River Song. Donna seems to have paved the way for Amy, who is independent, sexually attracted to but not in love with the Doctor, has faith in him but is well-aware of his failings, and wary of the fact that he lies to her. When Amy encountered the Doctor as an adult, she was younger than Donna, disillusioned by her imaginary friend's failure to return, but not as hard-bitten or as hard-used by life as Donna had been. Her strong personality matched well with the Doctor's, he came to trust her implicitly, and she and Rory loved the life of adventure in the TARDIS.

Donna's partnership with the Doctor also paved the way for River Song, who is first introduced as a completely independent adventurer. She argued and disagreed with the Doctor and was well aware that he lied sometimes. She didn't need the Doctor to get to where she wanted to go or to do what she wanted to do. As the series progresses, we (and the Doctor) find out just how close their complicated relationship is, that they are not only friends and lovers but a married couple.

But in the end, it was the Doctor and Donna Noble, together, who stopped the stars from going out.

The tragedy was that Donna saved the universe, but lost the memory of her life of adventure, her moments of transcendence, the Doctor's friendship, and all her heroism and self-sacrifice. The girl who was told she was a useless disappointment turned into a woman who was of key importance to the survival of the entire human race as well as every other species and world and universe in existence. "I was going to be with you forever," she told the Doctor. But she had to go back home, with no memory of any of it.

We saw later that she found love and the Doctor managed to give her a wedding present that took care of any money worries. She was still the same person, independent, tough-minded, in-your-face Donna, and it was good to see she found a man who loved her for it. But it was a shame that she couldn't have her life of adventure. And as we saw later, this incarnation of the Doctor didn't do so well without her.

But even if Donna never remembered her triumph, the Doctor did, and so did Donna's mother and grandfather and all the other people throughout the universe whose lives she touched. And more importantly, we remember.

We remember the time Donna Noble, the loud, abrasive, forty-something temp who became a loud, abrasive 40-something hero and space adventurer, saved the universe.

I'm From the TARDIS and I'm Here to Help You: Barbara Wright and the Limits of Intervention

Joan Frances Turner is the author of the novels *Dust* and *Frail*. Like many Americans, she was first introduced to *Doctor Who* via Tom Baker reruns on public television, and re-introduced by Christopher Eccleston reruns on... public television. She is still embarrassed about getting sniffly when the first Doctor regenerated.

"I feel afraid - as if we're about to interfere in something that is best left alone."

—Barbara Wright, *An Unearthly Child*

"You failed to save a civilization, but at least you helped one man."

—The Doctor, *The Aztecs*

Doctor Who, from its inception, has embraced a paradox: a protagonist inextricably intertwined with human history exhorts us repeatedly that tampering with time invites disaster. "You can't rewrite history," his first self famously declares. "Not one line!" The Doctor thus tacitly endorses the "butterfly effect" theory from Ray Bradbury's *The Sound of Thunder,* where a single foot put wrong in time alters all that follows, infinitely for the worse. The Doctor's own travels, however, and his irresistible urge to make people better, amount to millions of random footprints - and we know, as viewers, that he rewrites events wherever he goes. Even if one simply decreed it's different because it's the Doctor, his are far from the only footprints - dozens of companions have "wandered off" to make their own mark on the universe's collective history.

Barbara Wright, one of the Doctor's first companions (and, not insignificantly, a history teacher), is a forceful advocate of interference for the greater good, even after experiencing its negative consequences firsthand. So how does Barbara, in her first season on *Doctor Who,* embody the show's paradox of meddling non-interference? What are the actual constraints on intervention, rather than the mere stated - and often ignored - rules of disengagement? How does Barbara's attitude clash with the Doctor's and how are they in philosophical accord?

Barbara's interventionist tendencies announce themselves immediately in *An Unearthly Child,* when concern and curiosity leads her (and Ian) to 76 Totter's Lane. Barbara acknowledges she is seeking out what "is best left alone" and unhesitatingly does it anyway, crossing the TARDIS threshold with no idea what dangers lie inside. Barbara's instinct to intervene trumps her safety - she insists on aiding the wounded caveman Za, convincing a reluctant Ian to help her and unequivocally confronting the still-hostile Doctor: "You treat everybody and everything as something less important than yourself!"

The Doctor, however, scorns Barbara's actions as futile, and subsequent events seem to prove his point. The Doctor exposes the true killer of clan matriarch Old Mother, but Za - framed for the crime - repays them by taking them hostage. Ian teaches Za the coveted "secret of fire," but new chieftain Za immediately monopolizes this secret, assuring the bloody tribal conflicts will continue. Barbara's assistance saves Za's life, which then enables him to kill his rival Kal - as if the timeline required a man must die - and to become, like his father before him, complicit in a prehistoric arms race which may ultimately kill him in turn. None of it would have happened without Barbara saving Za, and yet it's simultaneously unclear if her intervention changed anything at all.

In *An Unearthly Child,* Barbara's behavior is arguably spontaneous Samaritanism. In *The Daleks,* however, her interactions with the Thals are more complex - equal parts pragmatism, a sense of fair play and unexamined willingness to manipulate others for a supposed greater good. In helping rescue a team of Thals from a Dalek ambush, Barbara merely repays a favor: "The Thals gave us the anti-radiation drug. Without that, we'd be dead!" When the travelers find themselves trapped on Skaro (because a vital TARDIS component was left in the Dalek city), however, her attitude changes. Ian and Susan initially oppose soliciting the pacifistic Thals' aid; it's unethical, Ian argues, to ask them to fight and die to retrieve a piece of TARDIS machinery, in the guise of self-defense. Barbara, though, argues relentlessly for this strategy. "You'd simply run away?" she asks Ian, and is unmoved when he insists he can't abide innocent deaths: "Except mine, and Susan's, and the Doctor's?" She chides both the Doctor and Ian for "wasting time with small talk... all you're doing is playing with words."

Significantly, the Doctor very much agrees with her: "We need actions," he declares, "not words!" He is coldly utilitarian; the Thals will be footsoldiers, with himself as their natural leader. Barbara's approach is equally self-interested, yet she also casts critical eyes on a central Thal cultural tenant. "Are they really pacifists?" she asks Ian. "Or is it a belief that's become a reality because they've never had to prove it?" Where the Doctor desires to "make use" of the Thals - even if converting them from pacifism is in their interest, that's not his essential concern - Barbara seems to believe Thal culture requires major change, consensual or not. What is good for her and her companions, and good in her worldview, is *ipso facto* good for the Thals; if they cannot see this, then more aggressive, underhanded means of persuasion are all for everyone's ultimate benefit.

This humanitarian interventionism of Barbara's will prove crucial to understanding not only her behavior in later stories, but her strongest clashes with the Doctor. For the Doctor, meddling due to higher idealistic motives means getting too involved. His fate and those of his companions, as he says, rest elsewhere, and intervention means seeking large-scale, long-term change, for the wrong reasons. Barbara, however, clearly believes that unless their presence leaves a lasting impact - an indelible footprint - it is essentially meaningless. They are not intervening, they are *assisting,* and where it's for the greater good (as defined by the TARDIS crew), it's wrong to do nothing. These opposed ideologies inevitably collide later in the season.

In *The Edge of Destruction,* the alien environment Barbara attempts to alter is the malfunctioning TARDIS itself; she does not simply acquiesce in the Doctor's increasingly paranoid theories, nor credit him with special expertise. She first suggests "another intelligence" has invaded the ship, but backtracks when the Doctor calls this "not very logical," and Ian openly laughs. *The Edge of Destruction,* in fact, brings gender issues to the forefront in a way little seen during the rest of the season, and in a fashion putting Barbara at direct disadvantage. The Doctor and Ian immediately dismiss her suggestions as irrational, and conceal from her and Susan - "the girls" - that the TARDIS has only five minutes' viable time left, on the apparent assumption they couldn't handle the knowledge. Even when the Doctor finally admits Barbara was correct in her assessment of the crisis, he couches it as a battle of the sexes, male rationality vs. female perceptiveness: "It was your instincts and intuition against my logic, and you succeeded." The TARDIS crew frequently encounters institutional sexism in alien cultures, but *The Edge of Destruction* drives the issue home to a disturbing degree.

Barbara's hesitation and enforced feminine diffidence, however, are short-lived. When the Doctor accuses her and Ian of sabotaging the ship, she explodes with overdue anger:

> How *dare* you! Do you realize, you stupid old man, that you'd have died in the Cave of Skulls if Ian hadn't made fire for you? And what about what we went through with the Daleks... because you tricked us into going down to the city! Accuse us? You ought to go down on your hands and knees and thank us! But gratitude's the last thing you'll ever have, or any sort of common sense either!

Once again, Barbara leaps into the breach with the Doctor, despite her and Ian's dependence upon his good will; in *The Edge of Destruction,* this risky tactic reaps growing returns. The Doctor finally admits he's underestimated Barbara. "We all owe you our lives," he tells her sincerely, and notes that "[as] we learn about each other, so we learn about ourselves." Also significantly, Barbara, the first human we ever see set foot in the TARDIS, now becomes the first character - human or alien - to credit the TARDIS with sentience: "The machine has been warning us [of its malfunction] all along!" (The Doctor himself, in direct contrast to his later communion with the "old girl," scorns the idea the TARDIS could ever have a mind of its own.) Thus within the tiny society of the TARDIS itself, Barbara has affected demonstrable change - which, judging by the show's later direction, will have lasting, mostly positive consequences - and her interventionism is successful. Outside the TARDIS, though, circumstances prove more complicated.

In *Marco Polo,* the question of intervention retreats to the background; the TARDIS crew upholds the accepted timeline, and though they agree Ping Cho's impending marriage is unjust, they don't try to prevent it. The ethics of intervention are also a seemingly minor concern in *The Keys of Marinus,* and yet for Barbara they will play a major role. When, during recovery of the titular keys, Barbara accidentally transports herself to the city of Morphoton, the rest of the TARDIS crew soon find her there lounging in bejeweled luxury. This scene will be echoed in *The Aztecs,* when Barbara again goes missing, and the other three again find her dressed and behaving like a queen. Notably - like the Doctor, with his expectations of taking charge - Barbara takes to royal treatment immediately.

However, while Barbara is the first seduced by Morphoton's evanescent luxuries, she is also the first disillusioned. The next morning, she rails against the squalor she perceives beneath the Mesmerers' fragile veil and tells her friends: "Try to see the truth... I must find a way to show you, I must before it's too late!" Barbara, now fully resistant to the brain-like Mesmerers' hypnotic power, subsequently fights off a mesmerized Ian, recovers the first microkey, finds the Mesmerers' control room and destroys their life support machinery; the TARDIS crew and Morphoton slaves alike are freed from captivity.

(Incredibly, after all this, Ian - with the same sexist "chivalry" he demonstrated in *The Edge of Destruction* - orders her and Susan to stay where they are and do nothing until he returns from exploring the next microkey location by himself. Barbara and Susan's reactions to this make an interesting contrast - a frustrated Barbara retorts, "I do wish Ian wouldn't treat us like Dresden china," while Susan responds that, "I think it's nice the way he looks after us." One can cogently argue both for and against the idea of Barbara as a proto-feminist companion, but it's clear that even as she attempts to impose her own values on other cultures, she doesn't embrace the foibles of her own wholeheartedly.)

Barbara has thus fomented a spontaneous, spectacularly successful one-woman revolution - she does not simply *believe* she's the only one who sees things as they are, she actually *is* that person, and thus only she can correct them. This places Barbara in a Doctor-like position - the lone actor who can see beyond the immediate moment, and muster the cleverness and force to achieve justice for the "little people." This sequence of events cannot have escaped Barbara, and it is that - along with a predilection for assuming authority - which will prove crucial in the subsequent story.

The Aztecs most directly, and famously, addresses intervention's limits and unforeseen consequences. Immediately upon the TARDIS landing, Barbara asserts a simultaneously protective and appropriative attitude toward the Aztecs - she deplores that people only remember their ritual sacrifices and discount the good in their culture, while she casually tries on potentially sacred jewelry in the tomb, including the fateful Yetaxa snake bracelet. Unbeknownst to the TARDIS crew, they've stumbled into an ongoing power struggle between Autloc, High Priest of Knowledge, and Tlotoxl, High Priest of Sacrifice, the latter insisting only human offerings can end the drought. Their argument over whether Barbara is the spirit of Yetaxa returned will be gasoline to the flame. Barbara's donning of the dead Yetaxa's bracelet is a classic trivial, yet gravely consequential, butterfly tread. Paradoxically, her more deliberate attempts to intervene in Aztec culture work no real change at all.

Just as she took to royal treatment in Morphoton, Barbara seems at ease with this deifying mirage. The Doctor repeatedly tells Ian to "let them get on with" the sacrifices, but Barbara refuses, inspiring one of the most memorable Doctor-companion confrontations in the show's history:

> **Barbara:** I can't just sit by and watch!
> **The Doctor:** No, Barbara! Ian agrees with me. He's got to escort the victim to the altar... they've made him a warrior, and he's promised me not to interfere with the sacrifice.
> **Barbara:** Well, they've made *me* a goddess. And I forbid it!... There'll be no sacrifice this afternoon, Doctor, or ever again! The reincarnation of Yetaxa will prove to the people that you don't need to sacrifice a human being in order to make it rain!
> **The Doctor:** Barbara, no.
> **Barbara:** It's no good, Doctor. My mind's made up. This is the beginning of the end of the sun god.
> **The Doctor:** What are you talking about?
> **Barbara:** Well, don't you see? If I could stop the destruction of everything that's evil here, then everything that is good would survive when Cortés lands!
> **The Doctor:** But you *can't* rewrite history. Not one line!... Barbara, one last appeal. What you are trying to do is utterly impossible! I know. Believe me, *I know*!
> **Barbara:** Not "Barbara." Yetaxa.

Barbara has progressed rapidly from impulsive intervention, to pragmatic tinkering with cultural values, to acceptance of a privileged, authoritative status within those cultures. Now, like the Doctor in his own hinted-at past, she rushes in full force; she will rewrite Aztec culture according to her own rules, using a borrowed, illegitimate authority, and thus - she declares, in a feverishly idealistic outburst - save it from its historical fate. Barbara thereby commits the exact mistake she decried in the Aztecs' critics, appointing herself their culture's ultimate arbiter; further, much as the Doctor assumes he will lead the Thals to victory, she is certain of success before she begins. "Just walk around like you own the place," the Doctor will advise another companion, far down the road; here, we see the consequences of Barbara embracing this philosophy.

Barbara's efforts, however, end in disaster. Tlotoxl - whom she fatally dismisses as less intelligent than Autloc - turns the sacrifice's disruption to his own advantage, easily convincing the erstwhile victim to throw himself to his death and declaring, more correctly than he knows, "This is a false goddess! And I shall destroy her!" Force having failed, Barbara attempts persuasion, warning Autloc that "famine, drought and defeat will come, and more and more sacrifices will be made. I see a time when ten thousand will die in one day... your civilization will pass forever from the land!"

What is curious about this all too truthful prophecy is Barbara's apparent belief that if she ends human sacrifice - if she "civilizes" the Aztecs, by a *conquistador*'s lights - history will spare them. But if Barbara, by her own account, specialized in Aztec history, she surely knows no indigenous culture, starting with the Arawak and Taino, was spared genocide for being peaceful. In the guise of reason, Barbara thus retreats into superstition, attempting to placate not rain gods but a chimera of Whiggish enlightenment and progress. This, more than the Doctor's warnings, demonstrates the worst hazards of chronological intervention - in imposing her own beliefs, Barbara helps bring about Tlotoxl's religious and political victory, exactly the situation she'd been determined to prevent.

Barbara's actions bring about in miniature the Aztecs' final fate; the arrival of Europeans, imposing their ways by force, persuasion and deceit, signals a twilight of the gods. Barbara's prophecies of doom, and Autloc's slow realization she betrayed his trust, shatters his faith; he abandons the priesthood for the wilderness, leaving Tlotoxl in charge with no moderating influence. The Perfect Victim is sacrificed and - given Tlotoxl's predilections - more and more sacrifices will indeed follow, and all is as if the TARDIS never landed.

In the story's concluding scenes, the Doctor and Barbara, at loggerheads throughout, are brought into sudden, unflattering accord. Barbara, literally and symbolically relinquishing a goddess's regalia, acknowledges the timeline required Tlotoxl's triumph, and demands, "What's the point of traveling through time and space, if you can't change anything? Nothing! And the one man I had respect for, I deceived." The Doctor - now gentle and compassionate - comforts her by declaring, "[Autloc] found another faith, a better. That's the good you've done: you failed to save a civilization, but at least you helped one man."

Given the emotional tenor of Autloc's retreat, and the Doctor's own prior statements, this conversation is disturbing. In praising how Barbara stripped Autloc of his faith, his trust, his cultural moorings, is the Doctor implicitly endorsing the interventionism he claimed to condemn? Why does the Doctor assume that Autloc will find a better belief system, rather than wandering in unrelieved disillusionment? Has the Doctor surmised that, since Tlotoxl's victory was inevitable, so was Autloc's exile or assassination - so at least now Autloc has chosen his inescapable fate? The mutually accepted subtext - that Autloc is fortunate in having his indigenous beliefs degraded - throws into confusion the Doctor's exhortations against altering Aztec traditions. He judges, as Barbara does, though he claims to stand beyond the fray, and his judgments are no less colored by innate prejudice; recall, in their earliest travels, his dismissing Ian and Barbara as "savages" and "red Indians." The Doctor may "walk in eternity" (*Pyramids of Mars*), but like his human companions he still steps firmly within a white, Western cultural landscape.

Another possibility is that these constant contradictions on the Doctor's part are quite deliberate - they are the perpetual inconsistencies of his own psyche, inevitable for anyone who must keep lookout for butterflies and yet stand aside while millions die. Despite his arrogance and temper, the Doctor has clearly come to like and respect Barbara; he is, perhaps, angered not only by her willfulness, but because just as she could not save the Aztecs, he cannot spare her the pain of the neophyte time traveler's hardest lesson. Barbara has, with startling speed, thus followed the Doctor's own implied psychological trajectory, and exhibits many of his same faults, biases and unwitting missteps. For all the unbridgeable distance between Gallifreyan and human, time traveler and history teacher, they reflect one another's best and worst with marked, and fascinating, regularity.

Interestingly, in *The Sensorites*, a key plot point concerns not Barbara's attempts at intervention, but Susan's. Susan pleads to accompany and negotiate with the Sensorites, noting her demeanor and strong telepathic abilities have won their trust. The Doctor, however, flatly vetoes this, becoming furious when Susan tries to defy him, and Barbara unhesitatingly supports the Doctor.[15] Is Barbara ceding to the Doctor's grandparental rights? Significantly, however, she does not merely tell Susan that the *Doctor* forbids her to go - instead she declares, "*I* abso-

15 Again, as in *The Edge of Destruction*, there is a disquieting gender-based subtext to the Doctor's actions: he dismisses Susan as a silly child and ignores her (entirely accurate) pleas that his belligerence is making things worse, as well as the Sensorites' admonishments that they can "read the misery in her mind." After all this, he seems genuinely amazed to discover Susan has telepathic gifts far surpassing his, much as he was shocked that Barbara's suggestions about the malfunctioning TARDIS might be correct. Susan's emotionalism and dependency in other stories makes greater sense in this context; the more she protests, "I'm not a child anymore!", the more aggressively her grandfather infantilizes her.

lutely forbid it!"[16] Barbara may just be concerned for Susan's safety - or, after *The Aztecs*, she may wish to spare the more emotionally fragile Susan from risking her own experiences. Ultimately, of course, matters are put to right, but what might have come of Susan's aborted attempts to intervene will never be known.

In *An Unearthly Child*, Barbara notes that Susan has borrowed a book on the French Revolution. "What's she going to do?" Ian quips. "Rewrite it?" In *The Reign of Terror*, the first season's final story, the show addresses exactly that question; it soon becomes apparent that Barbara's experiences have profoundly altered her approach to intervention. Barbara, Ian and Susan fall in with counter-revolutionaries - one of whom, Jules, kills the double agent Leon in self-defense. Though Leon had betrayed, wounded and imprisoned Ian, Barbara still unconditionally condemns his death: "He was a traitor to you, to his side he was a patriot... the revolution isn't all bad, neither are the people who support it. It's changed things for the whole world, and good honest people gave their lives for that change!" When Ian, (unsurprisingly) unmoved, dismisses Leon's death as "what he deserved," Barbara's temper flares: "You check your history books, Ian, before you decide what people *deserve!*"

Barbara's judgment of the revolutionaries echoes her earlier statements about the Aztecs: people remember only the bloodshed, and forget their accomplishments. However, where she formerly (and seemingly unconsciously) echoed the collective judgment, unilaterally attempting to end a tradition she found abhorrent, here she argues that neither she nor Ian is in a position to pass final judgment on the Revolution. This is a significant departure from her attitude in *The Aztecs*, both toward historical events themselves and toward the possibility of changing them or imposing justice upon their participants.

Barbara's admonishment of Ian is a Doctor-like appeal to chronology's inherent coherence: what has happened will happen, and though TARDIS travel makes footprints inevitable, they cannot trample on timelines outright. When Barbara and Ian reconcile, Barbara confesses the real source of her frustration and anger: "I'm so sick and tired of death, Ian - but I never seem able to get away from it." This is another classic time traveler's dilemma - not only must one let arbitrary violence

16 The Doctor himself, if only because he agrees, doesn't protest Barbara's show of authority. This is perhaps the darker side of his plea to Barbara in *The Daleks*, that she assist him by speaking to Susan "on [Susan's] level." It simultaneously implies that Barbara, the "savage" human, has the status of an overgrown child, and also permits him to muster further quasi-parental artillery against Susan should she defy him.

(however transformative) play out unimpeded, but also accept that all roads lead to one destination, all timelines terminate in death. "Everything has its time," Sarah Jane Smith would later eloquently declare in *School Reunion*, "and everything ends." Barbara, one can surmise, now perceives this truth as she never did before, and that it can be unbearable. Once again, even as Barbara and the Doctor seem at opposite poles, their shared experiences put them on a strikingly parallel track.

Barbara's subsequent behavior shows that she has thoroughly absorbed the lessons of *The Aztecs*. When Jules and company ironically contemplate trying to retain Robespierre - even he might be preferable to Napoleonic dictatorship - Barbara doesn't support their political plans (or Napoleon's), but tries to convince them that timelines are immutable and whatever they do, Napoleon will rule France. The Doctor's response to even these small efforts, though, is short and to the point: "Save your breath." Just as Barbara had to learn the hard way that history, and time, create their own momentum, so too will Jules and his co-conspirators; "events will happen just as they're written," and the TARDIS crew can only offer the possibility of change - however dubious, as in Autloc's case - to a very few souls along the way. Or, as the Doctor says in *The Reign of Terror*, "We can't stem the tide, but at least we can stop being carried away with the flood."

Barbara Wright desires to change history for what she believes to be the better, but her noble intentions have a darker side. More than once, she assumes her own ethics represent a natural, ideal order; just as the Doctor once dismissed her and Ian as "savages," she often expresses unquestioned, biased value judgments, particularly against cultures she judges less advanced than her own. Nonetheless, Barbara learns to look past her own prejudices, suppressing the urge to divide history into do-gooders and evil-doers, and to leave the final judgments to history and time.

In the end, the distinction between forbidden, butterfly-stomping interference and justified intervention on the side of right remains complex, contradictory, deeply contextual and largely undefined. Full-scale efforts to alter societies end in fate's and history's mandates asserting themselves - and yet the Doctor and his companions leave lasting cultural footprints, their actions implicitly endorsed by the show even when their motivations are less than selfless. Barbara Wright, the idealistic - and self-interested - history teacher who storms the chronological barricades, intervenes for grand principle, petty gain, the welfare of others and her own needs and desires. She experiences spectacular success, disillusioning failure, chastening setbacks and, ultimately, genuine hard-won enlightenment, all within the course of a single season.

It is no accident that this character trajectory suggests the Doctor's; history, and time, and how we affect them, are not straightforward Whiggish lines, but the proverbial, unpredictable "big ball of wibbly-wobbly." One may or may not save civilizations, or help individuals, but clearly the better part of time travel is simply showing up. "What's the point of traveling through time and space," Barbara asks in *The Aztecs*, "if we can't change anything?" By the end of her first season, she may have given up on being an angel of history, but she has learned the one clear rule of intervention: we can all do very little, but very occasionally, we can do something. The point, in other words, lies entirely in the possibilities, and Barbara, in all her own innate complexity and contradictions, is a companion always attuned to the art of the possible.

I Robot, You Sarah Jane: Sexual Politics in *Robot*

Kaite Welsh is an author, freelance journalist and critic whose work has appeared both online and in the national press. She is a contributor to BBC Radio 4's Woman's Hour and her fiction has been shortlisted for several international awards. She holds an MA in Sexual Dissidence & Cultural Change from the University of Sussex and lives in London.

Beginning with *Robot* and ending with *Revenge of the Cybermen,* Season Twelve introduced Tom Baker, a new Doctor with a wild mop of hair and a manic, toothy grin. Along with the new Doctor, a new tone was introduced - one that was both more surreal and darker than before.

Continuity was provided by the return of Sarah Jane Smith, played by Elisabeth Sladen. Established early on as the perfect foil to the third Doctor with his old fashioned charm and implicit sexism, Sarah resembled Liz Shaw more than she did Jo Grant. Clever, plucky and always ready to puncture the Doctor's ego, Sarah had a rapport with the Doctor that developed into a double act of Hepburn/ Tracey proportions when Baker replaced Jon Pertwee. The feminism she espoused in her first season was backed up by increased autonomy and a growing confidence - even nonchalance - in her ability to handle the bizarre situations in which she found herself.

The general consensus is that it took a few stories for Baker's tenure to really hit its stride[17], but although it lacks the menace of *Genesis of the Daleks,* the campy brilliance of *The Ark in Space* or the innovative structure of *The Sontaran Experiment,* many of the themes explored in those stories are first raised in *Robot.* The increasing emphasis on strong female characters is among the most noteworthy.

17 The prevailing argument is summed up on the BBC's website itself - "[a]side from the new Doctor," it claims, "there was little to distinguish Season Twelve's first story... from the type of *Doctor Who* to which viewers had become accustomed over the previous few years."

Girls on Top

"Well, I bet that did your female chauvinist heart a power of good. I mean, fancy a member of the fair sex being top of the totem pole."

—Harry to Sarah, *The Ark in Space*

Despite *Doctor Who*'s reputation as a show where the female characters are dismissed as screaming bimbos, Season Twelve is full of strong women. Along with Sarah Jane, who had proudly declared herself a feminist in the previous season, viewers were introduced to the deliciously evil Hilda Winters; Bettan, the courageous Thal soldier in *Genesis of the Daleks*; and med-tech-turned-station-commander Vira from *The Ark in Space.* Even the High Minister - or at least her voiceover - is a woman. It's a stark contrast from *The Monster of Peladon,* where Sarah had to reassure the young queen that "there's nothing 'only' about being a girl!" By Season Twelve, women occupy an equal footing to men - at least some of the time.

But rather than create a sexism-free utopia, the writers instead engaged with the struggles women faced to be taken seriously. As in the real world, women in positions of authority are still rare enough that even Sarah Jane assumes Hilda Winters is the assistant, rather than the leader, of Think Tank.

It probably isn't a coincidence that *Robot*'s real villain shares the middle name of another scientist-turned-politician who was about to become one of the most prominent women in the country. Margaret Hilda Thatcher wouldn't be appointed leader of the Conservative Party until February 1975, a month after the final installment of *Robot* aired, but was firmly on the nation's radar as the Education Secretary who abolished free school milk.[18] The name of Winters' organization is also telling - think tanks are policy institutes that advise the Government, such as the Centre for Policy Studies that Thatcher had recently established. Like Thatcher, Winters is the figurehead for a movement that features few other women and certainly doesn't champion their cause, if Mr Short's objections to Sarah's trousers are anything to go by.

Although the portrayal of a powerful woman as the villain is prob-

18 It was a theme that would continue - in the late 1980s, *Doctor Who* would challenge Thatcher's policies more directly in *The Happiness Patrol,* and Sylvester McCoy would later describe her as "far more terrifying than any monster the Doctor had encountered."

lematic, the idea of a woman who, despite her professional success, still internalizes misogyny is not a new one - nor, unfortunately, an unrealistic one. Like Thatcher, Winters is happy to reap the rewards of feminism, but disinterested in extending a helping hand when it comes to the sisterhood - especially not in the form of nosy young journalists. Unlike Vira in *The Ark in Space,* who is virtually indistinguishable from her male colleagues - her hair and clothing are identical, her gender is seemingly irrelevant - Hilda Winters does not disguise her femininity, but is not above treating it as a weakness in others. When she denigrates Sarah, she does so by implying that she is sentimental, "the sort of girl who gives motorcars pet names." On the other hand, the Doctor has done just that in recent memory, naming his yellow roadster Bessie - an indication of the delight the show is beginning to take in skewing the gender norms. The problematic nature of a woman wielding power only to misuse it is counterbalanced by the stronger depiction of Sarah throughout the story - female viewers are not asked to choose between the powerful villain and the weak heroine.

"That Journalist Girl"

> "I'm still a working girl, you know."
>
> —Sarah Jane, *Robot*

Feisty, brave, and not keen to be relegated to just making the coffee, Sarah Jane Smith frequently tops favorite companion polls, and was introduced to a whole new generation of viewers in 2006's *School Reunion.* The favorable fan reaction led to her own CBBC spin-off, *The Sarah Jane Adventures.* After Elisabeth Sladen's death in April 2011, journalist Viv Groskop described Sladen as "impossibly cool, the Meryl Streep of CBBC... She took a role which demanded ridiculous heights of emotion amid preposterous plots and turned it into something magical and believable." The reasons for her popularity are evident in *Robot* - where, despite the presence of not one but two new actors, Sarah is the driving force of the plot.

In the previous season, she had helped defeat Sontarans, battled Daleks and dinosaurs and introduced alien princesses to the concept of women's liberation, all whilst holding down a day job as a reporter for *The Metropolitan.* In the opener of Season Twelve, she acts as a substitute Doctor whilst he recovers from the aftereffects of his regeneration. Her trustworthiness is exemplified when the Brigadier breaks the Official

Secrets Act by telling Sarah[19] that the top secret plans for the disintegrator gun have been stolen, because without the Doctor, "there's no one else I can tell." Rather than waiting for the Doctor to recover, she heads off to investigate Think Tank - not just because she knows he would want her to, but because she knows she could get a good story out of it. Her independence extends to having a life away from the TARDIS, although that will eventually be sidelined.[20] Few companions are allowed or choose to pursue their own interests whilst travelling with the Doctor - Liz Shaw is a notable example - and however this aspect of Sarah's character is subsequently treated, in *Robot* her career is an important plot device.

Crucial to the development of Sarah's character is her relationship with the new Doctor. Whilst the third Doctor's chivalry veered dangerously close to chauvinism, his new regeneration will cheerfully throw her to the wolves knowing that she can take care of herself. Sladen has said on numerous occasions that one of her motivations for portraying Sarah as anything other than her strong, vibrant self - and no matter how she was written - was because having the Doctor put his faith in someone not up the challenge of exploring the universe made him look foolish. Although Sladen stated more than once that - unlike her character - she didn't identify as a feminist, here she tapped into one of the central tenets of the feminist movement: subjugating women damages men as well.

A Bit Old Fashioned

> "Call me 'old girl' again, and I'll spit in your eye."
>
> —Sarah Jane, *The Ark in Space*

Whilst Sarah had chafed against the third Doctor's protective paternalism in Season Eleven, this was nothing to her response when Harry Sullivan tries the same thing in Season Twelve. He quickly became a foil for Sarah, his bumbling stupidity highlighting her bravery and quick thinking. His function as comic relief also indicates on which side of the battle of the sexes the show places itself, even if this isn't always borne out in the writing. Harry represents the old era of *Doctor Who* - embody-

19 Although she is addressed as Sarah Jane in her post-2005 appearances, she is predominantly called "Sarah" during her original tenure, and so that is how I have chosen to refer to her here.

20 Whilst not explicitly addressed here, the consequences of this are examined in her post-2005 return.

ing a world where chauvinism and chivalry went hand in hand and, in the same way that *Robot* bridges the transition from one era of the show to the next, his presence in Season Twelve eases the way for the beliefs he espouses to go from accepted and promoted by the show itself to being the target of derision - just another hazard to overcome.

He lacks an alarming amount of common sense for someone who is both a doctor and a naval lieutenant, is clumsy and accident-prone (a "ham-fisted idiot," according to the Doctor). In *The Ark in Space*, the Doctor criticizes Harry's lack of agency; the Doctor's ego may not recognise an equal, but he values competency above all things. To paraphrase Liz Shaw, Harry's job is to pass the Doctor test tubes and tell him how clever he is. In essence, he is the traditional idea of the Doctor's female companion, and flipping the gender roles underscores what a problematic archetype this is.

Unlike the female companions, Harry possesses considerable privilege that he takes for granted. Dismissing Sarah's feminism as "female chauvinism" in *The Ark in Space*, he is oblivious to the struggle that lies behind the evolution of a world where women wield real power, and of the part he plays in society's progression to that end. Although when he calls Sarah "old girl" or "old thing," his intention is not to insult, he belittles her and is amused rather than concerned that she takes offence. And yet despite his position of power, Harry isn't equipped to cope with the situations he finds himself in - or the emancipated women whom he encounters. He is outsmarted by not only Sarah, but Hilda Winters and Vira. At one point, he nearly gets eaten by a giant clam - the symbolism speaks for itself.

As Sarah says before her exit in *The Hand of Fear*, "travel broadens the mind," and over the course of Season Twelve, Harry does evolve from the stuffy, old fashioned Establishment prop we meet in *Robot*, but his ingrained sense of male superiority doesn't fit with the increasingly equal footing of Sarah's relationship with the Doctor, or the introduction of female characters in positions of real power. Attitudes like Harry's, whether intentionally demeaning or not, have no place in the TARDIS with Baker's Doctor at the controls and, it is implied, no place in the modern world at all. It is fitting that at the conclusion of his story arc Harry and his outdated notions about women's place and competence are quite literally left behind.

Clothes Maketh the Woman (and the Time Lord)

Despite their claims of a rational new world order, the Scientific Reform Society remain mired in traditional notions of gender essentialism, ideas that feminists like Sarah were beginning to challenge openly. This is most clearly illustrated when her attire falls foul of the Scientific Reform Society, who consider it unsuitable for their new world order. As she points out, in their utopia "I would wear what you thought was good for me... and think what you thought was good for me, too." Historically, women's dress has always been policed as a means of restricting their freedom, so it is unsurprising an organization that so proudly boasts about elitism should be so rigid in their dress codes. Not only is Sarah adopting masculine dress, but the outfit itself is offbeat, an indication of individualism that the SRS cannot allow. Her outfit, with its androgynous tailoring and dramatic headscarf, echoes the costume of the 1920s flappers, who rejected the values of a world that treated them as the property of husbands or fathers and enjoyed newfound independence. In contrast, the uniform adopted by the SRS is just that - it is military, conformist and their logo resembles the Nazi swastika.

As the story that introduced the fourth Doctor, *Robot* is concerned with identity and presentation, but what is also notable is the evolution of Sarah's clothing. Whilst Sarah's outfits during Season Eleven were notable for largely consisting of unflattering jumpers, during her travels with the fourth Doctor she's notable for her unusual style, veering from floating, pseudo-Victorian dresses to dungarees in her final two stories.[21] In *Robot*, she has a delicate prettiness we're not used to - the jeans and argyle sweaters have been replaced by a lavender skirt suit, pearls and high heels, and yet she subverts her feminine image by climbing over walls, running for her life (in heels, no less) and breaking into buildings. The way she presents herself visually varies dramatically throughout the story, but this serves to overtly reject the implication that her femininity makes her weaker or less competent, or that her forays into androgyny have any relation to her bravery and strength.

The relationship between clothes and identity in *Robot* is complex, not least in the new Doctor's choice(s) of outfit. The subplot of the story is about establishing Tom Baker in the role, but rather than use a trope such as the tenth Doctor's "what kind of man I am" speech in *The Christmas Invasion*, writer Terrance Dicks instead focuses on the fluctuating nature of the Doctor itself - his identity is rooted in constant transformation. When the Doctor adjusts to his new regeneration, he goes

21 *The Masque of Mandragora* and *The Hand of Fear* respectively.

through numerous wardrobe choices before settling on the comparatively normal attire that would become synonymous with the role. Although the different personas he adopts - Viking warrior, a king and a sparkly clown - are all male, wardrobe changes highlight the volatility of his identity, and the Brigadier's reaction can be read as horror at the prospect of what all this dressing up might imply. Although in later seasons Romana will try on both different bodies and different species for size, and the 2011 story *The Doctor's Wife* confirms that Time Lords can regenerate into any gender[22], *Robot* is the first story to seriously examine this sense of fluidity.

Damsels-In-Distress

Despite the positive portrayal of Sarah's character in *Robot*, the plot still calls on her to revert back to the damsel-in-distress. Terrance Dicks, after all, was never one to advocate for the feminist movement when a cheap joke would do. Sarah becomes the Fay Wray to the eponymous robot's King Kong when he[23] scoops her up, and their short-lived "relationship" has some chilling parallels. Although he states his intent to protect her, he isolates her from her friends, threatens her whilst claiming to defend her - his line "You will be safe. See how I deal with our enemies?" is an implicit warning that if she fails to submit to his authority, she too will be crushed. At one point, he even hits her. Despite the frustrations inherent in having yet another "Sarah gets kidnapped" plotline - by time of her exit in *The Hand of Fear*, her travels with the Doctor will have been reduced to a litany of the times she's been shot at and possessed by one alien menace after another - the acknowledgement that this sort of behavior is wrong is welcome. Once again, oppressive actions disguised as being in her best interests are challenged.

Despite Sarah's continued role as victim of Alien of the Week, *Robot* sees the introduction of equal opportunities in victimhood. Whilst it is normally the role of the female lead to be kidnapped, threatened, tied up or otherwise come to harm in service of the plot, both Harry and the Doctor throughout Season Twelve need their fair share of rescuing. In *Robot* alone, Harry is tied up and imprisoned in a cupboard, and the Doctor is menaced by the robot in a scene that mirrors one of Sarah's in the previous episode. In *The Sontaran Experiment*, they both fall into a

22 Based on the apparent ability to regenerate into different species, they are also presumably not confined to a binary system of gender.

23 The robot is referred to in the script as "it," but as it is voiced by a male actor and has a quasi-romantic attachment to Sarah, it seems clear that "it" is in fact a "he."

ditch, the kind of silly mistake that Sarah would unfortunately become known for. Whilst the female characters are given increasing opportunities to prove their strength, the men are also given challenges that take them out of their comfort zone.

Conclusion

In a season with some of the best-loved stories - *Genesis of the Daleks, Revenge of the Cybermen* and *The Ark in Space* are among the strongest of Baker's tenure if not some of the best in the show's history - *Robot* is unjustly overlooked. Reflecting the gradual progression of women in British society, women played a more prominent role in Season Twelve and the increasingly outdated gallantry espoused by Pertwee found a satirical mirror in charming but old-fashioned Harry Sullivan.

Despite the story's title, it is the clash between the cold-hearted Hilda Winters and the irreverent Sarah that defines the story. They may be underestimated because of their gender, but that's not a preconception either woman allows to last long. Although none of their interactions would pass the Bechdel test, they accurately reflect a society where powerful women and feminism do not always see eye to eye - a considerable achievement for a show known for its love of the damsels in distress trope.

Referencing among other things *The Avengers, King Kong* and even James Bond, *Robot* sets the tone for a season where sexism is tackled head on in nearly every story and where women play an increasingly large role, from leaders to villains. Despite its flaws, *Robot* is an engaging opening start to Baker's era, and one that hints at the full potential of the companion's role.

Between Now and Now

Juliet E. McKenna's love of other worlds, other peoples, fantasy, myth and history was nurtured by childhood viewing of programs such as *Doctor Who*, *Star Trek* and *UFO*. After studying Greek and Roman history and literature at Oxford University, she worked in personnel management before a career change to combine motherhood and book-selling. Her debut novel, *The Thief's Gamble*, was the first of The Tales of Einarinn series (1999-2002). Two more novel series followed: The Aldabreshin Compass sequence (2003-2006, beginning with *Southern Fire*) and The Chronicles of the Lescari Revolution (2009-2010, starting with *Irons in the Fire*). Her diverse shorter fiction has included tie-in stories for *Doctor Who*, *Torchwood* and *Warhammer 40,000*, as well as contributions to anthologies in the UK and the US. Working from time to time as a creative writing tutor, she also reviews books for print and online magazines, notably *Interzone* and *Albedo One*. She served as a judge for the Arthur C Clarke Award 2011-2012. Living in Oxfordshire with her teenage sons and husband, she fits all this around her family and vice versa. Her fourth epic fantasy series, *The Hadrumal Crisis*, began with *Dangerous Waters* in July 2011, published by Solaris.

The final story of Season Nine explores the nature of time travel with reference to concepts owing as much to philosophy as to quasi-science. It's left to the ever-reliable Sergeant Benton to simplify the TOM-TIT device's function in *The Time Monster* as moving objects "through the crack between now and now." As we see intriguing glimpses of this space outside time, I realize that this is the most interesting and productive place for the viewer of classic *Who*.

Recalling the "now" of my first watching as a child in 1972 offers entertaining nostalgia, but little insight. I was as ready to accept a future of food reduced to pills and capsules (and oddly short on furniture) in *Doctor Who* as I was in the original *Star Trek*. What of it? The "now" of watching stories as an adult and comparing them to current TV offers little more than wry amusement at the contrast in production values, and a few good laughs and winces never intended by the writers or actors. The special effects can't compete with CGI, while the fight scenes are frequently risible. These future computers still have endearingly retro analogue dials and reel to reel tapes, while locations are pinpointed as "50 miles or so outside London" with paper maps and dividers. What does any of that tell us beyond the obvious?

The most interesting perspective is surely comparing and contrasting those visions of the present and future written 30 years ago in the dual light of the cultural climate of their own time and of ours today. That demands we step through that crack into somewhere outside both decades for the clearest view of both "now" and "now."

It would never have occurred to me as a six year old to wonder at the inherent assumptions of male authority evident in this season from the very first story, *Day of the Daleks*. But then, children of every decade are used to adult authority, male or female. As an adult who has experienced 30 years of feminism, though, the subordinate role of women in this 1972 world immediately grates. Miss Padgett the secretary is there to serve the great man, Sir Reginald Styles, just as Jo Grant is apparently present to facilitate the Doctor's work. Both here and in the third story of Season Nine, *The Sea Devils*, military women in UNIT and the Royal Navy seem strictly limited to taking dictation, operating radios or phones and making the tea. In the twenty-second century Earth ruled by the Daleks, we see not much has changed. Women operate scanning consoles in obedient silence for the human Controller. The only thing the Controller lacks compared to his 1972 counterparts is an authoritative moustache. Ah, but he's not really in control since he reports to the Daleks, which presumably explains his lack of facial hair.

Except when we see the trio of future freedom fighters coming back to try and kill Sir Reginald - to divert history away from the calamity of a Dalek conquest - they're led by a woman, Anat. More than that, as her juniors object and protest, she has no qualms about asserting her authority. This is a future when women in command of a mixed gender force is entirely accepted. We must step outside our own time to fully appreciate the impact of this, not as viewers accustomed to Colonel Samantha Carter of *Stargate SG-1*. Even if Anat herself ultimately reports to yet another man with a suitable moustache.

Once we step through that crack, we can also see the less overt but no less significant initiatives taken by other women in these stories. UNIT's radio operator insists on interrupting the Brigadier's phone call with a government minister to make sure he gets a vital message. Captain Hart's Wren/ secretary Jane Blythe in *The Sea Devils* decides to ring the treacherous Colonel Trenchard to check where the Doctor and

Jo might be, and then draws the Captain's attention to the implausibility of the story which Trenchard tells them. She doesn't even know the Colonel has been suborned by the Master.

The ways in which different men react to these women's actions are also well worth noting. Captain Hart, one of the good guys, pays attention to 3rd Officer Blythe's concerns. It's Walker, the bloodthirsty coward from the Ministry, ready to respond to a lost submarine with nukes, who sees her only as a source of tea and sandwiches. The Brigadier accepts his radio operator's reasoning, just as he is ready to accept and respect Dr Ruth Ingram's authority as a scientist in *The Time Monster*. Granted, he does occasionally revert to type, once barking at Jo and Ruth that females should take cover - but overall, Lethbridge-Stewart is impressively enlightened for a man of his time, class and career. Let's not discount the potential influence of this facet of a moustachioed heroic character on young male viewers in 1972.

Dr Ingram is the most overtly feminist character in this entire season, something highlighted in the script with references to "women's lib" in the mostly mocking tones of her assistant Stuart Hyde. It's soon clear that his attitudes don't reflect the scriptwriters' own views. It's Ruth Ingram who ultimately solves the technical challenge of the Master's machine while Stuart is looking after Sergeant Benton (who's been accidentally returned to babyhood), and it's Stuart who the Doctor sends to put the kettle on while he discusses the situation with Dr Ingram and the Brigadier. However, there's further nuance when Dr Ingram condemns all men as spineless and Stuart points out that he's not actually all men, but one individual. This reminder not to make sweeping generalizations is wholly in keeping with those aspects of *Doctor Who* common to both instances of "now" and at the heart of its enduring appeal.

Beyond the ancillary characters, Jo Grant is central to any assessment of the portrayal of women in this season, not least because in both *The Curse of Peladon* and *The Mutants*, Katy Manning's is essentially the only female role. Granted, there are two other women actors in the *Peladon* cast list, but the Alpha Centauri delegate is explicitly explained as a hermaphrodite hexapod, while the female Earth delegate only appears in the story's final moments (though let's not discount that unspoken assumption about women's future roles).

Jo's role throughout this series can look oddly uneven from both perspectives. In *Day of the Daleks*, she fetches and carries for the Doctor and for UNIT, is fearful of ghosts and seems naively trusting when the twenty-second century Controller tells her how wonderful life is. She arrives on Peladon in a posh frock and hairdo, ready for her date with Mike Yates. She spends a great deal of time in *The Mutants* being captured, rescued, captured again, swept up in the arms of a good-looking hero. In *The Time Monster*, she mostly tags along after the Doctor, to Cambridge and to Atlantis, where she's promptly sent off for another groovy frock and glam hairdo. It's so in keeping with 1972's expectations, and so alien to a modern viewer.

Except there are always hints that Jo is more than this. She's always well informed about current events, supplying the Doctor with key information from newspapers. She asks him lots of questions and when he asks her, she's ready with answers, up to and including identifying TARDIS components and other such tech. Their relationship is far more that of teacher and student than manager/ officer and secretary/ subordinate. When the Doctor has to introduce her as Princess Josephine on Peladon, he doesn't hesitate to involve her in this high level diplomacy, at one point putting her in charge of the vital conference. Why not? She's already proved she can climb a mountain in a storm wearing a maxi-dress and high heels, and find the tunnel to the top. He also listens when she argues he's misjudging the Ice Warriors' warlike intentions, and this is by no means the only time that the Doctor revises his own opinions in the light of her comments. Finally, Jo is the key figure who encourages the young king to assert himself.

There are repeated references to Jo's "escapology course," and this really comes into its own in *The Sea Devils*. Jo is in the thick of the action in this adventure from start to finish, in an indestructible and unstainable cream trouser suit which must surely be sewn from some alien fabric. She bribes a boatman to borrow his motorbike, evades pursuing soldiers, finds the imprisoned Doctor, signals her plan to him through the window, finds a way to break into the castle and successfully rescues him. She doesn't baulk at escaping through a minefield, at climbing through ventilation shafts, and rides a hovercraft along with a couple of dozen sailors into the final gun battle. Let's not discount the potential influence of such facets of a female character on all young viewers in 1972. Such behavior in the Doctor's female companions is definitely something I recall challenging those inherent assumptions of male authority all around me at the time.

If Jo returns to much more of a damsel-in-distress role in *The Mutants*, we should note that this script is already tackling a slew of issues, contentious then and now. This is one of those stories where universal themes speak boldly to viewers in both decades. The Earth Empire is withdrawing from the planet Solos, not because of any concern with the increasingly rebellious indigenous people's rights, but because they can no longer afford to maintain a presence on this world they have stripped of natural resources. Written in the last fading twilight of the British Empire, this story still resonates today as corporations and countries like China engage in a new scramble for Africa's mineral wealth. "One man's terrorist is another man's freedom fighter" is a debate still very much with us, as is the question of scientists' responsibility for the long-term effects of their actions. When the scientist Jaeger claims he is only following orders - and thus cannot be blamed for the global climate change ordered by the Marshal and lethal for the Solonians - the Doctor's condemnation of this infamous excuse is truly timeless.

The presence of a black actor, Rick James, in the very first scenes - as one of the Overlords loudly condemning the planet as a stinking rotten hole - still prompts a double-take today. Back in 1972, that would have been truly astonishing. The 70s was a particularly poor decade for ethnic minority actors' visibility across British TV drama, not only in *Doctor Who*. Moreover, while the cultural mix of the country had substantially increased through the 50s and 60s, visible ethnic minorities were still very much concentrated in the cities. I don't recall if this character would have been the first black face I'd seen as a child living in rural Lincolnshire in 1972, but I think it's a fair guess that his was the first West Indian accent I would have ever heard. Change since then has been slower than you might think; it's only in the past decade that black faces no longer prompt double takes on the High Street in the Cotswold market town where I now live.

So Cotton's presence is still thought-provoking, not least because no one makes any reference to his color and perhaps most of all when in the final resolution, with the corrupt Marshal now dead, the Earth Investigator blithely puts Cotton in acting command of the entire Skybase. Such color-blind casting was so very much the exception at the time and is still too rare nowadays. Though the character's name isn't some cunning post-modern ironic twist on Afro-American slavery as it would surely be today. According to the writers, the character was originally intended to be a Cockney, one of the varied accents among the characters showing the range of Earth people. Rick James was cast later simply to take that idea one step further. Knowing this certainly explains why some of the dialogue sounds distinctly odd in his delivery.

The key to solving the problem of *The Mutants* is knowledge. The Doctor and the anthropologist Professor Sondergaard finally unravel the life cycle of the Solonians in relation to the planet's 2000-year orbit. Though the realities of this solar system are not explained with anything like the detail that would surely be the case today. One distinct difference between "now" and "now" is the lack in all these stories of what can so often become tedious technobabble in later television SF. (*Star Trek: Voyager*, yes, I'm looking at you.) There are also far fewer of the morality debates that current characters so often indulge in. I find it particularly notable that no one agonizes over rewriting the timeline in *Day of the Daleks*, realizing that these brave future soldiers will now never have been born. That would surely be an intense and pivotal scene for actors to seize on in any modern version.

No one makes particular mention of the future soldier Shura's self-sacrifice in detonating the bomb that stops the Day of the Daleks. The attitude is very much "the job's done, let's move on." Is this superficial writing or is it more a reflection of a decade far less removed from the cold, hard reality of personal sacrifice and death in World War II? Let's not forget that Jon Pertwee saw active service in the Royal Navy, Barry Letts served aboard a submarine during the war, and many of the writers and actors, like Nicholas Courtney, would have been old enough to do National Service through such crises as the partition of Palestine and the Malay Emergency. As I clearly remember, 1970s TV and cinema were full of war dramas while the news was still covering the last years of US involvement in Vietnam, where deaths were far too numerous for individuals to be named. Numerous, but not so shocking to those who had seen much greater losses in WWII. Just as their forefathers would consider D-Day losses as grimly acceptable in the light of the far greater carnage they had known on the Somme.

When I was a kid in the 70s, everyone's parents and grandparents reminisced about WWII, and Great War stories were still common. My gran told me about her brother's experiences on the Western Front, and I had one great uncle who served in the Royal Flying Corps. These days, I am often the only person in a room with friends currently serving in the military, let alone with school friends who served in the Falklands War. Comparing personal and media attitudes of the 1970s to the reporting of twenty-first century military (mis)adventures in Iraq and Afghanistan definitely highlights key differences between these decades. I see that contrast reflected in early classic *Who*'s seeming indifference to death. For good or ill? I can see both sides of that particular coin. You will have to make up your own minds. Which is, of course, another recurrent and eternal theme of *Doctor Who*: individuals are always responsible for drawing their own conclusions and making choices.

There are always individuals in *Doctor Who*. Groups are rarely wholly benevolent or malevolent, okay, with the exception of the Daleks and the Master. There are honest and brave Earth Overlords on Solos to counter the Marshal's venal brutality, while neither of the most prominent Solonians - Varan and Ky - are entirely good or bad. Other characters are just as complex. The future Controller in *Day of the Daleks* may be a quisling, as the Doctor rightly accuses him, but his self-justification is rooted in the past sufferings of his people, and that makes him far more than a simple black-hat. Colonel Trenchard has been duped by the Master in *The Sea Devils*, but it's his better qualities, notably his patriotism, which has proved his Achilles' heel. Even a villain like Hepesh - the murderous priest on Peladon - wants the best for his people, just as the Atlantean Council in *The Time Monster* hopes to use the power of the Kronos crystal to benefit their people. It's only King Dalios who is old enough to remember how badly things turned out in the past. He's also old and wise enough to see that the Master is no emissary of the gods, and to resist his hypnotic powers.

A common thread uniting classic and New *Who* is that knowledge is always the key to making informed decisions. The third Doctor won't accept the Controller's assurances in *Day of the Daleks* any more than he yields to the High Priest's superstition on Peladon, establishing instead that Aggedor, the Royal Beast supposedly embodying the curse, is nothing more than a captive animal. Communication is just as important. Despite his own previous experiences with the Silurians, the Doctor insists on trying to negotiate with the Sea Devils, just as he tries to find common ground with rival factions on Solos. It's the Doctor who both saves the universe and condemns Atlantis by telling the Queen the truth about King Dalios' death, undercutting the Master's lies.

The Master may have a great deal of knowledge, enough to build devices to contact Sea Devils and to transmit matter through interstitial time, but he has no time for such two-way communication. Convinced of his own brilliance, he has no interest in anyone else's opinion, as he shows time and again. He cuts Colonel Trenchard short with open rudeness while his feigned courtesy to Dr Ingram does nothing to conceal his innate arrogance. The difference between the Master's patronising attitude to Dr Ingram and the Doctor's genuine respect for her as a scientist speaks volumes. These two stories, *The Sea Devils* and *The Time Monster*, are driven by the contrasts between the Doctor and the Master. This is made all the more compelling by the lead actors' performances, especially in their verbal jousting, if rather less so in their impromptu and otherwise inexplicable swordfight.

Roger Delgado does a superb job of making what could so easily have been a pantomime villain into a truly chilling adversary, up to and including the requisite evil laugh and gloating. His beguiling tones are central to the Master's manipulation of Colonel Trenchard and the Queen of Atlantis, and in his convincing assumption of authority over Dr Percival at the Newton Institute. Time and again, he's ready with quick and plausible lies to further his own ends, whereas the Doctor's innate honesty can be his undoing. Even the shortest scenes reveal so much with a silent glance, such as the Master's utter indifference when he finds an injured window cleaner, fallen from his ladder.

He has no interest in people, only in the pursuit of absolute power over time and space. If he cannot secure such power, he is ready to accept the destruction of the universe, whereas the Doctor is only bluffing when he threatens the Master with the oblivion of a Time Ram. Ultimately, of course, this arrogance proves the Master's undoing, as when he makes the mistake of treating the Queen of Atlantis like a maid. But none of this would convince us without Roger Delgado's performance. I remember him from my childhood just as clearly as I remember the third Doctor. The dark shadows of such villainy are vital for showing the Doctor's virtues so clearly, amid the other facets of his character so brilliantly conveyed by Jon Pertwee.

The first story of this season offers one of the best summations of the Doctor, now and now, through his own words. In *Day of the Daleks*, the Doctor is drinking a wine from Sir Reginald Styles' own cellar. He describes it as "sardonic but not cynical, a wine after my own heart." This perhaps more than anything else captures the appeal of *Doctor Who* for me, past, present and future.

What Would Romana Do?

Lara J. Scott has a degree in an Arts subject and thus is not very good with facts. She is a bit geeky and nerdy, and enjoys *Doctor Who* as well as proper hobbies like drumming and languages. But mostly *Doctor Who*. Yes, she owns an overly-long scarf. No, you may not wear it.

I don't know if I can capture the importance of a Doctor-like woman to those of us of the feminine gland. We're always being told that we can't have a female Doctor, for this reason or that. The main protagonist role is denied to us by our sex. Luckily in the case of *Doctor Who*, there are two things working in our favor: the Doctor's lack of cliché gender and the occasional appearance of a woman like Romana. She's completely capable of carrying the show on her own if needed (go forward a year and watch *The Horns of Nimon* if you don't believe me). You too can be the Doctor, ladies, albeit with another name.

Romana *is* the Doctor with tits. There's not really any getting round that. She's arrogant, witty, occasionally smug, hyper-educated, privileged, curious, compassionate, brave and more than slightly posh. But Romana is also something new. She's a mid-point between the stuck-up boring old farts of Gallifrey and the out-of-control rebels like the Doctor. When she first arrives onboard the TARDIS in *The Ribos Operation*, she appears to be a much more traditional Time Lord than the Doctor - but by the end of her tenure on the TARDIS, the Doctor's influence has allowed her to become her own Romana. Rather than return to Gallifrey, she finds a universe of her own to have adventures in.

In discussing Romana, people tend to overlook Season Sixteen and focus on Lalla Ward, to the detriment of the delightful Mary Tamm. I am not entirely sure why that is. It's like saying you like toast and then never talking about bread because bread isn't toast yet. So let me extol the virtues of bread for you.

Romana I is just as clever, witty and fascinating as her later regeneration. She has an arrogance that irritates the Doctor and wins over anyone who ever thought he was a bit too fond of himself. Everything that is great about Romana starts here, and her personal journey from naïve

debutante to universe-saving veteran is wonderful to watch. If you took out Romana I, then the Romana whole would be less interesting and less impressive in terms of change over time.

Mary Tamm is gorgeous and graceful - and if it's at all possible, I want to be her when I grow up, and not just because of her perfect eyebrows. Romana I has jagged edges to her that never get filed off, but become slightly less apparent as she gets used to the universe and the Doctor. Most of all, I love the sparks between her and the Doctor as they try to fit their egos into a finite space. These are the early days, where she's trying to work out how to approach him and he's working up the courage to ask her out on a date. (I'm sorry, it's just really hard not to see it as romantic in a season where she pulls him onto a white horse and gallops off into the sunset.)

Now, I always tend to argue that the Doctor isn't "masculine" as traditionally described. He's mostly non-violent, always willing to find a compromise, easily swayed by his emotions. He has a nurturing streak that draws him to take care of the entire universe in his own strange way. Does he need a feminine side? Does he need a Romana? Well, what are her contrasting qualities? In Season Sixteen, Romana is more by-the-book and she seems almost chilly by comparison on the emotional level. She's initially inexperienced, more academic and perhaps even more intelligent than the Doctor - in her first scenes, we learn that she graduated from the Academy with a triple first while the Doctor scraped by with 51% on the second attempt. Romana is not The Girl you may know from all those ensembles where the one woman is characterized entirely based on her gender. So it's not so much that they make a gender-balanced pair as it is that they make a new whole.

This isn't to say that Romana doesn't have her weaker moments - in Season Sixteen, she screams, she gets captured, she worries. But she never loses her confidence; she never becomes entirely a victim. She remains heroic and specifically she remains Doctor-like. While her first cliffhanger (in *The Ribos Operation*) has her calling for help as a monster threatens to eat her and she ends up clinging in fear to the Doctor, I see two things that make this not as awful as it seems. The first is that the Doctor is also in danger (rarely mentioned in discussions of that cliffhanger), and the second is that this is her first time out against the monsters. She's had a sheltered upbringing on Gallifrey and suddenly she's completely out of her element. (And, to be fair to her, *she's* not the one who got caught in a net trap partway through the first episode.)

Of course, as a Time Lord, knowledge of her race's power and position in the universe, as well as her own intelligence and education, has already privileged her with a bucket load of self-esteem before she even stepped into the TARDIS, helping to negate her lack of experience.

This privilege and growing confidence becomes apparent when she gets arrested in *The Pirate Planet* and her first action, while being threatened at gunpoint, is to coolly send K9 to get help from the Doctor. Thereafter, she's tremendously casual about it all, apparently completely unconcerned for her own safety. This confidence keeps her from being reduced to the victim role that has tended to plague the Doctor's companions from time to time. She acts pretty much like the Doctor would, and it's only her second adventure.

People say that Romana is posh - which, to be fair, she is. She's a Time Lord, you see. Time Lords are powerful, arrogant, well-educated, confident and... well, Romana's no different. Time Lords are the aristocracy, and you can't get round that. It's an intentional portrayal by the writers (especially Robert Holmes) to demonstrate the power of the unelected over ordinary people. The Doctor and Romana remain friends of the people by placing themselves as the ones put in danger by the whims of the powerful. *Doctor Who* is great because you never feel condescended to by these aliens. They aren't quite of us, but they have turned their backs on the things that oppress us. The Doctor has rejected the so-called "birthright" of hereditary power, and Romana has been irreversibly removed from it and is learning to see things from the Doctor's point-of-view rather than her people's, but they're still cruising along in a TARDIS with vast educations and no financial needs. The Doctor and Romana don't have to care about the class system because they are, well, posher than everyone. They're outside the system by virtue of their Time Lord status. The only people they have to defer to are beings on the level of the Guardians, things even more godlike than themselves. It's to their credit that they choose to interfere against oppression when they have no need to. It could be seen as adventure-tourism, but it's always obvious that they actually care about what happens to people. Class may be something that happens to other people, but it's not to be ignored just because it doesn't affect our heroes personally.

While later *Who* may have uncertainties about the privilege inherent in the Doctor's position, in the 1970s there's no problem of sources. *Doctor Who* is punk. Romana I may confuse with her cut-glass accent and her occasional tiara, but we know that she's on our side. Ironic that people seem to think of Romana II, played by a genuine aristocrat, as the "less posh" Romana, isn't it? I think that's just not seeing past the exteriors, the same unthinking acceptance that leads people to denounce the entire series as a colonialist daydream. *Doctor Who* is against the establishment and that's clear in Season Sixteen despite the number of aristocrats in the stories. It doesn't like it when you steal some other culture's stuff, it doesn't like it when you commit crimes against the masses.

Of course, our heroes don't care about money because they never have any need for it. It's an incredibly privileged position to be in, but they use this ability to help others and to belittle those who oppress in the name of capital. To the Doctor and Romana there is something futile and pointless about all of this - the quest for immortality and the accumulation of money are equally ridiculous when you get right down to it.

The very structure of Season Sixteen, framed by the Doctor and Romana's search for the Key to Time, allows us to see the petty nature of such upper-class concerns and examine the conflicts of the class structure.

We see this in *The Ribos Operation*, where the lower classes - at least when imitated - have regional accents. This has always been a bit of a thing with *Doctor Who*, as with most TV of its time, in that Received Pronunciation is set as the default and anything else is noteworthy. Here Garron and Unstoffe, the conmen trying to sell the planet Ribos, use accent as a deliberate marker of background and social status. It gives us a sideways glimpse of the class issues of Ribos and the local area. This is a planet thought of as so backwards, it can be bought and sold without any concern for the people who live there. They have no rights here, no say in their future which is played for by a dethroned prince. What's especially relevant here is that nobody really cares what happens to him. Garron and Unstoffe see only financial opportunity, and the Doctor and Romana are equally uninterested in the prince's claim.

In *The Pirate Planet*, the class system is more modern and capitalistic, yet the real ruler is a queen set on living forever through the destruction of others. She is the parasitic nature of her class, the dead worlds are the generations of people who suffer to maintain a monarchy and/or aristocracy. The people of the titular pirate planet don't question anything, because each destruction rewards them with "a new golden age of prosperity." They talk to Romana first because she's "prettier than [the Doctor]," being led by, and used to, shallow visions of the world around them.

The Power of Kroll is openly about colonialism, and it's worth mentioning that the oppressed "swampies" are as brutal as the people who seek to destroy them. They worship an angry god, and make living sacrifices to it. They aren't perfect, but we accept that whatever their own flaws this is their planet, and it shouldn't be taken from them by humans seeking to make a profit. Sometimes it comes down to armed struggle, and that's never pretty. There's an ugliness to the story, even a cynicism, that makes the conflict more nuanced than it might otherwise be. The masses are never to be seen as angels, always as people with their own problems and issues even as they suffer injustice from others.

The nature of modern warfare is criticized in *The Armageddon Factor*. While propaganda on the planet Atrios recasts the pointless deaths of ordinary people on the frontlines as glorious, the Marshall responsible for sending them to their deaths - and the aristocracy who will ultimately benefit most from victory - remain in relative safety far away from the fighting. And, in the end, even the trite promise of greatness in death proves false: their enemy, the inhabitants of Zeos, are gone and they are fighting a computer that - even had Atrios *won* the war - would have destroyed both planets were it not for Romana and the Doctor's intervention.

The Doctor ignites the rebellion in us all. In Season Sixteen, he gives Romana a purpose beyond dry academia, and tells us we have to get out there and change the world, not sit and read about it and act like people are theory. At the end of the season, we come to understand that the Doctor doesn't have to take the Key to Time to anyone; instead, he sends it spinning out into the gleeful ordered-chaos of the universe, a reflection of what he's doing to Romana as his influence helps her on her way to becoming her own Romana. We'll probably never get the Doctor's "origin story," so here's Romana's instead and isn't she an awful lot like him? She's more than a mere reflection of the leading man, but her existence and actions help to illuminate him a bit. Romana is now on the path that leads to her inevitable departure, where she turns into her own version of the Doctor and needs her own universe to explore and make better. She couldn't have done it without her Time Lord privileges, but she steps beyond that by connecting with the "normal people" of the universe and working to help them deal with the oppression that they face. Had I two hearts of my own, she would hold both of them in her beautiful hands.

The Women We Don't See

K. Tempest Bradford is a science fiction and fantasy author living in New York City. She spends her days surrounded by mobile technology, but has not yet found a suitable sonic screwdriver. You can find more of her essays on *Doctor Who* in *Chicks Dig Time Lords, Fantasy Magazine* and on her website: ktempestbradford.com

> "I'm a Time Lord. I walk in eternity. I've lived for something like 750 years. About time I found something better to do than run around after the Brigadier."
>
> —The Doctor, *Pyramids of Mars*

I came to *Doctor Who* late in life for a science fiction fan. Growing up, I somehow missed seeing it on my local PBS station and, for a long time, closeted myself with *Star Trek* fans. I had a vague idea about *Doctor Who* before I started watching the new series and have received a significant education in How Things Used To Be from fans of the original series.

Aside from all the good things they had to say about the show and the combination of the fourth Doctor (Tom Baker) and companion Sarah Jane Smith (Elisabeth Sladen) in particular, people did warn me about sexist overtones and some really disturbing instances of racism (such as *The Talons of Weng-Chiang* from Season Fourteen). I went into my first viewing of Season Thirteen (1975-76) with this knowledge and an understanding that *Doctor Who* is, and always will be, a product of its time.

Even with that preparation, I still found myself surprised by the mixed messages about women the show offered up. For most of this season, the Doctor travels alone with Sarah Jane - and in half of the stories, she's the *only* woman we see, with the exception of extras and background people. This erasure is as glaring as the stereotypes we get when women do eventually show up.

After watching Season Thirteen, a person could walk away from *Doctor Who* thinking that there was only one worthwhile woman in the universe.

The first story of the season, *Terror of the Zygons,* doesn't share the same feel as the stories that follow. Thematically, it better fits in with Season Twelve and is a continuation of the storyline that started with *Robot*. After *Zygons*, there's a noticeable shift in tone on several fronts. In contrast to the previous season, there are no stories featuring major, recurring villains like the Daleks, Cybermen or Sontarans. Harry Sullivan leaves the show as a regular companion and this is the last time fans will see Brigadier Lethbridge-Stewart for several years, leaving Sarah as the sole companion. *Zygons* is also the last story commissioned by the show's previous producer, Barry Letts. New producer Philip Hinchcliffe then steered *Doctor Who* in a decidedly gothic horror direction influenced in part by Hammer Horror[24] films. Because of this, I'm focusing on the stories between *Planet of Evil* and *The Seeds of Doom*.

The Girl

In *Planet of Evil*, the TARDIS lands about 30,000 years in the future. A human science expedition has been on the planet for months, and a spaceship manned by humans arrives to check up on them. None of these humans is female. Sarah is the only woman that appears in this story. *Planet of Evil* teaches us that, in the far future, women won't serve on starships and they won't be scientists. Not even a little bit.

About halfway through, I noticed that all the men in the show except the Doctor kept calling Sarah "girl" or "the girl" even after they knew her name. Once I picked up on this, I couldn't unhear it. And every time they did it *again*, it just made me madder. Even on a ship full of dudes, there must be someone who knows how to remember a proper name for more than five seconds, right? Not in this script.

This doesn't happen as much in other Season Thirteen stories. Sometimes people do refer to Sarah as girl, but usually after they know her name they address her as Miss Smith or Sarah. But, in many ways, Sarah *is* symbolically "the girl."

She's the only woman in the next story (*Pyramids of Mars*) as well. And though there are a couple of women in *The Android Invasion*, they are background/ non-speaking roles. Any time we get away from modern day Earth in this season, the likelihood of seeing a woman other than Sarah goes down to almost zero.

The only positive I could glean from this state of affairs is that, if we only get one woman, I'm glad it's Sarah Jane. It's easy to see why she's so many fans' favorite companion. She's smart, brave, skilled and com-

24 Hammer Film productions is a UK-based studio that was famous for horror films in the 1950s, 60s and 70s.

petent. And even when she has moments of all-too-human fear or the urge to run away, the Doctor explains to her why it's important to stay and fight instead of just putting her down or calling her a coward.

In *Pyramids of Mars*, when the Doctor, Sarah and Laurence Scarman finally get back to the TARDIS, Sarah suggests that they go on to 1980 as they'd planned - because, obviously, Sutekh failed to take over the world in 1911. The Doctor takes them to 1980 and shows her a ruined Earth, all thanks to Sutekh, and she realizes that they have to stop him to protect her future. That teaching moment not only illuminates something about the nature of time and why the Doctor must intervene when he comes across evil in the universe, it's also indicative of the respect he has for Sarah.

By this season, she's been with him for a couple of years and it's clear that he trusts her completely. As a New *Who* fan, I'm used to the Doctor being overly protective of his companions to the point of being frustratingly paternalistic. If he sends them off to the TARDIS on their own to get a tool, as he does with Sarah a few times, it's usually a trick to trap them inside and keep them out of harm's way.[25] The fourth Doctor is very protective of her, of course, because he cares for her. But the Doctor is also well aware that Sarah is a badass.

Other characters don't always afford her this same level of respect. Even knowing that Sarah is the Doctor's assistant, men ignore or glance right over her to focus on the Doctor, even when they don't yet have a reason to do so. The villains' underestimation of Sarah often works in her favor. In *The Brain of Morbius*, the evil Dr Solon and his lackey Condo don't even notice that she's missing from the front room, allowing her to roam around and then escape the house.

Being a woman that men don't see has its bitter triumphs.

I also noticed that even though she sometimes needed saving from the antagonists, so did the Doctor. And it was mostly her doing the saving when it came to that. This is even more important in light of what immediately preceded this season in terms of companions and long-running guests. After *Zygons*, we have no Harry (except a guest appearance in *Android*) and no Brigadier. Sarah is the only audience surrogate we get. Because she has the benefit of experience and a relationship with the Doctor based on mutual trust and respect, the show couldn't relegate her to the role of damsel-in-distress or other trite stereotypes all the time.

25 The two most prominent examples that come to mind are *The Parting of the Ways* (2005) and *The Doctor's Wife* (2011).

It's too bad that the other women who come into the Doctor's orbit don't get the same courtesy.

The Women Men Do See

"How many centuries have passed while you have remained unchanged? How long since anything here changed?"
"Nothing here ever changes."
"Exactly my point. No progress."

—The Doctor, Maren, *The Brain of Morbius*

The fifth story in the season, *The Brain of Morbius,* finally features women in speaking roles: the Sisterhood of Karn. As glad as I was to finally see more women on screen, I was equally angered by how quickly they descended into stereotype. It's as if the story's writers, Terrance Dicks and Robert Holmes (under the pseudonym "Robin Bland"), set out to explain in story form everything that's wrong with women by pulling out all the tropes and slathering them on thick.

In this story, the Doctor and Sarah land on the planet of Karn, having been forcibly sent there by the Time Lords to deal with an evil Gallifreyan who is supposed to be dead but, through the efforts of a corrupt scientist, is about to get a new body and live again. Their arrival is also noted by one of the Sisters of Karn, who reports to leader Maren that two people came to the planet even though their ship was not detected. Maren then correctly surmises that the Time Lords must have sent them.

We learn that the Sisterhood of Karn is a very old order that dates back centuries and the leader is as old as the Sisterhood itself. The key to their longevity (and possibly their power) is the Elixir of Life, which is generated by the Flame of Life. The sisters can sense spaceships up to a million miles away and have the power to make them crash if they come too near Karn just by using their minds. At one point, a sister states that "alone among the races in our galaxy, the Time Lords are our equals in mind power." So these women are powerful, perhaps as powerful as the Time Lords, and possibly come from as old a race. Yet they're portrayed as a bunch of silly, irrational women.

Maren jumps to the conclusion that the Doctor is there to steal the Elixir of Life because she'd had recurring dreams that the Time Lords would do such a thing (gotta love women's intuition, right?). The Flame of Life is dying and Maren doesn't know why; it hasn't generated Elixir in over a year and supplies are running low. No one knows this, not even the other sisters, but nevertheless that must be why there's a Time Lord around.

Based on this, Maren sentences the Doctor to death. She teleports him to the shrine, insists he confess to being sent there by Gallifrey, and won't listen to him when he says he has no idea what she's talking about. No big shock there, since his professions of innocence come with a giant dose of condescension. The Doctor belittles the Sisterhood's powers about two minutes after waking up with their knives pointed at his face. "You mean you still practice teleportation? How quaint." His ability to snark in the face of danger is usually charming, but at that moment I felt he got what he deserved when the sisters attempt to burn him at the stake. Lucky for the Doctor, Sarah Jane is able to save him.

Maren's irrationality can be explained away by fear. It could be that, given a group of monks in the same situation, they might also panic and make bad decisions. But the script drives the point home further by painting the Sisters as backward, ignorant and silly.

Later in the story, the Doctor returns to the shrine and insists that he can help figure out the problem with the Flame of Life. Again, he brings the not-helpful condescension to the table while telling the Sisters that there's nothing mystical about the Flame and, if it's dying, there must be a *rational* explanation for that. Maren relents and agrees to let him see the chamber where they keep the Flame. Within seconds, the Doctor deduces the chemical reactions that takes place to create the Elixir of Life. Seconds later, Maren dismisses his prattling, calling the Elixir-making process a mystery "beyond the reach of the mind."

At this point, I had to pause the episode so I could have a moment of incredulity. These women are hundreds of years old, maybe thousands. Their only job in life has been to take care of and protect this flame and drink the juice it generates so they can live forever. But they don't know how the process works? That doesn't even make sense. It's not as if the Sisterhood is completely sheltered from the universe. They're aware of technology, spaceships, even time machines. Are there no scientists among the sisters? Nor even philosophers?

Apparently not.

Collectively, they don't even understand the concept that fire needs air to burn. The reason the Flame of Life is dying turns out to be that there was some soot in the floo. The Doctor again surmises this in seconds, much to the surprise of everyone in the room.

This is ridiculous.

It's also frustratingly paternalistic. Though we later encounter female Time Lords (the first being Rodan in Season Fifteen, unless you count the female computer voice in *The Deadly Assassin*), up until this point in the show we've only seen the male of the species. When Maren deduces that the Time Lords sent the pair, she only orders the sisters to kidnap the Doctor, not Sarah. Time Lords represent male power, knowledge and rationality in the world of *Doctor Who* at this point. That attitude is very much on display here.

I realize that it's possible that the original idea may have been a commentary on religion and not women, especially with the speech the Doctor gives about the need for progress and change instead of clinging to old, ignorant ways. The negative stereotypes about women may have crept in unconsciously. However, the fact that all of this plays out as a conflict between the Sisterhood of Karn - not the Brotherhood or even the Non-Gendered Conglomeration of Karn - and the Doctor, a male Time Lord, is telling.

In the last story of the season, *The Seeds of Doom*, there's one other woman worth mentioning: Amelia Ducat. When we first see her, she comes off as a normal but absent-minded older lady who's just there to provide a clue and move the plot along. She shows up later in the story when Sarah and the Doctor are trapped in Harrison Chase's mansion. Turns out she's on a recon mission for the government entities trying to find the evil plant monster the Doctor is battling. Despite earlier impressions, Amelia turns out to be very shrewd and sharp, all while maintaining a detached, unassuming air. Go girl!

Unfortunately, the show then turns around and demolishes all that by portraying her, in her final scene, as a silly biddy the men can't wait to be rid of. It's almost a perfect allegory for the awesome/horrifying seesaw around the portrayal of women in this entire season.

The Horror, the Horror

How much of this is deliberate and how much due to the time period and reigning attitudes in Britain in the 70s is debatable. Sarah Jane is a feminist, that's stated outright, and in the previous season held her own against Harry when he initiated sexist conversations on the subject. The show runner at the time believed it was important for that to be an aspect of the Doctor's female companion, thus making it an issue on the show. Then again, Elisabeth Sladen is on record as saying that she had to flesh out the character herself because "if you didn't, no one else would."[26] So perhaps the credit for the things that make Sarah Jane more than just "the girl" rests with the actress who played her, not the writers who wrote her.

There's also the overall tone producer Philip Hinchcliffe cultivated starting with this season: gothic horror. Each of the stories he commissioned is easily traced to horror movie and literary influences. *Planet of Evil* incorporates elements of *The Strange Case of Dr Jekyll and Mr Hyde* and *Forbidden Planet; The Android Invasion* (and, to some extent, *Terror of the Zygons*) plays on the same themes as *Invasion of the Body Snatchers;* Dr Solon in *The Brain of Morbius* is clearly a movieverse Frankenstein-esque figure with his own Igor, even; *The Seeds of Doom* starts out as *The Thing from Another World* and morphs into *The Quatermass Experiment*.

The horror genre is not known for its feminism. Audiences are more likely to find rampant misogyny in the films produced then, just as now. With these gothic sugar plums dancing in Hinchcliffe's head, it wouldn't surprise me if he didn't notice or didn't care about what was going on with the portrayal of women in these stories. I'm almost surprised it wasn't worse. Then I remember that *Doctor Who* has to be mindful that children are watching. The kind of things that happen to women in horror films aren't suitable for family television. The show was already pushing the boundaries of what some people found acceptable for kids with these scary tales.

Sarah Saves the Day

Season Thirteen was the beginning of a very popular era in the history of *Doctor Who*, and its influences are apparent in the fandom as well as in New *Who* - which is written and produced by people who grew up watching and loving the show.

The Sisterhood of Karn immediately pinged me as a possible influence for the Sybilline Sisterhood in *The Fires of Pompeii* (2008). The fourth Doctor even mentions Vesuvius when talking about possible scientific reasons for the Flame of Life's issues. In *Pompeii*, the Sisterhood also become the victims of their own ignorance and the tenth Doctor takes his turn chiding them for their lack of judgment. Did James Moran have a bit of *Morbius* in his brain when he came up with that?

Most of the Doctor's companions are women, Sarah Jane Smith being one of the most popular - yet some male fans still don't realize, or are shocked to find, that the female fandom for *Doctor Who* is so large.

26 Robertson, Cameron "Dr Who's 'Cut-Out' Girl Back." *The Daily Mirror* (2006). www.mirror.co.uk/3am/celebrity-news/exclusive-dr-whos-cut-out-girl-621265

We can't be dismissed as only New *Who* fans enamored with the handsome modern Doctors before us. Most of the female fans I know are old-school Whovians to their core. They've been around since before *Planet of Evil* erased us from the future.

Looking back at these stories from the perspective of the twenty-first century, I can't treasure them the way old-school fans do, but I can appreciate the good in them. Like the way the Doctor and Sarah shared inside jokes and how she made fun of his maudlin moping about. Tom Baker's boss attitude with that hat, or the crazy faces he made when he tried to pretend he was in pain. I especially appreciated the fourth Doctor's vulnerability. When he made a mistake or found himself about to die, he wasn't just pretending to be caught and sure of his escape. When he couldn't save himself, Sarah was there to save him.

Sarah saved the season for me. No matter how much the scripts or the attitudes of the time tried to erase or cast women as inferior, by her very presence Sarah proved just the opposite.

The Ultimate Sixth

Tansy Rayner Roberts is the author of the fantasy novels *Power and Majesty*, *The Shattered City* and *Reign of Beasts*, and the short story collection *Love and Romanpunk*. She lives in Tasmania with her partner and two daughters, and enables their devoted *Doctor Who* fannishness. Yes, even the two-year-old. Tansy blogs at tansyrr.com, tweets as @tansyrr and is one of the three voices of the Hugo-nominated *Galactic Suburbia* podcast.

It's a generally held belief in fandom that Colin Baker's sixth Doctor was heartily redeemed by the Big Finish audio productions: the combination of a likeable performance, clever scripts and no one having to look at that damn coat all the time.

I love Big Finish, but as far as I'm concerned, *The Trial of a Time Lord* did it first.

The Trial of a Time Lord wasn't just my favorite sixth Doctor story when I was a kid; as far as I was concerned, it was all the Colin Baker in the world. Thanks to my mother's erratic (and at times, targeted) videotaping of episodes, I had entirely missed his previous run of stories, which meant *The Twin Dilemma* and *Timelash* remained entirely theoretical until I was well into adulthood.

While nothing can be done about the coat short of turning down the colors on your television, *Trial* provided Colin Baker with a variety of meaty material which suited his Doctor's pompous, demanding personality. He and Nicola Bryant credit themselves with changing the Doctor and Peri's relationship to something friendly rather than adversarial, which is noticeable from the first moments of *The Mysterious Planet*. What with that and Peri wearing actual grown-up clothes for both of the stories she took part in, I ended up with a completely different perception of her as a companion than those viewers who had witnessed the boobs-and-bickering season before.

The Trial of a Time Lord is flawed in places, but also works as an excellent showcase for Baker as a darker, more complex Doctor than had been seen since William Hartnell. Its strengths are the high concept of the season, and the excellent array of actors pulled in to play crunchy guest roles.

The potential of the trial format was huge. I can't help thinking how well this idea would work in the current version of the show, with a Doctor already established and beloved by the core audience (sadly something that Baker lacked):

A new series, and the eleventh Doctor trips from his TARDIS into a courtroom scene, discovering that he is on trial for meddling in the affairs of humanity. Benedict Cumberbatch as the Valeyard is obviously out to get him, the grave and dignified Inquisitor (Keeley Hawes) seems tough but fair, and the whole thing is rather amusing, so he stays to see what they have to offer... and of course, to discover what the hell has happened to Amy, Rory and his own memory.

So much of what almost worked in the original *Trial of a Time Lord* would be brilliant television with a few tweaks of modern storytelling. But on revisiting the story, I discovered that in fact there was plenty about the original which worked just fine, thank you. The scriptwriting is erratic, with brilliant moments and a few which made me gnaw my fist in frustration, but I was surprised at how well the season stands up as a whole - not only against my childhood memories, but against my current expectations of what *Doctor Who* is supposed to do.

The first episode is wonderfully complex and fast-paced. The TARDIS is beamed into a space station, the Doctor walks out and into a three-hander plot of political intrigue, Gallifreyan hypocrisy and witty banter.

I'm a sucker for witty banter.

The trial scenes, as a framing narrative for the whole season, get a bad rap from fans. Personally, I've always enjoyed them far more than the stories they introduce. Lynda Bellingham takes absolute control as the Inquisitor from the first few minutes of the story, in a role where she could have been nothing more than a talking head. She sits between the dynamic, accusatory Valeyard (Michael Jayston) and the outraged, huffy sixth Doctor like a cool-headed Hermione constantly keeping the peace between Harry and Snape. Meanwhile, Jayston and Baker posture and verbally duel with each other for 12 episodes straight, until we get the narrative payoff of the two of them physically hunting each other in the surreal Dickensian Disneyland that is the Matrix.

Jayston also benefits from getting the last line in nearly every episode - okay, many of them are the same line, but he gets zoom shots and threatening music and lots of attention from the camera before the traditional "Doctor looks shocked but undaunted" image and the closing credits roll.

Even before the grand revelation about who the Valeyard is, it's clear that he is a good match for the Doctor. Colin Baker is at his best when sending zingy putdowns at his opponents, and to have someone worthy of his sharp tongue giving as good as he gets is the key to making the sixth Doctor awesome - as opposed to the bully he appears when being all superior and mean to Peri.

Meanwhile, down on *The Mysterious Planet* (the first story pitched as evidence for the trial), we also get a more likeable Doctor to spend time with - and another fabulous guest cast. The standout here is Tony Selby as the rogue Sabalom Glitz, who steals the show from the warrior queen *and* the giant robot. Selby doesn't always get the best lines, but he has a sly charisma that makes even the ropiest piece of dialogue sound like it was handed to him by Raymond Chandler. (Glitz: "Five rounds rapid should do the trick!" Really, Robert Holmes? Really?)

I'm always a little surprised at how good Dibber is as well - he might be playing Glitz's dumb sidekick, but he has some lovely comedy moments such as helpfully explaining proper gun technique to the "primitive" warriors, which they promptly use against him.

But let's talk about the warrior queen. *The Mysterious Planet* brings us Joan Sims as Katryka - the casting of a comic actor in a dramatic role is always a risk, but she acquits herself with great aplomb. Katryka fascinates me - the red-haired warrior queen is the kind of role which would normally be totally sexualized, with a glamorous siren poured into bronze D-cups and a tiny skirt. Instead, we get a robust older peasant woman with a huge voice and a powerful sense of self, who makes a credible leader.

It's a part which could as easily have been played by a man - hell, if they didn't already have a role for Brian Blessed this season, he could take over the script with only a few minor changes. And as with Professor Lasky later, and even the Inquisitor herself, it might well have been written as a man in the 1970s.

The Mysterious Planet is all characters and ideas, many of which appear to belong to separate adventures. Glitz and Dibber are in a Guy Ritchie caper movie, while everyone else is in *Logan's Run*, *Soylent Green* or *The Viking Queen*. The Doctor and Peri flit from one to the other, exchanging chat with whomever is handy, and while the Doctor later claims to have saved the universe, it never really feels like anything was at stake. The tension comes from the smaller tragedies: Peri discovering the Marble Arch tube station beneath the planet and realizing the truth; the librarian who only has three books and considers them all to be holy, including the one about the life cycle of the Canadian goose; Merdeen having to shoot a friend and colleague who thinks he is a traitor.

It was the revelation of Ravolox as the Earth's future which socked me in the gut as a young viewer. Never mind the dystopia of the underground children ruled by a giant robot, never knowing there was real rain outside their nuclear bunker - I was devastated at the idea that something so final could happen to the Earth, and I loved the Doctor for likewise being stunned and angry about what had been done to his favorite planet.

The Mysterious Planet is a fairly ordinary *Doctor Who* story, lifted by some clever character moments and chilling themes. The most intriguing aspect, the bits of Glitz-Dibber dialogue which are edited from the Matrix, are left to tantalize the viewer, but it's clear that the real story is what is happening in the trial room, not on the courtroom screen.

The central theme to *The Trial of a Time Lord* - the ethical implications of superior civilizations experimenting on or in other ways generally screwing with those less privileged than themselves - runs through the trial scenes as well as the inner stories, tying them all together thematically even when it seems that they have little connection.

The other thing which both the framing narrative and the inner stories have in spades is some quality male posturing. I say with love that the sixth Doctor is a posturing Doctor, never happier than when giving a judgemental and self-congratulatory speech, or when butting heads with someone of equal strength and confidence. In the case of *Mindwarp*, a story which is deeply satisfying on some levels and irretrievably broken on others, he does at least get a whole cast of arrogant, bombastic male characters to play against: Crozier, Sil, Kiv and of course the shoutiest of them all, King Yrcanos himself. Indeed, the Doctor appears almost subdued at times in comparison to the other performers, and this story represents one of the only times in Colin Baker's whole run that you actually feel he might be under personal threat.

Unfortunately, while the scenes with these guest actors show the sixth Doctor as a more complex, manipulative and plotting Doctor than we are used to, this is undermined (largely through the script) thanks to his awful, simply *awful* scenes with Peri.

In the first episode of *Mindwarp* (the second story under the *Trial* umbrella), when the Doctor and Peri arrive at the psychedelic, pink-oceaned planet of Thoros Beta, Colin Baker and Nicola Bryant do their best to mitigate a regressive script which has them once again bickering with each other. They deliberately undercut several bitchy lines to each other with wry smiles and understanding looks, and I laughed out loud at the Doctor pretending Peri was a nurse so they could apply the "skedaddle test" to a dead body and escape the guards.

But once Peri realizes that this is Sil's home planet - and that the Doctor deliberately brought her here - there is no fixing things. Because of my lack of knowledge of other sixth Doctor stories when I was younger, I didn't realize the significance of the scene in which Peri shows her fear of what Sil did to her in the past - but looking at it now, you can see how deeply she feels betrayed. The idea of the Doctor bringing his companion to face a demon from her past as a storyline was used to brilliant effect (more than once) in the Sylvester McCoy era, but here it seems an unnecessarily cruel and dangerous thing to do.

Then comes episode two and the Doctor starts acting very strangely.

It's a clever twist that the Doctor in the trial room can't remember anything after the electric shock Crozier gave him, and so has to assume that he is behaving deliberately out of character on screen, rather than actually being evil. Even the Doctor can't entirely trust the Doctor! It could have worked marvelously in the modern structure of the show, with an actor as popular as David Tennant or Matt Smith. Sadly, I don't think Colin Baker had enough emotional currency with the audience to carry it off. I might not have been aware of it when I first watched this story, but "the Doctor is not acting like himself" had already been done with this particular Doctor, an experiment which had badly damaged the audience's trust in the Doctor and the show as a whole.

So the Doctor is (probably) pretending to be evil to save Peri's life - but the net effect is that he has to behave appallingly to her when she is unexpectedly turned into a harem girl, and then by tying her to some rocks on the pink beach and interrogating her viciously. We see evidence that he is performing for the cameras, but we also see him going much further with emotional cruelty (pretending to be his real self and then pulling the rug out from under her) than is necessary.

This is the first point at which the Doctor starts to challenge the evidence - no matter what he does or does not remember, the scene feels entirely wrong to him, and so it should. But Peri is devastated by the Doctor's performance, utterly taken apart by his betrayal, and it goes on for far too long, beyond the episode in which the idea is introduced.

If the story ended with Peri giving the Doctor hell for what he put her through, it might have been forgivable. But a very different ending is coming, so we as an audience never get that closure and never get the chance to forgive him ourselves.

When not actually in scenes together, Nicola Bryant and Colin Baker are marvellous. He gets to be all sneaky with the green wormy people and the morally bankrupt scientist Crozier, while Peri gets to banter in corridors with the utterly barmy King Yrcanos and his equerry Dorf. Bryant has more comic material here than in the entire rest of her run, and her interactions with Yrcanos show off her survival instincts as well as her sense of humor. This is a man who can't conceive of anything but war, who physically picks her up like she's the receiver to a telephone whenever he has something to say to her. Peri is in a dire situation but she rallies beautifully, naming herself Perpugilliam of the Brown, learning to speak fluent warlord and employing rudimentary dog training techniques to manage both Yrcanos' and Dorf's behavior.

For some reason I'm imagining their marriage as an eighties sitcom. *Me and My Homicidal Warlord*, with Sil and Kiv as the green same sex couple next door.

But that's the problem, isn't it? The marriage. Peri has two fates - to die twice at the hands of Crozier and Yrcanos, and to marry Yrcanos and live as a warrior queen. Neither of these are good options. The Doctor's behavior to Peri takes on huge repercussions (never dealt with) upon her death, but the alternative is that she gets to live on an alien planet with a crazy warlord king whom she never displays any attraction to whatsoever. The closest thing to affection we see from her is exactly what you might reluctantly offer a large, vicious dog who almost bit your arm off, but was distracted at the last minute by a packet of sausages and now thinks it is your friend.

"There's a good warlord" is not a basis for a lasting marriage. Neither is the moment when Yrcanos stops being funny for 30 seconds and strokes Peri's cheek. She flinches, and you see how afraid of him she is. It's chilling and creepy and I know it was the eighties but really, *really*? That's her happy ending? That's the best she can expect? I would so much rather hear that she went back to Yrcanos' home planet, introduced his culture to democracy and kicked his arse in the polls. Peri for President!

But this is *Mindwarp*, not *The Ultimate Foe*, and marriage is not yet on the cards.

Leaving aside the rebooted alternate ending, the clever thing about the final episode of *Mindwarp* is that it shifts Peri and Yrcanos' interactions into something which is intimate (though still not romantic) when they discuss his culture's views on death and the afterlife. It's a cute red herring, playing on his unrequited adoration and his desire to marry her, when in fact it's warning us of her impending death.

Much though I hated the ending of *Mindwarp* as a child, to the point that I avoided that episode whenever possible, I'm with Nicola Bryant on this one: Peri's death is a shocking, brilliant end to a companion who rarely got a chance to shine and she should have been allowed to keep it.

Colin Baker also shines here, when the Doctor puts everything together in the trial room and his memories finally make sense. His quiet "you... killed Peri" to the Inquisitor is as startling and emotionally effective as Bryant's own electric performance as Kiv before her second death. I find it interesting that not just the Valeyard but the Inquisitor justifies taking the Doctor out of time before he could save Peri. She claims that he was already too late and it was his own fault, and we see that for the first time she's not the moderate judge, but part of the corruption of Gallifrey.

And then, as the intensity of the story finally swells to a crescendo, with the past and the present colliding into gorgeous, messy clarity... we all take a four week break to watch a fizzy lemonade filler murder mystery featuring aliens who look like giant green penises.

Okay, that's (mostly) unfair, but having come to a new appreciation of *Mindwarp* (episode two notwithstanding), I found it very hard to forgive *Terror of the Vervoids*. The story seems to actively work at ignoring all the drama and tension built up in the previous episodes. In the trial sequence, we see that the Doctor has dealt with all that pesky emotional fallout off screen, between episodes, and apart from the Inquisitor being a lot sweeter and more sympathetic to him, it's as if Peri never existed.

Meanwhile, the story that the Doctor picks for his defence is from his future - a lovely conceit which the script does little of any interest with. The pacing of the whole thing is off - it might be because I leaped straight into this story on the DVD box set without waiting a week myself, but starting from scratch again at the beginning of a four-parter felt like walking through treacle. Even the characters themselves have noticed - in *Mindwarp*, it was quite cute that the Doctor pointed out the unnecessary introduction scene, and other problems with the narrative and that the story got to skip ahead in response. Here, the Valeyard quite rightly points that our time is being wasted and it's hard to argue with him when the vital point that the Doctor claims to be "getting to" (that he was asked for help) doesn't turn up in the evidence until halfway through the fourth episode.

Vervoids might not make as many outright mistakes as *Mindwarp*, but there's no getting around the fact that it's just not as clever.

There are some good guest performances - Honor Blackman plays a very flawed and driven scientist, Professor Lasky. I also very much liked the Commodore, a long-suffering former acquaintance of the Doctor, who allows him free rein of the ship and doesn't bother with all those tiresome "let's lock up the mysterious strangers" scenes.

The story itself is at its heart quite dark and has a lot of potential. The creation of the Vervoids definitely fits the on-going theme of the ethics in experimenting on lesser species, but the script is so banal and the production design so desperately bright and cheerful, the interesting bits get lost along the way. The glaring technocolor bubblegum palette makes you think you're watching a comedy, even when everyone's dying and horrible crimes are being committed. As with *The Happiness Patrol*, this is one which would have benefited from being screened in black and white... or sepia!

Then there's Mel. I like Mel. I really do. I think she had some useful traits as a companion, and after several years of Tegan and then Peri complaining so much, it's refreshing to have a companion who is cheerful, goes off on her own to investigate things and seems to actually like the Doctor. Her most important trait - that of getting people to open up to her and confess their problems - is shown off to good effect here.

Terror of the Vervoids, however, feels so desperate to cheer people up after the fate of Peri that Mel's relentless chipperness is a shock to the system. We're further hindered by the script clumsily tacking on regular details about her backstory, as if we're not going to notice that this is someone we have never been formally introduced to, when in fact that's the most interesting thing about her character.

(Actually the *most* interesting thing about her is that she is a paradox, the Doctor's first chronological meeting with her - from his point of view - being in *The Ultimate Foe* when she is called as a witness, and that she must then have two leaving stories like Tegan, going off somewhere into the sunset so he can meet her again, for the first time in her point of view, later on, which means that her travels with the seventh Doctor and later with Glitz could have all happened to her before she appeared in the Trial room, right? Right? River Song, eat your heart out.)

Terror of the Vervoids wants to be *The Robots of Death*, and it falls extremely short. The only real surprise here is that, while the Matrix is tampered with to suggest that the Doctor committed a more minor crime, the charges of genocide are legitimate. It's... an odd outcome, when it would have made more sense to have the tampering with the Matrix set him up.

The Trial of a Time Lord unexpectedly gets awesome again in episode thirteen, also known as episode one of *The Ultimate Foe*. With Robert Holmes wielding his typewriter for the final time, the Valeyard utters his quiet evil laugh, Glitz and Mel turn up as surprise witnesses, and the Master appears on the screen of the Matrix, all in the first five minutes. Everyone's on fine form here - the Doctor has a gorgeous speech about the corruption of the Time Lords, Glitz is acting like he just wandered in off the set of *Rumpole of the Bailey* (he's not the only one) and the Master is adoring his time in the spotlight. Oh, I do love Anthony Ainley.

Pace, pace, pace. It rips along like it knows it's going to be compared to New *Who* someday, the dialogue is smart again and, lo and behold, Mel suddenly becomes a sympathetic character - gung ho and good-humored without being grating. When the Valeyard is called out as the Doctor's darker self, however, and flees to the Matrix, it's not Mel but Glitz whom the Doctor drags along as his companion of choice - and what a brilliant decision that was!

With Glitz, we have the best on-screen companion the sixth Doctor ever had - even with the changeover of scriptwriters between the thirteenth and fourteenth episodes, he's far more consistently written than either Peri or Mel, and is a far more appropriate target for the Doctor's acidic barbs. Never mind Adric or Thomas Brewster, here's our Artful Dodger companion! Michael Jayston's Valeyard is a brilliant antagonist, and it's so good to see him and Baker finally acting against each other in a physical sense, no longer restricted to the courtroom. Ainley's suave and making-no-sense Master is icing on a great big black-and-silver iced cake.

This combination of horror and humor is exactly what we should have been getting all along - *Mindwarp* came closest to it, but the icky misogyny derailed my viewing experience. I've always found Dickens creepy as hell, so using Dickensian iconography as the fuel for a surreal horror piece works very well for me! The Popplewicks are excellent characters who foil and frustrate the Doctor at every turn. The story leaps from the Doctor being strangled by a barrel and buried alive at one extreme, all the way to a comedy sequence with the Master failing to hypnotize Glitz because he's using a shiny thing which might be worth a couple of grotzits (I will now be trying to use the word "grotzits" in casual conversation as much as possible) and the shifts in tone work so well against each other.

At the center of it all, we have Colin Baker as the Doctor and he's good, he's heroic *and* pompous *and* judgemental *and* funny, and he's barely even paying attention to the Master because the Valeyard is his true love nemesis. And, honestly, even after 14 episodes, I'm now sad that it's come to an end.

(Yes, the final resolution makes very little sense whatsoever, and the Inquisitor is being suspiciously kitten-like as she assures the Doctor that all charges are dropped, and it's all cuddles and carrot juice, and Peri's married to her stalker in a haze of rose-tinted light, isn't it lovely, but shhh, let's not get bogged down in details.)

Because this is it. They finally got the hang of the sixth Doctor, figuring out how to show him off to good effect without him coming off as a bully or an ass, and it's done. All over. Too little, too late. We're one wig and a shaky TARDIS away from Sylvester McCoy, and while I welcome the new regime and all it had to offer, I'm wistful about what could have been.

Thank goodness for Big Finish, who gave the sixth Doctor the stories he deserved. Because really, looking back at the highs and lows of *The Trial of a Time Lord*, at the messy bits and the triumphant bits, at the bits I want to hug to me and the bits I'd really like to set fire to, I don't think it was the coat that was the problem.

Maids and Masters: The Distribution of Power in *Doctor Who* Series Three

Courtney Stoker is a cisgendered white woman living in the United States. After getting her M.A. in English, she started working as an adjunct instructor to pay for her writing habit. Her research and writing focus on feminism, science fiction and fan studies. She is a bit of an expert on cosplay as a fan practice, particularly femme cosplay in the *Doctor Who* fan community, and has been interviewed on the subject at *io9* and the now-defunct *The Sexist*. She recently started *Doctor Her*, a group feminist *Doctor Who* fan blog (doctorher.com).

What's so compelling about the Doctor? Why do so many different kinds of people jump in the TARDIS to travel with him? Is it his boyish charm, his goodness, his sense of humor?

I would argue that for most of the companions in the new series, the most attractive part of the Time Lord is his power. To convince Rose to leave her life for adventure, the ninth Doctor expands on the power he has: "Did I mention that it travels in time?" Later, Martha says to the crowd in the tenement in *Last of the Time Lords*, "I know what he can do." That's her vote of confidence for the Doctor, how she convinces the people of the Doctor's importance: *what he can do*, not how good or brave he is. The adventure the Doctor offers his companion is inseparable from his power, from his ability to manipulate space and time, from his ability to threaten and fight enemies unimaginably evil and powerful.

Power impacts every relationship the Doctor has, but it's not something *Who* fans talk about often. We like to pretend, I think, that the Doctor's extraordinary power isn't important. We like to think that it doesn't affect him or his relationships with others. We like to think that if companions are "strong" enough, sassy enough, smart enough, they are his equals. But no matter how many times a companion saves the Doctor, or how many times a companion stands up to him, they don't have his power. The Doctor can manipulate space and time, travel through them in a manner even the humans of the future could only imagine. He can fix practically anything with his magic sonic screwdriver. He can hold the knowledge of infinite lifetimes in his head. He can read minds. He can (and does) force his will on others: he takes away Donna's memory; he disables Jack's ability to time travel; he traps a girl in a mirror. His power outstrips any possible capabilities of his companions.

The disproportionate power dynamic in the Doctor/companion relationships is something each companion in the new series[27] struggles with at some point or another. When Rose protests in *School Reunion*, "I'm not his assistant," she voices the frustration that many of the companions have felt with the Doctor. The truth is, they know that they are small next to the Doctor, who is practically a demigod. But they, along with most of the audience, resist that reality, insisting that they are as good as, as clever as, as important as the Doctor. And perhaps they are all those things. But they are not as powerful as him. And this crucial fact is never more evident than it is in Series Three, where it seems that unequal power distribution in close relationships becomes a near-constant theme.

It's interesting that this is the series where the writers explore power so thoroughly, since Martha is the only companion in the Russell T Davies era with much power in her own world. Rose is relatively poor and Donna is stuck in a series of dead-end temp jobs; both lack connections, opportunities and the hope of social mobility. Martha and her family, however, enjoy a marked level of affluence. Before she meets the Doctor, she's no aristocrat (like Lucy Saxon), and she has no extraordinary institutional power, like a government seat or a position as a high-ranking judge. But she is preparing to be a doctor and wields much more power over her life than the other companions. She has chosen a fairly well-paid and prestigious career and isn't stuck being a temp or a shop girl, with little ability to change her situation. After leaving the Doctor, Martha gets an officer position at UNIT (on the Doctor's recommendation), exercising a significant amount of military power for one so young and inexperienced. She's also the only companion to put the Doctor on a leash, effectively controlling when he shows up in her life again. And by leaving the Doctor, a moment many have pointed out as Martha's strongest, Martha does exercise the power she has and walks away. But all of this means only that Martha is more powerful than past (and some future) companions in the new series, not that she is as powerful as the

27 I am only analyzing the issues of Series Three in the context of the new *Doctor Who* series that began in 2005.

Doctor.[28]

The Doctor frequently fails to acknowledge the difference in power between him and Martha. In these moments, it's difficult to know if he is being willfully obtuse. For example, in *The Shakespeare Code,* Martha reminds the Doctor that she doesn't have the same amount of privilege and power that he does when walking willy-nilly into the past:

> **Martha:** Oh, but hold on. Am I all right? I'm not going to get carted off as a slave, am I?
> **The Doctor (looking genuinely confused):** Why would they do that?
> **Martha (pointing at her face):** Not exactly white, in case you haven't noticed.
> **The Doctor:** I'm not even human. Just walk about like you own the place. Works for me.

This set of dialogue is a handy example of the Doctor refusing to acknowledge even the small ways (compared to say, mind reading and time travel) in which he is more powerful than his companions. Martha recognizes that history is not necessarily a safe place for her, since she doesn't have the same privilege and power there that she does in her present. And the Doctor assures her that *he has less power and privilege* ("I'm not even human!"), which is a blatant misrepresentation of what is happening here. The Doctor has white privilege (and, more relevantly in Elizabethan England, male privilege), even if he isn't actually a human. It's easy for him to act like he owns the place, because in the vast majority of human history, *he could actually own the place,* while Martha couldn't. The Doctor's dismissal of her concern may be warranted in this situation, but he also refuses to acknowledge that there is a power differential between them. Not only does Martha not have the same power as a white man would have historically, she is also not as capable of getting herself out of trouble. If she was "carted off as a slave," she would not be able to sonic screwdriver her way out of physical restraints. She might be able to run to the TARDIS, but without the Doctor, she couldn't use it to escape. She doesn't have the extraordinary knowledge of the Doctor to help her if she's trapped or threat-

28 Note that I don't complicate her class privilege with her lack of race privilege; this is because the show refuses to do this in her present. The only times the show acknowledges her race, and the ways in which her race diminishes her power because of racial oppression, are in the past, as with *Human Nature/ The Family of Blood.* This suggests that the writers problematically believed racial oppression to be a problem of history, not something Martha has to face in the present.

ened. This kind of exchange is echoed in other parts of the new series, like when the Doctor assures Astrid Peth that he doesn't "have a penny" in *Voyage of the Damned*, and it is fundamentally dishonest. By looking like a white man and by being an alien with special abilities, the Doctor has more power and influence than Martha. When the Doctor refuses to recognize the role power plays in his relationships, he risks exploiting that power difference.

Even as a human, in *Human Nature/ The Family of Blood*, the Doctor has an uneven power relationship with Martha. Martha as John Smith's housemaid is not *that* different from Martha as the Doctor's companion. When we see Martha in a maid uniform, it's a visual amplification of her relationship to the Doctor, not a deviation from it.

Okay, I know that claim isn't going to go over well. But Martha has no actual power in the TARDIS or in their adventures. Her frustrated powerlessness as she watches John Smith fall in love with Nurse Redfern mimics the powerlessness that she feels while trapped in a car in *Gridlock* or in the escape pod in *42*. In the TARDIS, the Doctor is in charge; he makes the decisions. And, crucially, Martha's job in the TARDIS is to tend to the Doctor's emotional needs. She is there because he is lonely, and to keep him from misusing his power. ("I think you need someone to stop you," Donna tells the Doctor in *The Runaway Bride*.) That maid uniform signals to us not only her lack of power in comparison to him, but also her servile role in his life. (It's an exaggeration of that servile role, obviously.) She's a companion, a caretaker, a therapist. She is not a partner. I mean, you can be friends with your maid, and you might even pretend that makes you equals, but she's still your maid.

The relationship between the Master and Lucy Saxon makes it clear what can happen when a Time Lord pretends an equal relationship with a human. In modern Western culture, the ideal heterosexual romantic pairing is *the* relationship of equality. We like to think we've moved beyond the sexism of the past, where marriages were exchanges of women-property, and that marriages based in love are equal partnerships. So the fact that the Master marries Lucy is significant. What's interesting is that we never see the Master as purposefully manipulative with Lucy in *The Sound of Drums*. He seems to have, at least, a certain affection for her. Their body language in this episode is not that different from a couple in love. He doesn't lie to her about his plans, and they both seem to think that she is entering this relationship with her eyes open. Neither the Master nor Lucy acknowledge the extraordinary power imbalance in their relationship, which is why it's easy for him to end up abusing that power with her.

The relationship that the Master has with Lucy Saxon is horrifying, but it acts as a foil to the relationship the Doctor has with his companions, and specifically with Martha. It's an exaggeration of the Doctor/ Martha relationship, not a departure. In the new series, both the Master and the Doctor choose their companions because they need something from them (connections for an election, companionship to counter loneliness). Both are in charge of their companion's adventures. The Master takes Lucy to places that will shape her into what he wants: a person with little sympathy for human life. And while the Doctor often elicits and obliges his companions' requests, the number of times the companions ask "Where are we going now?" makes it clear that the decision of "where" and "when" to go is ultimately up to him. Finally, both the Master and the Doctor have an extraordinary amount of power over their companions, and both fail to acknowledge this, often pretending their companions are on equal footing with them.

In the Master/Lucy relationship, we see the exaggerated possible future of the Doctor and any of his companions. One year after the Master releases the Toclafane, his relationship with Lucy has altered irreparably. When we first see Lucy in *Last of the Time Lords,* she has a bruised eye and walks with a limp, indicating physical abuse from the Master. She is dressed in a low-cut red satin dress, obviously chosen by the Master. The dress sexualizes her, and signals possible sexual abuse. Her haunted and empty look also suggests emotional abuse. After all, the Master seems to have gotten bored of her, flirting with his masseuse Tanya in front of Lucy, promising Tanya he would take her traveling in the TARDIS. Lucy's ability to resist has been worn down by the Master's treatment of her. Even as she shoots the Master, she almost looks like it happened by accident, like she's in shock.

It's not a pretty picture; with the Master, Lucy has gone from a powerful agent (with wealth and connections) to a powerless victim. Could something like this happen with the Doctor and his companions? Doubtful. But the Doctor is not above taking advantage of his companions' lack of power. He removes Donna's memory, despite her resistance and clear *no.* He dumps the Doctor clone onto Rose, and Rose back in her alternate universe, despite her reservations about whether that's what she wants. He disables Jack's time travel device, knowing that Jack has no way to fix it. He doesn't do these things often, but he is always in a position to do them. His companions have few ways to fight back when the Doctor decides to do something "for their own good."

And the relationship between the Master and Lucy is not the only way in which the series finale draws clear parallels between the Master and the Doctor. The Master disables the Doctor in *The Sound of Drums,* taking away his sonic screwdriver and aging him so that he is physically weak. In the next episode, we see the Doctor crawl out of a tent, with a bowl reading "dog" outside of it. The Master delights in stripping the Doctor of his power and humiliating him. When the Master is disabled at the end of the episode, and the Doctor is at full strength, the Doctor says that he will keep the Master "safe" in the TARDIS. The Master is horrified; "You mean you're just going to... *keep* me?" he asks. The Doctor responds, "Maybe I've been wandering for too long. Now I've got someone to care for." While what the Doctor wants to do with the Master is far kinder than what the Master did to the Doctor, the comparison is unavoidable. Neither of these men enjoys seeing the other as an equal. The Master wants to keep the Doctor as a pet, humiliated and weak. The Doctor's plan to "keep" the Master sounds no less humiliating, and is predicated on the fact that the Doctor will be able to overpower the Master for the foreseeable future. Their relationship is a power struggle.

The Master functions as the Doctor's foil in this season, an exaggeration of the ways in which the Doctor often has the most power in his relationships. Like the Master, the Doctor wants a fairly equal relationship with his human companions, and this desire leads the Master to corrupt his wife. While the Doctor doesn't deliberately take advantage of his power like the Master does, the Master is an object lesson for the Doctor. He is a warning of what could happen if the Doctor continues to deny the difference of power with his companions, and Lucy Saxon serves as a reminder of how much harm the Doctor is capable of doing to his companions.

Think of all the relationships in your life where someone more powerful than you pretends you're equals. Your mother, telling you that you should treat her just like a friend, and tell her everything, without acknowledging that you could tell her something that gets you grounded. Your boss, encouraging you to treat her like an equal, despite the fact that she could fire you at the drop of a hat. Your teacher, the one who wears jeans and has you call her by her first name, who wants you to act like she doesn't give you your grades. All of these instances are dangerous, because by denying their power over you, these people leave you open to exploitation. Your mom may want you to tell her everything, but when you tell her about that time you went drinking after prom, she swiftly takes away your car. Your boss may want to take you out, like friends, but if you accidentally tell her you steal pencils from the office, you're fired. But what are you supposed to do? Tell your mom and your boss that you don't want to be friends with them? Because they hold so much power over you, you *have* to at least pretend closeness and friendliness. And that simply isn't fair. It's important in relationships to recognize the power we do or don't hold over our fellow human beings. The only character, and prospective companion, who really seems to recognize this in Series Three is Joan Redfern.

Joan is one of the only prospective companions in the new series to turn the Doctor down, and she does so because of power. At the end of *The Family of Blood,* Joan is coming to terms with the fact that the human John Smith no longer exists. In one of his more oblivious moments, the Doctor invites her to travel with him as his companion. "But that's not fair," she says sadly, "What must I look like to you, Doctor? I must seem so very small." In this scene, she recognizes that she will never be the Doctor's equal, and that she is "small" and powerless next to him, even though he denies it. She doesn't want to replace a relationship with John Smith, based on companionship and mutual understanding, with a relationship with the Doctor, the demigod who brought death and destruction to her home. Joan is more perceptive than a lot of the other characters who come in contact with the Doctor, and she doesn't seem to buy the Doctor's denial that she is small next to him. She recognizes that a relationship with the Doctor will never be "fair," no more than a "friendship" with your mom can be fair.

So what does all this mean? Is the Doctor despicable? Are the companions powerless? Well, no. The Doctor's intentions are good; he wants to connect with his companions. He wants to be equal partners with them, and that's admirable. But his solution, to gloss over the power he has, is dangerous. It leaves his companions open to exploitation; if he doesn't acknowledge his power, he can't be aware of how it affects his treatment of his companions. What I like about Series Three is that it tackles this inequity, from Donna to Martha to Joan to Lucy Saxon. In the climax of the series, we see a distorted and corrupted Master, who serves as a warning to the Doctor. His abuse of Lucy, of Martha's family, of the human race, is an admonition: *Don't ignore the power you have. Don't ignore how that affects your relationship with humans. Don't use it to manipulate and exploit others.*

Does the Doctor learn this lesson? Not exactly. The closest we see him to grappling with the amount of power he holds is in *The Waters of Mars*, but he doesn't radically change his behavior afterwards. He also comes face-to-face (again) with the power of the Time Lords in *The End of Time*, but seems to reflect very little on how this is related to his relationship with humans. And by the time we see the eleventh Doctor, bumbling into the home of the young Amelia Pond, the theme of power distribution seems to have evaporated. We're encouraged to see Amelia and the eleventh Doctor as the same - adventurous and childlike - rather than what they actually are: a small and vulnerable child and a powerful alien.

I keep watching, hoping that we'll see again an exploration of power distribution in the Doctor's relationships, of vulnerable companions and other humans, of the possibility of abuse and exploitation in relationships like this. Particularly while the Doctor is played by an actor in so many privileged categories (white, cisgendered male, abled, young) that hold power in our world, it's important for the writers and fans to grapple with the role power plays in *Doctor Who*. After all, why haven't we had a female Doctor or a Doctor of color? Is it because s/he would lose all that power associated with being a white man? Does he need the power to strut through Earth history and the rest of the universe without a worry, the power to command and control, even if he doesn't use it? Are we fans as attracted to the Doctor's power as his companions are? If so, then it's even more important that this theme resurface in the show, and that fans have a conversation about it.

And I, for one, look forward to that conversation.

Robots, Orientalism and Yellowface: Minorities in the Fourteenth Season of *Doctor Who*

Aliette de Bodard is a computer engineer who lives in Paris - in her spare time, she indulges in her love of mythology and history by writing speculative fiction. She is the author of the *Obsidian and Blood* trilogy of Aztec noir fantasies, published by Angry Robot. Her short fiction has garnered her a BSFA Award in addition to a Hugo and Nebula nomination. Visit aliettedebodard.com for fiction, language learning struggles and recipes involving plenty of garlic and fish sauce.

Season Fourteen of *Doctor Who* certainly does things on the grandest of scales: it sees the Doctor (Tom Baker) foil the Master's plot to take over Gallifrey (*The Deadly Assassin*), avert nuclear catastrophe (*The Hand of Fear*) and travel from nineteenth century London to a distant future where robots are ubiquitous (*The Talons of Weng-Chiang* and *The Robots of Death,* respectively). With such diverse backgrounds and settings, as well as the openness of mind that is meant to be an integral part of the show, the inevitable question is how well does the season fulfill its promise: how effective is it at representing the minorities of its time period?

For the purposes of this essay, I will examine the Others in a science fictional context, and include both aliens and robots within the examination: there are well-documented parallels between the depiction of aliens and robots in SF, and that of racial minorities. It is not the purpose of this essay, so I will not over-argue the point; but certainly, within the colonial framework of SF in the late 1970s, the aliens were often a barely-veiled extension and/or metaphor of foreign people and their "odd" customs, and used as such, either unconsciously or to deliberate effect (see for instance the deliberate though not entirely effective parallels drawn between the Vietnamese and the creechies in Ursula K. Le Guin's *The Word for World is Forest,* which was published as a novel in 1976, at the same time Season Fourteen aired).

Where Season Fourteen of *Doctor Who* excels is in its aliens, showing on screen complex and memorable species. The Kastrians in *The Hand of Fear* are seen only through the lens of extinction, and the psychopathic Eldrad, but they nevertheless give an impression of a technologically advanced society which predated the humans by several centuries (and a society strong enough to create technology that keeps working even in the present time). Faced between a choice of racial suicide and outward conquest, the Kastrians' noble choice to destroy themselves and their racial heritage, leaving nothing for Eldrad to exploit, both shrouds them in pathos, and gives them a moral high ground far above humans (as a species, we have so far shown more inclination to survive by slaughtering and conquering others than by committing suicide). By those lights, Eldrad and her willingness to enslave other planets become nothing more than a heresy doomed to die with her, neatly overturning the stereotype of aliens overeager to conquer (especially Earth).

Likewise, the season does some interesting things with the Time Lords - the Doctor's tumultuous, if not outright inimical, relationship with his own species is well established, but *The Deadly Assassin* takes this a step further. It shows us Time Lords as distant aliens in elaborate costumes that contribute to distancing them yet further from the viewers. In the absence of a companion, the Doctor (who only dons Time Lord attire when seeking to camouflage himself within the Panopticon) is the most human character on stage, an interesting reversal of his being the only alien when he travels to Earth or to human-dominated futures. And what we see of the Time Lords is, likewise, both fascinating and balanced: a powerful, advanced civilization without strife, with a variety of people ranging from the sheer evil of the Master, to the power hunger that characterizes both the ill-fated Chancellor Goth and his successor Borusa, to the wonderful stubbornness and pragmatism of Castellan Spandrell and Co-Ordinator Engin. Gallifrey might not be a place that welcomes the Doctor (though, in a later season, it will welcome companion Leela), but it's certainly a location that feels both lived-in and utterly different from the UK of the seventies.

However, all is not rosy in Season Fourteen. Ironically, where the depiction of aliens is particularly strong the show falters in its treatment of robots and non-western humans.

The robots feature in one story, the aptly named *The Robots of Death*. In it, they are machines, and treated as such by the humans on board the sandminer. They are, though, the personification of the fear the Other inspire: they look human, but do not think or act like humans. There is even a specific sickness, "robophobia," which can reduce a grown man to a gibbering wreck in the presence of robots: a rather ugly materialization and justification of prejudice bundled into a neat plot point. The story's party line is that they cannot and will not ever achieve self-awareness. The story's villain, Taren Capel, is ostensibly motivated by the need to free them from human bondage; and, when we see a more advanced robot, D84, who is clearly capable not only of logical thinking, but also of weighing ethical decisions (he chooses to sacrifice himself to save the Doctor), this raises doubts about the self-awareness of the robots. Is it all nothing more than programed behavior - and even if it were, can a being capable of making such choices be justifiably used as little more than a slave?

Probably the low point, though, is the show's treatment of racial minorities: there is only one story which prominently features them, *The Talons of Weng-Chiang*, but it basically manages to hit every single Orientalist trope in the book. It starts with the yellowface: the major Chinese characters are played by British actors. This would mostly have been fine - if the production hadn't attempted to compensate for the lack of "Chineseness" in the actors by applying liberal quantities of makeup to turn them Chinese. This is not only insulting and frankly bizarre, as the end result is far from convincing; it also ends up emphasizing the alienness of the Chinese, by accentuating only those traits which people think are "typically" Chinese, such as the epicanthic folds and the goatee (that last being a feature many Chinese, and indeed many Asians, do not have).

This is only the start: the story itself has stellar dialogue, wonderful characters (Litefoot, Jago); but falls flat on its face by treating the Chinese as raw Others. They are pictured as enigmatic and untrustworthy people - with every single Chinese character on screen turning out to work for the villain - and their customs are depicted only as fodder for plot points. Again and again, the Chinese are distanced from the narrative, portrayed as "unlike us," with marked insistence on their odd customs, their ridiculous superstitions: there is a strong subtext that only a Chinese peasant could have been gullible enough to believe that a time traveller is a god (presumably, an English peasant would have been much more pragmatic...). The villain's lair is pure Orientalism, with Chinese-looking furniture used as cool props without any nod as to its original purpose, feeling more like the Disney version of China than the real thing. The wardrobe is used as a time cabinet, the imperial dragon as a laser, and even a jade disk turns out to be a hidden key. The fake Chinese extends to the Oriental-looking chess board, which is meant to look exotic but utterly fails at authenticity by looking more like an odd version of Western chess than like Chinese chess or go.

There is a slightly more equalitarian treatment of minorities in *The Robots of Death,* which features a strong multi-racial cast; though there is a strong tendency to kill them off. The black woman, Zilda, and Cass, the South Asian crewmember, both die fairly quickly into the story, and are seldom, if ever, in direct interaction with the Doctor; while the survivors of the story could model for an all-White Britain.

Otherwise, minorities mostly shine by their absence: just like Time Lords have no women, they apparently do not have any other race but white European in their ranks. It's not surprising that *The Masque of Mandragora* wouldn't have any minorities, given that it is set in fifteenth century Italy (though even Italy was more diverse than this, with influxes of migrants from the nearby Arab countries, who fail to feature at all in the cast). It is, however, unjustifiable that the Time Lords would be racially homogenous; and an odd choice to make all the settlers of the planet in *The Face of Evil* Caucasian (it could be argued that the ship that crashed was all-Caucasian, but it's a contortion when we see how diverse some futures such as *The Robots of Death* can be).

All in all, then, this season of *Doctor Who* is not exempt from problems, and does not shine as a beacon of social progress. However, shows are not made in a vacuum, and I have been deliberately unfair by holding the season to the social and moral standards of 2011 - whereas it aired in 1977, more than 30 years ago. It must be remembered that the norms were very different back when the show was made: so, to ask the question again: how does it stack up against its own time period?

The answer is "not so bad" (and it is one of the reasons I enjoyed watching it so much). The racial attitudes, for instance, are very much of a time when blatantly worse shows were on display. *The Hand of Fear* has a South Asian doctor who takes care of Sarah Jane Smith; Zilda in *The Robots of Death* is one of the most informed and perceptive characters (this is what brings about her death). And *The Talons of Weng-Chiang* is indeed racist by today's standards; but to my mind, it is more through clumsy choices than anything else. It is evident as you watch the story that there is more to it, that it is attempting, however clumsily, to subvert its own Orientalism. The Doctor, for instance, gets out of the coach when Litefoot makes one of the most blatant Orientalist assertions about the Chinese being an "odd people," and refers to their burial of his father with fireworks as though it was a deadly sin. The Doctor is clearly disgusted by Litefoot's racism and lack of understanding, though he does not attempt to convince Litefoot otherwise (and this, I think, is where the narrative falters, because the Doctor has clearly shown before that he will speak against unfair customs, and his failure to do this now is inexcusable).

Likewise, Li H'sen Chang is not only aware of the era's racism against him (he dryly says to the Doctor that to the English, all Chinese look alike), but clearly plays on the perceptions of his audience: he speaks broken English when on stage, but his diction becomes perfectly fluent when he is out of his stage persona. His choice of show, which plays into the worst Victorian Orientalist clichés, is deliberate, and it is palpable that he treats it as a game, as something that allows him to rise in fame. Likewise, he uses the position of the Chinese within Victorian London, and their entries into London society to good effect: he hides his homunculus in the laundry that is washed at Limehouse; he has a good relationship with the police as an interpreter, which comes in useful when he has to dispose of a troublesome underling. And he is clearly the smarter man when compared to Litefoot or Jago, or even Magnus Greel: the latter's plans only start to fall to pieces once Li H'sen Chang has rejected him.

In fact, watching the story is like watching a train wreck in progress: you can clearly see where the writer was attempting to depart from the Orientalism, but a number of choices, from the lack of "good" Chinese to the alienation of the Chinese as a race, turn the story into a morass of racism. It would be inexcusable in today's climate to make this kind of story (not that this has stopped some series from trying); but in the context of 1977 and the other shows on television, *The Talons of Weng-Chiang* is actually more informed and well-meaning than most.

The robots are also a product of their time: *The Robots of Death* is a homage to literary SF, with a character named "Poul" (after Poul Anderson), and robots who give more than a passing nod to Asimov's own creations (the duo of investigators D84 and Poul are eerily reminiscent of Daneel and Elijah Baley in *The Caves of Steel*, down to the human member of the duo having an aversion that turns into a handicap - Poul is robophobic, Baley is claustrophobic). Once we get past the homage, one of the story's strengths is the spin it puts on the villain - Capel is so obsessed by the robots that he seeks to make himself into one of them (down to the make-up on his face), but he is also a megalomaniac who cares more about himself than the welfare of the robots he so casually uses, reprograms and discards. The story makes it clear that Capel is not needed by the robots; but also that he is a danger to them, both by reinforcing the phobia against the robots, but also by using them against their will. If robots are indeed sentient, forcibly reprogramming them so that they take orders from Capel is nothing less than mind-rape, and exposes Capel as the ugly, misshapen human being that he really is.

Season Fourteen, then, is very much a show of its time regarding its treatment of non-mainstream cultures and characters. It has huge flaws which cannot be ignored; but neither can its merits in attempting to subvert the stereotypes of its time period: though the results are ultimately mixed, its heart is in the right place.

David Tennant's Bum

Laura Mead is a *Doctor Who* fan with a tendency towards chaps with big hair and hi-top sneakers. She is one quarter of *The Ood Cast*, a podcast that celebrates the joy and endless creativity of the series (find it at theoodcast.com or on iTunes). Growing up without a television, Laura was a very late bloomer into the world of the Doctor. She maintains that the first episode of *Doctor Who* that she saw had a woman getting her head forcibly shaved by a chap in a holographic jumpsuit and yelling about it, but can't for the life of her remember when that was. She is very pleased that the possibility of a female Doctor is now canonical, and she likes to sing songs about time travel, cake and political apathy.

> "Oh, this one is tasty! I'll have lashings of him! Delicious!"
>
> —The Wire, *The Idiot's Lantern*

Ah, classic *Doctor Who*. That whirling mélange of history and imagination, of complex morality and basic truths. A noble vehicle of education, whimsy and flights of soaring fantasy. Launch-pad of a thousand burgeoning writers and exponentially more partially sofa-obscured nightmares. Instigator of nobility, pacifism and conversation.

And for me, instant narcolepsy.

Now, before an angry mob assembles outside my house brandishing flaming torches, pitchforks, and copies of *The Seeds of Doom*, I know it's a heretical thing to say, but I really did try. Quite a range of different Doctors, writers and eras, in fact: *City of Death, Ghost Light, Logopolis, Earthshock*, even *An Unearthly Child*. What all these classic stories have in common is an unerring capacity to send me to sleep, usually by the second or third installment.

This is as baffling to me as it is to the other Oods on *The Ood Cast*, a *Doctor Who* fan podcast I co-host. What could it be? I don't mind electronic bleeps as backing music. Hell, discovering Kraftwerk about 30 years late was a bit of a revelation for me. I love bombastic speeches; I'm a big fan of Shakespeare, and a good dollop of British character acting has always been just the thing to float my boat. I don't even mind convoluted space-babble; Asimov was bed-time reading for me as a child and my summers were as much Helliconian as halcyon.

So why, with all of these factors in great supply, was I not an instant convert?

Like many recent devotees, I came to *Doctor Who* from Russell T Davies onwards, as an adult (yes, really I am) trusting in the god-like prowess of the BBC to produce quality drama, but not knowing what to expect beyond explosion-filled trailers; rubberized, dribbling terrors; and the somewhat confusing combination of bubblegum pop sensation Billie and a gruff northerner in leather. With a cheeky nod to Knightsbridge snobbery, and a healthy injection of nightmare fuel, the rejuvenated *Doctor Who* burst onto our screens.

And it was good. Fairly.

I watched with modulating degrees of terror as the Doctor and Rose were chased by malcontented ghosts, gas masked zombies and the occasional pig - but still, when the next Saturday rumbled round, it would take a firm nudging from my husband to sit down to his favorite show, and missing an episode or two really didn't strike me as that tragic. In fact, there are still a few Eccleston outings I've never sampled. Now, I appreciate a good fart joke as much as the next puerile 20-something, but I only saw *Boom Town* for the first time a couple of months ago, and I don't feel like a missing puzzle piece of my life has finally dropped into place as a result.

Granted, Series One of New *Who* didn't have quite the lullaby effect on me as its predecessors. The differences were obvious. Comparing the classic and the modern series, I could talk about pacing, and storyarcs, and character development (particularly of the female companion variety) until I was blue in the box. But that still wouldn't hide the fact that until the arrival of the subject of this essay, my overwhelming reaction to *Doctor Who* was "meh."

So, Series Two of New *Who* begins, and the United Kingdom has turned over a new fig leaf. The Civil Partnerships Act is signed into law, finally granting gay couples a semblance of the rights afforded to their straight compatriots, whilst soon-to-be "defender of the faith" Prince Charles marries his former mistress.

And a new Doctor smoothly segues onto our screens. Has he "still got it?" Yes, indeed. He is, in his own words, sexy. Not only with a full head of post-coital hair, but "slim and just a little bit foxy" (Cassandra, *New Earth*). I'm not sure a series debut of a 900-plus-year-old genius has been made yet with more lashings of innuendo than were ladled onto *The Christmas Invasion*.

Even Jackie recognizes the allure of our freshly minted, vulnerable, unconscious hero. "Anything else he's got two of?" Be still my beating heart(s). If Rose drew the line at tucking him up in bed, a significant proportion of the viewing public, myself included, would have happily clambered in there too. This is the Doctor with "a new... everything," repackaged (oof, there's another story) for a new kind of fan, one with more than a passing interest in the wrapping around the greatest mind in the universe.

Call me cynical, but I'm sure that Russell T Davies knew exactly what he was doing when he picked this Son of the Glen to pilot us through history, peppered with knowing winks, a shameless shower scene within two episodes, and a very nicely fitted suit. There have been a great many Doctors with appeal, but this one's gib was a cut well above the average.

Before I could even attempt to rationalize my decision in terms of the feisty scriptwriting, the palpable sexual tension between the Doctor and his assistant, or the affinity I experienced with someone for whom the consumption of a well-brewed cup of tea was a matter of life or death, I was hooked.

I wasn't alone. Not by a long chalk.

Where once crowds of men of a certain age (no offence, chaps, but you know who you are) peopled conventions, the demographic subtly, but unstoppably, began to slide into the pink. This was particularly notable across the pond in America, where hordes of girls for whom the verb "squee" seemed to have been specifically invented began to invade. Slowly, but surely, the viewers switched on in their droves, with every Tennant episode averaging 8.33 million to Eccleston's 7.95. According to the *Radio Times*, the notoriously difficult to please 16 to 35 age group, the *Skins* generation, effervescent with hormones and burgeoning sexuality, certainly appreciated the new direction, with the audience share rocketing up from only 7% of the audience in 2005, to over 25% today.

With his new face, new hair and new teeth, this Doctor was most definitely "in." And why not? Ladies now had the vote, ostensibly equal pay, and the right to wear trousers in public without being labeled a "hussy." Wasn't it about time that someone started (ahem) trying to tick our boxes?

What was it about the tenth Doctor that particularly piqued my interest?

It wasn't David Tennant, or even particularly his perky bum, a thing of joy and inspiration though it is.

I'd seen him before, pirouetting his way through *Blackpool* and *Bright Young Things* and placed him firmly in the "talented" camp, but even his role as the famously lascivious Casanova had failed to get my motor running. It was something else, an extra *je ne sais quois*, an added piquancy, that met my tastes.

Undeniably, incontrovertibly, Tennant had suddenly become more attractive in not just my eyes, but those of most of the viewing public of the UK; a mean feat to achieve, armed with only a bed-head hair-do and a pair of Converse trainers. So something else was going on.

Here was a previously low-profile actor, now being voted as *Attitude*'s man of the year, and ranked Sixteenth Most Sexy Man worldwide by *Cosmopolitan* in 2008. Men wanted to be him, women wanted to have him. If I'm being truly inclusive, quite a few men wanted to have him (and women wanted to be him - now possible thanks to the now delightfully canon tale of the Corsair) too. The Doctor had become not just a figure of admiration, but an object of desire.

Now, partially, this increase in attractiveness could be attributed to the Doctor's Benjamin Button-esque charms. Although there have been a few bumps in the graph here and there (step forward Mr Davison, taking over the role fresh-faced at 29, before Colin Baker and Sylvester McCoy bucked the trend back up again), the average age of actors playing the Doctor has decreased by around 1.8 years each time. The Doctor started out as something much closer to the "pompous, ancient, dusty senators" of Gallifrey, but has evolved into someone far more vivacious.

William Hartnell was 55 when he made his debut, but being white-wigged, grandfatherly and stern, he played up traits of seniority and experience that made him seem far older than his years. Ironically, the new, chronologically older Doctor is a far more likely candidate for a relationship with a companion, without any of the lecherous overtones a more obviously elderly figure would usually induce. This is something picked up on by Sarah Jane as she somewhat jealously mocks him after meeting Rose in *School Reunion*: "You can tell you're getting older - your assistants are getting younger..."

What Rose, Sarah Jane, Reinette Poisson and even Cassandra - wildly different women (or flaps of skin, albeit with remarkably good taste) - all recognize in Tennant's Doctor is that he is, well... incredible. As Reinette says in *The Girl in the Fireplace*, "One may tolerate a world of demons for the sake of an angel."

Inevitably, most of the ladies he comes into contact with are more than prepared to help him fall to Earth. Gussets have not been so universally moistened since the arrival of James Bond but, despite gratuitously flaunting a tuxedo on more than one occasion, the Doctor is no 007.

What are the characteristics that make him the target of so many heaving bosoms?

Just for the sake of clarity, I'll list them.

He loves life so much he'll go to any lengths to preserve it. He faces down the barrel of a gun with an anecdote about a children's television program (*Balamory*, for connoisseurs of CBeebies). He is brave and inquisitive even in the face of terror. Where your nobler, more classically heroic protagonist would dash in with a sword (and end up as noble, classically heroic mincemeat, a la *Tooth and Claw*), the Doctor thinks, talks and runs his way out of sticky situations. But this isn't down to cowardice: equally, he will run towards danger without batting an eyelid, hurtling into bottomless pits, one-way portals and alien-infested schools.

His desire for discussion, debate and peaceful compromise is fed by a love of life, and also from self-awareness of his capabilities when his back is against the wall. Only when all other options, including surrender, have been exhausted will he strike. When he does, it is with finality, with uncompromising, deadly force. There will be no boring 20-minute slow-mo slug-fests for him.

To him, books are "the best weapons in the world" - which leaves him disarmingly unprepared for a strong left hook, and yet stronger by far than his brawnier, brasher opponents. This is something recognized by Mr Finch, the demonic headmaster of *School Reunion*: "Your people were peaceful to the point of indolence. You are something new." And this is aptly true.

The Doctor is not afraid to admit he's scared. He is proud of his ability to feel and act on emotion. Even those emotions which would normally be considered negative: fear, pain and loss all act as a spur to his genius. In fact, he would rather die than not feel. If he is proof that emotions destroy you, he is also proof of their power to rebuild a soul.

His deductive prowess is unmatched; he is observant and intuitive to an uncanny degree. He appreciates science and technology, but not only that, he wants others to appreciate them too, and takes the time to explain his theories and actions. In a way, he's like Professor Brian Cox, but with better hair and a sexier voice. He might explain things at 90 miles per hour, and he is intellectually fearsome, but he doesn't balk at recognizing the same brilliance in others who shine. He basks in the glow of knowledge and loves to be challenged, to learn, and to share the joy of discovering the peccadilloes of the universe. This is in stark contrast to the typical Hollywood blockbuster belittling of intelligence. We all know the trope of the psychotic genius/ dark professor ranting in Machiavellian code in their ivory tower before being felled by a single punch.

He's a socialist with a dislike of Margaret Thatcher (whose policies were, in my not especially humble opinion, nowhere near as good as the concept of a female prime minister) who fights the system, throws out the rule book and refers to those working with him as his "comrades," directing and encouraging them with a firm but coaxing authority. He enables the best in people, inspiring instant trust and loyalty; probably because that's what he expects of others. He's radical, a rule breaker. If offered the universe on a plate (of chips) he would turn it down, standing as a defender of worlds, not a god. At least, not yet.

He's eloquent to a fault, with speeches full of ice and fire and... well... melty water. He never has difficulty in conveying exactly what he means, how he feels and what he intends to do about it, in language as poetic as Rushdie but without the pompous alienation. Yet he is prepared to recognize his fallibility. His constant quest for knowledge is more about being challenged, surprised and proved wrong than it is about asserting his dominance over time and space. In fact, as he puts it in *The Impossible Planet*, "... the day I know everything, I might as well stop."

He prefers to neutralize or deconstruct a threat rather than destroy it, recognizing beauty even in the most frightening, disgusting or unexpected of situations. And he is incredibly tactile: touching, stroking and investigating his way through close encounters with other life-forms.

This brings me to another charming feature, one so crudely unsubtle it must have had the writer's room in hysterics: this is a Doctor who is well experienced in the oral arts. Any unidentified object, thing or substance, his first reaction is to lingeringly, lasciviously, lick it. And his tongue is so talented it is able to distinguish any element or compound, including mistletoe, Krillitane oil or Bakelite, to name but a few.

He is steadfast, loyal and honest, giving his word that he will fix, solve or think of solutions to any problem. Given the belief and respect of his companions, he could accomplish anything. He is passionate, sweet and uncompromisingly moral, unarmed but never powerless. In fact, this Doctor's flashes of darkness are almost always centered around a morally impregnable core.

He is comfortable, relaxed and huggy around everyone, but particularly women, and knows how to appreciate the female form, nobly managing not to address the décolletage of Reinette as he stutters, "My, how you've grown..." He views women as equals, bastions of resourcefulness and intellect, not victims. He's prepared to leave them to rescue themselves, although he can just as easily double as a knight in shining pinstripe, riding through the mirror of their dreams, and making the ultimate sacrifices of freedom, indeed of life itself, if called to. Sure, he might balk at the idea of a mortgage, but that doesn't mean he won't let his admiring companions spend the rest of their lives with him, no matter the personal emotional cost of watching them wither and die. Stick that in your sparkly pipe and smoke it, Edward Cullen! (Apologies for genre-hopping there, I don't know what came over me.)

The fact remains that even Mickey Smith trussed up in his boxers in front of a blazing fire (a sight to warm the cockles of even the flintiest heart) can't hold a candle to the Doctor, fully clothed, popping on his "sexy specs" to examine a data download or delightedly snogging a spark-plug. And when Mickey tells Rose: "All the time you've been saying he's different, but the truth is, he's just like any other bloke," he couldn't have been more wide of the mark.

David Tennant's Doctor, the Doctor of Series Two of New *Who*, is an entirely new kind of sex symbol, redefining sexy for the noughties, for a more technologically savvy, liberal, free thinking generation. He is ideally sculpted for the ladies (and gents, no judgment here) who have grown tired of the kind of "alpha male" figure constantly thrust upon the viewing public as the masculine ideal, everything that women are supposed to find attractive, but almost exclusively forged in the crucible of a very overtly male industry.

Your typical hero: muscled, bare-armed and stubbly, walking calmly away from an explosion (come on now, who the hell wouldn't *run*?) without looking back. Happy with a revolver, a set of nunchuks or even their bare fists. They are gruff, incommunicative, deadly and definitely not into hugs. And the idea of shedding a tear over the loss of a companion? Impossible. Screaming into the rain whilst holding a limp body, yes. An intense frown courtesy of the "smell the fart" school of acting, or perhaps even a terse *gawd dammit!* with a customary fist smashing into the wall? Even better. But burning up a star to say a two-minute goodbye?

Instead, with the Doctor, we have an emotionally intelligent, expressive, pacifist figure finally arriving on the scene with a quip, a wink and a mind that can invent the world's first VCR whilst running full pelt through north London.

And not a moment too soon. The Doctor is trailing in the wake of a wave of testosterone. Think of just a few of the men of stage and screen (large and small) held up as the aspirational "beefcake": James Bond (pre Daniel Craig), the A-Team, Jason Bourne, any Bruce Willis or Jason Statham character.

These are the kind of men who would much rather overcome an obstacle by starting a punch-up rather than a soliloquy.

Excuse me for a moment. Who decided that a bulging bicep was sexier than the ability to solve an equation? Who picked the AK-47 as a weapon of seduction over wide-eyed enthusiasm and affability? Who thought that the way to get women to let the protagonist into their heart or their bed was to strip them down to a wife-beater and cover them in a strategic layer of grease?

Frankly, why that would make women want to do anything other than force them into a hot, soapy bath with a loofah? I don't know.

In the sleeve notes for the DVD box set, Julie Gardner, the executive producer of Series Two, describes about *Doctor Who*: "There's wit and love and pain and adventure[...] Your actions count. The universe is dangerous and your moral choices, your actions define you. If we all had a little more of the Doctor in us, our world would be a better, braver place." Amen to that, Julie. We can all agree we'd like a little more of the Doctor in us.

I'd go so far as to argue that the advent of the Doctor as a new kind of sex symbol, the intelligent, pacifist hero, has led to a whole Christmas hamper of other similar characters speckled throughout popular culture, such as Benedict Cumberbatch's Sherlock Holmes. The watershed moment of the "Perfect Ten" Doctor has enabled fans to reappraise the hidden gems of genre television and the other rough diamonds including kindred roles such as Hugh Laurie's House and Nathan Fillion's Malcolm Reynolds. Even the more traditionally swashbuckling roles of Captains Jack Sparrow and the new Kirk now come complete with side orders of emotional angst and ennui. The alpha male, in all his bullet-spraying glory, is now frequently just a thin veneer over the more cerebral kind of hero women have grown to demand. And the reasons why are crystal clear.

We've grown savvy as to what happens after the closing credits of the latest blockbuster. No matter her qualifications for the role, or the intensity of the passion displayed in whatever clinches or couplings, the "love" interest never makes it to the next film of the franchise (or if she does, she'll meet a grisly end less than five minutes in). A relationship based on such an unequal pairing as a squealing damsel and a grunting safety net is, we know, unlikely to last past the first shopping trip to Ikea, let alone conversations about life, the universe and everything.

Strong and silent might have sufficed when there was more of a gender boundary, but now the lines between traditional male and female roles are not so much blurred as totally porous. Why continue to color the world in such overbearing shades of pink and blue and expect half of the viewing public not just to buy it, but actively desire it?

I for one am very, very tired of machismo being standard, the join-the-dots guide to inspiring female desire.

Crucially, I am tired of machismo, but I am not tired of men.

And that is why David Tennant's bum was such a draw for me. Because it was attached to the greatest, most eloquent, most intuitive mind in the universe. And that's what's really sexy.

Superficial Depth?: Spirituality in Season Eleven

Caroline Symcox, in addition to being a Curate and a writer of *Doctor Who* audio adventures for Big Finish, is also married to some guy named Paul Cornell. They live in the UK.

On being offered the opportunity to write about a season of *Doctor Who,* I immediately jumped at the chance to focus on Season Eleven. Why? Because reputedly it contained a theme very much relevant to my interests, being as I am a priest in the Church of England. This season has often been considered the place where Barry Letts gave more concrete expression to his particular religious and spiritual leanings, in particular, his interest and belief in Buddhism. I was also interested to see if other spiritual themes would get an airing, and what the treatment might be of religion in general. So it was with a hopeful heart that I stuck the first DVD into the machine and embarked on a fresh viewing of a season of *Doctor Who* that aired significantly before I was so much as a gleam in my parents' eyes.

Two things need sorting out before we can really get into exploring spiritual themes in Season Eleven. First, I need to clarify what I mean by "spiritual." In today's pluralistic world, there is a great deal of confusion and suspicion around the terms "religious" and "spiritual." Notably, "religious" has gained a negative connotation which "spiritual" seems to have largely avoided, even though self-identifying "religious" people might contend that the two terms actually refer to the same reality. To avoid getting into a heavy discussion of all that, I'll start this section by unilaterally declaring how I'm intending to use these terms. In this essay, "religious" refers to the state of being part of, or concerned with, an organized system of belief, action and, indeed, spirituality. "Spiritual" refers to the state of being concerned with transcendence and with a search for overall meaning and purpose. Both terms will be useful in exploring themes in Season Eleven.

Second, setting out to look at spiritual themes in this season raises an immediate question. Namely, *should* there be religious or spiritual themes in *Doctor Who* at all? The program has always been family viewing, largely interested in adventure with the odd snippet of education. Does spirituality have a place in that set up? I would argue that it does. Spirituality, in the broader sense I've outlined above, is a part of the human condition. Humanity naturally looks for meaning and purpose in the universe, and searches for greater truths beyond what's directly in view. Religion, on the other hand, has been part of the historical human experience for centuries. To understand a given human society, we have to understand its beliefs, and the organized systems of belief that had a hand in shaping that group of people in time. *Doctor Who*, as it follows the adventures of our hero through space and time, naturally meets with systems of belief. The story may skirt around them, or it may get to grips with them, but like it or not, the two should and do come into contact from time to time. What the series does much more rarely is investigate the spirituality of the Doctor himself, and in Season Eleven the show comes perilously close to doing just that.

All that said, in the first story of the season, spiritual or religious themes are conspicuous by their absence. *The Time Warrior* is an unabashed romp, four episodes of sheer adventurous fun, which would go some way to explaining why there's little in the way of an exploration of deep spiritual concepts. Nevertheless, I might have hoped for more than a mere passing recognition that religion might have been something of importance to people in the twelfth century. Sarah Jane and the Doctor dress up as alms-seeking monks at one stage, and the word "demons" is thrown around liberally, but that's about the height of the religious imagery put to use. Considering how central the Christian establishment was to the lives of everyone in Britain at this point in history, it wouldn't have been too much of a push to show a little more of that reality. What is interesting is the manner in which the religious imagery is skirted or lightened in the service of the humorous tone. What might have been identified as religious belief in the historical characters becomes surface superstition. Anything scary and unidentified is the product of "demons." Anyone doing unidentified things is a "magician." Notably, negative strange events are attributed to the negative aspects of religious belief systems, but positive strange events are not attributed to positive aspects of those systems. Why is the Doctor a magician rather than a saint? Why are his tricks thought of as magic rather than miracles? With this in mind, it becomes clear that the already skimpy religious imagery on show is lopsided as well. It comes across as an afterthought, something to add to the historical flavor of the dialogue, but not worth any serious consideration.

This basic lack of thought when it comes to religious themes continues in *The Monster of Peladon*. Back in *The Curse of Peladon*, when we were first introduced to the planet and its people, we learned about the firm religious views of the locals. They worshipped the spirit of Aggedor, the Royal Beast of Peladon. The beast's statue had pride of place in their temple, and to touch it was death. As it turned out, of course, the beast that had been periodically appearing and killing people was none other than a real live animal, trained by the high priest, and not remotely godlike. When we return to Peladon some 50 years later, this paradigm-destroying theological discovery appears to have made no difference at all to the local religion. Aggedor is still worshipped, and when he apparently appears in corridors killing people (déjà vu?), there is no doubt that this must indeed be the Spirit of Aggedor. Worse, as we go through the story, we discover the extent of this strange double thinking. Aggedor is kept in a cave below the temple, where he is able to feast on careless blasphemers who can be conveniently disposed of via trapdoor. It seems to trouble the local clergy and believers not a jot that the god they worship is nothing more than a handy means to reduce the blaspheming community. Instead, the various miners and aristocrats continue to piously invoke the will and wrath of Aggedor as if he were a disembodied spirit, and not, as in reality, a shaggy bear-like creature living under the floorboards. If I were to be generous, I could assume that this situation is presented by design rather than accident. Perhaps we are right in finding the peoples' double thinking to be unacceptable, written as a deliberate flaw in the society on Peladon, rather than any lack of thought on the part of the production team. However, it doesn't feel like this is the case.

Rather, this set up has the feel of an automatic reluctance to take religion seriously, with the result that a half-drawn religious institution sits irrelevantly and illogically on the sidelines until it's needed to motivate people for the political shenanigans that are the real heart of the story. Even Aggedor's death lacked any kind of impact. This absence of a religious theme was noted by the BBC's incoming head of serials, Bill Slater, although too late to influence the story itself. In his notes to the production team, he questioned the lack of Aggedor after episode three, and highlighted the issues noted above. He said:

> I was given no idea how it [Aggedor] ever came to be there, its relevance to Peladon society, why they worshipped it, were afraid of it, and what they were to do without it. It seemed an area of storytelling that might have been fruitful and enriching. Gods

> have origins. It seemed a pity to reduce poor Aggedor to the status of Palace Pet, whose eventual demise was no more meaningful than that of the family cat.

Religious themes - that is, narrative that is interested in systematic and organized believing societies - thus seems conspicuous by its absence in this season. Of course, this is not to say that other seasons serve such interests any better. *Doctor Who* in general shies away from particularly religious comment, unless "religion" in a story functions not as a belief system, but as an element of political society. On some levels, this is understandable. *Doctor Who* is, after all, a family show, and deep religious discussion would just slow and unbalance more adventurous stories. At the same time, why risk courting controversy by referencing existing world religions, when it's easy enough to create your own when the story demands it?

But still, even with these good reasons for avoiding explicit or lengthy religious themes, the lack of deeper thought when handling the created religion of the Peladonians smacks of pure bad writing. You don't need to put a great deal of effort into exploring religious elements, just as long as they make reasonable sense within the rest of the narrative. Sadly, this is something *The Monster of Peladon* simply doesn't achieve.

Where things get more interesting is when we broaden our scope from looking at religious themes and images, and look at spirituality more generally. Instead of focusing on existing or created organized groups believing certain things about the universe or how one should act, it allows us to look at concepts. In the course of a story, a full-blown organized religion may be unwieldy and over-heavy for a younger audience, but more general explorations of questions about meaning and morality are much easier to get into. The Doctor's spirituality is something that has attracted a lot of discussion. Just what is it that the Doctor believes? We can pick out general themes, although given the lengthy history of the show, each theme will usually have its notable exceptions. The Doctor seems to be largely anti-war and anti-violence, for example. In *The Time Warrior,* he has little time for either the warriors of Irongron's castle or Linx and the warlike Sontaran race. All the same, he's not above using a little violence in self-defence, as his liberal use of "Venusian Aikido" indicates, and his respect for the soldiers of UNIT shows at least a tolerance for people who use violence on a regular basis. He's vocal too about the sanctity of all life, although "sanctity" wouldn't be a word he would use. He prefers brain over brawn, and is keen on the notion that actions have consequences that must be accepted. What he isn't is a member of any recognizable religion. His spirituality is his own, and can only be discerned through his actions rather than his words.

With all this in mind, the end of Season Eleven is particularly interesting in that it explicitly deals with questions about the Doctor's spirituality, and the nature of the universe in which he lives. *Planet of the Spiders* has its down points (hovercraft chases and infodump dialogue disasters spring to mind), but where it grabs me is its open exploration of spiritual themes. It is, of course, Barry Letts' penultimate story as *Doctor Who*'s producer, and there's an argument to be made that in this, his last story with Jon Pertwee, he gave vent to some of his own concerns and beliefs, and let his own Buddhism show clearly. Indeed, *Planet of the Spiders* has been called a "Buddhist parable." But is it really? What can we say about the spirituality that's shown through these six episodes?

The first things to notice are the explicit Buddhist trappings of the retreat center in "deepest Mummerset." We see meditation being practiced on numerous occasions, both the more ominous meditative practice of the rebellious group led by Lupton, and briefly, the practice led by the Buddhist clergy of the center. Neither of these practices were created purely for the show. The mantras recited are genuine Buddhist mantras, such as the *Jewel of the Lotus* mantra led by Lupton. The use of mandalas, an example of which is the circle image that sits at the center of Lupton's group as they meditate, is a regular part of Buddhist practice. Were this another story in the course of *Doctor Who*'s long history, we might expect the explicit spirituality and religious activities on display to be brought into question and possibly debunked by a Doctor intent on getting to the true heart of the matter through science. After all, throughout his long history the Doctor has done his fair share of god killing. But not here. Certainly, Lupton and his cronies are using the power of meditation for evil, but for once, it's those individuals that are wrong, and not the whole system. Others who follow the same practices are shown to be fully good, and even in a better moral position than the Doctor himself. It is the Abbot, after all, who points out the Doctor's own fault and weakness, and sets him on the right path.

More than simply making use of religious trappings and practices, however, *Planet of the Spiders* shows itself interested in spirituality on a narrative level. The story as a whole is concerned with issues of the misuse of power, the responsibility that comes with action, and the need for both self-awareness and humility. Obviously, Lupton's naked greed for power is punished over the course of the story, as that greed is turned back upon him by the spiders he sought to use for his own ends. But so too is the Doctor's own interest in power punished. Knowledge is power, so the saying goes, and the Doctor is nothing if not interested in knowledge. It is this thirst for knowledge as a possession, and implicitly, the power that goes with it, that results in both his downfall and that of the Spider Queen.

For once, as happens only very rarely in *Doctor Who,* we see the Doctor recognise that his whole mindset was at fault. In his conversation with the Abbot, he accepts that his desire for knowledge was controlling him, and that he wasn't self-aware or humble enough to recognise the danger in that. He doesn't mention it in that conversation, but my mind instantly went back to the opening episode of the story, when he effectively causes the death of the mind-reading "Professor" in his own relentless search for more knowledge. I'm not sure we could have a clearer illustration of the callous abuse that concern for one thing and one thing only might bring about.

What makes up for this lapse in the Doctor's own spiritual well-being, because that is how the situation is clearly drawn, is his acceptance of the consequences of his actions, and his courage in facing those consequences. His drive for knowledge led him to steal the Metebelis Crystal. It is his desire for atonement that leads him to return it, even at the cost of his current incarnation. The moment of the Doctor's realization that this is what he must do, as he speaks to the Abbot, has been equated to the image of Christ in the Garden of Gethsemane. In both cases, a person looks death square in the face, with the fear and revulsion that must come of facing death, and continues on anyway. The major difference, I would suggest, is that the Doctor was aware that his previous actions demanded this consequence. His penance was something he brought on himself, in contrast to Christ's situation. The virtue on display here then is courage, or dauntlessness, one of the "glorious virtues" of Buddhism. It is this virtue that is shown to triumph.

Is the Doctor Buddhist? No, I don't think so. But the ethical and spiritual concerns included in not only Buddhism but other of the world religions are clearly part of his make-up. Self-awareness, self-restraint, love of others, service to the world: all these things are part of most of the spiritual systems to be found in the world, and in world religions. And here at least, the Doctor lets us see through his façade just enough to recognise those concerns at work in him.

As a watcher of this show, I can't help but find this kind of treatment of spiritual themes attractive. The presentation of spiritual concerns is sympathetic, not out to attack, but not out to proselytize either. Letts and writer Robert Sloman aren't trying to sell us the idea of the Doctor as a Buddhist, but rather are taking the time to explore the questions of meaning and balance in the world. Nor are they, as is often the case in family shows, wanting to make clear distinctions between good and bad. In *Planet of the Spiders*, with the possible exception of the Abbot, nobody is perfect, and our hero himself is shown to be one of the people most clearly at fault.

Of course, the story has its problems. Much of the spiritual content is simply delivered in lines, which often leads to large indigestible tracts of dialogue unbalancing the movement of the story. It also suffers from the fact that it's Jon Pertwee's last story as the Doctor, and there seems to be a desire to indulge him with a few of his favorite things. It's not an over-exaggeration to say that a full episode of this could have been dumped without any real loss to the story as a whole. But even with these flaws, I would say *Planet of the Spiders* is worth a watch. It's a rare opportunity to see spiritual themes explicitly explored in *Doctor Who*, and definitely educational if you'd like to learn more about Buddhism.

With regard to the spiritual themes I've identified and explored through the stories of the season, I have to admit to being a little disappointed. Spirituality had the possibility of being given a decent outing through the explicit inclusion of religion and spiritual discussion in two out of the five stories of the season. However, the overwhelming impression is that these discussions were superficial at best. The strange lack of systematic thought given to religious structures in both *The Time Warrior* and *Monster* is a weight on the scales against the more measured treatment of Buddhism in *Spiders*. Overall, this means that Season Eleven may have the beginnings of a consideration of spiritual themes, but fails to deliver on closer inspection. That said, it's good to see the series even begin to delve into this area. Given that faith and spirituality forms such a key part of human experience for people throughout many different cultures, it's fitting that some of that experience at least should be reflected in works of dramatic fiction, *Doctor Who* included. I would suggest, too, that no subsequent production team thus far has done as well as Letts and his fellows in exploring themes of spirituality. A challenge for the future, perhaps?

The Problem with Peri

Jennifer Pelland lives outside Boston with an Andy, three cats and an impractical amount of books. She's a life-long lover of science fiction thanks to her dad, who started her on *Star Trek* repeats in her infancy, and who brought her to the expensive movie theater outside town to watch the first *Star Wars* film instead of waiting for it to come to the cheap seats. She was introduced to *Doctor Who* on her local public television station about the same time she discovered Duran Duran, and she still loves both. Her short fiction has garnered two Nebula nominations, and 11 of her stories are collected in *Unwelcome Bodies* from Apex Publications, who have also published her novel *Machine*. Because spare time is for the weak, she also has a full-time job, is a performing belly dancer and is an occasional radio theater actor.

When I was offered the sixth Doctor's first full season to review for this book, my initial thought was that I'd write an essay called "Peri vs. the Rani," which would highlight all the reasons why this feminist had identified more with the new villain than with the companion. I hadn't watched the sixth Doctor since the 80s, and what I mostly remembered was Peri's whining and the Rani's awesomeness. But after watching a friend's DVDs, I realized that the real problem wasn't that the Rani was more awesome than Peri, but that *every single named female character she appeared with* was more awesome than her. And that's a damned shame.

Let's just take as read that Peri's American accent is terrible and that her character is a caricature of the worst of American entitlement. Those are easy and obvious nitpicks, and to be fair, I've seen worse. The real problem with Peri is that as a teenager, I couldn't get into her at all. Yes, I was raised in a feminist household, and yes, I'd had issues with most of the companions, but Peri? I had nothing *but* problems with Peri. She was the first "modern" (to me) companion whose sole purpose was to be eye candy, and for that, the teenaged me despised her.

Peri, plainly put, failed the most basic function of the companion. Not the oft-stated "the companion exists to give the Doctor a reason to explain things to the audience" role, but the "the companion gives the audience someone to identify with" role. I'd been willing to give the pre-1970s companions a pass on this. While I understood that feminism hadn't just popped out of nowhere with the fight for Equal Rights Amendment, teenaged me figured there was a reason that *The Mary Tyler Moore Show* had been considered revolutionary, so I didn't let myself get angry about how *Doctor Who* and other shows had treated women before I was born.

So, who were the "modern" (to me) female companions?

• **Liz Shaw:** scientist. I looked up to her for her smarts and professionalism, and quite frankly, I also looked up to the actress for landing such a plum role despite not being a classic beauty.

• **Jo Grant:** member of UNIT. She may have been something of a ninny, but she was plucky and loyal and did her very best to be brave.

• **Sarah Jane Smith:** journalist. Sure, she screamed a lot, but I liked her investigative instincts and the fact that she didn't think "feminist" was a dirty word.

• **Leela:** warrior. The original tough broad. The Proto-Xena. And the only time she screamed was when being dragged into the sewers by a giant rat. I was willing to give her a pass on that one.

• **Romana:** Time Lady. I adored the first one, because she was an icy, hyper-intelligent beauty that didn't take any crap from the Doctor; and was willing to accept the second one, because despite her silliness, she was still smarter than anyone else in the room.

• **Nyssa:** scientist. She was young and brainy and willing to run towards danger. Or, to put it a different way, she was everything I aspired to be at her age.

• **Tegan:** flight attendant. True, she was in a traditionally female profession, but she was a brassy broad who wasn't afraid to make her needs known, and I loved her for it. Plus, we shared a fashion sense.

• **Peri:** bikini-clad rich brat.

Was I missing something? Was that *really* all there was to her? What drove them to create the character in the first place? Maybe it had just been lost in the translation from the drawing board to the screen. Going straight to the primary source, we have this quote from then-producer John Nathan-Turner[29]: "She'll often be wearing leotards and bikinis. A lot of Dads (sic) watch *Doctor Who* and I'm sure they will like Nicola."

Dads. She'd been written for the dads, as a thank you gift for the onerous task of watching television with their children. She hadn't been written for the kids. She hadn't been written for me.

What makes this even sadder is that Nicola Bryant was just as unhap-

29 *Doctor Who: The Key to Time*, Peter Haining, W.H. Allen & Co., London, 1984

py about this as I was. At WishCon in 1994[30], she said, "I think everybody kind of knows that I was no friends with my costumes! [...] I mean, basically, the problem as far as I was concerned with the wardrobe was that my character got started in a bikini and never got dressed, it seemed! What a good start! And I think that's alright if you're, you know, playing Leela, because you're from another planet and you're a kind of primitive. But when you're supposed to be representing, you know, a student of the 80s, I just thought, 'Where are these high heels and the shorts from?'"

It may seem like I'm saying that the way she dressed was the main problem. But that's not it - it's that they didn't bother developing her beyond what she wore. As Bryant said in *TV Zone* (special issue #8, 1993), "When I first saw the script, I thought that Peri could have been an accurate reflection of young students in the late 80s. But I soon found out that this wasn't going to be the case, when on location, one of the make-up artists asked what nail polish I wanted, and I replied that I didn't think Peri would wear any, only to have them insist she would."

In other words, yes, her appearance *was* her characterization. Period. End of story.

So there I was, a high school feminist in the mid-80s, faced with a companion who spent a good deal of her screen time prancing around in a leotard, shorts and high heels, and flapping her arms like a chicken every time she broke into a run. And who, to add insult to injury, spent most of her non-screaming time complaining about the irritation of traveling through time and space. I loved *Doctor Who*. What was I to do?

Looking back at this season through adult eyes, I now see that I was meant to identify with the female guest stars. In every story that season, Peri is surrounded by interesting, complex, strong and utterly identifiable female characters. It's a wonder that Nicola Bryant didn't resign in disgust after three episodes.

Don't believe me? Fine. Let me hit you with another list, a rundown of the stories in Season Twenty-Two:

• ***Attack of the Cybermen***: This brings us the Cryons, one of the very few all-female species in science fiction television. (Go ahead, think about it. Most SF species are largely, if not wholly male, with a token female thrown in every so often so you don't start wondering how they reproduce.) The Cryons are waging a seemingly hopeless guerilla war against the Cybermen, but they're nowhere near ready to admit defeat.

---

30 A Panel Interview With Nicola Bryant, November 19, 1994. Transcribed by Andrew Gurudata. Originally printed in *The Foreman Report* #15 (March, 1995).

And even knowing that a horrific death awaits her, their captured leader Flast saves the Doctor and strikes another blow in her people's long battle. What does Peri do? Gets rescued a lot, and runs bouncily while dressed in a leotard, shorts and heels.

• ***Vengeance on Varos***: This episode brings us the freedom-fighting Areta; along with Etta, a hyper-patriotic woman who takes her responsibilities as a citizen quite seriously, and who doesn't take any guff from her less-than-enthusiastic husband. What does Peri do? Gets captured, then gets partially transformed into a bird (maybe the chicken arms were foreshadowing). In fairness, Areta also gets captured, but only after convincing a guard to help her escape from prison, then rescuing the Doctor and Peri from capture.

• ***The Mark of the Rani***: Oh, the Rani. The awesome, awesome Rani. She's brilliant, powerful, ruthless, mature and has cheekbones to die for. Not only does she rule an entire planet, but she's also clever enough to have figured out how to exploit Earth history to her own gain. Rewatching these episodes as an adult, I was also struck by the way she made gender stereotypes work for her. No one suspects an old woman of being up to no good, because no one ever pays an old woman any attention. Brilliant. What does Peri do? Walks around dressed like a cake topper while wearing fuchsia heels and matching tights and goes off on an unnecessary trip to collect flowers to make a sleeping draught. She even has to get saved by a tree. Yes, a tree.

• ***The Two Doctors***: What's not to love about Servalan... I mean, Chessene? She's another hyper-intelligent, elegant, mature, driven woman who, despite all the problematic talk about "savages," knows what she wants and will stop at nothing to get it. And lest we forget the brave Anita? The woman gently, but firmly, puts her male companion to shame by constantly running toward danger in case there are people who need her help. Peri? The producers stick her back into a bikini top, and someone tries to eat her.

• ***Timelash***: Vena isn't the strongest of characters, and yet she still has a good plot arc. After being initially too afraid to act, she steals an amulet in an attempt to save her lover's life, falls back in time and meets H.G. Wells, then comes back with the Doctor to help fight a revolution against the tyrant ruling her planet. And Peri? The poor girl finally gets to wear actual clothes. With no spandex And that's pretty much the highlight of this story for her, considering she's in more than one scene where she cringes back against a wall screaming and is saved by someone pulling her sideways.

• ***Revelation of the Daleks***: This story gives us a whopping three major female characters. There's Natasha, the daughter willing to risk death to find her father, and who goes on to kill the man to save him from being tranformed into a Dalek. There's Kara, a scheming, yet deceptively elegant businesswoman who will stop at nothing to get her business back under her own control. And yes, there's the lovelorn Tasambeker, who is not exactly a positive role model for a young girl (although she has far more agency than Bella in *Twilight*), but she does manage to give a creep his due. Peri? She's so unhappy to be traveling with the Doctor that her opening monologue consists of her grumbling under her breath about how much life sucks. But hey, she's more dressed than ever, thanks to the wardrobe department tossing a shapeless coat over the outfit they gave her in the previous story.

How could adult me have forgotten all of those amazing guest stars? As I rewatched the season, I kept finding myself going, "Oh my god, Chessene!" And, "Anita! I love her!" And, "Seriously, how the hell did I forget Kara?" The only explanation I can come up with was that my brain clung to the memory of the Rani and pushed the rest to the background out of a sense of self-preservation. Twenty-two seasons' worth of guest stars is a lot to store. But as I came to know them all again, I could still remember how much I loved all of them back when I saw them for the first time.

So, faced with all of that awesomeness, how was I, a student, feminist and all-around-nerd, supposed to identify with a scantily clad rich girl? A girl who constantly complained about traveling through time and space? A girl who used her education solely to admire pretty flowers? A girl who shrank back against walls and waited for other people to save her? More plainly put, how was I supposed to identify with a girl who was not only the opposite of everything I was, but also the opposite of everything that I wanted to be?

Meanwhile, there's the Rani, going for exactly what she wants, not caring what her peers think about her, and not apologizing for any of it. There's the sisterhood of the Cryons, showing the universe that women can hold their own against the militaristic and oh-so-male Cybermen. There's Chessene, with her ruthless ambition and drive, and the brave, selfless Anita who thinks of other people's safety before her own. There are the revolutionaries Areta, Vena and Natasha. There's the successful businesswoman Kara. So what if half of them are villains? They are all strong and interesting, and none of them had to wear spandex to be memorable. Of course I loved them. Of course I identified with them.

Of course I wanted to be like them when I grew up.

Why would I even look twice at Peri when I had them?

The tragedy of Peri was that she could have been awesome. An American college student, traveling abroad with her family, striking out on her own for the first time by running off with a time-traveling alien - it certainly sounds good on paper. If they wanted to end their run of young scientist companions, she could have been an anthropology student - the study of extinct civilizations could certainly have come in handy when dealing with alien cultures. Or she could have been a political science major and used her knowledge to help the Doctor work through thorny diplomatic problems. Or why not have had her be a curious history major presented with the opportunity to see first-hand the events she'd studied in books? No matter what her major, they could have coupled her academic curiosity with the reasoning skills she'd developed in school to help the Doctor solve the mystery of the week. She could even have kept the fashion victim wardrobe - it was the mid-80s, after all, and I was wearing fluorescent, knee-length blouses and had a poodle perm, so I couldn't really throw stones at her neon-colored leotards and across-the-forehead headbands. Giving her abilities, enthusiasm and a sense of agency would have made her someone I could have identified with.

But they didn't do any of that.

The teenaged me abhorred Peri. The adult me pities her. No modern companion has been such pointless, blatant eye candy, and to have the actress be so horrifyingly aware of it only makes it worse. Even Amy Pond, the walking uterus and kiss-o-gram (which I just learned isn't actually a coy way of saying "stripper," like many of us Americans assumed it was) looks good compared to her, if only because she actually *enjoys* traveling with the Doctor. I don't mind disliking characters because they're taken in directions that I don't agree with (Rose Tyler and the tenth Doctor), or because they're written to be entertainingly unlikeable (Melanie Bush, Adric, Owen Harper from *Torchwood*). Hell, I don't even mind characters who are designed for maximum sex appeal (Six from *Battlestar Galactica*, Leela). But I'm intensely unhappy when a show I love writes in a character for purely prurient reasons and ends their character development there. And then to highlight it by lavishing loving attention on complex and interesting secondary characters... well, that's just plain mean.

So in the end, I feel for Peri. I wish the show had given her more instead of giving all the good stuff to the guest stars. And part of me feels that I should be grateful that they gave me so many strong, complex, and interesting women in every single episode of Season Twenty-Two. After all, how many shows have that good a track record with their female characters even today? But doing so at the expense of the companion, at the expense of the character that all the young female viewers *want* to identify with, well, that leads me to believe that the show runners didn't actually care about that segment of their audience.

And that's a problem.

All of Gallifrey's a Stage: The Doctor in Adolescence

Teresa Jusino is an East Coast transplant living in Los Angles and the writer of your future favorite book/show/comic. She is a contributing writer at Tor.com and a pop culture columnist for *Al Día*, Philadelphia's No. 1 Spanish-language newspaper. She also examines issues of gender in media and pop culture at *The Gender Blender* (tumblwithteresa.tumblr.com), and she writes a travel column as Geek Girl Traveler (geekgirltraveler.wordpress.com). Her horror short story, "December," can be found in the literary magazine *Crossed Genres* (issue #24), and her fan fiction can be found at *Beginning of Line*, the *Caprica* fan fiction site she founded and edits (beginningofline.weebly.com). Her essay "Why Joss is More Important Than His 'Verse" is included in *Whedonistas: A Celebration of the Worlds of Joss Whedon By the Women Who Love Them*. Keep up with her at The Teresa Jusino Experience: teresajusino.wordpress.com.

Last scene of all,
That ends this strange eventful history,
Is second childishness and mere oblivion,
Sans teeth, sans eyes, sans taste, sans everything.
The sixth age shifts
Into the lean and slipper'd pantaloon,
With spectacles on nose and pouch on side,
His youthful hose, well saved, a world too wide
For his shrunk shank; and his big manly voice,
Turning again toward childish treble, pipes
And whistles in his sound.
And then the justice,
In fair round belly with good capon lined,
With eyes severe and beard of formal cut,
Full of wise saws and modern instances;
And so he plays his part.
Then a soldier,
Full of strange oaths and bearded like the pard,
Jealous in honour, sudden and quick in quarrel,
Seeking the bubble reputation

Even in the cannon's mouth.
And then the lover,
Sighing like furnace, with a woeful ballad
Made to his mistress' eyebrow.
And then the whining school-boy, with his satchel
And shining morning face, creeping like snail
Unwillingly to school.
As, first the infant,
Mewling and puking in the nurse's arms.
All of Gallifrey's a stage,
And all the Time Lords and Ladies merely players:
They have their exits and their entrances;
And one Time Lord in his time plays many parts,
His acts being thirteen regenerations.[31]

He stole a vehicle and ran away from home. He kidnapped his first companions to spare himself the trouble of being discovered. He taught a pacifist species the art of war so that they could help him defeat an enemy. He blew things up, or caused things to go awry, and when they did he'd find a way to blame his companions. And if he was proven wrong about something? He'd apologize. Reluctantly. The first Doctor was a crotchety old man prone to mood swings.

Or was he?

Despite William Hartnell's age, we are seeing the Doctor at his youngest. He's spoiled, obstinate and impulsive. He leads with his emotions; well-intentioned, but dismissive of the people he cares about. He doesn't take responsibility for his mistakes and gets upset when he doesn't get his way.

The first Doctor is a far cry from the Doctor we know today, and while the BBC had no idea that *Doctor Who* would be around for decades, it's interesting to look at this early version of the Doctor in the context of a Time Lord who is now 900-plus years old and has spent his time maturing under the guidance of his companions. In this context, the first Doctor is a bratty child who's finding himself. In Season Two, the Doctor experiences the tug-of-war between childishness and maturity that is true of adolescents everywhere, no matter what their planet of origin.

---

31 With all due respect to William Shakespeare and his wonderful play, *As You Like It*.

Don't Trust Anyone Over 30

The Doctor's relationship to his younger companions mirrors the time in which the show was made. The 1960s, in the United States and in the United Kingdom, were all about youth pushing the world forward, and like activist Jack Weinberg said in 1964, they didn't "trust anyone over 30." From the beginning, the Doctor has personally benefited from travelling with a young person, and the relationship between the Doctor and Susan - or the Doctor and Vicki - was much less a mentor/ mentee or guardian/ ward relationship than it was a relationship between compatriots. We see this in how he cares for their emotional needs in a way he doesn't with his older companions, Ian and Barbara. He cares for their needs, because he understands them.

While this is true of Susan, it's most evident with Vicki - a human teenage girl from the twenty-fifth century, whom we meet in *The Rescue.* The fact that she is a teenager is important, because she fills the void left by Susan's departure, and the Doctor would much rather hang out with a teenager than with the Old Fuddy-Duddies. In *The Romans,* the Doctor and Vicki become impatient with Ian and Barbara being perfectly content to lounge around for weeks. When the Doctor announces that he's decided to go to Rome to explore, Vicki begs him to take her along, and he enthusiastically agrees. When Barbara suggests that they all go, the Doctor refuses, having said that he was looking forward to taking this trip, because he "can't wait to get away from [them]." He then proceeds to get into a little rant about how they think he's not capable, and how they're acting like his nursemaids. Typical teenage tantrum. *Mooooooom! Daaaaad! I wanna do my own thiiiiiing!* In *The Web Planet,* the Doctor and Vicki spend much of the story exploring separately from Ian and Barbara. Barbara and Ian's parental role is solidified when they talk about "what they're going to do about" the Doctor privately, the way parents would discuss a child.

Kids! I Don't Know What's Wrong With These Kids Today!

Season Two of *Doctor Who* is all about growing pains, and before we see the mature Time Lord of which the Doctor is capable of being, we're treated to plenty of epic brattiness.

We are used to the Doctor giving new species a chance or a choice, and never jumping to conclusions based on superficial observations. Yet the moment the first Doctor encounters the large, dying insects in *Planet of Giants,* he assumes that "the people here are murderers." He paints a picture of a savage, bloodthirsty people. This may be the show's commentary on humanity, but the Doctor we know today would never negatively judge a species with limited information. This is the Doctor as a snotty teenager, making quick judgments and assumptions based on limited knowledge of the world.

The Web Planet is chock full of moments like this. As the Doctor and Ian emerge from the TARDIS to look around, happening upon an ancient pyramid, the Doctor says "It's old, so old! Look at the state it's in!" It's the kind of throwaway comment that a teenager would make when coming up against a history he doesn't understand or doesn't fit within his experience. When Vicki names the Zarbi they capture "Zombo" and asks the Doctor if he agrees that Zombo is cute, he says, "Since you mention it, no. I don't think so" in a tone that both makes fun of Vicki for thinking so and implies that the Zarbi are ugly. Later, when asking for the mental communication device through which the Animus communicates with him, he demands that the Animus "drop this hair dryer, or whatever it is." These flip, insensitive and disrespectful comments about an alien culture are ones that future Doctors would be reluctant to make. At least, not without the cultures demonstrating that they were really horrible first.

The Doctor's insensitivity and self-centeredness isn't just limited to his views on alien races. In *The Romans,* the Doctor goes along with being mistaken for a murdered famed musician, Maximus Petullian, in order to get to meet Nero. He is more concerned with meeting the Emperor than he is with Vicki's safety or his own. He also namedrops Hans Christian Anderson in the same story. Later, when Ian and Barbara have been brought to Rome by slave traders, the Doctor narrowly misses Barbara's sale to the highest bidder by leading Vicki away from the slave auction as something that "wouldn't interest" her. The Doctor we've come to know would never find something as unjust as a slave auction "uninteresting." But this first Doctor ignores "boring" things like injustice in favor of solving the mystery he's hopped up on, telling Vicki, "I've decided for my own sake I must get to the bottom of it."

Later, we see that Barbara has been purchased as a handmaid to Nero's wife. Nero has taken to her and chases her around the palace trying to make a move on her. The Doctor sees this, not realizing it's Barbara and says, "What an extraordinary fellow!" Like a horndog teenage boy, he watches in awe as a powerful guy makes moves on the ladies, apparently not too concerned with consent, or its apparent lack.

In *The Crusade,* he does want to save Barbara by going to King Richard for help, but he also just seems really jazzed about meeting the king. It's as if, while he might have experience with time travel, all this "meeting famous historical figures" business is still very new to him and the star-struck Doctor hasn't yet become jaded about it.

And then there's the mischief for mischief's sake! Much like in *The Romans*, the Doctor being in Earth's past seems to make him more mischievous than usual. In *The Crusade*, he comes up with this overly-elaborate plan to steal clothes from a merchant. Rather than simply taking advantage of the moment the merchant is distracted by a conversation with someone else to slide clothing to Vicki, he ties ropes to the clothing stand, knocks it down, and uses *that* as the distraction in a painfully obvious way. One gets the feeling that he was really attached to his original plan - and was determined to go through with it no matter what - because it allowed him to knock things over. In *The Romans*, the Doctor reacts to every situation like a boy in a man's body. He thoroughly enjoys getting into a fight and says to Vicki, "I am so constantly outwitting the opposition, I tend to forget the delights and satisfaction of the gentle art of fisticuffs."

You Take the Good, You Take the Bad, You Take Them Both and There You Have... The First Doctor.

It wasn't all bad behavior, though. As I said, this season was about growing and even as the Doctor was being a huge brat, he was also developing good qualities. A major mark of maturity is taking responsibility for one's actions and in *Planet of Giants*, the Doctor acknowledges his bratty behavior for the first time, and genuinely apologizes for it. After snapping at Barbara and Ian while trying to figure out where they are, he follows up with an apology saying, "I always forget the niceties under pressure." He feels the need to explain his behavior to people who are becoming his friends, rather than clinging to an image of superiority. By spending more time with his companions, he's started learning humility. The world doesn't revolve around him and his cleverness, and this is an idea he's never faced.

Throughout *Planet of Giants*, the Doctor displays a joyous, youthful exuberance that we are used to seeing in more current Doctors. What sets it apart in the first Doctor is that it doesn't jibe with his elderly body, giving his determination to do certain things a teenage willfulness. When he insists on climbing a wall so that Barbara "doesn't hurt herself," it's like a boy who insists he can drive the family car by himself with only a learner's permit. There's also his gleeful pyromania as he exclaims "There's nothing like a good fire, is there!" after helping to cause a conflagration to get the attention of the normal-sized humans. There is troublemaking, yes, but there's also the sense of wonder and adventure that will stick with him and evolve along with his better, more mature qualities.

It's established pretty early on that he's got it in him to be better. By the end of *The Dalek Invasion of Earth,* the Doctor has noticed that Susan is in love and is sacrificing her feelings out of loyalty for him when she agrees to return to the TARDIS. Despite Susan's insistence, the Doctor leaves her behind, moving on with Barbara and Ian. This seems callous at first, taking away the agency of a character who already had very little. However, as the Doctor clearly has no problem with stealing TARDISes and kidnapping companions, it is unclear how willing a passenger Susan really was to begin with. This was the Doctor making amends, allowing her not to feel forced to stay out of obligation to him. He shuts her out of the TARDIS because he knows that, though she would never decide to stay behind, she would be much happier on Earth with David, starting an adult life of her own rather than remaining "the child" on the TARDIS.

While this act shows that the Doctor has the emotional maturity to recognize that sometimes the needs of other people are more important than his own, it also marks the Doctor's hubris as something that he will continually need to keep in check. Before leaving Susan, it was an accepted part of his character that, for all his brilliance, he was conceited and selfish. Once he's demonstrated the love and compassion of which he is capable, it becomes something viewers can hold up as a standard. Just as, once a child becomes a teenager and is old enough to "know better," we become less tolerant of their childish flaws.

In Series Five of New *Who,* River Song explains to Amy Pond that she knew leaving the Doctor a message in a museum would get to him, because museums are how the Doctor "keeps score." Season Two sees the first Doctor visit his first museum in space ("I always thought I'd find one one day!"), and it is here that he not only begins keeping score, but starts to become the kind of Time Lord he's going to be.

In *The Space Museum,* two recurring phrases pop up numerous times in the Doctor's dialogue: "I don't mind admitting..." and "I must confess..." Up until now, the Doctor has had trouble acknowledging shortcomings and flaws - but in this story, he's overly-enthusiastic about doing so. When the Doctor and his friends come across the empty Dalek shell in the museum, he says to Ian, "I don't mind admitting, my boy, that that thing gave me a start, coming face to face with it again." When attempting to figure out the mystery of the time-track the TARDIS jumped, the Doctor says, "I don't mind admitting I've found it difficult to understand the Fourth Dimension." Later, he "must confess" that he is lost, and can't find the way out by going the way they came. Apparently, there's no zealot like a convert and once the Doctor has learned that humility is prized over superiority, he overcompensates.

However, the thing that really defines the Doctor in this story is his being captured by the Moroks. He is subjected to a deep freeze so he can be put on display as a museum exhibit, but he's still alive and able to hear everything that's going on. It is a vulnerable and frightening position for the Doctor. When Ian forces the Moroks to reanimate him, the Doctor emerges from his immobility by lashing out like a cornered animal. He is changed. Whereas he started this story as someone who could be amused by hiding from the Moroks in a Dalek shell, being made truly helpless has hardened him, forcing him to grow up faster than he might have liked. The Doctor is a defiant survivor as he says to Ian, "Thanks to you, dear boy, I'm now *de-iced*, and I think I'm quite capable of facing up to the climate once more." The scene is heartbreaking as we see the air of an assault or rape victim in Hartnell's performance. He's trying to convince himself as well as Ian and the Moroks that he's okay. He allows his bitterness to take over just once when he suggests that the Moroks could test the machine's effects on its victims by getting into it themselves. But then the Doctor says, "You think yourselves lucky. My conscience won't allow me to do that. It's a pity, isn't it? It's a pity!" And there is the Doctor we've come to know; a Doctor who's had horrific experiences, but who still has the strength to let his conscience be his guide and do what's right despite what he might *want* to do. The Doctor has grown up.

There comes a time in every Time Lord's life when he can't live with his parents anymore. In *The Chase*, after a quest through several worlds with the Daleks in pursuit, Ian and Barbara have the opportunity to go back to their own time by using a Dalek time machine, and they want to take it. The Doctor is furious, saying he can't abide a "suicide mission" that uses equipment with which they're unfamiliar. But it's actually about all the feelings it's more difficult to talk about: the fact that he loves his friends and will miss them, the fact that he doesn't want to be alone. Eventually, with Vicki's encouragement, he helps Ian and Barbara use the machine, then lets them go. After he sees that Barbara and Ian have made it back home safely, he says to Vicki, "I shall miss them. Yes, I shall miss them. Silly old fusspots."

The Seven Ages of Time Lord

It's interesting that *Doctor Who* managed to have the oldest actor ever to play the Doctor play him at his youngest, and now the youngest actor ever to play the Doctor playing him at his oldest. Yet for such a timey-wimey existence, it's appropriate. The Seven Ages of Time Lord wouldn't happen when they're supposed to. So what if the "whining school-boy" is living in the body of "second childishness and mere oblivion?" That doesn't mean we can't relate to each stage.

The eleventh incarnation of the Doctor said, "My friends have always been the best of me." The Doctor has a long history of being shaped and guided by his companions. However, they were never more important than at the beginning, during the Doctor's formative years, helping him navigate the choppy waters of Time Lord adolescence and steering him toward becoming the adult he was meant to be. It takes a village to raise a child. Or in the case of Time Lords, a TARDIS full of people. Once the Doctor and Team TARDIS are safe at the end of *The Space Museum*, having changed their future, the Doctor cheerfully says, "The future doesn't look too bad after all, does it?" All these years later, the Doctor's future is as bright as ever!

All the Way Out to the Stars

Iona Sharma is the product of more than one country. She loves science fiction, politics, writing and travel, and is currently working on her first novel. She lives in New York.

It's David Tennant's final year in the role and the Doctor travels alone. The five *Doctor Who* specials broadcast in 2009 feature characters who take on the traditional companion role for a single story, but, after the day is saved, there will be no invitation from the Doctor to take a trip in the TARDIS. This Doctor, grim and brooding, wants only his own company, no matter how self-destructive it becomes. His adventures, and his characterization, are dark enough that some would argue that this is the year *Doctor Who* was no longer *Doctor Who,* as it moved too far from the traditional joy and essential optimism of the show.

Part of that came with the territory. The Doctor without a companion is a rare thing; they are part of how the show works. The companions are there when the Doctor needs to explain exposition to someone, or when the plot threads require people going in different directions. More crucially, the companions are a mediating factor when the Doctor arrives in some strange new place and has to explain who he is and what he's doing; with a companion in tow, he isn't nearly so threatening. (See, for instance, how quickly the passengers turn on the Doctor when he doesn't have Donna with him in *Midnight.*) And, of course, it's his companions that keep the Doctor going. In *The Curse of Fenric,* it's faith that repels vampires - and, touchingly, the Doctor drives them off by reciting the names of his companions. If the Doctor has faith in anyone, it's them.

So how do we do *Doctor Who* without them?

At one level, *Doctor Who* is about a madman in a box. The young Doctor steals a Type 40 TARDIS, a rickety old thing just perfect for rattling around the galaxy and having adventures. He takes people along with him - people who become his friends, people whom he risks his life for - and together they save the universe with sealing wax and string.

But despite the title, is the show really about the Doctor? He doesn't, for the most part, have character development - each incarnation has quirks of his own, but in a lot of ways the Doctor as played by David Tennant is the same character as played by William Hartnell.

But Rose, Martha, Donna and the rest - they grow and change during their time with the Doctor. The stories became *their* stories as much as the Doctor's. Rose saves the world at the end of *The Parting of the Ways;* Martha saves the world in *Last of the Time Lords;* Donna saves the world in *Journey's End*. The Doctor is a catalyst for change, but they find their potential within themselves. In other words, *Doctor Who* is about how ordinary people become heroes.

As the first of the 2009 specials (albeit shown at Christmas 2008), *The Next Doctor* opens with a sense of chocolate-box promise. This is London, 1851, all gaslight and mistletoe and softly-falling snow. When the Doctor arrives, he has to run around by himself for a while, and look around wide-eyed much as the companion he doesn't have would have done. The look and feel is all lush period detail, vivid imagery, and literary flourishes: "tim'rous beasties" chase the Doctor across a roof, and there's a *Wizard-of-Oz* flavor to the hot-air balloon. Even though this is a Cybermen episode, the writing revels in the historical setting, which gives it a certain originality. The sequence where the Cybermen run riot in the graveyard against a background of black mourning garb and snow, to pick an example, is oddly surrealist and compelling.

But it's Jackson Lake, the man running around Victorian London in a fugue state, convinced that he *is* the Doctor, whom this episode is really about. The writing is playful, first giving us the obvious answer that Jackson is another Doctor, a future Doctor. Then a fob watch appears, much like the ones from *Human Nature* and *Utopia* - but sometimes, a fob watch is just a fob watch. Finally, the Doctor gently explains the truth - that something so terrible happened to Jackson that he had to escape, to become someone else. With the Cyberman info-stamp in Jackson's hand containing all known information about the Doctor, the route his mind took was obvious.

"But info-stamps are just facts and figures," the Doctor points out to Jackson. "All that bravery, saving Rosita, defending London Town, the invention, building a TARDIS - that's all you."

I once heard someone in fandom comment that all the incidental characters on *Doctor Who* are treated as though they've crossed over from an as-yet-unmade show where they're the star. This is especially true in the year of specials. With no regular companions, the characters who appear in each episode get the bulk of the character development.

When Jackson discovers he's not the Doctor after all, but an ordinary man who suffered something terrible, he still steps up - brave and human - when the Doctor needs his help. And it's interesting that Jackson acquires a companion of his own while he believes he's the Doctor. He understands that an essential part of being the Doctor is having companions, to make people around you do brave and extraordinary things. Rosita doesn't need an info-stamp to make her into a hero as she saves both the Doctor and Jackson from the Cybermen.

The next outing is the Easter special, *Planet of the Dead* - and it's perhaps the weakest of the five specials, mostly because the one-episode companion, Lady Christina, is something of a misfire. It's hard to feel much sympathy or commonality with an aristocratic jewel-thief who just steals for the thrill of it. While Donna proves that you can have a beloved companion with a somewhat abrasive personality, Christina doesn't have Donna's warmth or compassion to offset it.

But this episode, too, has its incidental heroes. Take Nathan and Barclay, the guys on the bus who don't panic when thrown through a wormhole to another planet, and instead ask what they can do to help. Take Malcolm, the socially inept scientist, who flounders and panics and somewhat ridiculously names units of measurement after himself, but who also stands up to UNIT rather than let the passengers on the bus be sacrificed. And there's Angela, who begins the episode crying into her hands, but ends up ready to learn how to drive a bus through space and time. The Doctor, even this sadder, angrier Doctor, understands the potential in people. "Chops and gravy," he says, "that's special" - because getting people home for dinner is important, because people and their lives are important.

If we did not know that the characters on the bus play the lottery every week, that they take turns cooking dinner, that they go to visit their girlfriends and they're worried about their daughters - in short, if we didn't know about their *ordinary* lives - we wouldn't care about those lives becoming extraordinary. Lady Christina doesn't arouse much of the viewers' interest primarily because she isn't one of these characters who finds something greater in herself. Nevertheless, there is the point where the Doctor should be saying to Christina, with a winsome smile, "Come with me." Instead, he says: "People have travelled with me and I've lost them. Lost them all. Never again."

This isn't a version of the Doctor we can be altogether comfortable with. But it doesn't mean the individual people whose lives have intersected with the Doctor's in this episode aren't changed. Again, the

Doctor himself is aware of this - recommending Nathan and Barclay to UNIT as "good in a crisis." Even though he rattles off into time and space on his own, he leaves on the right sort of high point: the Doctor's come and gone, but the people he met have found a universe that's full of wonders.

The notion of people becoming heroes around the Doctor reaches its logical conclusion in *The Waters of Mars*. The Doctor arrives in 2059 at the first human base on Mars - on the day that it's historically fated to be destroyed. Yet more time without a companion has made the Doctor even more grim and strange, but when he discovers where he's landed, he becomes all excited and fanboy as he rattles off the name and rank of every person on the expedition. It's one of the lighter moments of the episode, although there are a few others: the "No trespassing" sign put up outside the base, and Yuri's cheerful anecdote about his brother Mikhail's marriage to his husband George. As before, the small details bring these characters within reach, and *Doctor Who* knows how to show us their humanity.

As the crisis on the base escalates, the characters show us their inner fortitude - the technician Steffi, cut off from the others by a sheet of contaminated water, waits for death; Ed Gold blows up the escape ship and himself with it rather than let the water-monster reach Earth; and Roman, the youngest of them, touched by just one drop, merely says quietly, "You'd really better go without me."

They are all incidental characters, again stepping in from those unmade shows where they're the stars. And the real hero of this piece is Captain Adelaide Brooke, the leader of the expedition. She's determined, a little humorless, and not patient with others' foibles and weaknesses. She doesn't let anything distract her from the mission and expects nothing from anyone that she doesn't offer of herself. Even before the story begins, she's sacrificed so much of her life to reach Mars, "to stand on a world with no smoke, where the only straight line is the sunlight." The Doctor, sounding entirely like his ordinary self, grins and says, "That's the Adelaide Brooke I always wanted to meet. A woman with starlight in her soul."

"Imagine," the Doctor also tells her, aware of her importance to history, "if you began a journey that takes the human race all the way out to the stars. It begins with you. And then your granddaughter, you inspire her, so that in 30 years, Susie Fontana Brooke is the pilot of the first lightspeed ship to Proxima Centauri. And then everywhere, with her children and her children's children forging the way."

So when Adelaide learns that her *death* is what inspires her granddaughter and ignites human exploration of the galaxy, she knows what the right thing to do is even if the Doctor doesn't. There are rules pertaining to fixed points in time such as this - meaning that the Doctor has no choice but to walk away, even as everyone dies.

And yet, in *The Waters of Mars*, he doesn't. He makes the decision that human history will be *better* for being done his way. He changes the fixed course of events by stepping in, saving the three surviving crewmembers, and bringing them to Earth in the TARDIS. What's evident in the other specials, but brought forth here in all its glory, is the Doctor's hubris and destructive anger - it's unsubtly symbolized by the rising flames of the base around him, and drives him to do something he wouldn't have done with a companion as a moderating influence. So it's left to Adelaide (who has learned much about her importance to history) to rebuke the Doctor and tell him, "No one should have that sort of power... the Time Lord Victorious is *wrong*"... just before she walks into her own house and shoots herself.

It's clear that this is not traditional *Doctor Who*! The Doctor, you can easily argue, is meant to be a kindly, benevolent force; he's not meant to have this unsettling sense of self-importance, this terrifying way of working out his own issues from the Last Great Time War. Most damning of all, *Doctor Who* is meant to be a family program - and an episode that ends in this horrible, upsetting way, with a suicide, is very far from that familiar modus operandi.

But what *is* traditional *Doctor Who* is ordinary people becoming heroes - even when the Doctor himself is not. Adelaide does the right thing and the bravest thing. She's not a Time Lord, but rather an ordinary person whose parents were killed by the Daleks, whose own dedication took her to Mars, and who doesn't need the Doctor's permission to do what she thinks is right.

We go into the last two specials of the year - the last tenth Doctor story period - with a sense that something is *really* different. The first half of *The End of Time* has an elegiac, melancholy feel, opening with gloomy narration about "the last days of planet Earth." Meanwhile, the Doctor arrives on the planet of the Ood wearing a lei and a straw hat - but his usual cheerful babble about ridiculous adventures and namedropping of historical figures ("Good Queen Bess! Let me tell you, that nickname is no longer... anyway.") falls flat. "You should not have delayed," states Ood Sigma, and solemnly leads the Doctor away.

There are frightening things afoot on Earth, including the resurrection of the Master. The Doctor's return, however, is intercepted by Donna's grandfather Wilfred Mott, who has chartered a bus, enlisted the help of all his friends and set out to find the Doctor. All in one afternoon.

It's clear that if this episode has a hero, it's Wilf. The scene where he gets reacquainted with the Doctor is particularly bleak - the Doctor's mind is on his own foretold death, and on Adelaide's recent demise, and he struggles to talk about it with Wilf over the coffee. Taken on its own merits, this becomes a claustrophobic piece that's an effective exercise in creating a mood - it's a vision into a different sort of *Doctor Who,* with a pessimistic philosophy of life rather than the more usual refrain of the wonders of the universe. Then the Doctor encounters the Master again, resulting in a confrontation that ends with the Doctor on his knees at eye level with his opponent, talking disconnectedly about Gallifrey, about who they used to be, and how the Doctor now has more in common with the Master than he's had in years, centuries even. This Doctor has lost his moral compass, down there in the dirt.

By the end of the episode, it's superficially become more of a "normal" *Doctor Who* episode, with the Doctor running around trying to save the Earth. But there's still that bleak flavor, that disaffect about it all. Wilf is astonished and delighted by the view of the Earth from a spaceship, even as the Doctor half-heartedly tries to fix the vessel's heating system. The ship drifts, dead in space. There are no miracles here.

And it's Wilf - with his dynamism, with his determination - who takes on the role of the Doctor's missing moral compass. If the Master is killed, all the billions of people he's transformed into carbon-copies of himself will revert to normal. When the Doctor balks at slaying his old friend/ foe, Wilf hands the Doctor a pistol and tells him: "Don't you dare, sir. Don't you dare put him before them." The Doctor saves the Earth from the Master and the return of the Time Lords, but then Wilf fatefully knocks four times on the inside of the radiation chamber in which he's trapped, and the Doctor knows that his own death is close...

This is still a strange and unpredictable Doctor. He rages against the dying of the light, at the lack of a reward. But in the end, Wilf returns him to who he really is. The Doctor, who has been talking about "little people" (to Adelaide's fury), now sacrifices himself to save just one elderly man. Because Wilf *is* important, because people are important. And it sticks. A year later, in *A Christmas Carol,* the Doctor will comment: "Nine hundred years of time and space, and I've never met anybody who wasn't important before." The eleventh Doctor is very different from the tenth, but that particular change is one Wilf has wrought.

And the Doctor, now dying as his regeneration starts to take hold, sets off for his real reward: a glimpse into what his companions are making of their lives. Suddenly, all rings familiar - the Doctor makes sure Donna and Wilf are happy, that Martha and Mickey are happy, that Sarah Jane is happy, that all of his friends are happy, because he cares about them. And when he visits Rose, it's New Year's Eve, 2005, and she hasn't met him yet. In her eyes, he's just some passing drunk...

"I bet you're going to have a really great year," the Doctor tells her, and everything comes full circle, just for a moment.

The Doctor's companions have made lives for themselves beyond him; but he's been a catalyst for change, even in his darkest times, and in their turn, his companions have sustained him. Because at its heart, *Doctor Who* is about people, about how brave and wonderful they can truly be.

Build High For Happiness!

Lynne M. Thomas is the editor-in-chief of the Hugo-nominated semiprozine *Apex*. She co-edited the Hugo Award-winning *Chicks Dig Time Lords*, as well as *Whedonistas* and *Chicks Dig Comics*. She is also the moderator for the Hugo-nominated SF Squeecast, a monthly SF/F podcast, and chaired the 2011 James Tiptree, Jr. Award Jury. In her day job, she is the Curator of Rare Books and Special Collections at Northern Illinois University, where she is responsible for the papers of over 60 SF/F authors. You can learn more about her shenanigans at lynnemthomas.com.

Sylvester McCoy is *my* classic series Doctor. His era made me a fan of the series (see *Chicks Dig Time Lords* for details of my conversion experience). You *will not* convince me that I am wrong and that the terrible seventh Doctor era deserves scorn. (Please don't try. You will only create a very cranky fangirl wishing for Ace's baseball bat.)

Despite *my* love for them, the first four stories of the Sylvester McCoy era (Season Twenty-Four) are consistently ranked among the worst of the series, if *Doctor Who Magazine*'s all-time polls are to be believed. Received Fan Wisdom (a vocal portion of the long-term *DW* fandom community who write extensively about such things) collectively agree that Season Twenty-Four mustn't be held up as an example of what makes *Doctor Who* great. We endure it, but we certainly don't celebrate it.

Received Fan Wisdom is *wrong*.

Much of my love for Season Twenty-Four comes out of its context of following directly upon Seasons Twenty-Two and Twenty-Three. *Doctor Who* constantly changes tone over the course of its run: new actors, new script editors, new production teams. Each envisions *Doctor Who* a little bit differently. And that's great. Different stories appeal to different people. *Doctor Who*'s brilliance comes through its storytelling flexibility.

Unfortunately, after Seasons Twenty-Two and Twenty-Three, I felt much like Tegan at the end of *Resurrection of the Daleks*: traveling with the Doctor stopped being *fun*.

Colin Baker's Doctor was supposed to be an alien Mr Darcy at the beginning of *Pride and Prejudice* (his description), whose actions would teach us to love him despite his brusque manner. Unfortunately, his stories do no such thing.[32] He and Peri argue *constantly*, and don't seem to enjoy each other's company very much. They keep arriving on planets full of selfish people who have all turned on one another when the Doctor turns up to shout at them, dragging a whiny Peri along for the ride. Eric Saward (the script editor for those seasons) preferred dark stories that put the Doctor into situations where any victory he could claim was Pyrrhic at best.

This doesn't really work for me. I reject the notion that telling a darker, more nihilistic story *always* equates to telling a *better* story. For me, the most effective stories have both dark and light elements; they heighten one another. (As a point of reference, I enjoy Joss Whedon's work, but not the new *Battlestar Galactica*.) I stopped caring what happened to these people and planets. Why mourn what is lost if there's nothing worth losing?

Season Twenty-Four marks a transition to a new era. In addition to the change from Colin Baker to Sylvester McCoy's Doctors, we have the addition of the novice, 20-something script editor Andrew Cartmel to the series, replacing Eric Saward after his infamous Season Twenty-Three meltdown, resignation and public tantrum. Cartmel brings a new sensibility to the series, favoring younger writers and seeking to incorporate the concepts of contemporary comic books (especially those by Alan Moore).

Producer John Nathan-Turner *thinks* that he's leaving *Doctor Who* any minute now for a soap opera gig, but doesn't quite manage it, despite his best efforts. This leads to a different atmosphere behind the scenes where he starts to loosen his micro-managing style of production.

The four stories of Season Twenty-Four have a decidedly 1980s look and feel. They begin very bright and cheerful, both in terms of design and tone. As their plots progress, we see the dark underbelly of this enforced cheer, reflecting the shift from the vaguely clownish version of McCoy's Doctor in these stories to his darker interpretation in later seasons. These stories take the Doctor to explore a society that has everything it could possibly need, a perfect place to live, an exciting holiday camp and a malt shop on a pristine ice planet.

Unlike Seasons Twenty-Two and Twenty-Three, though, this season

32 I note here for the record that I think that Colin Baker is a lovely person, a good actor, and that his interpretation of the Doctor was completely rehabilitated in his run of Big Finish audio adventures. You should seek them out and listen to them, for they are absolutely *splendid*. Particularly the ones with Evelyn Smythe as a companion.

is filled with manic energy and excitement. Things aren't perfect by any stretch. The tone shifts all over the place in each story, characters often lack understandable motivations (such as the Doctor's infamous literal cliffhanger in *Dragonfire*), and the directors, actors and writers clearly envision different stories as they're creating them (hello, *Paradise Towers*).

And yet, Season Twenty-Four makes me care again. It makes up for its decided lack of perfection with moments of joy, verve, adventure and a sense of humor. It reminds us that traveling with the Doctor is also supposed to be about having *fun*. The Doctor and Mel encourage those they meet to find their *own* happiness.

That begins with Mel, the most relentlessly chipper, trustworthy companion in *Doctor Who* history. She's like something out of *Babes in Toyland*. For Mel, happiness comes through caring and building community through mutual trust, which she models throughout Season Twenty-Four.

Traveling with the Doctor challenges Mel's trusting nature. Every time she wanders off to do something that *sounds* fun (Holiday camp! A lovely cool swim in a pool! Milkshakes at the mall!), bad things happen. She's kidnapped and threatened with a toasting fork (*Paradise Towers*), suspended upside down (*Time and the Rani*) and threatened by soldiers (*Dragonfire*). On the bright side, a dragon defends her for that last one. So there's that.

Mel cares about everyone she meets - assuming they aren't actively trying to kill her - and she tends to give even *those* folks the benefit of the doubt. She cares about Pex, the Kangs, Ace, Delta, Mr Burton and Sabalom Glitz, but not just them. The nameless ordinary people on the fringes of the story matter to Mel: the Lakertyans in *Time and the Rani*; the holiday camp-goers in *Delta and the Bannermen*; the residents of *Paradise Towers*; everyone in the mall on Iceworld in *Dragonfire*. The wanton destruction of innocent lives horrifies her.

Mel's insistence upon trusting everyone and being completely trustworthy serves as an example for a society that has forgotten how to trust *anyone* in *Paradise Towers*. The Doctor exhorts the Paradise Towers' residents to work together; Mel models *how* to do it. A bit of Mel's pluck is sometimes just what a character like Pex needs to decide to do the right thing, the brave thing, rather than earning the moniker of "cowardly cutlet" from the local girl gang. Likewise, Delta trusts Mel with her secret of the last Chimeron, and asks for help (*Delta and the Bannermen*). The Rani uses Mel as an example of trustworthiness, *imper-*

sonating her to gain the Doctor's trust (*Time and the Rani*). Ace, deeply suspicious by nature, accepts Mel when she meets her (*Dragonfire*).

Most importantly, Mel cares about the Doctor, who has gone from brusque to a bit barmy with post-regeneration amnesia. Mel carries on, cautiously believing that he is indeed the Doctor until he has the opportunity to prove it in my favorite scene in *Time and the Rani,* where the Doctor and Mel verify each others' identities by feeling one another's pulses (one for her, two for him). That moment between the two defines both characters as they truly connect. In this, we know that this pratfalling fool really *is* the Doctor, and the Rani will be defeated.

This Doctor certainly differs from his predecessor. He uses malapropisms and throws himself about. He plays the spoons *on the Rani's chest.* More polite than the last bloke, he tips his hat to inanimate objects, just in case (*Paradise Towers*). He connects easily with children (*Dragonfire*), logical considering that John Nathan-Turner hired a children's entertainer to play the Doctor.[33]

The seventh Doctor has slightly more subdued dress sense, too, which means that Mel's fashion sense now comes across as bright and perky, rather than merely trying not to disappear behind the glare of the sixth Doctor's coat. It makes her much easier to spot when she and the Doctor get separated, too.

The seventh Doctor's cliffhanger facial expressions are rather reminiscent of Jon Pertwee's, and his antics are similar to those of Patrick Troughton. He smiles quite a bit. In fact, he's sort of... pleasant.

I rather like him.

Over the course of the season, the Doctor begins to show the astute intelligence and cunning that we expect of him, but he never loses that sense of warmth and caring for those he's trying to protect and help. In this incarnation, there's no doubt that he and Mel enjoy their adventures together, carrot juice or no. They help people, together.

He's still ruthless, though. He has no compunction about defeating the Rani and leaving her to the mercies of the Tetraps, driving Kane to self-immolation or destroying Kroagnon with an explosive trap. However, he also recognizes Pex's self-sacrifice, and stays for his funeral - the kind of act typically avoided by previous Doctors. The Bannermen's slaughter of the tour bus full of Navarinos angers him deeply. There's darkness in this Doctor, but at this point, it's balanced with hope.

33 Sylvester McCoy began his career in Ken Campbell's Roadshow stuffing ferrets down his pants and playing the spoons, and moved from there to children's television, which required broadly comic physicality, before getting the *Doctor Who* gig.

(Maybe Mel rubbed off on him, a bit.)

Mel leaves the series in *Dragonfire*. And what would make someone who insists upon being cheerful and trustworthy and trusting decide at the drop of a hat to leave the Doctor behind, and travel with Sabalom Glitz, the least trustworthy person in the known universe? Perhaps she decided that Glitz needs her, in a way that the Doctor doesn't. After all, if Glitz wouldn't know trustworthy if it bit him on the nose, isn't she exactly the person to demonstrate how it ought to work?[34]

As Mel leaves, we meet Ace, the new companion. Seeing Mel and Ace interact, their differences could not be more starkly drawn. In her first five minutes on screen, Ace calls Sabalom Glitz a bilgebag, then dumps a milkshake over a customer's head.[35]

Ace comes as close to a "real" teen as the series had ever had at that point - her bedroom is strewn with dirty laundry that reflects contemporary fashion choices. She lies about her age, bemoans that her previous school didn't understand that blowing up the art room was an act of creativity, runs about blowing ice dams up with great glee while shouting "Ace!" at their destruction, and *insists* upon being included in the Doctor's plans - rankling particularly when women are excluded for some reason.

Where Mel is the soul of innocence and trust, Ace is already hardened, suspicious, and frighteningly smart and independent - and so very angry and broken. She makes explosives for fun. She fights back if she thinks she or her friends are being threatened (hell, she'll take the first swing).

She is, in a word, *magnificent*. And *modern*. The closest we can get to a new series companion in the classic series, really, which suits the Doctor just fine. He has big plans for Ace. (Stay tuned.)

These characters tell their stories this season with style, zest, energy and a little silliness, all bright colors and earnest synthesizer music, immersing us in the 1980s, with a wink and a smile, direct from the opening credits. There's more nostalgia in the first few minutes of any Season Twenty-Four story than an *I Love the 80s* marathon on VH1.

Time and the Rani boasts possibly the silliest regeneration scene in

34 In Steve Lyons' New Adventures novel *Head Games*, it is revealed that the Doctor used psychic persuasion to get Mel to leave, so that he could become Time's Champion (the darker, more mysterious version of the Doctor that defends time using occasionally unsavory methods, Andrew Cartmel's vision for the series going forward) without her interference. (But I like my theory better.)

35 Ace's anger at Glitz implies that he seduced her; this is later confirmed in Paul Cornell's New Adventures novel *Happy Endings*.

Doctor Who history, with Sylvester McCoy donning a curly blond Colin Baker wig, followed by the traditional Doctor makeover sequence as he chooses his new costume. Mel and the seventh Doctor begin building their relationship anew in this story, and this incarnation of the Doctor spends much of his time trying to connect with the individuals he encounters, an endeavor with which his previous incarnation didn't always bother. Also, revel in Kate O'Mara's delicious, ruthless performance in the titular role. She pulls off some *serious* shoulder pads with aplomb, despite never telling us how exactly she escaped that dinosaur. I feel like everybody on this show is having fun. They want to be there, and I get caught up in their joy.

Paradise Towers, the first story truly script edited by Andrew Cartmel, walks the line between smart, nihilistic, post-apocalyptic speculative fiction and more high camp than a *Mamma Mia* Sing-Along. When I say "walk," I actually mean drunkenly stumble back and forth without rhyme or reason. Paradise Towers' Great Architect needs to transplant his brain into a suitable replacement body, taken from among the Towers' three dysfunctional groups of inhabitants. Like you do. The color-coded girl gangs "Kangs," possess names like "Bin Liner" and "Fire Escape," along with a slang all their own.[36] The Doctor and Mel really connect with the Kangs, taking the time to introduce them to an important aspect of teen life, soda pop. That scene in particular demonstrates the new warmth and joy of the series.

The Caretakers, in true conformist fashion, can't think their way out of a paper bag (check out the actors' look of triumph when they nail the very long regulation codes).[37] The rezzies, Tabby and Tilda, a couple of lovely older ladies that (ahem) cohabitate, keep trying to *eat* the others. (Did you know that crocheted tablecloths work well as restraints? You do now.) Pex, bless him, only looks large and imposing next to Bonnie Langford, who still saves *herself* from the cutest killer robot in the swimming pool *ever*. The Chief Caretaker/Great Architect staggers through the second half of the story chewing the scenery with *adorable* Cleaner hench-bots, a performance nearly to *Torchwood* Series One levels of camp. Much of this doesn't work together, but a brilliant story screams for release underneath the whiplash tonal changes.

Delta and the Bannermen defines fluffy historical romp with aliens.

36 Kang slang is *excellent* convention badge ribbon fodder, and Kangs work really well for group cosplay. You're welcome. Ice Hot!

37 The caretakers were supposed to be out-of-shape older guys who lumbered about (i.e. unfit for the war they aren't off fighting). The casting office sent bog-standard young, fit guards instead. Oops.

Mel prepares to hit the happiest place on Earth, 1950s Disneyland, with the Doctor, but settles for a 1950s Welsh holiday camp, Shangri-la. The Doctor once again demonstrates his softer side, *dancing* and dispensing hugs to Ray (a motorcycle-riding Welsh lass), as well as comforting her after her crush, Billy, tosses her aside. The Doctor emphasizes trying to keep the campers and staff safe as he foils the Bannermen using the sweetest tool in his arsenal: an attack of *honey* from the local beekeeper's supply. No story of Season Twenty-Four better demonstrates the new joy of *Doctor Who*. Nostalgia, weird characters (one of them played by Stubby *Guys and Dolls* Kaye!), and rock and roll combine in a fresh way that makes you almost forget the story is about genocide and interspecies sex.

Dragonfire, a story of beginnings and endings that closes the season, sends Mel warmly on her way, and introduces Ace, with a heart of fire on an ice planet. The story revolves around human emotions: love and revenge. Mel parts from the Doctor as she came in, reaffirming their warm friendship. She goes freely with Sabalom Glitz, cheerfully ready to reform him, as she tried to do with the Doctor.

The Doctor's relationship with Ace begins here, based on mutual admiration, respect and a bit of collective destruction. They just... *click,* with instantaneous rapport, as though they had been friends for years. She insists on calling him "Professor," specifically to needle him, but there is underlying affection and trust there. She's ready to take the scenic route back to Perivale with him, facing monsters along the way.

In many ways, *Dragonfire* succeeds for me. It blends dozens of SF/F tropes like an intergalactic malt, but it works because I *care* about these characters. I believe in the relationships and friendships between the leads. They're adventurers, exploring the universe for knowledge and fun. And yet, they still embrace their heroic natures when villainy rears its head.

Season Twenty-Four may not always be the most consistent in terms of performances and casting, but it provides a necessary respite, a light side, between seasons that, on either end, demonstrate the Doctor's darkness. Like duct tape, you need both sides to properly bind the universe together. There is no Black Guardian without the White Guardian; there can be no Seasons Twenty-Three and Twenty-Five without Season Twenty-Four.

And that's indeed worth celebrating.

Nimons are Forever

Liz Barr is the daughter of a Trekkie and a Whovian, which, as far as she's concerned, explains everything. She lives with her three best friends and an emotionally-stunted cat in Melbourne, Australia, and spends far too much time on the Internet.

Popular wisdom has it that *Doctor Who*'s seventeenth season is either a complex inter-textual post-modernist take on mainstream science-fiction, or a disgrace to all that came before it, bringing shame and dishonor to everyone involved in its production.

But there is also a third option: that Season Seventeen represents the triumph of chemistry and character over uneven scripts, tight budgets and some highly questionable acting choices, with the ultimate emotional focus of the series being placed firmly on the relationship between the Doctor and his companion. In short, for better *and* for worse, it's quintessential *Doctor Who* for the twenty-first century, which just happened to be made 25 years ahead of schedule. And it is wonderful.

Initially the subject of considerable vitriol in the fandom (although ratings were high and audience responses were generally positive[38]), the season was eventually somewhat rehabilitated. David Owen, in *In-Vision* #45, described it as a season "which, miraculously, manages to be *less* than the sum of its parts." On the other hand, Gareth Roberts - then an author of tie-in novels, now a scriptwriter for *Doctor Who* and *The Sarah Jane Adventures* - wrote that it was "hugely, magnificently and squarely entertaining."[39]

With the revival of *Doctor Who* in 2005, Season Seventeen found a new, largely female audience who felt little if any connection with the fandom debates of yore (we now enter the realm of essay as autobiography). Perhaps arrogantly, we were less concerned with traditional

38 Justin Richards, in the fanzine *In-Vision* #43 (1993), noted that *The Horns of Nimon* got high ratings despite being "one of the failures of the Whoniverse," and was regarded by the BBC as having been highly successful.

39 Gareth Roberts, "Tom the Second," reprinted in Paul Cornell (ed.) *Licence Denied* (Virgin 1997).

sources of fannish rage, like the practical implications of Romana's regeneration scene in *Destiny of the Daleks* (which one-time continuity adviser / writer / composer / professional fan Ian Levine called "unforgivable"[40]) and more interested in what it indicated about her relationship with the Doctor and her own self-image. Season Seventeen has its undeniable weaknesses, but the central relationship between Romana and the Doctor is a strong thread that unites the season internally, and fixes it firmly in its place in the wider context of the series.

> "I suppose the best way to find out where you've come from is to find out where you're going and then work backwards."
>
> —The Doctor, *City of Death*

Season Seventeen marked Graham Williams' third and final year as executive producer of *Doctor Who*. His tenure was strongly marked by what would now be called network interference, as the BBC responded to accusations of gratuitous violence and horror elements, and budgetary restraints were exacerbated by inflation and widespread industrial action of the late seventies. These problems came to a head when production on the six-part season finale, *Shada*, was halted due to strike action, never to resume.

The season also faced a further, unique problem, in that script editor Douglas Adams' attention was divided between *Doctor Who* and *The Hitch-hiker's Guide to the Galaxy*. *Doctor Who* required more intensive work than he had anticipated, including complete script rewrites, putting the notoriously deadline-shy writer under considerable pressure.

In addition to all this, 1979 was Tom Baker's sixth year playing the Doctor, and under Williams he had begun to take an active - some said over-active - role in making changes to scripts and adding his own improvisations. With the departure of Mary Tamm the previous year, he was joined by Lalla Ward as the second Romana. Baker and Ward were infamously married for a brief period after they left the series, and separately or together, they were formidable creative forces themselves. Indeed, one of the criticisms of Season Seventeen is that Baker and Ward had too much influence over the series, encouraging a certain silliness that traditionalist viewers believed was inappropriate for *Doctor Who* - which was prior to this, of course, a very serious program with no inherent absurdities whatsoever.

---

40 John Tulloch and Manuel Alvarado, *Doctor Who: The Unfolding Text* (St Martin's Press 1983) p.66.

"If they have to x-ray it to find out whether it's good or not, they might as well have painting by computer."

—The Doctor, *City of Death*

Despite - or perhaps *because* of these problems and pressures - Season Seventeen captured the strengths of *Doctor Who*. Where the plots themselves were weak (as with *The Creature from the Pit*) or where good scripts were let down by low production values (such as *The Horns of Nimon*), they were consistently uplifted by the strength and charisma of the performers. And in the special case of *City of Death* - where the script, performances and Paris locations combined to overcome the occasional weaknesses of the special effects - the result was something almost magical.

Whatever tensions existed during filming, Season Seventeen contained some of Tom Baker's finest performances, matched and sometimes exceeded by Lalla Ward's portrayal of Romana. There's a popular belief that only modern *Doctor Who* contains strong companions who advance the plot without getting captured and screaming a lot. The myth of the old "mini-skirted screamer"[41] still turns up occasionally in the press, and promotional material for a new companion invariably implies that the new character will be the very first independent, clever and useful companion in the series, and her similarly-touted predecessors were a bit rubbish actually. In fact, companions have always been varied and interesting in their own ways, very much products of their eras, but often with surprising and unexpected strengths. And the claim that Companion X is a much stronger, braver and more dynamic character than the characters who preceded her has been made at least since Elisabeth Sladen replaced Katy Manning in 1973, and probably well before that.[42]

Although this era of *Doctor Who* was not character-driven in the way the modern series is, with plots specifically revolving around the companion's life or psychology, Season Seventeen is completely dependent on the relationship between the Doctor and Romana for its emotional meaning. Romana's three seasons - one with Mary Tamm in the role,

41 If we're going to be pedantic, both Rose Tyler and Amy Pond have worn mini-skirts and screamed, and have also screamed while wearing mini-skirts. Which only goes to prove that a character is more than her fear response and clothing, and also that some clichés are too powerful to die.

42 Obviously the very first strong-minded, career-defined companion who stood up to the Doctor without fear was Barbara Wright, and all subsequent characters have to some extent stood in her monochrome shadow.

two with Lalla Ward - offer an unusual opportunity to see the Doctor interacting with a character who shared his background and abilities, but whose goals and experiences are not necessarily congruent with his. The closest the series otherwise comes to this dynamic is with the Master and River Song, neither of whom are likely to become full-time companions. (River because part of her appeal comes from the way she drops in and out of the Doctor's life; the Master because... well, it would be awkward, to say the least.) The Doctor and Romana's scenes together, particularly Romana's commentaries on the Doctor and his methods, provide a knowledgeable outsider's perspective on a long-established character. Their dialogue tends towards witty interplay and intellectual one-upmanship, reminiscent of classic black and white film partnerships.

> "Hearts? How many have you got?"
> "One for casual, one for best."
>
> —Tyssan and Romana, *Destiny of the Daleks*

The relationship between the Doctor and Romana developed over three seasons, from the initial antagonism and wariness of their first meeting to the slow cooling of their relationship and eventual separation in Season Eighteen. Season Seventeen is their honeymoon period, with moments of pure joy slipping in between the interstellar wars, genocides and overdue Gallifreyan library books. These moments don't deny the terrible things to which the characters have been exposed, but give them meaning and perspective.

After Romana's regeneration, she and the Doctor are visibly taking pleasure in each other's company. To younger, contemporary viewers accustomed to the overtly romantic framing of the Doctor-companion relationship in New *Who,* including the retconning[43] of the Doctor and Sarah Jane's relationship in *School Reunion,* it seems more surprising that the Doctor and Romana were *not* intentionally written as a couple. For fans who watched the classic series after first watching the 2005 revival, this was certainly the logical conclusion. As L.M. Myles put it:

---

43 Retcon: abbreviation of "retroactive continuity," in which a fictional universe's established history is altered or reinterpreted. "Retroactive continuity" was first used in print in the seventies, and by the twenty-first century, the shorthand version of it - "retcon" - was mainstream enough to be used as the name of Torchwood's memory-wiping drug.

> Encouraged by the new series playing on the possibility of a romantic relationship between the Doctor and Rose, classic *Who* fans and new series fans applied the new rules of How To Interpret The Show to the classic series... a touch or glance, a shared smile or a desperate hand-holding run was now more than enough subtext to prompt a ship[44] fic.[45]

Season Seventeen is full of scenes encouraging these revisionist tendencies, being full of moments emphasizing the great joy the Doctor and Romana take in simply being together. Whether they are debating temporal physics in a Parisian café and art in *City of Death* or being cheerfully condescending in the face of interstellar drug squads, they're behaving like a couple in the early phases of their relationship, willing to put up with almost anything so long as they can do it together. This would be unbearable if they took each other seriously - but, luckily for the audience, Romana never hesitates to tell the Doctor off for being portentous, or to gently puncture his ego if she thinks he needs it. In *The Horns of Nimon*, for example, we hear:

> **The Doctor:** I'll tell you something interesting. When I mentioned the black hole to Soldeed, he didn't seem to know what I was talking about.
>
> **Romana:** Ah, well, people often don't know what you're talking about.

John Nathan-Turner, on taking over as executive producer in 1980, called their interaction "bitchy,"[46] but this overlooks the genuine affection that underlies their relationship (and his use of such a gendered label, along with his remark in *Doctor Who Magazine* #51 that Romana's intelligence "threatened the Doctor," suggests that the real problem was that Romana was not only willing to disagree with the Doctor, but that she was quite likely to win the argument).

If the author is dead, or at least looking a bit peaky, it stops mattering whether the bond between the main characters was intentionally written, or whether it stemmed from the relationship between the actors -

44 Ship/shipping: from "relationship," referring to fannish engagement with a romantic bond (canonical or intentional or otherwise) between two characters.

45 L. M. Myles, "Renaissance of the Fandom" in *Chicks Dig Time Lords* (edited by Lynne M. Thomas and Tara O'Shea, Mad Norwegian Press, 2010) p.140.

46 John Tulloch and Manuel Alvarado, *Doctor Who: The Unfolding Text* (St Martin's Press 1983) p.217.

or, as Lalla Ward has suggested, the other way around.[47] In *Nightmare of Eden,* they finish each other's sentences and, clutching hands, leap together into an unknown virtual world. *Shada* starts out with the iconic punting scene: the Doctor and Romana trading Cambridge trivia and scientific theorems while they punt down the Cam, like a science-fictional Peter Wimsey and Harriet Vane.[48] Douglas Adams was inherently incapable of writing stupid characters (even Duggan in *City of Death,* bless him, had his own brand of intelligence, although it didn't extend to corkscrews), and his scripts frame the characters as people who, like Wimsey and Vane, are attractive because they are clever. Taken too far, this runs the risk of alienating the audience, but generally speaking, Season Seventeen goes just far enough. Whether they are simply close friends or four hearts beating as two,[49] the Doctor and Romana were the very soul of *Doctor Who* in 1979, and the series is richer for it.

> "You're a very beautiful woman, probably."
>
> —The Doctor, *City of Death*

To underscore the significance of the Doctor-Romana relationship to the stories, Season Seventeen is full of couples and individual characters who act as parallels and foils to the leads, particularly Romana. This begins in *Destiny of the Daleks* with Agella, the Movellan woman whose imperturbable intelligence stands in stark contrast to Romana's terror in the face of Dalek interrogation.[50] Both women are powerful and competent, and both are apparently "killed," then later resurrected. Behind the scenes, actress Suzanne Danielle even encouraged a perception in the mainstream media that she, not Lalla Ward, was the Doctor's new companion.[51]

47 *Doctor Who Magazine* #217 and again in issue #341.

48 As immortalized in the series by Dorothy L. Sayers, although Lord Peter and Harriet went to Oxford, and Lord Peter would never have countenanced the Doctor's scarf.

49 Credit where credit is due: the phrase was coined, to the best of my knowledge, by nostalgia_lj on LiveJournal sometime in 2006.

50 The interrogation scene, in which Romana goes to pieces regrettably quickly, according to the DVD's text commentary, was originally intended to show that she was suffering the effects of radiation poisoning. With that explanation lost in revisions, it simply looks like the script has lapsed into a standard sexist depiction of a damsel-in-distress being menaced by alien monsters.

51 As Ward herself discusses in the commentaries, along with casting aspersions on Danielle's talent and professionalism. One gets the impression that Ward holds a

The strongest parallel comes in *City of Death* with the Count and Countess Scarlioni. Here, just as Russell T Davies would do with the Master and Lucy Saxon in 2007, we have a couple who invert the whole concept of the Doctor and his companion: an ancient, brilliant alien and his beautiful and glamorous female partner. The Scarlionis' marriage even shares the curious asexuality of the Doctor-companion relationship. Many have wondered over the years how Scaroth maintained the illusion of humanity in a marriage, or how the Countess could have been married to an alien without realizing. The obvious answer to the twenty-first century viewer, of course, is that the Countess believes her husband is gay, reinforced by their dialogue in episode one:

> **Count:** I trust you will be...
> **Countess:** Discreet? Of course.

Discretion is the whole foundation of their relationship. This is further shored up by her reaction (annoyance, but no surprise) when told that her husband is (as usual) down in the cellar with Professor Kerensky, and later in an exchange with the Doctor:

> **Countess:** Discretion and charm. I couldn't live without it, especially in matters concerning the Count.
> **The Doctor:** There is such a thing as discretion. There's also such a thing as wilful blindness.
> **Countess:** *Blind?...*
> **The Doctor:** Yes! You see the Count as a master criminal, an art dealer, an insanely wealthy man, and you'd like to see yourself as his consort. But what's he doing in the cellar?
> **Countess:** Tinkering. Every man must have his hobby.
> **The Doctor:** Man? Are you sure of that? A man with one eye and green skin, eh? Ransacking the art treasures of history to help him make a machine to reunite him with his people, the Jagaroth, and you didn't notice anything? *How* discreet, *how* charming.

Theirs is a transactional relationship: the Countess enjoys a life of luxury, and the pleasure of being the consort of a master criminal; the Count has the respectability of a marriage to a beautiful woman, and an assistant in his endeavours. It's a neat twist on the relationship between the companion and the Doctor: a (usually human) woman gets to see the universe and discover reserves of skill and courage not realized by

---

grudge for some reason.

her day to day life, and the Doctor has a friend who can act as a buffer between his eccentricities and the smaller minds they encounter,[52] and through whose eyes he can see new pleasure in things and places he has seen many times before. And, of course, they save the world a lot.

Obviously, the Scarlionis are more a parallel for the generic Doctor-companion, rather than the fourth Doctor and Romana specifically. However, at the same time, at nearly every turn we see a continuous, obvious contrast between the Countess and Romana. Romana is a girlish and immature figure wearing a school uniform the way a child dresses up in her mother's best outfit. By contrast, the Countess is played by the astonishingly beautiful Catherine Schell and costumed in a series of fashionable skirts and play-suits, with prominent jewellery and her ever-present cigarette holder. She addresses Romana as one would a child ("Yes, it's a very rare and precious Chinese puzzle box. You won't be able to open it, so put it down"), and her jaded manner is juxtaposed with Romana's squeak of pleasure and wide grin as she does, in fact, open the puzzle box. Their differences are even referred to unconsciously by the Doctor himself: the Countess may be a very beautiful woman (probably), but he later describes Romana, without qualification, as a pretty girl. The irony, of course, is that the Countess is dealing with an alien woman in her second century, and judging by the way the Countess' accent slips when things begin to go bad, even her aura of upper-class sophistication is as much a façade as everything else in her life.

> "You meddlesome hussy!"
>
> —Soldeed, *The Horns of Nimon*

More than *City of Death, The Horns of Nimon* is the archetypical Season Seventeen story: a character-driven script marred by poor production values and some very unfortunate acting. (In fairness, the script, with lines like "Weakling scum!" and the line quoted above, almost seems to have been written with over-acting in mind. Faced with lines like "Don't dare blaspheme the Nimon!", what self-respecting actor wouldn't grab a bit of scenery and start chewing?) It's notable for the way Romana essentially takes over the Doctor's role while he assists

52 The 2008 episode *Midnight* amply demonstrates how much the Doctor needs that buffer when faced with a room full of hostile and fearful people, and the 2009 specials are a perfect example of how dangerous the Doctor can become when he's alone and emotionally isolated.

and makes foolish errors.[53] Here the lead characters are paralled by Seth and Teka, teenagers offered as sacrifices to the Nimon. Seth is a runaway forced to become a hero; Teka is an upper-class girl whose faith in his abilities is as unshakable as her own much-underestimated will.[54] Like the Scarlionis, they follow the pattern of the standard Doctor-female companion duo. Seth himself comes to act as a sort of sub-assistant to both Romana and the Doctor, standing behind Romana and looking pretty while she drives off the villains, and feeding her straight lines for jokes:

> **Seth:** "If we don't pay tribute, the Nimon will destroy us."
> **Romana:** "Sounds like an insecure personality to me."
> **Seth:** "He lives in the power complex."
> **Romana:** "That fits."[55]

It might seem strange to have two teenagers acting as mirrors to such advanced and long-lived aliens such as Time Lords, but *Doctor Who,* and the fourth Doctor's era in particular ("There's no point in being grown up if you can't be childish sometimes," he says in *Robot*) tends to regard the distinction between adults and children as purely arbitrary. (The fandom generally takes a similar attitude to the distinction between adult and children's television.) Teenagers in love feel mature and grown-up; adults in love feel younger; Time Lords laugh at our petty lifespans and go in search of new adventures.

> "Well, come on, old girl. There's quite few millennia left in you yet."
> "Thank you, Doctor!"
> "Not you, the TARDIS!"
>
> —The Doctor and Romana, *The Horns of Nimon*

---

53 It's also notable for the scene where a character's pants split as he dies, revealing his white underwear. Look for it in the final scene of the first episode and the recap at the beginning of episode two.

54 The Teka of the completed story was ultimately a much stronger, braver character than the one in the script, mostly due to Janet Ellis' performance.

55 This marvellous exchange is echoed, probably unconsciously, in Steven Moffat's *Sherlock*: "You know, Mycroft could just phone me, if he didn't have this bloody stupid power complex," remarks John Watson, as the camera cuts to the designated meeting place: Battersea Power Station (*A Scandal in Belgravia*). A few months earlier, *Doctor Who*'s *The God Complex,* also produced by Moffat, had made overt reference to the Nimon. One begins to suspect he's had Nimons on the brain of late.

"Oh, it's all right, Joe. It's all right. It's my dog. And, uh, my wife."

"Well, you might have mentioned me first on the billing."

—Nick and Nora Charles, *The Thin Man*

Like other periods in *Doctor Who*'s history, Season Seventeen owes a heavy debt to the great film partnerships of Hollywood's golden age. Witty dialogue is cheaper than special effects, although not necessarily easier to create, and the relationship between the Doctor and Romana is largely based on witty repartee laced with a competitive edge. Most particularly, as they meander through the universe, fighting villainy in company with their robot dog, they echo the iconic partnership of William Powell and Myrna Loy as Nick and Nora Charles in the Thin Man movies.

Originally an adaptation of Dashiell Hammett's last published novel, the series depicts a charming one-time private detective, now married to a wealthy woman who shares his passions for alcohol and crime-solving. The son of a Greek immigrant in the novel, for the films Nick was given a more acceptably middle-class white Anglo-Saxon Protestant background against which he had rebelled. (He came, in fact, from a family of doctors.) Much of the comedy of their partnership comes from the contrast between Nora Charles' upper-class mannerisms and the delight with which she throws herself into the criminal milieu.[56] For example, upon finding herself playing hostess to the reporters and petty criminals of New York, she throws her arms around her husband and cries, "Oh, Nicky, I love you because you know the most lovely people!" With Hays Code restrictions banning the depiction of even a married couple sharing a bed, the Charleses even share the curious informed asexuality that marked *Doctor Who* until the TV Movie in 1996.

Similarly, there is an interesting tension between the Doctor's careless dismissal of Gallifreyan law and tradition (in *Shada,* Romana is amused but unsurprised to learn that his boyhood hero was a notorious criminal) and Romana's more conventional approach. This was, of course, part of the initial brief for the character, that her academic success and real-world inexperience would highlight the Doctor's less disciplined but more successful attitude. ("Is that why you always win?" Romana asks in *Destiny of the Daleks,* "because you always make mis-

56 She also shares her husband's love of liquor. *Doctor Who* is sadly lacking in scenes of competitive martini consumption. On the other hand, the Charles' dog wasn't a robot.

takes?") With Romana's adventures and achievements in Season Sixteen, coupled with the replacement of Mary Tamm, she has grown in experience, but also taken on a new, more aristocratic persona. Lalla Ward is the daughter of a viscount, and though she herself does not emphasise her background, it's evident in her speech and mannerisms when she plays Romana. This plays well against the Doctor's persona as the rebellious aristocrat, a ne'er-do-well who has rejected his background in favor of a more bohemian lifestyle. "I don't work for anyone," he claims in *Nightmare of Eden*, "I'm just having fun." Like Nick Charles, he is not quite a man of leisure and would be stifled by a peaceful life - and, like Nora Charles, Romana is far happier living outside the rules of her society than she would be in a more conventional situation.

Even the body language of the two couples is similar, with Nick and Nora literally skipping arm in arm as they set out to solve a mystery, or pulling faces at each other over the shoulder of an attractive young woman who has thrown herself into Nick's arms. The comedy, too, is full of echoes. Nick's line in the first film, "Would you mind pointing that gun somewhere else? My wife doesn't mind, but I'm a very timid fellow," would not be out of place coming from the fourth Doctor. And the hoary old "Sugar, no lumps" joke repeated throughout *Shada* is of much the same ilk as Nora's "Waiter, will you serve the nuts? I mean, will you serve the guests the nuts?"

Of course, much of this similarity derives from common origins; *City of Death*, the defining story of Season Seventeen, was conceived as a pastiche of exactly the same hard-boiled detective stories that the Thin Man series was subverting. Wealthy, glamorous and corrupt dames, tough-guy detectives, disposable thugs and the heroes who are drawn into the action literally at gun-point: these are the conventions of the genre. But having the action revolve around an established and happy couple was a twist first conceived in the creation of *The Thin Man*. *City of Death* marked the first time that twist had been applied in a science-fiction context, and it set a tone for Season Seventeen that carried through until the end.

> "Marvellous. Absolutely."
> "Absolutely marvellous."
> "Well, I think it's marvellous."
>
> —The Doctor and Romana, *City of Death*

Was Season Seventeen conceived with the intent to portray a relationship between the Doctor and Romana? No. Such a thing would have been unthinkable.

Does intent matter? No.

It's the nature of an ongoing series that new stories will cast a different light on the old. The Doctor can kiss his companions, contemplate spending a human lifetime with a French courtesan, flirt with and marry a roguish time travelling archaeologist. He has confessed to being rubbish at weddings, especially his own. To suggest that he and Romana shared a brief, ultimately bitter-sweet love story does not narrow his character, but expands it.

Season Seventeen contains a series of love stories, conventional (Della and Stott in *Nightmare of Eden*, Seth and Teka in *The Horns of Nimon*) and decidedly otherwise (the Count and Countess Scarlioni). For the Doctor and Romana, it's the middle chapter of their story, the year in which they're in sync with each other and the universe. Season Eighteen will bring entropy, separation, regeneration and Adric, but for five (and a half) stories, we have the pleasure of silly, clever, flawed adventures, and two leads who are utterly content to be together.

Exquisite. Simply exquisite.

Ace Through the Looking-Glass

Elisabeth Bolton-Gabrielsen used to be a housewife, but is now an Office Admin in a local College and is finding it not entirely dissimilar. She is also happily married and has three daughters, all of whom she - somewhat to her husband's despair - has managed to turn into avid fangirls. However her *Doctor Who* appreciation wasn't a given; hailing from Scandinavia, she had never even heard of the show before arriving in England, and what she subsequently (before the show's return) found out through cultural osmosis could easily have fitted on the back of a postage stamp. She has spent entirely too much time since then making up for this deficit.

There is an old story about a girl who fell down a rabbit hole and met a Mad Hatter. It has been retold many times, because it's a very good story. The girl was bored, and thus noticed something her sister didn't... and because of this ended up having a great adventure, meeting all kinds of fantastical creatures as she travelled through another world.

When it comes to *Doctor Who*, this story is the one we hear over and over again. In the words of current show runner Steven Moffat:

> The story happens to the companion, not the Doctor. It's only when he's got someone to show off to that it's happening. That's why I think the story starts again every time a new person takes that decision to go into that blue box.[57]

When it comes to Ace, there is a twist. Before she met the Doctor, she was swept up in a time storm and transported into the far future to the planet Svartos. The Doctor was not the one to entice her down the rabbit hole - she was already there. Except their meeting wasn't random - unbeknownst to Ace, she was a "Wolf of Fenric," one of many descendants of a Viking tainted with the genetic instructions of the ancient evil known as Fenric. In order to escape from prison, Fenric uses Ace as a pawn in a game played against the Doctor across time and space. As Ace's story progresses, the Doctor also begins moving her across the board in his own game to defeat Fenric.

57 Source: 2009 annual Screenwriters' Festival in Cheltenham.

The Hatter in *Alice in Wonderland* is a mad man who is best friends with Time. Ace's Hatter is not so different. The Doctor changes the lives of everyone who steps into the TARDIS - he is a trickster, a manipulator, an unpredictable storyteller who turns up and changes people's lives, often by leading them onto new adventures.

While every regeneration brings out a different aspect of the Doctor, the seventh Doctor's particular brand of manipulation is very much that of a chess player. This motif is woven throughout Season Twenty-Five as he plays on a metaphorical chessboard encompassing entire worlds with people or planets as playing pieces, employing the same sure touch for his opponents and allies as he does the chess pieces on the board.

In *Silver Nemesis,* the Doctor *literally* intersperses saving 1988 Earth with a chess game played against someone (possibly his past or future self; we're never given a definitive answer on this) who keeps visiting Lady Peinforte's house in the seventeenth century. Although we never see the outcome of that game, in the story's final scene - after the day has been saved - the Doctor and Ace are seen playing a game with the same chess set... and Ace wins. The Doctor, however, chooses to deliberately ignore her victory and listen to the music instead. He sees her as a worthy player and on a course to win, but pretends not to notice.

Chess also plays an integral role in *Through the Looking-Glass, and What Alice Found There.* As Alice gazes out over the world in the Looking Glass, she notices that the whole country is a giant game of chess. She longs to play - especially if she can have some say in matters. The Red Queen lets her know that she is allowed to move across the chessboard landscape on her own - and that if she can get to the eight square she will no longer be a pawn, but become a Queen herself.

Alice eagerly embraces this idea, and her journey across the chessboard is what gives the story its structure - her crossing is even mapped out, move by move, at the beginning of the book. Even more aptly, she moves between the different squares "as if by magic," leaving one place and turning up in another without quite knowing how - very much the same way that Ace finishes one adventure and starts another in a very different place, thanks to the TARDIS.

But Alice's goal is firm in her mind, and as Ace's story arc - cut short by *Doctor Who*'s cancellation in 1989 - was to conclude with her entrance into the Prydonian Academy on Gallifrey to train as a Time Lord, Alice's journey from pawn to Queen is a very fitting parallel save for one crucial exception: Ace doesn't *know* that this is her journey. She is kept in the dark as the Doctor withholds the truth and manipulates her from square to square.

The Doctor doesn't really see a problem with those sort of machinations. It isn't so much a question of secrecy as that people can't seem to grasp the overall picture the way he can. It's simply easier not to tell them what's going on - except, perhaps, as it affects their immediate situation. Maybe. Possibly. This is particularly well illustrated in *The Happiness Patrol,* where he orchestrates the overthrowing of a whole society in a single night through a combination of working behind the scenes and fomenting dissent in the wider population, never letting any of the people of Terra Alpha know his master plan as he moves them all into position for the checkmate.

But when the game is played out on a chessboard comprising the whole universe, and the pawn is a companion, the issue becomes more complex. Although Ace is unknowingly part of a bigger game, as we learn in *The Curse of Fenric,* she is only given scraps of information about the Doctor's true plans in *all* of the stories in Season Twenty-Five. In *Silver Nemesis,* even the tape deck the Doctor has built for her (as a replacement for the one destroyed by the Daleks in *Remembrance of the Daleks*) doubles up as a multi-purpose tool, and can now jam the signal from the cyber ship. It's a prime example of the Doctor using and adapting something innocuous for his own ends, and he does the same with something as simple as words...

In *Alice's Adventures in Wonderland,* language is unreliable. Words are twisted, meanings and interpretations changed at a whim as the characters see fit. The Doctor also has a tendency to use coded, poetic or impenetrable language, often only comprehensible to himself. As time goes on, Ace learns - and even becomes used to the fact - that the Doctor not only uses language as a blind, he also blatantly lies or withholds information. This takes us into uncomfortable territory - how much agency can Ace retain if she is frequently manipulated and kept in the dark as to the Doctor's motivation?

The Greatest Show in the Galaxy is an especially interesting story in that regard, and is populated by creatures every bit as mad and unusual as those in Wonderland. Ace is the driving force in this story as she immediately senses there is something wrong with the circus - a neat bit of role-reversal as it is generally the Doctor who has odd feelings or strange hunches. While it's unclear whether the Doctor *genuinely* doesn't sense anything wrong or whether he's just testing Ace, his role in *Greatest Show* is mostly to provide a distraction while Ace does the real work: retrieving the amulet needed to defeat the Gods of Ragnarok.

In a story about a circus, with emphasis placed on the significance of names and costumes, it's notable that Ace briefly wears both the fourth Doctor's scarf as well as previous companion Mel's top. This beautifully illustrates her metamorphosis from questing visitor, moved about without much say in the matter, to a fully integrated part of Wonderland. Later - in *Survival*, the last classic *Doctor Who* story, and so Ace's last TV appearance - we will see her briefly don the Doctor's hat and umbrella, clear signs that she considers herself the one to take up the reins. She's become a Mad Hatter in her own right. But what's crucial to this process is that Ace isn't *granted* agency, she assumes power on her own.

But neither power, nor agency, were alien to Ace when she first came to Wonderland - the seeds of these qualities were firmly planted, and only needed the right environment for them to grow and flourish. She already had a capacity for defiance, and the confidence to rely upon herself - a trait she shares with the contrary Alice. And not only defiance, but the ability and willingness to lie about her actions (much like the Doctor himself). In a season filled with deceptive language, the Doctor trusts Ace to deliberately go *against* his direct instructions, knowing that she will do as he does, not as he says. In *Silver Nemesis*, the two of them resolve a problem with:

> **The Doctor:** I don't suppose you completely ignored my instructions and secretly prepared any Nitro-9 [explosive]?
> **Ace:** And what if I had?
> **The Doctor:** Naturally, you wouldn't do anything as insanely dangerous as to carry it around with you, would you?
> **Ace:** 'Course not. I'm a good girl, I do what I'm told.
> **The Doctor:** Excellent. Blow up that [cyber] vehicle.

Language is used as a cover, communicating true purpose under the guise of an ordinary conversation, every word carrying another meaning. Ace and the Doctor are in perfect understanding, and the implicit meaning beneath these words is that Ace is *dangerous*. And the Doctor, despite proclaiming to dislike violence, has no qualms about using Ace as a weapon. On the whole, he doesn't shield her from the darkness of his methods - if Ace doesn't always know that she's being manipulated, she's well aware of the Doctor's methods. She's already learned that Wonderland is not always safe and she, in turn, casts herself in the role of the Doctor's protector. He even assists her in that endeavour, imbuing her baseball bat with the power of the Hand of Omega, which she subsequently uses to attack a Dalek.

It's fortuitous that this happens during the first story of Season Twenty-Five, *Remembrance of the Daleks,* a story which pays homage to the very first *Doctor Who* story of all: *An Unearthly Child.* Not only is *Remembrance* set in 1963, when *An Unearthly Child* takes place, the Doctor and Ace revisit the now-iconic junkyard where Barbara and Ian first encountered the Doctor and his granddaughter Susan.

Although many of the Doctor's companions have filled the "substitute granddaughter" role in one way or another, there is a case to be made that Ace fits the mold more than most. Not only is Ace brave, inquisitive and bright - qualities the Doctor always prizes - her life experiences to a certain extent mirror the Doctor's own: she doesn't have much of a home to return to, her childhood was traumatic and she was a known troublemaker. The first Doctor remarks upon how both he and Susan are "wanderers in the fourth dimension of space and time, cut off from our own planet and our own people," and whilst Ace fits this description, she is a very willful young woman, changing a traditionally supportive role to one of defender and right-hand (wo)man.

Even her name is something *chosen,* like the Doctor's own. It isn't hard to see why the Doctor was taken with her, and how he felt inclined to move her further along the path he found her on - much like he can't walk by a chessboard without moving a piece, imposing his own will on the outcome of the game, intuitively trusting that his strategy is superior to the original.

Usually at the end of a companion's journey, they return to their own life, older and wiser. But the Doctor's plans for Ace went beyond this. He did not intend for her to return to her own world - at least, not until she had completed a journey longer and more complex than any other companion's. He wanted her transformation to be complete. When we look at her role as a "Wolf of Fenric," lifted through time, and marked as part of the Doctor's world before they even met, it's not hard to see why her journey needed to be more comprehensive than that of so many other companions.

So the Doctor's behavior towards Ace - insisting that she go the slow route, forcing her to figure things out for herself or even outright manipulating or lying to her - is all done with the knowledge that Ace could be the one companion to stay in Wonderland for good, eventually complete the training the Doctor is putting her through and enter the very same Academy the Doctor himself graduated from. She's the pawn that has to get to the eight square on her own.

But the Doctor genuinely *cares* about Ace. He is, at heart, a good man; a marked contrast to the warped mirror Doctor-companion duo - the famous explorer Captain Cook and his travelling companion Mags - seen in *The Greatest Show in the Galaxy*. Unlike the Captain, who has no qualms sacrificing everyone around him in order to save himself, the Doctor has every faith in the people around him, Ace especially. If he hides the greater truth from her, leaving her no option but to do things the hard way, it's in many ways a token of his high regard for her. He trusts her to make the right calls, despite only holding a few of the relevant cards.

Forcing someone you love to go through something like this is obviously not a *nice* thing to do, but metal has to first go through the fire to become tempered. And what a fire this lifestyle is - there's endless wonder and danger, a world full of madness and impossibility and treacherousness; a world of Mad Hatters, Cheshire Cats and living chess pieces. It's a world where a little girl can become anything she wants to be, and if the end of *Doctor Who* in 1989 left Ace's journey incomplete, all the signs are there that *this* little girl went on to become Queen Ace.

Hey, You Got Science in My Fiction!

Laura McCullough, Ph.D., is a professor and department chair of physics at the University of Wisconsin-Stout. She has studied gender and science issues for 20 years. She enjoys science, science fiction, cats, video games, friends and being social, along with many other things. Her husband is science fiction author Kelly McCullough, and she is always excited to read things no one else has seen yet. She enjoys breaking stereotypes, yet recognizes that a female physics professor with long red hair may be uncommon in science, but in science fiction she is hardly a rarity.

As a physics professor researcher in gender and science, I am amused by the connections between gender, science and technology in the loosely scientific Season Eighteen. Or do I mean bemused? This season had a lot going on: it was a fresh start for a new producer; it had a new opening sequence, a new logo and more modern, synthesizer-heavy music. It bid farewell to one companion, introduced three more, and lost and gained a Doctor.

And it had a lot of science.

Whether the writers had help from scientists or whether they were just your standard "science is cool" type geeks, they got a lot of the science language right. They draw on the flashiest words and the shiniest technology to make you feel like the characters know a lot more than you do. And yet they aren't showing real science; it's just the dress-up version for showing off.

After all, *Doctor Who* is science fiction. That means it isn't real and doesn't have to be. What? You're willing to accept time travel, alien planets and races, and Time Lords, but want to quibble over a little question of scientific accuracy? Nope. The science in *Doctor Who* is fiction. There are lots of science words and science tools, but they rarely add up to science. And for this physicist, that's much of the pleasure in viewing these older stories. In a context of science and technology, I can feel at home while not needing to worry about whether or not they are getting the science right. It's not science, it's sciency!

The concept of entropy, in particular, is one sciency idea that the producers and writers chose to emphasize several times.

What is entropy? Why is it so interesting and so unlikely in a series about time travel? A simple definition: things get worse. Rather like many writers' definition of plot. Entropy actually has many different definitions, and if you're a chemist, you might find my physics definitions look wrong. Try a web search for entropy and you'll find five definitions for five different sites. I look at entropy from the view of classical statistical physics: entropy is a way to measure possibilities. It's how well we know what's really going on at an atomic level. Well, actually, it's more of how well we don't know what's going on. One of the important things about entropy is that it always increases or, at best, stays the same. In general, you can't go from knowing very little about a system to knowing a lot about a system, not unless you're willing to put in a lot of work - i.e., add a lot of energy to the system.

The silliest example of entropy is in Logopolis itself - a city of people devoted to calculations. Calculations done via a hive mind. In this story, we discover that Logopolis has been keeping entropy from increasing in the Universe. This is accomplished by creating little vent holes and tossing the built-up extra entropy outside the universe proper. An entropy garbage disposal. It's a lovely idea and, depending upon how you define your parameters, might have merit. But physics gets in the way. It would still cost something to open up the vents and spit the extra entropy out, which would increase the entropy in the Universe a bit. Though you can argue that it would increase much more slowly than normal. In any case, the idea of a Universe where entropy doesn't increase is delightful. Ice cubes in a glass of water might not melt. Or if they do, the glass next to it might spontaneously form ice cubes. A splash of rum in a glass of Coke might not mix up without some external help. Your body heating up during exercise might mean your companion is cooling down.

But even though the science isn't always what you'd call accurate, *Doctor Who* makes science fun and cool. In *Doctor Who*, science solves problems, explains mysteries. The show uses technical words and science terms in this season, demonstrating for the viewer that science is the answer... or, sometimes, the problem.

The Leisure Hive is full of scientific language tidbits: tachyons and tachyonics (the term "tachyon" only being about 20 years old at that point), anti-baryon shields, eigenfunctions and oscillators. While the language is mostly appropriate to the context, the details remind the viewer that we are watching science fiction.

In *Full Circle*, we first encounter the concept of "E-space." The Doctor and Romana are heading back to Gallifrey when they encounter a wobble in space-time that messes everything up. The TARDIS is flipped into E-space, where there are "negative coordinates." I liked this explanation for how E-space differs from N-space; it has a nice simplicity to it, and I can come up with ideas in my head for how it might work. Although I struggle to figure out how the sensors might be able to detect this shift in readings. The functions of the TARDIS should be built on positive coordinates; they shouldn't be able to show negative coordinates. It's like a car's speedometer: one direction only.

There is also a lot of time technology talk in *Warrior's Gate*. How to escape from E-space; how to fix the warp drives; how to move between the two spaces. The use of the negative coordinates for E-space is wound up beautifully with the discovery that the TARDIS is set at zero coordinates. The discussion that zero isn't negative or positive but in between, crossing both worlds, wraps up the E-space trilogy nicely. Other fun language feels appropriate to the context: dimensional contraction of the microcosm system; space-time instability; dwarf star alloy; mass attraction (whatever that might be); triangulation.

We also have some fun physics with K9 making a few snarky comments. A crewmember fires an energy weapon at the gateway mirror. It bounces off, and K9 says "angle of incidence equal to angle of reflection." Then when the captain kicks at K9 and the mirror, K9's response is "Newton's third law of motion: action and reaction are opposite." Absolutely appropriate physics used to make snide comments: priceless.

A crewmember also appears to have charge of a "portable mass detector" machine. I had to smile when I heard that. It's so wonderfully *Doctor Who*. Lovely scientific language that adds up to nothing more than a neat phrase. Though in the light of the recent discovery of the Higgs boson, perhaps this is less fictional than we thought.

The science in *The Keeper of Traken* is, again, mostly absurd but uses good scientific language. Strange frequency readings are clarified using a Fourier analysis, a mathematical method for separating out different wave frequencies (like sound waves) that are jumbled together for some reason, which seems a perfectly acceptable technique for this sort of thing. The scanner that Tremas uses is an unknown device - the best kind of toy in *Doctor Who*. "Bioelectronics" is mentioned a few times, and plasma fields, and gamma mode encryption. It's all the pretty language thrown in without any need to make cohesive sense.

And, of course, we get our fill of science in *Logopolis*. This story is so much fun! There is great science here and, as I previously mentioned, some of it even makes sense. What a way to close up the season: the

Doctor working with, then against, the Master to save the universe. With science!

In *Doctor Who,* science is respected and valued. Or, at least, it is in most of the stories. Science gives the Doctor the tools he needs to combat the problems wrought by ignorance and superstition. *Meglos* is an interesting variation on the normal scheme. Here we have science and religion pitted against each other with mystics and savants arguing over the Dodecahedron, the source of power for the compound.

The religious leader tries to solve the problem with human sacrifice. Or, rather, Time Lord sacrifice, while the scientists work with the Doctor and his companion Romana to bring about the satisfactory explosive conclusion. Here we see religion treated as an obstacle to the rational solution of problems and science as the antidote.

While science is mostly treated positively in this season, occasionally the picture is negative. Science is responsible for the murder of a tourist in *The Leisure Hive,* but then later it saves the day, with the troublesome duplicating/ rejuvenating machine bringing the dictator Pangol back to infancy and the female chairman Mena back to robust health. In *Full Circle,* the scientist who gets hold of a swamp creature cares nothing for his hostage's comfort. In fact, he's so determined to learn about and understand the alien that he loses all empathy for it as a fellow living creature. The elderly rebel in *State of Decay* is also completely focused on learning and understanding the world around him, but he has not lost all his empathy for his companions. Instead, he is (ironically, given the title) frozen in indecision since he does not feel they have enough information to rise up against their vampire overlords.

State of Decay is also where, after two strong women protagonists, we get a strong woman enemy. The vampire queen is stronger than the king, more active, more forceful. She tells the king to shut up; she pushes for action. She is the one to say to the king that the Doctor is not unarmed; he has the greatest weapon of all: knowledge.

Thinking of gender as I watch or read something is second nature to me. I am a physics professor, I am a woman, and I do research on gender and science. These three focuses make for some interesting viewing and occasionally leads me to strange observations. For example, as I was watching the *Warriors' Gate,* I noted the open grid flooring in the ship. Not a very welcoming place for someone wearing a skirt. In fact, of all of Romana's wonderfully outrageous outfits in Season Eighteen, she only once (in *Full Circle*) wore a skirt. Romana's clothing isn't ever so fashionable as to be confining or restrictive. She wears sensible low-heeled boots and shoes which allow her to run - and not just away. Her clothing often is better for running than the Doctor's dragging scarf and flapping coat. She always looks great and her clothing never gets in the way. She is a partner, rather than a damsel in distress.

In other areas, Season Eighteen has a strange mix of traditional science stereotypes and counter-typical gender roles. Yet overall, the portrayal is fair and provides some good role models both for women and for scientists in general.

The Leisure Hive has two male scientists whom Romana helps, and her work saves both the day *and* the Doctor. In science classrooms 30 years later, girls are still more likely to take on a passive role while letting boys play with the equipment. It is a pleasure to see this reversal of roles.

In *Meglos,* the lead scientist is male, but the secondary and more active science role is played by a woman. She is also captured by the villain and ends up working with Romana. The vampires in *State of Decay* include a stronger queen and weaker king, a nice change although the science-type character here is male, elderly, white and has disarrayed hair. Stupid stereotypes.

On the world of Traken, we do not have people devoted only to science, though the leaders do need to have technical knowledge. And Nyssa's father is obviously the one who knows the system best. Most of these portrayals are quite positive and with one exception do not feed into the common stereotypes of scientists as weirdos, and women as rescue objects.

Then, in *Logopolis,* we get a real treat.

In the city, you have two genders sitting and doing the calculating on their simple little abaci. Male and female Logopolitans are depicted, though it's hard to spot any women among the calculators. No clothing differentiation among those calculating, which is itself kind of cool. Equitable gender roles are displayed despite the shortage of women in the overall cast. And the Logopolitans aren't in white lab coats, don't have glasses, don't have beakers of colored fluid. I suppose they do have weird hair, though. But we conquer most of the stupid stereotypes!

There is such an imbalance of men and women in the casting of *Doctor Who,* it is hard to argue that there is a worse imbalance in the scientists. Unlike in our world, where women are still quite under-represented. Can you, dear reader, name a famous female physicist? Perhaps you come up with our radioactive friend Marie Sklodowska. You probably know her as Madame Curie. Now can you name a second? It gets harder, doesn't it?

Season Eighteen puts some of the science back in the science fiction show, yet it doesn't lose its fictional quirkiness. We have vampires and aliens and robots and space travel. At the same time, the stories include situations which might give modern TV producers pause: evolution, genocide and slavery are potent examples. The majority of the cast is male, yet gender is a non-issue for most of the characters. All of this is wrapped up in science clothing, with some humor as a colorful accessory. That effort to deal with a myriad of problems by bringing science and humor to bear on them is what makes *Doctor Who* great and compelling even after 30 years. And for this scientist, it makes for some wonderful leisure time.

Seven to Doomsday: The Non-Domestication of Earthbound *Doctor Who* in Season Seven

Mags L. Halliday started in *Doctor Who* fandom in the early 1990s, writing for the *Skaro* fanzine as well as being an active member of online fora like rec.arts.drwho and the Jade Pagoda. In 2002, she joined the then-literal handful of women to have a *Doctor Who* novel published, and has since written for the Faction Paradox, Bernice Summerfield and Iris Wildthyme ranges. She also helped to form a couple of female networking groups - one in *Doctor Who* fandom and one for creative women in her home city. She currently works as a civil servant, having given up being a scientific doctor's assistant. Yes, really. The hours were terrible. She lives in Devon with husband and fellow *Who* author Mark Clapham and their young daughter. They fear the oncoming tyranny of pink. She can be found at magslhalliday.co.uk

Ah, the UNIT family. Cosy cuppas, quirkiness, ditzy girls, a little light patriarchy and, as Jon Pertwee himself put it, Yetis on the loo in Tooting Bec.

Except that comfortable scenario belongs to Season Eight, not Season Seven. The first attempt at making *Doctor Who* Earthbound resulted in a quasi-military world filled with Cold War paranoia, violence and hard rational science. One of the shocking things about *Inferno*, the season's final story, is not that the parallel world is so different, but that it's such a simple step away from the normal one. Jo Grant's "good morning starshine" business wouldn't have stood a chance in Season Seven.

Luckily, Season Seven has Liz Shaw. She's a smart, rational career woman who regards Brigadier Lethbridge-Stewart, and the unearthly world she's suddenly dragged into, with wry amusement.

In some ways, Season Seven is a hangover of the late 1960s more than the start of the 1970s. The budget-saving expedient of exiling the Doctor to Earth means this one season contains as many "alien invasion of near-contemporary Earth" stories as the entire preceding six seasons.[58] Malcolm Hulke, one of the writers of the season, pointed out that there

58 The four previous stories being: *The Faceless Ones, The Web of Fear, Fury from the Deep* (presumably; the weed creature's origins are never established) and *The Invasion.*

are only two stories you can do with a grounded Doctor: alien invasion or mad scientist. He then promptly found a third, using the Erich von Daniken[59] idea that the aliens have been here all along.

Within the first two tropes, there are a range of themes that could be explored. Instead, Season Seven sticks closely to three Cold War themes: military hubris, rational people acting irrationally and the concern that people may turn to the "other side." It echoes with fears around communism, fascism, nuclear or biological warfare and energy crises. It's not entirely surprising, given the period that the stories were produced in. The doomsday clock, an indicator of the risk of nuclear Armageddon, was at seven minutes to midnight in 1969, and US peak oil, the point at which oil production reaches terminal decline, was reached in 1970. Britain was a few years off the oil crises that meant I was going to bed by candlelight as a kid, but the early signs were there. The Season Seven stories reflect real world fears not through stories set in the distant future, but set in a pretty much contemporary Britain.[60]

Spearhead from Space introduces the Nestene Consciousness. The Nestene plans to colonize the planet through animating plastic facsimiles of senior civil servants.[61] And shop dummies. It's about the fear of identity-theft, of finding someone can look the same but be totally different. And, at the same time, the Brigadier discovers someone can look totally different but be absolutely the same.

Doctor Who and the Silurians is Malcolm Hulke demonstrating how to break the story limitations by suggesting the aliens have been here all along. This twist is one that recurs in *The Daemons* and *Pyramids of Mars*. When the sleeping reptilian race is awoken, they are horrified to discover the apes have developed civilization. It's an essay on different Cold War engagement policies; the Doctor's rational argument for detente is overwhelmed by military mindsets on both sides.

The Ambassadors of Death has astronauts on a Mars mission replaced by radiation-emitting creatures who have come in peace but are exploited as weapons by a madman and a criminal. The science is a struggle to believe and the direction is more like an ITV action series than *Doctor Who*. Yet again, a rational man behaves irrationally, leading the world to the brink of war.

And *Inferno* takes the militaristic theme to the final level, showing

59 Von Daniken's *Chariots of the Gods* was published in English in 1969.

60 I'm not getting into UNIT dating.

61 It remains a source of great amusement to me that Tussauds would have a whole room containing waxworks of top civil servants. And that Liz Shaw would recognise them.

the Doctor a world that's tipped into a fascist dictatorship maintained by military brutality. UNIT are advising on *another* top secret energy supply project, this time drilling below the Earth's crust. The Doctor slips sideways into a parallel world which is destroyed by the powers unleashed when the project director refuses to heed the warnings of others.

This is all a long way from an amusing tea time adventure serial for children, and into the adult fears of *Doomwatch* and *Quatermass*.

In one sense, Season Seven is the most domestic season yet. The Doctor is tied to a single world. His support - the Brigadier and Liz Shaw - don't travel with him because he doesn't travel. It's recognizably our world with just minor twists. It has villages and high streets, cottages and commuters. But these stories aren't actually domestic. They are all about workplaces and secretive people in positions of power. The Nestene make copies of civil servants. The Silurians are awoken by a miniature CERN being used as a new energy source. The Ambassadors are astronauts. And Inferno is another top-secret power station.[62]

Compare this to the circuses and domestic interiors of Season Eight. *Terror of the Autons*, where the Nestene animates chairs, daffodils, telephones and a troll doll, was a story that so alarmed people by putting the alien into the domestic realm that there were questions in the Houses of Parliament. Or look at the traditional character types - the vicar, the local crazy old lady, the publican - who fill Devil's End village in *The Daemons*. In *The Ambassadors of Death*, the Doctor only stops working to watch TV because he spots the Brigadier in the background - whereas one season later, Mike and Benton are settling in with cuppas to watch the opening of the barrow in *The Daemons*.

UNIT doesn't seem to have found a single permanent base in Season Seven. They have moved on from operating out of a military cargo plane, but they've yet to have a manor house. Instead, the Brigadier commandeers rooms to be based in, just as he commandeers Liz Shaw into UNIT. The Doctor has lost whatever domestic home he had - he's exiled from his home planet, and even lacking the TARDIS interior with its furnishings and steadying hum. And he's yet to build himself an urban family from the people around him.

The difference between Season Seven and "cosy UNIT" even shows in the costuming: for most of Season Seven, UNIT still wear the mushroom uniforms designed for Season Six's *The Invasion*. The uniforms are

62 *The Hungry Earth*/ *Cold Blood*, Chris Chibnall's pseudo-remake of *Doctor Who and the Silurians*, replaces CERN with a giant drill seeking a new energy source.

sleek, futuristic and unfamiliar even if the Brigadier does have various medal ribbons on his and carries a swagger stick. By *Terror of the Autons,* Lethbridge-Stewart himself has swapped to standard British army kit wearing woolly jumpers with elbow patches, or regular army officer uniform complete with archaic leather straps. He becomes the comedy British army officer, a reactionary Colonel Blimp rather than the visionary military man looking out for future threats.

Even the Doctor's costume is more austere in Season Seven. It may have a cape and a silk cravat, but he's otherwise in black opera clothes not the vibrant Edwardian smoking jackets and increasingly bouffant hair of later years.

As the clothes become more familiar, the relationships become more familial. This is still a long way from the domesticity of twenty-first century *Who* and the Doctor settling in for Christmas lunch with the Tylers, but the UNIT "family" of Season Eight onwards is the start of that journey.

When fans talk casually of the cosy UNIT era, it is the later Pertwee stories that are being referred to, not the cold, hard world of Season Seven. They mean the Brigadier as patriarch with Mike Yates, Benton and Jo Grant as the dependents. And the Doctor as the maverick, exotic uncle who shows up with tall tales and strange presents. There's no room in that comfy family portrait for an independent woman, for Liz Shaw.

Co-opted into UNIT against her will to act as the Brigadier's scientific consultant because she has every PhD in the book, Liz stands out as one of the few female regulars from all the TV series to be a feminist role model. By which I mean she expects/ demands respect and equal treatment from others regardless of anyone's gender or position.

Her first question to the Brigadier is whether "all that nonsense" involving secret locations and searches is really necessary, and she consistently regards him with amusement. She rolls her eyes in contempt at hearing the Brigadier say "she's not just a pretty face," a reaction that can be contrasted with Zoe's pleasure at being told she is "far prettier than a computer" in *The Invasion*. On being told she can't go to the caves in *Doctor Who and the Silurians,* she archly asks the Brigadier, "Have you *never* heard of female emancipation?" On being told she is to man the Brigadier's phones, she retorts that "I am a scientist, not an office boy." And when the Brigadier suggests getting medical treatment for a comatose Doctor in *Inferno,* she drily asks if he remembers that she "happens to be a doctor"?

But what really stands out is not Liz Shaw's dialogue, but that she gets on with things. She devises and runs experiments, she puts forward theories, she works on escape plans. After being attacked by a fleeing Silurian, something that has caused two other people to revert to Neanderthal behavior, she calmly details what she saw to the Doctor and the Brigadier. She actively participates and seeks solutions, using her initiative rather than passively waiting to be rescued. She depends on no-one but herself.

She is not, in short, a screamer.

When I was growing up with *Doctor Who* - a late-comer in the 1980s - I was constantly told that this or that new companion would be "different." She wouldn't be a screamer in need of rescuing, or ditzy, or any of those other clichés. So you can imagine my surprise when I started to read about the history of the show and found women like Barbara Wright and Liz Shaw as regular characters. Women, not girls. They were professionals. They had careers they rather wanted to get back to, and they were unafraid to argue with the Doctor. Not just emotionally, not just about feelings or instinct or any of that perceived "female stuff," but rationally, using logic and intellect to advance an opposing view.

Yet, over 30 years after I first read a Target novelization and discovered these role models, such women are still rare delights in *Doctor Who*. The Doctor-Donna was so dangerous she had to be erased. "But she was better because of you," Wilf cried, and I cried too. The problem is that smart, independent women don't make good companions, and that's a painful realization. I don't like the idea that my favorite series has, as a fundamental part of its set-up, no room for the kind of women I want to see.

Liz Shaw isn't the only female scientist in Season Seven. But what distinguishes her from the others is that she doesn't allow emotions to overwhelm her rationalism. Miss Dawson, a senior scientist at the Wenley Moor installation, keeps Dr Quinn's contact with the Silurians secret because she is in unrequited love with him. And, when he is killed, she becomes a ruthless advocate of destroying them all. Petra Williams at the Inferno project is also devoted to her superior, in both universes, but eventually defies Stahlman because she's falling for another man. They are dependent, emotionally attached on someone else for their self-worth.

Liz's loyalty to the Doctor is solid, but there is no suggestion it comes from emotional attachment rather than rational engagement. She does tend to acquiesce when the Doctor suggests she does as the Brigadier asks, but she also manipulates the Doctor into doing what the Brigadier wants. Contrast that nuanced relationship with Martha Jones, a professional woman whose unhealthy infatuation with the Doctor means she literally walks around the entire world to help him.

What's noticeable is that acting irrationally due to passion is not portrayed as a feminine trait in Season Seven. Dr Lawrence, Dr Quinn, General Carrington and Professor Stahlman all refuse to listen to reason and pay the price with their lives or minds. Or both. Since irrational or misplaced loyalty is not a feminine trait, Liz's emotional detachment is not shown as a weakness or failing - as it might be in later seasons, where companions are always loyal, always dependent, always expecting to be rescued. Instead, it's a sign of Liz's strength that she alters her world view to accommodate the facts of aliens, the Doctor and physics beyond her current understanding.

Yet despite all her scientific qualifications, she's addressed as "Miss Shaw," "Liz" or "m'dear." For production purposes, this is clearly so you don't end up with two people addressed as "Doctor" all the time, but it still feels like a demeaning of Liz's qualifications and intellectual rigor.[63] This can be seen in the context that one of Barry Letts' first actions as producer was to "soften" Liz Shaw, making her visually less severe. The hair came down, the hemlines went up.

Caroline John tells of arguing that Liz Shaw would wear trousers to go exploring the Wenley Moor caves in *Doctor Who and the Silurians*. It's right for her character to be practical, even if she favors a cowl-necked lab coat in the first two stories over the more traditional lapels. The actor was told that she'd be doing those cave scenes in a mini-skirt and high-heeled boots, no matter what she said. Tellingly, it was only when Jon Pertwee intervened that the producers agreed to her wearing a boiler suit.[64] Then, during the filming of *Inferno,* Letts told John they were looking for another "girl."

And "girl" is the right term. They don't replace Liz Shaw with another smart grown-up woman, but with the childlike naïf Jo Grant. Jo gets her place because her uncle is someone important, not for any actual skills she may bring. In fact, she's deliberately introduced as being the opposite of Liz. She's someone who clearly wouldn't have her job without her family connections. She took A-level science but didn't

63 An alternative theory is that she is not merely a doctor of medicine but a surgeon, at which point the form of address reverts to Miss. This theory can be supported by the fact Liz introduces herself as "Liz Shaw" to someone in *Spearhead from Space.*

64 See *The UNIT Family* extra on the *Inferno* DVD set.

pass, she ruins the Doctor's experiments, is mesmerized by the Master, gets taken hostage and so on. She talks about the Age of Aquarius, is irrational and eventually leaves to get married. In *The Green Death*, she even admits she is swapping her dependency on the Doctor for "a sort of younger" version.

The casting of Katy Manning as Jo Grant was based on her own personality at a shambolic audition, but Pertwee himself called her "perfect" on looks alone. Compared to Caroline John, Manning is tiny. Jo Grant has to literally look up to the Doctor. The recent confirmation that April Walker, the original actor cast as Sarah Jane Smith, was rejected by Pertwee in favor of the smaller, less dominant Lis Sladen indicates that there was a desire in the early 70s to avoid another female companion who might equal the Doctor.

Sarah Jane Smith, for example, is touted as a feminist, but she talks about equal rights for women more than she demonstrates her equality through actions. Unlike Liz, Jo's pluck and Sarah Jane's initiative frequently gets them into trouble and neither "girl" really challenges the Doctor on his actions or ideas.

Question him? Yes. Act as a child's viewpoint into the narrative? Yes. But not challenge him on an intellectual level. The trouble is, as Season Seven exposes, that kind of equal companion doesn't leave anyone to be the child's identification figure, or to ask questions the average viewer, who may not have taken any science O-levels, has.

Season Seven is a cold adult world not only because of the prevailing theme of betrayals and warring ideologies, but because the possible identification figures are either militaristic or too knowledgeable to ask the "what's going on, Doctor?" questions. Liz Shaw beats the Doctor to it on occasion - she connects events back to the Auto Plastics factory; she suggests possible antidotes to the Silurian toxin; she understands what the computer is warning of in *Inferno*. It makes her a great character, and a great role model, but that role isn't of being someone to guide viewers through the story.

And the Doctor, when surrounded by nothing but other adult characters, loses a little of his quirky charm. So Liz Shaw heads back to her research projects at Cambridge between seasons and Jo Grant, the archetypal companion, joins UNIT instead. The Doctor's avuncular relationship with a "girl" is re-established, the Brigadier and the Doctor have someone to be protective about and UNIT gains a cosy, family vibe. There are still alien invasions and mad scientists, of course, but the tone moves from warnings of political doom to jolly action-adventures.

The Sound's the Star

Emily Kausalik is a doctoral candidate at the University of Texas at Austin where she is completing a PhD in music theory. She is currently writing her dissertation on the music and sound design of *Doctor Who* (both classic and new series), and participated on the 2011 "Murray's Gold: The Music of *Doctor Who*" and 2012 "More Magic of *Doctor Who* Music" panels at Gallifrey One. She presented a paper on the use of stock music in classic *Doctor Who* at the Music and The Moving Image Conference at NYU in June 2012. These activities all cut deeply into her knitting time.

The first decade of *Doctor Who* can be quite nebulous for current-day fans. As most of us know, up until the late 1970s, the BBC lacked a consistent methodology for keeping episodes once they aired. In fact, a whole book called *Wiped! Doctor Who's Missing Episodes* by Richard Molesworth is dedicated to illuminating the BBC's attitude towards episode retention as a result of funding, technology and many other internal factors (and is an absolutely fascinating read). *Doctor Who* wasn't the only program to suffer, but due to its incredible tenure in broadcasting, and its immensely passionate fanbase, a relatively typical occurrence has become a point of utter outrage.

Of all the actors to play the title role, Patrick Troughton's era suffered the most from the destruction or loss of tapes by the BBC Engineering Department, which at that time was in charge of housing and managing all of the BBC's videotapes. Out of Troughton's 14 stories in Seasons Four and Five, only *The Tomb of the Cybermen* remains completely visually intact. Yet in spite of that, there is plenty to be gleaned from Season Five through its audio remnants.

But first, it's important to know why we have to rely on these audio remnants in the first place. While I won't go into too much detail about why certain stories or certain years suffered so greatly (you can get that in *Wiped!*), I will say that in the 1960s, the Engineering Department had no policy of any kind requiring they keep *any* videotapes once an episode had aired. For something to stick around, someone had to file a request to keep it. If the BBC Drama Department felt a story could be sold overseas or re-aired, they would file a retention request. But if no one specifically asked for tapes to be stored long-term, they were fair game to be destroyed or wiped for re-use. Because of this policy, the episodes that have survived the test of time seem rather arbitrary - the video archive for Season Five includes one episode of *The Abominable Snowmen*, four of *The Ice Warriors*, one of *The Enemy of the World*, one of *The Web of Fear* and two of *The Wheel in Space*. Some of these were rescued from overseas networks, including *The Tomb of the Cybermen* from Hong Kong's Asia Television network in 1991. Others were found in the late 80s when the BBC was clearing out Villiers House, the home of the BBC's Video Tape and Film Archive during the 70s and 80s. Ultimately, there is very little rhyme or reason to what was or was not kept by the BBC.

Although these sound-only copies can feel like a lesser version of the episodes, there is a lot that can be said about the show, in terms of both production and reception, by looking at what we have left: fan recorded audio. Fans didn't know that the BBC's retention of episodes of *Doctor Who* was so inconsistent during the 1960s and early 70s, because those expectations didn't exist at the time. They pulled out their tape recorders to preserve episodes for themselves, as this was the only guaranteed way they could enjoy an episode more than once. This wasn't unique to *Doctor Who*; many different shows in the US, UK, Japan and beyond had fans recording the audio. Part of this has to do with the novelty of the then-newly available and affordable audio recording technology, and part of it had to do with finding a way to revisit an episode after it aired. In fact, these two elements create a causal loop of sorts; because they could record the episodes they did, and because they liked the stories enough to want to save them, they recorded them. While technological determinism is usually an unsatisfactory reason for something to happen, it's undeniable that commercially available technology often changes the way we consume media and the way we participate in the discourse around media.

Comparing and contrasting the soundtracks from the earliest years of the show to Season Five illuminates some interesting changes in sound design and production attitude in *Doctor Who*'s formative years. One of the defining features of the earliest seasons of *Doctor Who* was its use of electronic and modernist music newly composed for the program. These cues were typically used for transitions and scene/ location changes. However, by Season Three, *Doctor Who*'s sound editors found themselves pulling stock music tracks from the BBC Production Library more and more frequently. These tracks ranged from short, quirky, eccentric cues lacking a noticeable melody (more like the show's earlier sound profile) to bigger orchestral works with longer sections of music and larger ensembles than any newly composed music had used up until that point.

The reason for the use of stock music was often practicality: paying a composer to write new music often went outside their allotted budget. In *The Tomb of the Cybermen,* this seems to be the case because of the ambition in editing and post-production. The BBC mandated that only five cuts were allowed on videotape per episode, with any additional cut (yes, physically cutting the tape into pieces) costing them £60. Even now, that sounds like a lot of money. With the cuts between film and videotape, the changes in location, larger sets and more complex villains, I'm sure the production team burned through their budget before music was even considered.

So stock music was an easy way to save money. Yet because stock music could be more melodic - with longer phrasing and larger, more noticeable instrumentation than music written specifically for an episode of *Doctor Who* - any chosen cue could change how and for how long the sound editors could use music in an episode. The earlier years of the show frequently had long spans of time without any music in its episodes. The sound editors tended to avoid using music as underscoring and preferred to use it at transitions. The main narrative reason for this was to avoid overpowering the dialogue, but there was an important production reason as well: before the BBC adopted click track technology for television production, its programs had music and effects ported into the studio mixer as the episode was filmed-in one day-in their television film studios. While low-level sound effects and special sound ran throughout scenes when needed, music and dialogue were often kept separate out of concern that the music would distract the viewer from the dialogue.

For cues to be used in an episode, they had to be composed before recording. To give the production staff the most flexibility in the studio, composers frequently provided either short tracks that were abstract, amelodic and could be played on a loop, or longer, amorphous, musical soundscapes that could be faded in and out without noticeable breaks. While the stock music in the BBC production library was created specifically for television and radio, it frequently used bigger ensembles, longer musical lines and larger repeated musical sections than *Doctor Who*'s previous music. Directors and sound technicians sought out stock tracks that worked best for their stories, but often found it didn't conform to the characteristics of transitional cues and had to be relegated to other roles in the program. They had less control over stock music, and to avoid making the ins-and-outs of the musical cues obvious by cutting into the middle of a musical phrase, the production team would let a song play for a few minutes, sometimes throughout an entire scene. The result is a more cinematic treatment of the music, though being truly cinematic was beyond their means. But it did change the aural aesthetic of the show, and this is relatively consistent throughout the episodes in Season Five.

The origin of the ad hoc Cybermen theme, named "Space Adventure," is a perfect example of this. The piece was composed by Martin Slavin in the early 1960s, and was taken out of the BBC sound archives to be used as stock music for the Season Four story *The Tenth Planet*. In its original appearance, "Space Adventure" was used to underscore the very first appearance of the Cybermen in a dramatic approach scene. The music's slow crescendo and steady percussive beat underline the approach beautifully, and the swell at the end lines up almost perfectly with the Cyberman's attack. Because of these elements, along with its melodic trajectory, the cue works best as underscoring. And I wouldn't be surprised if the sound technicians sought out a track that could play throughout an entire scene and add to the drama, rather than play a more structural, transitional role in the format of the episode.

The "Space Adventure" track would return in both *The Moonbase* and *The Tomb of the Cybermen*, and would be used for the same purpose in the latter. As the Cybermen are released from their catacombs in *Tomb*, the opening segment of "Space Adventure" is used again for their approach, yet plays out even longer this time through a musical section with more intensity and excitement than the Cybermen seem to be showing through their labored escape from their cryo-sleep chambers. This would be the only obvious, recurring musical cue throughout the 1960s of *Doctor Who*, meant to recollect the Cybermen's previous encounters more than represent the characters themselves. Because syndication did not exist at this time, it's quite likely that some viewers would miss the repeated use of "Space Adventure" with the Cybermen; if they hadn't seen *The Tenth Planet* or *The Moonbase* in their original broadcast, they may not have ever heard the tune before. We can look back at it now and understand the connection, and it seems safe to surmise that the production team intentionally made the musical linkup.

Ultimately, the greatest impact the use of stock music had on *Doctor Who* was increasing the overall presence of music in the program. As the production team became more proficient with their visual recording and editing, they began using music to reinforce their ambition. Music helped bolster what could be considered a desire to be more cinematic than theatrical as the program grew and evolved in the 1960s. While being truly cinematic was beyond its means, *Doctor Who*'s production staff started using music to highlight longer, dramatic, and narratively crucial sequences of each episode rather than reserving it for moments where it wouldn't step on the toes of the dialogue. They used stock music to save money, but the stock music also had the added effect of adding a new style of musical treatment to the show.

The increased presence of music carried over into Dudley Simpson's score for *The Ice Warriors*. Though the music was newly composed, there was a more noticeable presence of this new music throughout the episodes, especially in the very melodramatic scoring of its title cards. His fantastic, though stereotypical, survival/horror scoring for that story gives a great indication of what the show would sound like during his incredible tenure in the years to come.

The one story that truly stands apart from the rest of Season Five is *The Abominable Snowmen*, because it uses practically no music at all. To establish the setting of the remote monastery, the editors used tracks of chant from the BBC's internal disc library. The tracks were "Morning Prayer" (1,2,3,5) and "Offering to God of Sakya" (6) and the record was listed on the production paperwork as *Monks of Sakya Set* (BBC Library LP 27579).[65] It almost goes unnoticed, as it is used very sparingly and always off screen, implying the chanting is off in the distance. *The Abominable Snowmen* is an example that the attitude of dialogue ruling over all other elements of the soundtrack is still prevalent even with the inclusion of more music in other stories. The lack of music also helps set the stark, remote setting of the Himalayas. The downside is that the lack of music makes the audio remnants surprisingly difficult to listen to all the way through.

With such a long passage of time between *The Tomb of the Cybermen*'s original transmission in 1967 and the VHS release of the newly reclaimed story in 1992, there were inevitably fans of the program that experienced the serial in audio form having never seen the visuals. Now that the visuals are available, it's interesting to see what worked aurally, and what did not. In the *Doctor Who* guidebook series *About Time*, authors Tat Wood and Lawrence Miles remark on the difference between what

65 "Doctor Who Classic Episode Guide - The Abominable Snowmen," www.bbc.co.uk/doctorwho/classic/episodeguide/abominablesnowmen/

they perceived in the recording and what is eventually seen on screen in the first episode of *The Tomb of the Cybermen*. Early on in the episode, there is an intense, frenetic musical track followed by an explosion, to which they remark, "all of this was rather unsettling, and left us with the impression that strange and terrifying things were happening throughout."[66] When the visuals resurfaced, however, the result was much less action than the audio might imply. Wood and Miles do highlight, however, the very clever use of the dial on the explosive device. "There's one inadvertent stroke of near-genius at the start, when expedition leader Parry sets the explosives and twiddles a knob on his control unit, seemingly to turn off the soundtrack."[67] These longer spans of music, without the visuals, can paint a completely different picture of the action than we might gather from a complete episode. But what that longer musical cue does, very effectively, is grab our attention and tell us something incredible is about to happen.

Luckily for current-day fans of the program, reconstructions and soundtrack versions of these missing episodes provide a viable way to revisit the stories. Part of what makes them so effective is the careful attention sound technicians paid to music, dialogue and effects during this era. They made a conscious effort of avoiding overlapping aural elements, which helped retain their clarity and understandability. The consistency in the treatment of cues in the earlier years of *Doctor Who* helped train regular listeners to anticipate certain narrative and structural elements of the story, like changes in location, action scenes and the organic or mechanical nature of different settings based on the placement of musical cues. As stock music became a regular component of the sound design, music was relegated to other roles, changing it from being a signifier of structural change to an enforcer of on-screen activity. Or, at least, that's what the music can lead us to believe. For while we have reconstructions that provide bridging narration to fill in blanks left by the visuals, we ultimately have to rely on our imagination to make sense of what we're missing. Luckily, the increased presence in music helps engage our mind's eye as we listen, and aids us in recreating the visuals for ourselves until someone travels back in time and saves those precious adventures for us.

Although much of Season Five is lost in the ether, we can glean so much from what was fortunately retained and rediscovered. We begin

---

66 Wood, Tat and Miles, Lawrence. *About Time 2: The Unauthorized Guide to Doctor Who* (Seasons 4 to 6). (New Orleans: Mad Norwegian Press, 2004): 115-116.
67 Ibid., 115.

to see changes in the production team's attitude about the show. With programs like *Lost in Space* and *Star Trek* forging new ground in US television (and in color, no less), *Doctor Who* really had no choice but to head in a new direction. The use of stock music as true underscoring, rather than punctual incidental music, was a result of budgetary concerns, but also shows the willingness of the production team to try something new. To experiment and branch out. To make do with what they had, and to utilize their resources to their greatest extent. This flexibility would become *Doctor Who*'s greatest asset. It has managed to stand the test of time because of its willingness to evolve, try new things and reinvent itself.

Harking Back and Moving On

Jenni Hughes works in a library and lives in a chilly basement in Bristol, which she shares with an ever-growing collection of *Doctor Who* merchandise and spinoffery. Her earliest *Who*-related memory involves racing home from Brownies on Friday evenings to watch the 1993 repeats with her father. (She also read the novelization of *The Faceless Ones* at an impressionable age and has viewed air travel with suspicion ever since.) When not watching (or reading, or listening to) *Doctor Who*, she is often found reading comics or working on her Masters degree. When watching *Doctor Who*, she is frequently found knitting, ideally something geeky. She blogs at shinyjenni.dreamwidth.org.

The first story with a new Doctor is always a hard sell. You've got fans of the previous Doctor tuning in, eyes narrowed, ready to hate the new one for the slightest transgression. You've got people who didn't like the last Doctor all that much crossing their fingers for someone they'll like better. And then there're all the people who don't usually watch but have switched on to see what all the fuss is about, and who might just stay, if you catch their attention.

Now factor in that it's Tom Baker who is being replaced in Season Nineteen: he's vastly popular, long running, and, for a lot of people, basically synonymous with the part. And if that isn't enough, the program is being moved from Saturday nights to weekday evenings. Sacrilege!

To make matters even more difficult, ratings for Season Eighteen hadn't exactly been stellar - though, to be fair, by 1982 none of the Saturday night TV timeslots were the ratings goldmines they used to be. Would it be possible for this new Doctor to revitalise *Doctor Who*, bring in new viewers, *and* hang onto those loyal fans who were still watching? Change is inevitable, but what if this means sceptical fans turning off in droves, muttering about how it's not as good as the old days?

Consciously or unconsciously, Season Nineteen harks back to previous seasons, through direct references and the shape of the show itself. "Don't worry," it seems to say, "the things you love aren't going away. We remember and love them, too." But this can be a double-edged sword - a source of joy and reassurance when done well, dragging down the storyline when it isn't. In itself, continuity isn't a problem, it's all about how you handle it.

Continuity Done Right

Castrovalva picks up, naturally, right where *Logopolis* left off. As a starting point for new viewers, this isn't exactly ideal, so the first episode throws in some exposition to get everyone up to speed, then zooms off as quickly as possible into a story that more or less stands alone. (Like a couple of other stories this season, it also falls neatly into two halves: one in the TARDIS, one on Castrovalva itself. A perfect format for the new twice weekly time slot.)

While *Castrovalva* stood alone plotwise, the first episode is full of explicit references to the program's past. The new Doctor is struggling to work out who he is just as much as we are, and he's doing it the same way: rifling through his past personalities, trying to see if any of them fit the man he's becoming. Loyal fans of the series would have just watched *The Five Faces of Doctor Who* repeats, and would for the first time have had *all* the previous Doctors fresh in their minds as they settled down to watch the latest incarnation. Chances are, they'd be mentally matching the new Doctor's mannerisms, speech patterns and personality to the previous Doctors, just like I did whilst watching *The Eleventh Hour*, many years later. In both episodes, the writers are one step ahead - they've written the previous Doctors right into the script.

Peter Davison's impressions of his predecessors are a joy to watch, a delightful gift to fans, and a reassurance for us too. It shows viewers that not only is this New Doctor essentially the same one we know and love, the new actor knows what he's doing. He knows what the previous Doctors were like and he cares enough to get it right. And the companions he mentions: Vicki! Jamie! The Brigadier! When the Doctor calls Tegan and Adric by the names of his past companions during his post-regenerative confusion, it tells us that they're still on his mind - they still matter to him. It just took a tricky regeneration to shake them back to the surface. It's noticeable that the Doctor doesn't mention Leela, Sarah Jane or Harry, the companions that viewers are likely to be most familiar with. (Romana does get a mention, but her departure was recent enough that she'd be on a lot of viewers' minds anyway.) Calling to mind mostly older companions suggests a connection with the program's *history*, not just its recent past, and marks a definitive break from the fourth Doctor era.

Castrovalva also gives the newest companions, Nyssa and Tegan, a chance to win us over by putting the Doctor and Adric out of action for much of the story. Like Ben and Polly in *The Power of the Daleks*, Nyssa and Tegan share our uncertainty about this new incarnation. Is this stranger really the Doctor? If they're worried, it makes it okay that we're worried too. Our concerns aren't trivial, it says, they're right there, in the program. By taking the audience's worries seriously, it helps us to feel like things will really be all right.

Look for continuity, not difference, we're told. The Doctor brings us on board by addressing our fears that this regeneration will be a change for the worse, and by telling us that we can help. "This regeneration's going to be difficult, and I shall need you all, every one of you." He's talking to Nyssa and Tegan, of course, but he's talking to the viewers as well. It's our faith in him that will make him the Doctor, and it's our faith in the program that will keep it going. "He's coming unravelled in more ways than one," worries Tegan, when she and Nyssa find the remains of Four's distinctive scarf. But that's not all that's going on. The Doctor isn't falling apart, he's deliberately putting his most recent past self behind him so he can find out who he is now. Knots, tangles and complications can be unravelled as well as scarves. And in the end, it's the Doctor's destroyed scarf that leads Tegan and Nyssa back to him.

This very first story in Season Nineteen involves the TARDIS being pulled back to Event One, dragged almost to destruction by the overwhelming weight of the past, and only able to escape through immense effort. (Though unlike the last time the Doctor started ditching bits of the TARDIS, the bit that disappears is only plot-significant, not emotionally significant. In *Logopolis*, the Doctor deliberately chose to jettison the departed Romana's bedroom.) Like the TARDIS itself, *Castrovalva* manages to escape the pull of its own history, incorporating it without being dragged under. Other stories this season, unfortunately, aren't quite strong enough to entirely escape that fate.

Continuity: Less is More

Earthshock, like *Castrovalva*, tells us that the program's history is important. But *Earthshock* appeals to *Doctor Who*'s history without really engaging with it. The Cybermen's cybervideo account of their history with the Doctor gives them weight and legitimacy as a threat; these are not just generic baddies, it tells us. But since the story itself has them act entirely out of character (I'm fairly sure smugness is an emotion), *and* completely ignores what's really scary about them, it's ultimately an empty statement. Yes, *Earthshock* has the Cybermen come to life and burst out of their pods, echoing iconic moments from the sixties stories, but this imagery's not enough. Without the body horror element, their unique menace is squandered. (The decision to wrap them up in cellophane like unusually lethal gift baskets may also have been a mistake.) Though credit where credit's due, I do like the way *Earthshock* opens, reassuringly, in a nice traditional quarry.

Kinda and *Time-Flight* handle their continuity references much more smoothly. The Doctor's mention of K9 in *Kinda* is a lovely surprise and feels completely natural; it's a nice bit of off-hand camaraderie between the Doctor and Adric. Invoking UNIT in *Time-Flight* is a handy plot contrivance (no need for the Doctor to spend ten minutes convincing airport security that no, really, I'm here to help, please stop arresting me), and it grounds the story firmly in the larger world of *Doctor Who*. Nothing happens in a vacuum.

In episode two of *Time-Flight*, it's the *recent* past that pops up. Both Adric and the Melkur (from *The Keeper of Traken*) reappear, as well as a Terileptil from *The Visitation*, but their scenes are disappointingly devoid of emotional resonance. Their appearances are first and foremost a puzzle to be solved, not a chance for Tegan and Nyssa to confront their grief over Adric's death and, in Nyssa's case, over the loss of her father. Adric's appearance should have built on the first TARDIS interior scene earlier in *Time-Flight*, in which our heroes begin to deal with the fallout from *Earthshock*, but it's a missed opportunity.

That earlier scene does double duty. First, it connects *Time-Flight* and *Earthshock*, locating the former story as taking place directly after the latter. And second, it tries to maintain the emotional continuity between them. It manages the latter better than a lot of stories this season do. The transition into planning a visit to the Great Exhibition is a little awkward, but otherwise, the scene feels like it's showing us the conversation that the Doctor, Nyssa and Tegan might really have had in that situation. It's not just a recap of what happened last week - it's motivated by the characters' genuine responses to Adric's death.

Outside of that scene, character development in this season suffers from the fact that what we're told doesn't always match what we're shown. Tegan is a case in point. Every now and then she announces a change in her attitude towards TARDIS life, and while it's perfectly plausible that she'd be won round over the course of the season, it's a bit strange that it's seemingly her experiences in *Kinda* and *The Visitation* that change her mind. After all, neither story is exactly fun for her. And then there's Adric's argument with the Doctor in *Earthshock*. Again, it's not completely out of the blue, but it's clearly included because someone decided that it would be a good idea if this story started with them falling out, rather than their argument being the natural climax of the increasing tension in their relationship. Having characters stand around talking about how they've developed is not the same as actually developing them.

Everything Old is New Again

All but one of Season Nineteen's stories either directly continue the previous story or begin by referencing it. Like the early seasons of *Doctor Who*, a lot of the stories in Season Nineteen follow directly on from one other. (Probably *not* a deliberate attempt to annoy future fanfic and spin-off writers by leaving only a limited number of gaps in which to fit new stories, but you never know.) Unlike the early seasons, however, it's mostly done with references at the beginning of each new story, not with cliffhangers at the end of the old ones.[68] This isn't just a cosmetic change. Cliffhangers, whether between or within stories, are a fairly straightforward way of making the audience want to come back next week. Referencing the previous adventure, on the other hand, is a reward for regular viewers (a slightly dubious one, given how contrived some of those conversations are) and a way of letting casual viewers know what they're missing. (This can also be a risky strategy as it has the potential to make anyone who *hasn't* seen all the episodes feel unwelcome.) The early seasons sometimes seem a bit like one continuous adventure divided into story arcs, because the stories frequently flow directly from one to the next. Season Nineteen, however, never does - each adventure is finished off neatly before the next one starts. Even where there is a cliffhanger - between *Four to Doomsday* and *Kinda* - there's a gap, both in time and location, before the second story starts.

Nevertheless, linking the stories together reconnects us with the early seasons and with memories of how *Doctor Who* "should" be. Season Nineteen also brings us the familiar sight of the Doctor trying to get his inadvertently kidnapped companion(s) back home. Even the four-person TARDIS team harks back to the earlier seasons, though it's nigh on impossible to map the Season Nineteen characters and their

68 There *are* two final episode cliffhanger endings this season, one at the end of *Time-Flight* (to make us all tune in next season) and the other at the end of *Four to Doomsday*. Though anyone watching *Kinda* to find out what's wrong with Nyssa would probably be disappointed to discover that the answer is "nothing that can't be fixed with four episodes asleep in the TARDIS."

relationships onto Season One's set up.

This concern with how the program works, or "should" work, pops up in the individual stories too. *The Visitation,* for example, is pretty much a checklist of all the things that should appear in a "historical with monsters" type story. But that's all it is: it doesn't do anything new with the elements it assembles, and so it all feels a bit hollow. Once again, rerunning the past isn't enough - change is vital to keep the program alive. This is similar to the problem with *Earthshock*: both stories contain aspects drawn from *Doctor Who*'s past (explicitly in the case of *Earthshock,* implicitly in *The Visitation*), but neither actually do anything with them. The borrowed elements just sit there, as if that's enough.

Similar again are the appearances of the Master which bookend Season Nineteen. He's rediscovered his third Doctor-era penchant for overcomplicated plans and elaborate disguises: it seems that, like the fans, the program is very aware of what a story containing the Master usually looks like. But just doing things because that's how they've always been done isn't necessarily a good idea: the best bits of *Castrovalva,* after all, are the bits *without* the Master.

Finding Balance

Throughout Season Nineteen, it's clear that the program's struggling to find a balance between its past and its future. Sometimes this works, as in *Castrovalva,* where the continuity references are integrated and meaningful. Other times, it's not so successful. It'll still be a while before the fifth Doctor era finds its feet, but given the challenges it had to overcome, I think we can forgive it for being a bit unsteady. And in the end, there's enough promise for the future that it's hard not to agree with the Doctor when he tells his companions that "whoever I am - it's absolutely splendid."

Anything Goes

Deborah Stanish first discovered *Doctor Who* in 2005, and has done nothing but look back ever since. She is the co-editor, with Lynne M. Thomas, of *Whedonistas: A Celebration of the Worlds of Joss Whedon by the Women Who Love Them*. Her essays have been published in the Hugo Award-winning *Chicks Dig Time Lords*; in volumes two and three of the *Time, Unincorporated* series; and in the forthcoming *Outside In: 160 New Perspectives on 160 Classic Doctor Who Stories by 160 Writers*. She is also a regular columnist for *Enlightenment*, the award-winning bimonthly fanzine of the Doctor Who Information Network. She can be found at deborahstanish.blogspot.com

It's hard to remember that television wasn't always a predictable beast. We've become jaded as to plot twists, mid-season cliffhangers and the surprise guest stars. But there was a time when television was a new frontier, a wild west of ideas and potential. In Season Three of *Doctor Who*, it was (at least for one story) a literal wild west where companions had as much staying power as chalk on a wet sidewalk, and the production teamed toyed with the idea of producing a story that completely excluded the main characters of the show. Season Three was when the nut cracked open, and the potential and possibilities of the show came rolling across our television screens. It laid the groundwork for *Doctor Who* to transcend from simply a popular television series to a beloved institution.

That is not to say that *Doctor Who* was a slouch in Seasons One and Two. Even for a show with a frankly fantastic premise, the stories were fresh and exciting. Still, there was a sense of consistency - the Doctor began travelling with a young girl and neatly replaced her with another young girl when she departed. When Ian and Barbara left, they were replaced by Steven, a companion of similar age, though now with an action-hero make-over. Even the first story of Season Three, *Galaxy Four*, feels like a continuation of Season Two - a standard "factions at war" with a now clichéd twist of beauty harboring the deepest evil.

Then came *The Daleks' Master Plan* and the playing field shifted.

This behemoth of a tale, 13 episodes in total, snuck up on viewers with its introductory story *Mission to the Unknown*. Whether this story is

Terry Nation's version of a backdoor pilot, a filler episode required after *Planet of the Giants* was reduced from four episodes to three, or simply a one-off story written to accommodate the actors' vacation schedule, the result is one of the most unusual stories in *Doctor Who* history. Neither the Doctor nor any of his companions appear in this story, it is told out of synch with the previous and following stories and yet serves as a prologue to the longest story told in the show's short history.

Given its odd beginning, *The Daleks' Master Plan* encapsulates nearly every innovation the writers and producers attempted in Season Three. Don't get me wrong, it's not a good story by any means - it is more often than not clunky, tedious and nonsensical. At times, it feels like The Daleks' Never Ending Master Plan. (This is a case of the sum being so much longer than the parts - marriages were formed and dissolved, babies conceived and born, nations rose and fell by the time this story ended.) But as far as breaking new ground, you have to respect its challenge and scope.

First, we have the companion experiment. Where there was a sense of consistency in Seasons One and Two when it came to the sidekick role, *The Daleks' Master Plan* played with the idea of interchangeable companions - it flicked a switch and moved companions across the playing field, using them at their best advantage for both the narrative and production convenience.

At the beginning of the story, we are saddled with the hapless Katarina - a handmaid to Ancient Troy's Cassandra, and someone who joins the TARDIS crew after Vicki, at the conclusion of *The Myth Makers,* inexplicably runs off with boy-toy Troilus. The Doctor seems to accept this switch with little emotion, although, to be fair, the limitations of the available media may play into this perception. This coming and going - sometimes for the flimsiest of reasons, sometimes in ways that shook the show to its core - is a recurring theme in Season Three and served to explore both the role and story-telling capabilities of the companion.

Katarina, however, was a failed experiment. It was, and is, generally accepted that the companion is the viewer's proxy, asking the questions we're unable to. With a companion from Ancient Greece who believes the TARDIS is a temple and that the Doctor is Zeus, the questions are less likely to be of the "is it possible to circumvent time in order to save lives?" ilk and more along the lines of "what magic makes these vapors, Oh Mighty Zeus?" While Katarina does show a bit of initiative in dealing with the Space Agent Bret Vyon, the writers soon realized the limitations of the character and quickly wrote her out of the show. Because of these very limitations, the series would only once more dabble with historical companions - Season Four's Jamie and Victoria - and would, in the future, stick with contemporary, future or off-world companions.

What made Katarina's short run as companion rise above a footnote in Whovian history was her exceptional departure. For the first time, we saw a companion die - violently and shockingly. Up until this moment, viewers lived in a cocoon of comfort. It's not that horrible, violent things didn't happen, it's that they always happened out "there," to the Others, never within the protective bubble of the Doctor's inner circle. Katarina's death ripped that veil of naivety from the viewer's eyes and brought an edge of uncertainty to the show.

This scenario would be revisited with the next companion to board the TARDIS: Sara Kingdom, *Doctor Who*'s first BAMF. Ruthless and lethal, Sara was a stone-cold killer. As a member of Mavic Chen's Space Security Agency, she was a dedicated soldier who killed her own brother without blinking an eye in the name of the law. Her transformation from enemy to ally isn't nearly as compelling as a modern narrative would make it, but she opened the door for the Warrior Companion, for a woman with brawn as well as brains. Despite the scope of *Doctor Who*'s storytelling, the unfortunate reality is that many of its early stories remain grounded in the values and sexual politics of their time. Yet, with Sara, we have a companion fighting side-by-side with the traditional male "muscle." Her strength and skills are admired by Steven and he treats her as an equal as they battle Egyptian warriors in *The Daleks' Master Plan* episode eight ("Golden Death").

Sara's physical prowess doesn't detract from the smart, capable female companions who came before, but it does add a layer of complexity that paved the way for a more physical companion such as Leela. This makes her death (yes - the *second* companion death in this story) all the more shocking. It is horrific to see her strength and vitality stripped away as she is aged by the time winds while attempting to help the Doctor manipulate the Time Destructor. The description of her death is chilling, and a part of me is glad that the only record of this is the audio track and still shots, as the actual tape of this must have been heartbreaking.

While both of these companion departures happened within the scope of *The Daleks' Master Plan*, they were representative of the comings and goings of companions throughout Season Three. Vicki's inexplicable departure and Katarina's arrival - nestled between *Mission to the Unknown* and *The Daleks' Master Plan* - is later echoed in Dodo Chaplet's arrival and departure. Dodo (another kind soul who, frankly, gets a bad rap in Whovian lore) wanders into the TARDIS and takes a matter of fact view of events, much as Katarina did, though their world views were centuries apart. Dodo's departure at the end of *The War Machines,* though she actually leaves the screen much earlier in the story, is a truly headshaking moment, nearly as headshaking as Vicki leaving all of the modern conveniences behind after a brief acquaintance with a cute Trojan boy. (Indoor plumbing? Modern dentistry? Love is grand, but really...) As with Vicki, the Doctor accepts Dodo's leaving the TARDIS for "a rest in the country" with aplomb and moves onto the next set of companions: Ben and Polly.

Steven also bids adieu to Team TARDIS in Season Three's *The Savages,* although this time it is at the Doctor's urging. During his run with the Doctor, Steven served as "the action companion," often finding himself in physical situations that befitted the vision for his character. Despite this beefcake façade, he also displayed surprising emotional depth, though it typically manifested itself in chivalrous gallantry. His emotional outburst and anger toward the Doctor regarding the fate of Anne Chaplet in *The Massacre* is one of Season Three's most honest moments and allows Steven's empathy to take center stage. Because of this moment it is less of a shock that, after brokering peace between the Elders and the Savages, the Doctor encourages Steven to take the mantle of Mediator and stay behind in order to help both races form a united society. Although this isn't a heroic death, it is a heroic gesture and Steven ends his run, just as Sara Kingdom did, helping the Doctor complete his mission.

Another element of Season Three that is explored in *The Daleks' Master Plan* as well as *The Myth Makers* and *The Gunfighters* is farce coupled with horrific violence. Once again, we begin in that fantastic "in-between" story, *The Myth Makers.* The ribald banter of Odysseus is a delightful foil for the Doctor's growing agitation as he realizes the inevitability of his becoming the architect of the Trojan horse. Meanwhile, in Troy, Paris is played as a poncy coward, Steven gets to play Greek soldier and Vicki is taken under Priam's wing as a prisoner of war in silk chains. The story is played broadly, with liberal doses of laughter and humor, and as a viewer (or listener in this case as, once again, the story is only available via stills and audio) is lulled into a sense of complacency that ignores the historical outcome of the story.

This makes the punch, when it comes, even more brutal. The battle cries of the warriors, the screams of the dying and the accusations of betrayal are shocking. As viewers, we *know* how the Trojan War ends, but we push that knowledge aside. As a *modern* viewer experiencing this classic series story, we almost anticipate the Doctor stepping in to fix things - to somehow mitigate the horror - even though, intellectually, we know this won't happen. As a result, we're forced to witness the fall of Troy from a very personal place.

In *The Daleks' Master Plan,* we get this same emotional whiplash when Bret Vyon is shot dead in episode four ("The Traitors"). In short order, we move from the horrific revelation that Sara has killed her brother for all of the wrong reasons to the camp of episode seven ("The Feast of Steven") and its whacky silent movie-era highjinks. As the Doctor, Sara and Steven scamper from movie set to movie set - complete with jangly piano soundtrack and Rudolph Valentino-esque lotharios - the viewers are left with a sense of disconnect that is jarring. There is no emotional resonance to Sara's revelation, which does a disservice to both the character and the story.

This disconnect is also present in *The Gunfighters.* While there is some debate as to the intent of the tone of this story, to a modern viewer it plays as a delicious farce of the westerns that were so popular in the early sixties. "The Last Chance Saloon," a hysterical ballad sung by Lynda Barron, pushes the story along in a way that nearly defies definition. The repeated attempts by nearly every character to give the Doctor a gun is reminiscent of a screwball comedy, and the sprightly banter between Dodo and Doc Holliday made this story a delight. The central premise of the Doctor being mistaken for Doc Holliday is a bit thin, but the heart of this story isn't about the Doctor - rather, it comes across as a spoof of the clichéd storytelling of the western genre. It is a fun romp, punctuated with moments of comedic horror, and you can almost imagine that at the end of this "play" all of the characters - even the barman Charlie, who is shot dead by the wonderfully over-the-top gunslinger Johnny Ringo - will rise up for a jaunty closing dance number.

Until, of course, you get to the final scene and, just as in *The Myth Makers,* the historical reality of the OK Corral sets in and you find yourself in the middle of a bloodbath. Yet, the Doctor, Steven and Dodo seem curiously unaffected by these events, which gives these stories (along with the grim *The Massacre*) the added taint of historical voyeurism. The Doctor isn't there to change events or to assist in righting some great wrong, he is there by accident or, worse, as a sightseer.

There is a sense of futility to *The Massacre* that further compounds this idea. For all of the efforts expended by Steven to assist the

Huguenots, his efforts are for naught and hundreds are slaughtered, just as history dictates. Once again, the Doctor's presence has either precipitated events or had no effect whatsoever. This story, along with *The Myth Makers* and *The Gunfighters,* builds upon the rules of time travel first advocated by script editor David Whitaker, and they collectively help to set up the idea of "fixed time" events which cannot be changed. This is a concept that Steven and, as a result, the viewers struggle with, but which later becomes a somewhat permanent tenet in the Doctor's romp through time.

While the body count was high in this season, nothing is as groundbreaking as removing a body from the show completely, particularly if that body belongs to your lead character. Just as in *Mission to the Unknown,* there are several stories that experiment with removing the Doctor from the story altogether. In *The Massacre,* the Doctor is absent for a great deal of the story, leaving Steven to carry on the narrative. When he does return, William Hartnell is playing a completely different character, the Abbot of Amboise. In *The Celestial Toymaker,* we find the Doctor first reduced to merely his hands and voice, and then rendered completely mute and invisible while Steven and Dodo play the Toymaker's cruel games. Finally, the body switch trick played in *The Massacre* is flipped in *The Savages* when the Doctor's "essence" is transferred to Jano, leader of the Council of Elders. As a result, William Hartnell is absent for the majority of the story, although his "character" continues to influence the plot, a move that is prescient to Season Four's regeneration of the title role to Patrick Troughton.

It is fairly well known that things were a little tense on the set during William Hartnell's final season. While these storytelling devices were employed to help offset Hartnell's health issues and backstage concerns, they also served the purpose of exploring the boundaries of the Doctor's role. Without the storytelling risks in Season Three, it is very possible that *Doctor Who* could have ended with Hartnell's departure. However, because the production team for whatever reason pushed the envelope as to the potential and scope of the show, they were able to successfully negotiate a change in lead actors, a move that gave what could have been a limited series a heretofore unimagined run that has lasted for decades.

Season Three took risks - sometimes those risks produced diamonds, and sometimes a slag heap of spent coal, but those choices all served a greater purpose. Whether the risks were based on story direction or the result of behind-the-scenes drama, they served to create a TV property like no other. Season Three expanded the scope of its stories, laid the groundwork for the ever-evolving role of the companion and, most importantly, for the concept of regeneration. It is one of the odder seasons in *Doctor Who* history, but to dismiss it as archaic and inaccessible does it a great disservice. Season Three unlocked the potential of *Doctor Who,* and the show has never been the same.

How the Cold War Killed the Fifth Doctor

Erica McGillivray is a die-hard geek who spends a ridiculous amount of time being nerdy. She was a late-blooming *Doctor Who* fan who fell in love with Sarah Jane Smith and her robot dog. Erica is president and marketing director of GeekGirlCon, a nonprofit that celebrates and supports geeky women with events and conventions. In her other life, she's a community attaché for SEOmoz, an Internet marketing software company; which in lay speak means that she tweets, blogs and answers Q&A about online marketing and tech for a living. She lives in Seattle with her cat Winston Zeddemore.

Welcome to 1984. "Greed is good." Margaret Thatcher and Ronald Reagan work as the gatekeepers of capitalism and keep the Cold War alive. Miners strike in the UK. Imperialism reigns, and *Doctor Who* is full of death.

Wait a minute... isn't the Doctor a Time Lord? Can't he just take Tegan, Turlough, Peri and everyone else away from contemporary concerns, to far away planets, the future or the past? Yes, but for better or worse, the writers for Season Twenty-One - Peter Davison's final season as the Doctor - are so heavily influenced by the issues of their day that the Cold War, capitalism, echoes of Thatcher's battle with the National Union of Mineworkers, the legacy of Stalin and the "hot war" in Afghanistan stalk the Doctor and company through time and space.

As a result, Season Twenty-One has its fair share of double-crosses, spies and would-be dictators; but mostly, there is death. These stories contain some of the highest body counts in *Doctor Who*'s long history (especially *Resurrection of the Daleks,* with nearly 75 individual fatalities). And the loss of life isn't limited to "red shirts" - several major characters in this season meet their doom: Kamelion, the Master, Davros and, ultimately, the Doctor himself.

I came away from Season Twenty-One reeling with depression. It felt as if this "really nice" Doctor can't save anyone. He'll hold your hand while you die and if you're really special, he will sacrifice himself so you can live; but if he doesn't like you, he'll watch you die without making a move to save you. As a Whovian who started with the new series, I was pretty shocked to find that the fifth Doctor's appearance often signaled death and destruction, and his last hurrah lacks the whimsy expected of a man with a piece of celery pinned to his lapel.

So why can't the greatest of the Time Lords unbury himself from death? You'd think this Doctor, who Peri later refers to as "almost young" and "sweet," would find that happy ending, that just once he'd be able to lead everyone to safety. Instead, this Doctor comes across like Britain itself, fighting the bad guys while coping with being a former superpower.

Most of this season's plots are convoluted, with healthy doses of saboteurs, mind-control and other plot devices right out of Cold War spy fiction. But the Doctor is not a spy. Spies have plans, *secret* plans even, and they're not known for kindness or mercy - but the Davison Doctor, thrust into a Cold War situation, fails to meet any of these criterions even more so than his previous incarnations. While almost *all* of the classic series Doctors (the seventh Doctor being the exception) rarely have well thought out plans, they are generally fairly good at thinking on their feet or playing to their Time Lord superiority as needed. In the case of the Davison Doctor, it's telling that in *Frontios*, the one time the fifth Doctor tries to play double agent, his cover is blown within a few minutes.

Season Twenty-One kicks off with *Warriors of the Deep*, a dry, literal Cold War analogy in which the Silurians and the Sea Devils launch a surprise attack to capture the human-inhabited Sea Base 4. These future humans refer to each other's sides as "blocs," echoing a Western Allies/Eastern Bloc conflict. And the fifth Doctor tries to help. He really does. When faced with a direct "hot war," the Doctor puts himself and his companions' lives on the line - but here, it's too late.

As the soldiers on Sea Base 4 give in to their Cold War suspicion, they accuse the Doctor, Tegan and Turlough of being enemy agents. When the *real* invaders - the Silurians and their Sea Devil shock troops - are revealed, those aboard Sea Base 4 are thoroughly outgunned, overwhelmed and largely slaughtered by them. The Doctor tries and fails to act as a peacemaker, and due to his "nice" persona, he doesn't become a *de facto* leader of either side. Thus, his actions become increasingly ineffective, to the point that he can't even convince Tegan and Turlough to hide in the TARDIS. Finally, the Doctor improvises two different weapons: an ultraviolet ray, and a weaponization of hexachromite that he deploys in an attempt to force the Silurians to abandon the base rather than launching missiles to kill humanity. When the Silurians refuse to capitulate, everyone lies dead on Sea Base 4 except for the Doctor, his companions and a single human survivor (Bulic).

Warriors of the Deep looks like a full-on Cold War story with undertones of the 1980's war in Afghanistan. The Afghanis, like the Silurians and the Sea Devils, were determined that neither the Western Allies nor the Soviets would win their country. The result was over two million Afghan deaths and untold amounts of destruction to their infrastructure and political systems. Silurian and Sea Devil society may be safe from harm in this type of a "scorched earth" tactic, but the analogy is apt and not even the Doctor can fix this Bear Trap.

Despite resorting to weapons and (however temporarily) acting like an arrogant super-powered Time Lord, the fifth Doctor's problem is that however much he tries to play the part, that's just not who he is. The Doctor may wield a gun against a Kaled mutant in *Resurrection of the Daleks,* threaten to personally assassinate Davros in the same story, and let the Master die in *Planet of Fire,* but he walks away from all these encounters (and massive body counts) tired: tired of fighting, tired of death and tired of mourning his losses. With exception of the Master, when he comes up against other tyrannical Cold War-type villains, he ignores the larger problem for as long as he can - determined to become no one's savior or destroyer - and eventually becomes an innocent casualty of a greedy military-industrial complex.

In *Frontios* - a story that is a medley of paranoia, oppression and the extinction of humanity - the Doctor, Tegan and Turlough find a group of people engaged in a decades-long war with an unknown aggressor. After the Earth collided with the sun, humans who escaped have launched a failing attempt to terraform the planet Frontios into a new home. Forced to live in a barren wasteland where food and medical supplies are strictly rationed and electricity is unreliable at best, the colonists also have to contend with mysterious disappearances - the records of which are kept secret by the state - and regular meteor shower attacks. In an attempt to calm the remaining population, their original leader, currently thought to be dead, placed the colony under martial law. And as events play out, the colonists move further toward anarchy.

The paranoia and propaganda that overtakes Frontios is very much in line with the fear of Communism, and the colony's second-in-command, Chief Orderly Brazen, has a very McCarthy-like approach to dealing with outsiders and dissenters. He distrusts everyone and automatically assumes the colony is under attack, immediately labeling the Doctor, Tegan and Turlough as enemy spies (only relenting when the

Doctor saves the life of the new colony leader).

Instead of addressing the problems of martial law or discovering the origins of the meteor showers, the Doctor initially treats Frontios like a vacation from all of his adventures - his primary goal is to tend to the sick and do odd jobs. He fears that anything more would invite the displeasure of the Time Lords. It's only because the TARDIS disappears that the Doctor is around long enough to follow Turlough down below the surface, into the realm of the burrowing Tractators. The Gravis, the Tractators' leader, is the Stalin-like villain in this Cold War play. He not only uses the kidnapped humans to power his machinery, but his fellow Tractators are unquestioning followers with no discernible personalities of their own. The Gravis plans on conquering the galaxy with both the Tractators' gravity-controlling powers and their ability to spread their influence just by breeding, the end result being a display of technological prowess and the "power of the people" through sheer numbers.

The Doctor moonlights as a Tractator sympathizer when dealing with the Gravis, and thus ends the Gravis' control of the Tractators and his plan to convert/kill the remaining humans. Arguably, he's somewhat successful as a secret agent - at least, long enough to fool the Gravis into getting back the TARDIS, and maroon him to break his control over the Tractators and end the assault on Frontios. However, this Cold War role isn't one that the fifth Doctor takes to naturally; while the Doctor "wins" in the end, the Gravis sees through the Doctor's bad subterfuge. Once back in the TARDIS, the Doctor's innate passivity comes back into play, along with his fear of violating the laws of time, so he and his companions leave Frontios behind.

No story brings out this kind-hearted Doctor's passive nature as much as his final stand, *The Caves of Androzani*. He and Peri land on Androzani Minor and become the innocent bystanders of a stand-off between military forces from Androzani Major and the scientist Sharaz Jek and his small army of androids. Meanwhile, the greedy capitalist Trau Morgus has been exploiting the Androzani workforce for the benefit of his corporation (the Sirius Conglomerate). He'll stop at nothing to contain and end the rebellion on Androzani Minor - if for no other reason than the vendetta that exists between himself and Jek as a result of a business betrayal. Despite being only a corporate head, Morgus' power extends into the highest echelons of the Androzani military-industrial complex; it's easy to see this as a parallel to the government contracts awarded to so many corporations in the 1980s. In the Al-Yamamah arms deal, for example, the UK government received 600,000 barrels of oil from Saudi Arabia in exchange for British Aerospace airplanes, making the private company £43 billion in 20 years while British citizens suffered a recession. Like the citizens of the UK, the people of Androzani also suffer recessions and hardships while Morgus and his conglomerate prosper. It's possible that Thatcher's own battles with the National Union of Mineworkers over cutbacks and closures loomed heavily in the minds of writer Robert Holmes and script editor Eric Saward as they crafted this tragic, operatic and far-reaching story.

Peri and the Doctor literally stumble into the middle of the conflict over the life-extending substance called spectrox, and start off their journey by accidently poisoning themselves with the miracle-drug in its unrefined state. Morgus and Jek become the micro-drama playing out the great macro-drama for control of Androzani Major and Minor and, ultimately, capitalist control of spectrox. Both Morgus' "greed is good" stance and Jek's union rebellion look equally damaging and unappealing to an audience cheering for Peri and the Doctor to live.

Morgus and Jek's battle for power turns into a zero sum fight to the death. As Androzani Minor is wracked by huge mud bursts, the surviving soldiers and Jek's androids are presumably plunged into chaos. With Jek gone, the supplies of spectrox will most likely resume, a triumph for the Cold War military industrial complex and its corruptions. If the Doctor influenced this outcome, it's only by virtue of people (such as Morgus and Jek) once again assuming, wrongly, that he is an enemy agent. Ultimately, it is an outcome that even the Doctor cannot fix.

Finally, with Peri in his arms, the Doctor staggers back to the TARDIS, paralysis overtaking his body. They barely make it inside the Ship before boiling mud bursts forth in an apocalyptic moment. But the Doctor - who failed to help anyone on Androzani - also loses his own life. In his final act of kindness, he gives Peri the remaining antidote for the spectrox poisoning affecting them both before he succumbs and begins his regeneration.

The Caves of Androzani says goodbye to the nice Doctor. The Doctor who ends up stuck in the Cold War. He doesn't see himself as a god, only as a powerful weapon he struggled against releasing; his writers never could make him fix the 1980s, no more than they could themselves.

Those of us looking at this story from outside the early 1980s know there's a world beyond the Cold War. Superpowers don't stay superpowered forever. We've seen great nations crumble and the Berlin Wall fall. In a perfect world, the Doctor would have been able to see a solution to the problem of two sides locked in battle with no end in sight except annihilation. But the fifth Doctor has no plan. He doesn't know how to heal the world(s) or take on McCarthyism or end corporate greed. And, unlike his other incarnations, the fifth Doctor lacks the arrogance to even pull off an attempt.

The fifth Doctor can't see beyond the sadness of power struggles that crush and kill. He can't save the world any more than he can save himself. He resorts to shooting Daleks, letting the Master die, and creating weapons of mass destruction as a last resort. He lives in a world of "acceptable losses," and it takes too much of a toll on his spirit. In *The Caves of Androzani,* his death is inevitable. He's been pushed to the edge of what his kind nature will tolerate.

Perhaps, like the people the fifth Doctor couldn't save, he also wants out. His sweetness couldn't keep Tegan traveling with him once she becomes overwhelmed by the horror and death in *Resurrection of the Daleks,* or let him "return home a bit of a hero" as Turlough does in *Planet of Fire,* or resoundingly save the last of humanity in *Frontios.* So many of Season Twenty-One's stories see people, towns and worlds ripped apart by villains and issues that represent 1980s Cold War politics and dramas. In the very end, the sweet Doctor can only save one person - Peri - before he regenerates into the sixth Doctor. The Doctor who would knock down the Berlin Wall without a thought.

Waiting for the Doctor: The Women of Series Five

Seanan McGuire watches too much television, which does not explain how she also writes three books a year (as two different people, no less), dozens of short stories and endless blog posts. It has been posited that she may be a Time Lady herself, or possibly an alien pod plant. Both seem equally likely. McGuire has been nominated for a variety of genre awards, and won the 2010 Campbell Award for Best New Writer. She lives on the West Coast with three bonsai Yeti she pretends are cats, a great many books, and an assortment of deeply creepy toys. *Doctor Who* has now been her favorite show for over 30 years, even if she no longer thinks it's actually a documentary. McGuire is currently the author of two ongoing urban fantasy series published by DAW Books, and writes science fiction medical thrillers as Mira Grant for Orbit. Again, she doesn't sleep. And this is why.

> "You wanted to come 14 years ago. What happened?"
> "I grew up."
> "Don't worry. I'll soon fix that."
>
> —The Doctor and Amy Pond, *The Eleventh Hour*

We first meet the newest Doctor - number eleven, played by Matt Smith - when his out-of-control TARDIS goes whizzing through the sky over London, slamming into things and generally presenting a hazard to life and limb. Meanwhile, Amelia Pond, a seven-year-old Scottish girl living with her aunt in the small English village of Leadworth, is praying to Santa Claus for a solution to the crack in her wall.

Santa may not be involved, but someone must hear the prayers of lonely little girls, because there's a great crashing from her garden, and Amelia rushes outside to find a strange, raggedy man in a big blue box waiting for her, like the best Christmas present ever left without a card. He is, he tells her, the Doctor, and he needs her help as much as she needs his. By the end of that first encounter, he has managed to change her life forever, and he doesn't even seem to notice. He tells her to pack her bags; he promises to come right back as he dives into his big blue box and disappears. The last we see of young Amelia Pond is that of her sitting in the garden, eternally hopeful, waiting for the Doctor to come back to her.

The story of the women of Series Five is an old one, as old as Penelope and Odysseus. It is a story of waiting. Amelia Pond dies waiting, and is replaced by Amy Pond, who grew up understanding one thing above all else: you can't count on magic. It comes and goes as it pleases, and when you need it most of all, it always lets you down.

Amy Pond is not only defined by her wait, she is created by it. Without the Doctor's intervention, Amelia would not have started to wait; would not have been replaced by a version of herself who knew nothing *but* the waiting. Amy Pond is brave and strong and loyal and true. All of these are good things. She is also, eternally, waiting. By the time her "raggedy Doctor" makes it back to her, 12 years have passed; a little girl has waited her way into womanhood, creating a person who does not know or understand a life not lived anticipating some event that has, as yet, failed to happen.

To his credit, the Doctor seems to realize that what he did to Amy, however accidentally, was wrong, and he does his best to make it up to her, taking her on an adventure through what he describes - in typical Time Lord fashion - as "all of time and space." By the end of the first episode of Series Five (*The Eleventh Hour*), it seems as if Amy's waiting is at an end. The rest of the series, however, proves this to be an illusion; Amy is still waiting. Amy is always and forever waiting, although what she is waiting for takes some time to become truly apparent.

The final scenes of *The Eleventh Hour* establish that the TARDIS is still malfunctioning, enough so that five minutes for the Doctor is another two years spent waiting for Amy Pond. She goes with him anyway, and we see her wedding dress hanging on the closet door. Amy will spend the majority of Series Five waiting for her wedding to arrive. Whether she anticipates or dreads it, she's still waiting for it.

As is the current tradition for new companions, the first place the Doctor takes Amy is the future - a place she could never have reached without him. Once there, we meet one of the more interesting women of Series Five: Liz Ten, the reigning monarch of *Starship UK*. Liz Ten believes herself to have been on the throne for a fairly short time, and has been waiting for someone to arrive and help her unravel the secrets of her kingdom. Liz Ten's characterization is reasonably scant. We know that she lives in an obscure corner of her own palace; we know that she is smart enough to have begun piecing together the truth behind the ship's façade; we know that she goes armed, everywhere, and is willing to shoot her own Smilers if necessary. (Liz Ten is Queen of the United

Kingdom. The United Kingdom is now *Starship UK*. The Smilers are thus her property, and she can shoot them if she damn well wants to. It's good to be the Queen.)

Liz Ten is a woman bound by her own duties - she can't free the star whale without destroying her people - but also bound by her own morality. Time and again, she discovers that there is a secret at the heart of her nation, and time and again, she tracks it to the point of being forced to choose between freedom and survival. Liz Ten is waiting for a miracle. That doesn't mean she's willing to endanger her subjects to get it. In fact, the circuitous nature of her personal journey can be seen as a form of time travel - didn't find the answer this time? Well, start over. It's okay. I can wait.

(Interestingly, it is Amy Pond, and not the Doctor, who brings Liz Ten's long wait to an ending. For a girl who spends the majority of her time waiting for something to happen, Amy does a lot to end the waits of others.)

The next major female to be encountered during Series Five is, in her way, as central as Amy herself: River Song, originally introduced in Series Four in *Silence in the Library.* As River herself might say, "Spoilers!", but for purposes of discussing Series Five, I must assume that the reader has seen Series Four. So: in her very first appearance River - who is encountering the Doctor for the last time even as he is meeting her for the first time - dies. She sacrifices her life to save his and, presumably, to preserve the timeline the two of them will eventually be able to share together. That's the problem with living in reverse. Eventually, you have to say goodbye if you want hello to be possible.

The River we encounter in *The Time of Angels* is not the River from Series Four; that River is in her future, and in the Doctor's past. This River is brash and cocky, seeming utterly certain of her place in the world. This River is not yet a Professor, and certainly isn't leading any archeological expeditions. Instead, she's a part of a military/ clerical mission intended to contain the last of the Weeping Angels. And she, like all the other women of Series Five, is waiting.

In River's case, the wait is at once more concrete and more nebulous. She's waiting for the day when the Doctor doesn't know who she is, because that will be the day that she dies (something she had to know in Series Four, when the Doctor greeted her with confusion, instead of with the recognition she clearly expected). She's waiting for him to come back to her, again and again, until the very last time. If Amy is the Penelope of this *Odyssey,* River is the Circe - wiser than she seems, bound by her own strange limitations. She can't tell the Doctor what is coming - "spoilers" again, something she is severely adverse to, as changing the Doctor's future would change her past.

But she knows that one day, the Doctor will discover who she really is, changing their relationship forever. She knows that one day, he will reach the point where he leaves her. Maybe worse, she knows that one day, he will meet her for the first time, and, whether she likes it or not, *she* will have to leave *him*. Most of the Doctor's companions have the luxury of going through their adventures without knowing when they're going to end. River knows exactly when it will end, for him; the only question is when it will end for her. She is waiting, eternally, for time to run out.

In some ways, River's story is the great tragedy of Series Five. There is a measure of hopelessness in her acts, as if she can see time running out between them. She can't know exactly when her death will come - spoilers! - but if the Doctor is this uncomfortable around her, it has to be soon. She is, from our perspective as viewers, traveling backward through the series, from death to life to whatever lies ahead of her. Amy waited for her life to begin. River is waiting for hers to come crashing to an end.

Not all the women of Series Five are heroes, or human. *The Vampires of Venice* introduces us to Signora Calvierri, the last female of her species, who is determined to preserve her race at all costs. She is, perhaps, the exception to the theme of woman-as-waiting: while she's waiting for the day that her girls will be ready to go into the water, she's also taking immediate and concrete action to bring that day about. For her, humanity is only worth what it can provide in nourishment and in fresh genetic stock. To this end, she has opened an exclusive school for young ladies... and that is where the waiting comes in. The young women who are entrusted to the Signora's care are waiting for a way out of their lives, trapped in a time and culture that limits their opportunities for advancement.

We deal most specifically with Isabella, one of the Signora's students, who is enrolled in the school by her father. He's trying to supply her with a better life. Instead, he supplies her with a grisly death. Isabella is the only one of the Signora's girls who doesn't seem to embrace her transformation into a new, utterly inhuman species - she fights back, she struggles, and she dies for her trouble. All of Signora Calvierri's girls die, as does the Signora herself. In an odd twist on the waiting which haunts the women of Series Five, it is the males of her species who must wait, forever, for wives who will never come.

Continuing on from Venice to the modern day, we arrive at *The Hungry Earth,* where we meet Alaya. She, too, has been waiting, but her wait is for the day when her people, the Silurians, can rise from their slumber beneath the earth and reclaim their world from the mammals that have infested it. It's easy to view her as an absolute villain - she's planning to kill all the humans, after all, and our sympathies generally lie with humanity. There's even a human woman to balance her: Ambrose, a faithful wife and loving mother who just wants what's best for her family.

What we may forget is that Alaya also wants what's best for *her* family. She wants them to come out of the dark, back into the light where they belong. She wants her sister, and their descendants, to walk on the surface of the world without fear. It's not that bad of a goal. Alaya is a hero in her own story; it's just that her story happens to intersect with one that casts her as the villain.

We'll get back to the human women of this installment in a moment. First, I want to contrast Alaya with her sister, Eldane. Both of them acknowledge that they have been waiting for the time when they could return to the surface. Eldane takes the more patient approach, being willing to wait until such a time as humanity is ready to learn about sharing. Alaya wants what she wants, and she wants it now. Alaya pays for her unwillingness to wait with her death. That, too, is a theme. While there are very few female deaths in Series Five, outside of *The Vampires of Venice,* all of them have a common veneer of impatience. The women who die are the ones who were not willing to wait until the time arrived for their stories to be told. Eldane chooses patience, and is thus able to live on with the others of her species, waiting for the day when the Silurians can rise.

Wait, and be rewarded. Penelope waited, and was rewarded with the return of her husband. Amy Pond waited, and was rewarded with the return of her Doctor. Even River waited and was rewarded; when the time of her death comes, the Doctor will be there to save her for the first time one last time. Only the impatient fall.

Sophie, in *The Lodger,* may be the ultimate expression of waiting being treated as superior to impatience in Series Five. As long as she was waiting for the man she loved to realize her affections, she was safe, protected by her own stasis. As soon as she began to move past her wait, to explore her own ideas of what she wanted to become, her life was put into danger. It took a return to her original goal - to the thing she had been waiting for in the first place - for her to be safe again. Sophie's story is a short one, encompassing only a single episode, but it illustrates the themes that run through the women of Series Five very clearly. Wait, or die. Wait, or be unmade.

Wait, because one day, the war will end, and Odysseus will come back to you.

The series finale, *The Pandorica Opens/The Big Bang,* brings the waiting to a new extreme as Amy Pond literally waits for centuries to bridge the two episodes and bring everything home. She is, and always will be, the girl who waited. River waits for rescue in the TARDIS; Amy waits for herself to free her from the Pandorica; Penelope and Circe, each on her own island, each hoping that this time, Odysseus will make it back to them before time runs out. Both of them wait faithfully, and carry out the terms of their positions without flinching away from what this will require. Both of them are rewarded with survival. Only the impatient die.

Amy Pond, the girl who waited, finally gets married in the series finale - the event she has been waiting for since the first episode. But this is an Amy who is closer to Amelia, who never sat in the garden waiting for a man in a funny blue box to carry her away through space and time. She is waiting, at the end, to remember what she's lost, what she traded for the safety of a white dress and a golden ring. Once again, Amelia has to be buried, has to be replaced by Amy, if she wants her wait to be worthwhile. To have the Doctor back, she has to have everything back. There is always a price at the end of a journey.

To Amy's credit - and I love Amy as a companion, she's one of my favorites - once her wait is over, she grabs her new husband and runs for the TARDIS like a bat out of hell, ready to find a new adventure, and a new purpose. But that is another series, and that story is outside my reach.

A Christmas Carol is technically an episode of Series Six, but in terms of both production order and theme, this Dickens-inspired fable belongs more with Series Five, and so I have treated it accordingly. This tale is half *Doctor Who* adventure, and half fairy tale, complete with singing fog and a beautiful girl in a coffin made of glass. Her name is Abigail. To hold with the *Odyssey* comparisons I have been drawing throughout this series, she is the Calypso of the story - captive on her island, knowing from the beginning that she will be unable to stay with the man she loves, no matter how much he loves her. (To be clear, she's the only one whose Odysseus figure is a man other than the Doctor - her romantic affections are given to Kazran - but as she, like Amy and River, spends some time as a companion, she is a valid entry into this particular triptych.)

Unlike the original Calypso, Abigail is all-too-mortal, and is already dying when we first meet her. Abigail is waiting for the end. When given the opportunity to prevent it - either by demanding to be re-frozen as soon as the Doctor thaws her, or by simply saying "I'm sorry, Doctor, I don't mean to be a bother, but you have a magic box that travels through space and time... do you think it could travel me to a hospital? If it's not too much trouble?" - she refuses the chance, choosing to continue her wait. She is the only woman of Series Five whose waiting is guaranteed to bring about her death, rather than delaying or preventing it... unless you choose to consider the years she spends frozen as the thing that she is really waiting for. Calypso is immortal as long as she remains on her island. Abigail is immortal as long as she stays frozen in her box.

Abigail is faithful. She is patient. She is the ideal of the woman in waiting, bound to react only when the men in her life call to her - and because Amy spends the episode in peril, outside the main story, Abigail only *has* men in her life. The Doctor and Kazran are her world, the only things she has to wait for. She waits until they choose to save her, and when the time comes that there is no more salvation, she goes willingly.

The female characters of Series Five are diverse. They are strong and they are weak, they are deep and they are shallow, they are flawed in a dozen different ways - they're people, which is what I always hope for in a fully-realized female character. But they are unified in their loyalty, in their faithful wait for something they may not even understand, and in the price they pay to bring that wait to an end.

They're all waiting.

> "We're all stories, in the end. Just make it a good one, eh? Because it was, you know, it was the best: a daft old man, who stole a magic box and ran away. Did I ever tell you I stole it? Well, I borrowed it; I was always going to take it back. Oh, that box, Amy, you'll dream about that box. It'll never leave you. Big and little at the same time, brand-new and ancient, and the bluest blue, ever. And the times we had, eh? Would've had. Never had. In your dreams, they'll still be there. The Doctor and Amy Pond, and the days that never came."
>
> —The Doctor to Amy Pond, *The Big Bang*

Timing Malfunction: Television Movie + the BBC Eighth Doctor Novels = a Respectable Series

Kelly Hale is the author of several short stories, a play, some overwrought poetry, a bunch of fanfiction, a co-authored TV tie-in novel of the *Doctor Who* variety (*Grimm Reality*), and her own book, *Erasing Sherlock*, that was published by Mad Norwegian Press as part of its *Faction Paradox* range, then languished out of print for two years, and is now available on Amazon Kindle. She lives in a crazy little place called Stumptown - jewel of the Pacific Northwest - where the streets are paved with espresso beans and the garbage recycles itself. She used to fantasize about doing the sex with vampires, Time Lords, Vulcans, etceteras. Now she fantasizes about making them a nice bowl of soup.

Doctor Who - The Movie was my gateway drug into the world of *Doctor Who*. Oh, I had dabbled in the eighties of course, like many others, stoned on a Saturday afternoon watching Tom Baker's antics on the local PBS. ("Oh my god, he's a Time Lord? What's a Time Lord?") Years later, when I saw that a new *Doctor Who* movie was going to be on the Fox network, I was enthusiastic. Fox had co-opted British television many times already. It seemed like the perfect fit and a perfect time to re-launch an iconic British show for an American audience.

Americans had their own quirky cult hits by this time. *Twin Peaks. The Simpsons. The X-Files. Buffy the Vampire Slayer* was just around the corner. All of these sly, hip shows, actively engaging us emotionally, intellectually and culturally. Shows that demanded our attention and got it. A *Doctor Who* reboot was favorably positioned to tick all the right boxes for a new young audience, and still retain the flavor and appeal of the original.

I made sure I was home on the evening it first aired, all settled in with popcorn and a glass of wine, for what I hoped, nay - *assumed* - would be the start of a brand new television obsession.

As we know, that did not happen. I mean, the obsession happened, but not right away, and certainly not in the way I expected. The movie was intended as a backdoor pilot for a new series, but as I was one of the few people viewing (5.5 million is only a few in America), there would be no new series. Something else happened though. At least for me.

Books.

In 1997, the BBC began publishing a series of Eighth Doctor Adventures novels based on the Doctor in the TV Movie (TVM). They published 73 in all, right up until New *Who* - our current happy obsession - returned to the BBC with Christopher Eccleston as the ninth Doctor. The ninth Doctor was presented to new audiences as having a terrible secret, the full extent of which we don't learn until the series is well under way. That secret has everything to do with what he did in his previous life, the life of the eighth Doctor, that handsome fellow from the TVM. A movie that launched eight years worth of novels and inspired a lengthy series of audio plays is worth a mention, I think.

In 2001, Big Finish released the first of many, *many* audio stories featuring Paul McGann in the role of the eighth Doctor, but I came to the series primarily through the novels. I even co-authored one, *Grimm Reality*, with Simon Bucher-Jones. Despite a long history and huge story arcs, very little of the books and audios have been included in the "canon" since the show returned in 2005. But one vital aspect of New *Who*, a significant motivating force in the show's current mythology, was first established in the Eighth Doctor Adventures novels. It is an event that informs the Doctor's character more than anything else, a connecting thread that weaves the three latest iterations together, a truth that each one cannot escape or avoid - much as any one of them might try. That is the destruction of the Doctor's homeworld Gallifrey and all her people by his own hand. The reasons for it are different in the show than in the novels - much simpler for one thing, but no less effective for the level and depth of emotion this provides the current series. The Doctor is the last of his kind and he is also the cause and the reason. Pretty powerful stuff.

I suspect that part of the reason the BBC wanted to take the publishing rights back from Virgin Publishing (who had a small but avid following of fans for their New Adventures novels featuring the seventh Doctor) was based on the idea (possibly erroneous) that there would be lots more fans clamoring for anything *Who* after the TVM. I have no idea if the book series made money, lost money, or barely broke even, but the reasons for publishing these novels must have had some notion of profit. The fan base was not huge, but included a lot of compulsive "completeists." Seventy-three novels based on a one-off TV Movie is a lot of break-even.

When I first proposed writing about the TVM for the collection you're holding, one of the editors asked, "oh god, why?" I get that reaction a lot from the old school *Doctor Who* fan base. She seemed horrified that anyone would willingly watch it, let alone actually want to write about it. The TVM is often a source of embarrassment, anger, outrage and other hyperbole in online forums. Still, a lot of people loved it - me for one, and Colleen Hillerup (former editor of the Doctor Who Information Network's fanzine *Enlightenment*) for another. She remembers watching the original episodes of *Doctor Who* with her dad back in the sixties and she adored the movie. Like her, there were some fans of the original show who were happy to hand-wave away the half-human references, embrace the romance and the American setting in the hope that a television movie meant their beloved show was making a comeback. But those that hated the movie are still very vocal about how much they hate it, and it's been 16 years since it aired. Fact is, even those people that hate it still watch it. And these same hate-filled fans were also those buying every eighth Doctor novel as soon as it came out. Remember, that number is 73. That's a lot of money for books based on something you hate.

A friend of mine who really really *really* hates the TVM has nevertheless seen it five or six times since it aired in 1996, usually as research for an article or book, but at least once, he admits, just to find something to like about it. "And, for avoidance of any doubt," he tells me, "the reason I hate it is because it's fucking awful." He cites lazy production values, bad script, terrible acting and other stuff that clearly did not bother me as much. Also, I disagree. Not all the production was lazy, not all of the script was bad, and not all of the acting was terrible. In fact, having just watched it again, some of all those things were surprisingly good. Perhaps the problem is: why should it have been *surprising*?

I believe that the revived series, going on seven years now, would not exist as it does without the television movie and the 73 novels it inspired. After all, it was Paul McGann dressed all Victorian gentleman with his steampunk TARDIS and his gleeful enthusiasm that brought the sexy to *Doctor Who* in the first place, a sexy that had not existed before in all the years it was on BBC television.

The Sexy Doctor, How He Came to Be, and Why He is Here to Stay

There was nothing sexy about the Doctor in the old BBC show. He was not written with sexiness in mind. He was written for family viewing. Even when he was engaged to (some might even say "using")

Cameca in *The Aztecs* way back in his first incarnation in the 1960s, he was no Captain Kirk. Later, when played by a sexy young man (29-year-old Peter Davison), he was still not some time and space traveling Lothario. Peter Davison's Doctor was an old man in a young man's body. He was very clear about that acting choice.

Despite years and years of hot young babe companions dressed in miniskirts, kilts, shiny unitards, leather loin cloths and teeny bikini tops, the Doctor - no matter his incarnation - was not a lecher. He was meant to be your mad, beloved uncle who swept in and took you away for crazy dangerous adventures and returned you safe again to the stodgy homestead. Sadly, that kind of character does not work as easily in a world mindful of sexual predation and molestation, but we still long for a madcap mentor. What we got instead was something the Doctor hadn't been before. When the eighth Doctor, portrayed by an attractive Paul McGann, bared his chest to Dr Grace Holloway's cool stethoscope, a whole new kind of Doctor was born to a whole new generation. He was now officially available for objectification. We were given tacit permission to fantasize about him and we did.

In the BBC's Eighth Doctor Adventures, he was made to bare his chest at least 14 times for a variety of reasons, some only flimsily germane to the plot, many plainly gratuitous. "I think it's safe to say the eighth Doctor was objectified in official channels far more than any previous Doctor. And only Tennant has been *as* objectified - within official channels - as much since," says Mags Halliday, *Who* novelist and official tally keeper of gratuitous torso moments.

In the movie, the Doctor did something else he had never done before - and this is probably the most common reason cited by old school fans for why the TVM sucked - he kissed Dr Grace Holloway full on the mouth. In fact, he initiated said kiss.

A recent *Who* convert (whose first Doctor was Matt Smith's Eleven), was surprised when I told her people were really upset by that kiss when the movie aired. Her surprise wasn't merely because she was accustomed to seeing the Doctor kissing and being kissed either. She had read the scene quite differently. "He just got his memory back! He was happy. He would have kissed anyone who was standing in front of him at that moment." This is a valid reading of the scene, of course. But the Doctor had, prior to that kiss, been mythologized by many fans as an asexual being (despite being a grandfather to Susan).

Now, in the twenty-first century, we are accustomed to a television world that over-sexualizes the life of every character represented, certainly in situation comedies, but pervasively in everything we watch. You might wonder how real people ever get anything done if they spend as much time looking for sex, having sex or lamenting their lack of sex as do characters in television shows (and I'm including reality shows here). An adult character not remotely concerned with all *that* might actually be refreshing - not as a comedic naïf foil for others (Sheldon in *The Big Bang Theory*), but as someone who is fun and funny and smart and clever and *still* not obsessed with, nor actively pursuing, sex. The Doctor is that character. Right now. That doesn't mean he's not sexy. Mr Spock, another cultural icon, was sexy without being remotely interested in sex (most of the time). In the world of fiction and fantasy, there is nothing sexier than a guy who isn't interested.

In New *Who*, sexual overtures towards the Doctor usually catch him by surprise (*New Earth, The Girl in the Fireplace, The Unicorn and the Wasp, Flesh and Stone, Day of the Moon*), and any attempts at seduction are rejected (*Flesh and Stone*) or derided (Ten's response to Lilith in *The Shakespeare Code*: "That doesn't work on me"). A guy who's above all that, whose brain power cannot be overridden or diminished by an ordinary biological need, is, let's face it, kind of inspiring. The Doctor seems to be able to switch it on and off at will without diminishing his mental faculties in the least. Take that, Mr Spock!

Although the Doctor kissing or being kissed is kind of a non-issue since the Christopher Eccleston season, the Doctor's "sexiness" is not and has never - even in New *Who* - been a defining quality of the character. Nevertheless, the eighth Doctor kissing Grace Holloway changed something about the show and the character forever. It resonated in the Eighth Doctor Adventure novels long after and carried over into the new series.

A Brief History of How the TV Came to be Made (as Documented by Committee on Wikipedia)

Executive producer Philip Segal is accused of referencing too much of the original series in detriment to the actual story of the TV Movie. And yet, the friend referenced earlier (Matt Smith is her first Doctor) watched the movie with her daughter and was thrilled with what she described as "that *Teenage Mutant Ninja Turtles* movie vibe"; *Buffy the Vampire Slayer* would use a similar vibe only a year later.

After years of dragging the property around with him to various production companies, Segal got Fox to commission a one-time television movie with the hope of getting a series out of it. Written by

Matthew Jacobs, directed by Geoffrey Sax, the original US transmission was on May 14, 1996. I have nothing but praise for the production design by Richard Hudolin. The sets for the TARDIS were Steampunktacular, evoking a sense of something vast and grand and gothic with flying buttresses and decaying leaves - ancient and alien and yet, somehow, a home.

But *Doctor Who* must also have its whimsy, wit and monsters to pull us in. The longest running science fiction show on television is, after all, about a strange man who travels through all time and space in a blue box that is bigger on the inside than the outside. He has adventures. He saves the Universe. That is his reason for being. He is both the Magician and the Fool in the Tarot cards. He is always about to step off the precipice into the unknown with a little dog nipping at his heels.

A Synopsis, Neither Brief Nor Without Sarcasm

The seventh Doctor (Sylvester McCoy relaxing with a cup of tea, a good book, and listening to the *actual* Ella Fitzgerald, or someone who is supposed to sound like her) is taking the Master's remains back to Gallifrey. The Master, as usual, is not really dead, and gets his essence all up in the temporal bits of the TARDIS, causing a Timing Malfunction. In a universe in which time travel mishaps such as Chronic Hysteresis happen, anything called a "timing malfunction" would be terrifying by the very fact of its simplicity.

The TARDIS makes an emergency landing on Earth, in China Town, San Francisco on December 30, 1999. The seventh Doctor steps out into a hail of bullets. Down he goes. All the gang members flee except one, Chang Lee, who calls an ambulance. The Master (who at this point resembles a liquid mercury snake) manages to get into the sleeve of a coat belonging to the EMT, Bruce, played by Eric Roberts.

Meanwhile, Dr Grace Holloway and her non-speaking-part boyfriend are at the opera where we are treated not only to an aria, but a close-up of a single, glistening glycerin tear on Dr Holloway's cheek, so moved is she by great culture. Grace is a renowned heart surgeon on call that night. She rushes down the corridors of the hospital in her beautiful blue ball gown, her bosoms heaving. We are forced to listen to more of *Madame Butterfly* as she flounders around in the Doctor's chest. He has already begged her not to operate. He has begged the nurses and attending not to sedate him. But they do and she does and they kill him. Dead. He gets a toe tag and trip to the morgue freezer.

Down in the morgue, attendant Pete (played by the fabulous Will

Sasso of *MADtv*) witnesses the resurrection of the eighth Doctor. And lo, he appears unto Pete complete with a Jesus-do and matching shroud.

The Master has managed to possess Bruce's body and gets Bruce's wife all hot with his new masterful ways before killing her. Dressed in evil-appropriate leather, he finds Chang Lee and uses him to gain access to the TARDIS. There he discovers that the Doctor is half-human - a previously unknown (to legions of fans anyway) characteristic. (It is one of the aspects of the TVM that the new series showrunners chose to ignore.)

In the hospital sub-basement (where hospitals apparently store abandoned baby dolls and broken mirrors), the Doctor sees his reflection (from many angles due to the broken mirrors) and falls to his knees in anguish, unable to remember who he is. (This scene is pretty over-the-top and is one of the only scenes that actually makes me squirm.) Later, the Doctor seems to have come to terms with the loss of memory as he rifles through the lockers of hospital employees looking for something a little less shroud-y. He rejects his past identity in the form of a multicolored scarf (made famous by Tom Baker as the fourth Doctor) and embraces his moral identity when rejecting the fake Colt 45 that accessorizes the costume he "borrows." Our new Doctor has no qualms about breaking into lockers and stealing clothes, yet finds a gun, even a fake one, objectionable. By this single, seemingly unconscious, decision he establishes himself as "the" Doctor, *our Doctor* - a man of action whose weapons of choice have always been wits and words. In a later scene, when he and Grace try to commandeer a police motorcycle, he threatens to kill *himself* with the cop's gun - like in a Bugs Bunny cartoon.

Because the Doctor is half-human (on his mother's side, always on the mother's side in these things, isn't it?), the Master can use Chang Lee's human retinal pattern to open the Eye of Harmony. I am still not sure if the actual Eye of Harmony was opened or just a link to it. The Eye of Harmony (as established in a fourth Doctor story, *The Deadly Assassin*) is a naked singularity - a black hole - captured by the ancient Time Lord progenitor, Rassilon, for use as a power source. Having used up all his regenerations, the Master intends to use this power source to take over the Doctor's body and live out the remainder of the Doctor's regenerations. I do not presume to know how this works. It is obviously the kind of science so advanced that it looks magical and McGuffin-y.

The Doctor finds Grace Holloway and convinces her to take him home with her (by pulling the probe out of his chest she lost in his body during surgery). She discovers her boyfriend has moved out. Conveniently. She is now officially unattached, so everything that happens after this point, with the kissing and running around and jumping out of windows in the arms of handsome strangers, is all right. He bares his chest to her stethoscope and she discovers two hearts beating in it. He finds a pair of shoes that fit perfectly and also remembers who he is.

But the Master can see what the Doctor sees, and the Doctor freaks out and starts babbling about the end of the world. His reaction causes Grace to flee from him, thinking he's insane. She calls an ambulance and when it shows up, so does the Master. The Doctor and Grace manage to escape, there's a vaguely exciting car chase, and eventually we get to the atomic clock that the Doctor needs to save the world from being sucked into the naked singularity that powers his TARDIS. I think. (This part of the plot is hazy to me, I still don't quite understand how it all works and I *just* watched it. *Again.*) They get the chip or whatever and race off to the TARDIS, but alas the Master has poisoned Grace. Just as they're about to make everything okay, she is possessed by the Master and conks the Doctor on the back of his head.

I thought the scenes in the Cloister Room were pretty cool actually (despite Eric Roberts' entrance as Ming the Merciless). Because the Cloister Room set was awesome and the Doctor hung from the rafters in that weird tortuous device was a little bit breathtaking. It is the kind of scene that gets repeated over and over in the Eighth Doctor Adventures. He just suffered so beautifully and fought so hard here - first with desperate truths, and then with actual physical punching and kicking - that the urge to explore this aspect of his character was hard for writers to resist. Seriously, the eighth Doctor was tortured by the writers in so many ways that it's difficult to count them all up. (Although I'm sure someone has, and has also posted it on the Internet somewhere.)

The Doctor convinces Chang Lee that the Master has lied about everything. The Master kills him. Grace overcomes her possession and manages to "jumpstart the TARDIS." The Master kills her, then tries to kill the Doctor but ends up falling into the Eye of Harmony. Right before the Eye closes up again, it releases some kind of energy that revives both Chang Lee and Grace. Everyone lives. The Master has been defeated - yet again. Chang Lee, gang member with the heart of gold, gets to keep bags of gold. Grace Holloway chooses to stay rather than travel with the Doctor. They kiss farewell (with New Year's fireworks going off overhead) and then he gets back into his TARDIS with his book, his tea and comfy chair ready for new adventures in his brand new body.

Television Movie Plus Eighth Doctor Adventures Equals a Series Worthy of Respect

Despite any missteps, production blunders and over-the-top performance choices as documented above, I believe that any uncertainty or awkwardness in Paul McGann's portrayal of the Doctor would have been eased had he the opportunity to develop the character and make it his own. Fans of the Big Finish audios think he has done just that. Over all, he had a good beginning on television that would only have got better over time. In his brief appearance, he captured the essence of that guy who manipulates Time and Space, the Word and the Will, with effortless ease. As it happened, much of his character was developed between 1997 and 2002 by writers of novels. But these writers began with the template Paul McGann and the television movie laid out for them. Instead of a television series of Eighth Doctor Adventures, we got audio stories and books, lots and lots of books. The back story and essential characterization of our twenty-first century Doctor is drawn from the rich, complex and fraught mythos the many writers of BBC's Eighth Doctor Adventures established for him.

The novel franchise was running out of steam by the time the announcement of a new series came along. It was time for a new Doctor. The eighth Doctor might have been killed off and regenerated in the books, or ceremoniously handed over to Big Finish Productions if the series revival hadn't come along. Happily, we got Christopher Eccleston's ninth Doctor with his PTSD and his death wish; David Tennant's tenth Doctor, charming, fast-talking, and terrifying; and the eleventh Doctor played by Matt Smith, who, despite his youthful appearance, seems to embody a practical and hard-won wisdom. In my humble opinion, they owe it all to Paul McGann, the TV Movie, Big Finish audios and 73 episodes in book form.

Guten Tag, Hitler

Rachel Swirsky holds an MFA from the Iowa Writers Workshop. Her short fiction has appeared in Tor.com, *Subterranean* magazine, *Clarkesworld* and many other venues, and also been nominated for the Hugo Award, the Sturgeon Award, the World Fantasy Award and the Locus Award. In 2011, she won the Nebula Award for best novella. She likes New *Who* a lot. A lot.

The teacher sighs. "Mels..."

A slim teenager wearing a short red-and-white-striped tie over her white button-down stands in front of her high school classroom. She twists her braids as she answers her teacher's question.

"A significant factor in Hitler's rise to power was the fact that the Doctor didn't stop him." [69]

I don't remember the first time I learned that I was Jewish. I don't remember the first time I learned about the Holocaust either. I do remember sitting in an elementary school classroom at age seven or eight, reading a passage in a history book which claimed that the Nazis had thrown Jewish babies into the air like clay pigeons and used them for target practice.

What was just a history lesson to most of the other kids in the room wound a tight coil around my viscera.

"We're not religiously Jewish," I said later to my mom. "So we'd be okay, right?"

(I probably didn't use those words. I was seven or eight.)

"No," Mom informed me. "They thought Jewishness was a taint you couldn't purge."

(She probably didn't use those words. She was speaking off the cuff.)

Of course I've read about many atrocities since then. I've empathized with many victims, those who resembled me and those who didn't. I've tried to come to terms with the knowledge that sometimes the people who resembled me were the ones committing the atrocities,

---

69 Italicized passages taken from *Let's Kill Hitler, Doctor Who* Series Six, 2011. Directed by Richard Senior, written by Steven Moffat.

and that I, as an upper-middle-class woman who lives in the United States, still benefit from many of them.

Nevertheless, that first burr still pricks its way down my limbic system.

A shiver.

It was my ancestors' blood they poured into trenches.

It was my ancestors' flesh they turned into numbers.

They'd have done it to me, too.

Some of them would do it still, if they could.

Mels turns to the Doctor, pulls out her gun, and clicks off the safety.

From off-screen, Amy shouts "Mels!" as the Doctor puts up his hands.

"For God's sake!" shouts Rory; simultaneously, Amy demands, "What are you doing?"

Mels glances over her shoulder. "I need to get out of here now."

The Doctor asks, "Anywhere in particular?"

Mels' arm draws a perfect line toward the Doctor, the barrel of her gun foreshortened as it angles out of the frame. "Let's see. You've got a time machine. I've got a gun. What the hell. Let's kill Hitler."

In "Why There Is No Jewish Narnia," an essay published in the Jewish Review of Books, Michael Weingard asks the following question: "why are there no works of modern fantasy that are profoundly Jewish in the way that, say, *The Lion, the Witch and the Wardrobe* is Christian?"[70]

Although his claim that there are no Jewish equivalents of Narnia proved controversial, one of his proposals struck a chord with me:

> ...there is a further historical reason why twentieth century Jews have not written much fantasy literature, and that is, inevitably, the Holocaust. Its still agonizing historical weight must press prohibitively upon Jewish engagement with the magical and fantastical. It is not that fantasy writers must be innocent naifs. Tolkien and Lewis were deeply influenced in their portrayals of evil by what they knew of twentieth century political barbarity. As Shippey notes, Tolkien especially grapples in his novels more seriously than many supposedly more sophisticated modern literary works with the evils of the twentieth century. Nevertheless, for Jewish writers working after the Holocaust, classical fantasy must have made redemption seem too easy. Certainly, the notion

70 Weingrad, Michael. "Why There Is No Jewish Narnia?". *The Jewish Review of Books*, Spring 2010. www.jewishreviewofbooks.com/ publications/ detail/ why-there-is-no-jewish-narnia

of magic and wizards existing in our own world - as in, for example, the Harry Potter books - becomes all but impossible. (Or at least must raise the question of why Hogwarts, like the FDR administration, never tried to bomb the railroad tracks.)

Jews have actually written a fair amount of fantasy fiction (although whether or not it's "quintessentially Jewish" is another question). Nevertheless, Weingard illuminates a concern that would affect any of the sociological minorities who've experienced historical devastation.

Of course, it's meta-fictionally obvious why the Doctor never bombs the symbolic railroad tracks. *Doctor Who* is presented as a world that could (mostly) coexist with ours, one that (mostly) shares our history.

If, however, one takes the show on its own terms, the question nags.

If there is a force for good in the universe that possesses powers both awe-inspiring and strange, one who like a superhero saves the world on a near-episodic basis, why is our history riddled with tragedies that there's no evidence he even tried to prevent?

The Doctor is usually shown saving small groups (and even then with casualties), but he's also depicted as having the power to influence much larger events. When Donna alters the Doctor's trajectory by failing to *Turn Left*, the whole universe is threatened.

The Doctor can't rewrite fixed points in time - but is every single tragedy a fixed point? Every genocide? Every disaster?

Why hasn't the Doctor tried to kill Hitler before?

"Thank you, whoever you are," Hitler says to the Doctor. "I think you have just saved my life."

The Doctor stares, stricken, a strained expression on his face. "Believe me... it was an accident."

At the end of the scene, Hitler is still alive.

The Doctor has an ambiguous relationship with the concept of normal human lives. On one occasion, he'll shout indignantly, "There is no such thing as an ordinary human!" only to later complain, "I'm stuck. On Earth, like... Like an ordinary person, like a human. How rubbish is that?"

In *Amy's Choice*, the Dream Lord creates a vision in which Amy and Rory live in a small village. Amy is pregnant; Rory is a medical practitioner. On waking, the Doctor calls their vision-lives "a terrible nightmare."

The Doctor doesn't save people from the all-too-real horrors of trenches and machetes. He rescues them from malfunctioning hordes of robots. He brandishes his screwdriver at invading alien forces. He outfoxes futuristic technologies and braves spatial anomalies.

His domain is the stuff of science fiction.

He doesn't stir himself to stop the merely ordinary tragedies that end merely ordinary human lives.

Hitler protests as the Doctor orders Rory to shove him into a cupboard. "But I am the Führer!"

Later, as the onslaught of comic misunderstandings pauses for a moment, Rory frowns. "Is anyone else finding today just a bit difficult? I'm getting a sort of banging in my head."

Amy's got the punch line. "Yeah, I think that's Hitler in the cupboard."

They leave him there, the comic relief, trapped for a televised moment.

A well-known writer once told a friend of mine in workshop that her stories weren't really science fiction. "Real science fiction," he explained, "is about rocket ships. It's about escaping from home. It's not about mothers and kitchens."

Sometimes mothers want to escape, too, but there's no room for them to do so in this formulation. One is either a person who travels on rocket ships or a mother, either a person who cooks in the kitchen or a person who escapes from mundanity.

The new series Doctor, with his alternating veneration and contempt for ordinary human experiences, lives the adventurous, rocket ship life. He's the bodily incarnation of privilege; even when he changes forms, he remains static along the axes of oppression. He's always white, male, able-bodied, cisgendered. When he's shown as possessing romantic attraction, he's captivated by women.

His less-powerful companions are not only ordinary human beings without the ability to manipulate time and space, but also sociological minorities. They experience his power second-hand, at his indulgence. When the Doctor is done with them, they lose their ability to escape. They must return home, to the sphere of women, to pursue lives among mothers and kitchens.

"The old man prefers the company of the young," the Dream Lord says contemptuously, and the Doctor, the man who cannot look at the computer-simulated faces of his companions without guilt, has nothing to say in return.

A miniature man in the eye of a robot leans over to speak into his microphone. "Throughout history, many criminals have gone unpunished in their lifetimes. Time travel has... responsibilities."

In the real world, the outer world, the Doctor laughs. "What? You got yourselves time travel so you decide to punish dead people?"

He doesn't seem to fathom it. Why would anyone punish dead people?

The Doctor doesn't punish. He doesn't even kill. He leaves Hitler alive in the cupboard, thumping to get out.

When I was a child, I never wanted to be the princess. I always wanted to be the queen.

I'd have taken the fairy dust from the magical-gender-change wand if it had been offered to me. I wanted the power that came with men's roles. But I never had a tom boy streak; I was happier imagining myself as a powerful woman. I wanted to straddle the twilight space between femininity and power, the place where one need not choose between kitchens and rocket ships.

From the time that River Song pulled off her helmet in *Silence in the Library*, shaking loose her curls, I was mesmerized. I've always loved Alex Kingston as an actress, but there was more than fine acting to River Song. She's mysterious, powerful, funny, keen-eyed, sharp-witted, charismatic. Like the Doctor, she possesses secrets: the name she was born with, the blue book that's always to hand.

At first I was disappointed that she wasn't a future incarnation of the Doctor, but in some ways what she turned out to be is equally interesting. She's something new - somewhere between Doctor and companion, human but not ordinary, an inhabitant of liminal space.

Like the Doctor, she's allowed to continue adventuring throughout her life. Although the fact that she's serving a prison sentence prevents her from having as much freedom as he does, she's never sent "home" in the way that the companions are, never forced to leave the science fictional world. Her power is inherent rather that contingent; she never loses access to it.

River Song is not the only assay toward diversity in Moffat's *Who*. Mels' transformation into River establishes canonical confirmation that one can trans-racially regenerate. A passing line in Neil Gaiman's *The Doctor's Wife* indicates that Time Lords can change sexes between incarnations. Someday, the Doctor may be something other than what he always has been.

As the companion, even Amy herself presents unconventional feminine possibilities. *Amy's Choice* puts her at the center of the dichotomy between rocket ships and kitchens when the Dream Lord attempts to force her to choose between them, but ultimately, he's revealed to be offering a false choice. Amy's real world is one in which she doesn't need to inhabit either extreme, one where she can both be married to Rory and travel with the Doctor, both have a baby *and* still have adventures.

"Sir, that blue box!" The man in the robot's eye leans over to examine a screen on which a blueprint of a blue police box spins, slowly. "Got a match. We're trying to bag war criminals, we've got the biggest one ever right under our noses. Forget Hitler. We take this one down, the Justice Department will give us the rest of the year off."

He's referring to River Song, the woman who killed the Doctor.

Because if there's any sin more grave than instigating the deaths of eleven million people in camps, it's killing a dude who won't stop wearing a bow tie.

It requires a certain blindness - assisted, though not necessitated, by privilege - to imagine history as a place of adventures where one's biggest concerns are aliens shaped like trash cans.

The Doctor, aided by his skin and sex, masters this nonchalance.

It's Mels - the black teenager - who thinks to question the Doctor's cavalier attitude toward human disasters.

It's River - the supposed psychopath - who wants Hitler dead.

The Nazi commandant, all sleek in leather, extends his gun. "What are you doing here?"

A sly smile spreads across the face of the newly incarnated River Song. "Well, I was on my way to this gay gypsy bar mitzvah for the disabled when I suddenly thought, 'Gosh, the Third Reich's a bit rubbish. I think I'll kill the Führer'."

They open fire. Her grin only widens as she takes the bullets. She spreads her arms. Orange light explodes from her body, hot and bright, tumbling the Nazis to the ground.

Reversing Polarities: The Doctor, the Master, and False Binaries in Season Eight

Amal El-Mohtar is an Ottawa-born Lebanese-Canadian, currently pursuing a PhD in the UK. She is a Nebula Award nominee and a two-time winner of the Rhysling Award for Best Short Poem, as well as the author of *The Honey Month*, a collection of poetry and prose written to the taste of 28 different kinds of honey. Her fiction and poems have appeared in multiple venues online and in print, including *Strange Horizons*, *Apex*, *The Thackery T. Lambshead Cabinet of Curiosities*, *Welcome to Bordertown*, *Stone Telling* and *Mythic Delirium*. She also edits *Goblin Fruit*, an online quarterly dedicated to fantastical poetry. You can find her online at amalelmohtar.com

I first met the Doctor in a small mountain village called Zabbougha, in Lebanon. I was seven years old. My Doctor wore what looked like a crushed velvet jacket in plum purple, sported extravagant lace cuffs that seemed the sartorial echo of his unruly grey curls, and leapt out at me from the cover of a novel titled *Doctor Who and the Planet of the Daleks*, by Terrance Dicks.

I had no idea that *Doctor Who* was a television show. I would continue to have no idea that it was a television show until New *Who* came around. At that point, I was bouncing off the walls with excitement, telling anyone who'd listen that these obscure novels I'd read as a kid - of which they could not possibly have heard - were being made into a show! Wasn't that cool?

I had never read anything like it before. Sentences and images have tangled themselves into my sense-memory. I remember tasting the sour tang of unfamiliar fruit a Spiridon feeds to Jo Grant; I recall feeling the strange, spongy stones that warmed the rebels at night with heat they'd stored during the day. What I remember most clearly, though, is that this book taught me the difference between courage and bravery. Bravery, said the Doctor to a fellow prisoner while they turned out their pockets to see what in their possession might aid them to an escape, was a simple matter of not feeling afraid; courage, on the other hand, was the capacity for doing something in spite of feeling afraid.

It shook me to read that. I felt I'd been taught something very important. Here was a distinction that not even all adults were aware of, but that I, a seven year old girl catching lizards in Zabbougha, now understood. I've had cause to think of it time and again over the last 20 years - every time I've felt afraid, in fact. *You may not be brave,* I would think to myself, before a recital, or an exam, or a transatlantic move, *but here is a chance to be courageous.*

Seeing Christopher Eccleston bring the Doctor to life was something of a paradigm shift for me. I hadn't yet entered into the culture that would teach me to call one incarnation or another *mine,* and am still unsure of how to go about it. I loved the ninth Doctor, loved his accent and his leather jacket and his desire to dance - but I also loved the tenth Doctor, with his enthusiasm and kindness, with his hair and his glasses and his way of stretching the word "well" out over time zones. But is the third Doctor actually my Doctor? The third Doctor, with his air of vague disdain for almost everyone around him, with his red-lined cape and his lace cuffs, his remote-controlled car and propensity for sassing the Brigadier?

Having now watched Season Eight, I am inclined to say yes. The third Doctor is my Doctor, if only because of an offhand remark he made during *The Daemons* that brought everything full circle for me. Separated from UNIT's scientists by a heat barrier, the Doctor has to talk them through the building of a denouement-device; after much benevolently snarky tut-tut-ing on the Doctor's part, the following exchange takes place:

> **The Doctor:** No, man, no. You're trying to channel the entire output of the national power complex through one transistor. Reverse it.
> **Sgt. Osgood:** Reverse what?
> **The Doctor:** Reverse the *polarity*!

There it was. The phrase that I'd spent much of childhood using as the ultimate means to doing the impossible - the phrase which made me the cool science-geek among my cousins whenever we played make-believe. "Oh no," they would exclaim, "the ship's going down, and there's no way off - we're going to crash, *and* we're running out of oxygen! Quick - what are we going to do?"

I would frown. I would poke invisible buttons, twist invisible knobs. "Stand back," I would say, grimly. "We're going to reverse the polarity."

It never occurred to me to wonder what exactly I was reversing the polarity of. Clearly, everything had one. It made perfect sense, intuitively. After all, I knew how magnets worked; I knew they had poles; I knew that reversing poles made them work differently, and thanks to *Planet of the Daleks*, I knew that polarity reversal had a very wide range of applications. It was my very own Moon Tiara Magic at least five years before I watched *Sailor Moon*; my Captain Planet; my Power Ranger Mecha smack-down. Three beautiful words so dear to the third Doctor taught me that when the situation before you is untenable, when it offers you no means of escape or success, change its parameters. Flip it turn-ways. Reverse its polarity. If your requirements are impossible, do something impossible to make them possible. If you've missed the boat on being brave, it's okay - you can still be courageous.

Season Eight is very much a season of reversals. It occurs to me that, in spite of the vast differences in plot, threat and coherence across the stories, reversing polarities is consistently the dynamic by which the Doctor gets things done. After all, everything has a polarity to be reversed; it isn't only the province of gadgetry and magnets. People have poles, and Jon Pertwee's Doctor is constantly flipping them; and in some cases, people are poles themselves, presenting theses and antitheses, binaries that are never so much synthesized as inverted.

In the first story, *Terror of the Autons,* we are introduced to a new companion, Jo Grant, who is initially dismissed by the Doctor on the grounds of not being a scientist like his previous assistant, Liz Shaw. In fact, far from being a scientist, she cheerfully admits that she failed the subject in high school. But Jo quickly shows herself to be fierce, kind and devoted to the Doctor, as well as being far more field-and-action oriented than Liz: she wields a gun, fights like a soldier, quells prison riots, makes friends with charming ease and will not stay where the Doctor tells her to. In fact, in possibly the ultimate reversal where Liz is concerned, Jo saves the world in *The Daemons* not by being clever, but by being irrationally, unreasonably altruistic.

But the most noticeable set of poles (as it were) in Season Eight is, of course, that of the Doctor and the Master.

As an avid watcher of New *Who,* I am used to the show's idea of the Good being created or debated in a tension between Doctor and companion. Doctors Nine, Ten and Eleven share a theme: they are old enough that their patience and compassion are wearing thin, and they need their companions to keep them in touch with, for lack of a better word, their humanity.[71] The ninth Doctor needs Rose to approach a dying Dalek with pity; the tenth Doctor needs Donna to stop him from committing genocide; the eleventh Doctor needs Amy to remind him of his title when he's about to make the Space Whale extinct. But in Season Eight, the Good is instead always posited by the Doctor and opposed by the Master. Where I am used to a story testing the Doctor's limits and convictions, the stories in Season Eight confirm him, time and again, as the moral arbiter of an environment being negatively influenced by the Master.

Just in case we aren't clear on how opposite the Doctor and the Master are, their titles help illustrate it for us. The Doctor wants knowledge for its own sake, to help people, to construct; the Master wants knowledge for power, to command minions, to destroy. There are endless jokes to be made about their titles academically: the Master is bitter that the Doctor completed his dissertation; the Doctor is bogged down in his research while the Master dominates the private sector; the Doctor went on to a PhD, but in fact the Master - according to the Time Lord leprechaun who pops in and out of existence in *Terror of the Autons* - received better grades in the Academy. Their titles also hint at the power dynamic they have with each other: the Master wants explicit control over the Doctor, but in spite of the multiple scenes of bondage that involve him wiggling phallic objects at the Doctor while tying him up, leaning over him while staring intensely into his eyes, or torturing him into a dazed sweat, the Doctor tops from the bottom. He is always resisting, escaping, reasoning and redefining the terms of the scene. If the Master seeks to rule, the Doctor seeks to undermine - and while he doesn't desire the power the Master seeks, the terms of the game they play require the Doctor to, however temporarily, gain power over the Master.

But this dynamic suits the Doctor's preferred problem-solving methods just fine; he almost always succeeds in outwitting the Master by reversing one polarity or another. If the Doctor has been passionately opposing the Master all story, he might reverse his own role and pretend to be as callous and careless as his nemesis, acting for his own gain, as in *The Claws of Axos*. Most often, however - so often that it was satirized in Steven Moffat's *The Curse of Fatal Death* - the Doctor dissuades the

71 Martha is a noteworthy exception to this general pattern, especially in *The Family of Blood*, where she has to forcibly remind the Doctor that he is *not* human. I'd suggest that this has potentially disturbing implications for the treatment of the only TV companion of color, but that's surely the subject of another essay.

Master from pursuing his schemes by holding up a mirror. He repeatedly reverses the Master's self-image, showing him that far from living up to his title, he is the dupe of those who pretend to serve him only as long as he is useful to them.

The simple elegance of a binary and its potential for reversal has its problems, of course. In spite of the Doctor's professed pacifism, you can't use a magic bullet without firing a gun; you can't focus on a binary without ignoring a potential spectrum. Setting the Master up as the wrong to the Doctor's right often distracts our attention from other quite disturbing conflicts where the alignment of their surroundings is concerned.

Colony in Space offers a good case in point. In it, beleaguered humans fleeing an overpopulated Earth are given leave by Earth's government (problematic in and of itself - who governs Earth?) to colonize an uninhabited planet. The planet is, however, inhabited - by green-skinned "primitives" who don't speak, and are conveniently just telepathic enough to understand what's spoken to them without being able to return a reply. They get along well enough until an Evil Mining Corporation (EMC) turns up wanting to exploit the planet's mineral resources, and tries to scare the colonists off through a series of incidents that escalate in violence until they force a confrontation which requires an impartial adjudicator.

Enter the Master, masquerading as adjudicator. The Doctor immediately focuses on him as the most pressing problem to be solved, and the conflict becomes polarized as between EMC and the colonists, debating which of them has more right to the planet. One imagines the primitives quirking non-existent eyebrows at this, in a "Guys? We're still right here" sort of gesture, while the magnanimous, gregarious, world-wandering Doctor, who gives speeches about justice and reason, sees no problem at all with the invasion and colonization of an inhabited planet, so long as the invading colonists are suitably hard-working, earnest, sympathetic folk who aren't working alongside the Master. In fact, in the most wince-inducing possible move to anyone possessed of a social conscience, the colonists can only work the land to their benefit once the indigenous inhabitants commit mass suicide, removing the remnants of underground technology that, as it turns out, were poisoning the planet's soil and preventing crops from growing. The only thing reversed during that denouement was my expectation of something better.

Because I have always known the Doctor as demanding better. The Doctor arrives on scene, finds a problem, and works the impossible to solve it. He appreciates ingenuity and rewards kindness. He asks more questions than he provides answers; he asks people to figure things out rather than tell them what to think. The Doctor who turned out his pockets in a cell in Spiridon is too wise to deal in certainties. Certainties exist to be questioned, challenged and complicated.

Given that, it may at first seem difficult to reconcile Season Eight's wry, patronising, authoritarian sort of Doctor with the nurturing wunderkind of New *Who.* But my Doctor likes things to be complicated, even while he claims they're very simple. And what it comes down to is that the Doctor's third incarnation, *my* Doctor, taught me to look at the world and see more than opposites; he taught me to find ground between them and connect them in order to make something different. Bravery and fear are opposites, but fear is a necessary condition of courage, which is not the opposite of bravery. And I think, ultimately, that what seems like a stark, impossibly reconciled difference between Season Eight and the New *Who* is solved very simply. The Doctor himself contains poles. Everything does, after all. We look at the Doctor, awkward and impossible in a given time and place, old-fashioned, beset by lace cuffs and red-lined capes and jingoism, and we reverse him. We reverse his polarity until he works the way he's supposed to, over and over and over, and makes us better so that we, in turn, can make him better - bravely, courageously, with conviction.

Acknowledgements

An anthology is a complex project that requires many hands, and this book is no exception. In addition to our families and friends who supported us throughout this project, we would like to thank Hazel Bell, Graeme Burk, Jessica Dwyer, Barnaby Edwards, Katrina Griffiths, Simon Guerrier, Kirsty Myles, Rob Shearman, Erik Stadnik and Damian Taylor for all of their help and encouragement. We couldn't have done it without you.

CHiCKS DiG COMiCS
mad norwegian press
#1
EDITED BY
LYNNE M. THOMAS
SIGRID ELLIS

About Time vol. 2: The Unauthorized Guide to *Doctor Who* Seasons 4 to 6... $19.95

About Time vol. 3 (2nd Ed): The Unauthorized Guide to *Doctor Who* Seasons 7 to 11... $29.95

About Time 1: The Unauthorized Guide to *Doctor Who* Seasons 1 to 3, by Lawrence Miles and Tat Wood...$19.95

About Time vol. 4: The Unauthorized Guide to *Doctor Who* Seasons 12 to 17... $19.95

About Time vol. 5: The Unauthorized Guide to *Doctor Who* Seasons 18 to 21... $19.95

About 'About Time'...

In *About Time*, the whole of classic *Doctor Who* is examined through the lens of the real-world social and political changes – as well as ongoing developments in television production – that influenced the series in ways big and small over the course of a generation. Armed with these guidebooks, readers will be able to cast their minds back to 1975, 1982 and other years to best appreciate the series' content and character.

Running a cumulative length of 1.7 million words, the six *About Time* volumes examine nearly every conceivable topic about *Doctor Who*, and include a breathtaking myriad of essays on topics ranging from the philosophical ("How Buddhist is This Series?") to the scientific ("Why are Elements so Weird in Space?") to the fannish ("Did They Think We'd Buy Just Any Old Crap?") to the historical ("Why Couldn't They Just Have Spent More Money?") to the whimsical ("Was There Any Hanky-Panky in the TARDIS?") and to the slightly bizarre ("What Do Daleks Eat?").

www.madnorwegian.com

wanting to believe

a critical guide to ***The X-Files***, *Millennium* & *The Lone Gunmen*

Out Now...

In "Wanting to Believe," acclaimed science-fiction writer Robert Shearman critiques and examines the whole of Chris Carter's "X-Files" universe, including the spin-off series "Millennium" and "The Lone Gunman." As such, this is one of, if not the only, guide of its kind to cover all 13 seasons of Carter's masterwork.

With this unauthorized guidebook, "X-Files" fans will be able to reevaluate Carter's TV series with Shearman (World Fantasy Award winner, Hugo Award nominee, renowned playwright, writer on the new "Doctor Who" series) as he diligently comments upon all 282 episodes (and the two "X-Files" motion pictures) of this property, which was one of the most notable TV works of the 1990s - and is every bit as enjoyable today.

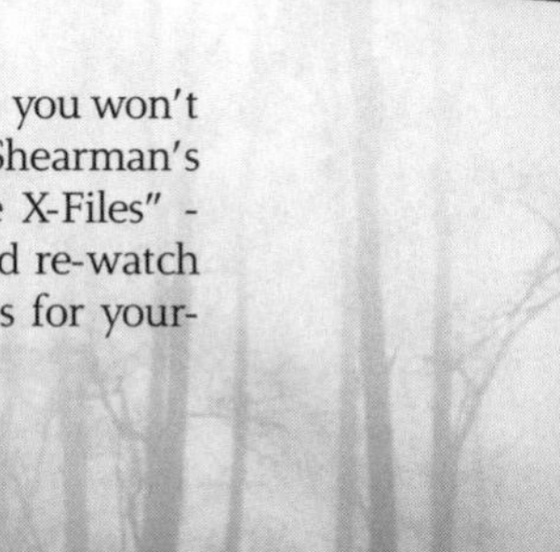

Armed with "Wanting to Believe," you won't just find yourself mulling over Shearman's insights and opinions about "The X-Files" - you'll want to pull your DVDs and re-watch this amazing and impressive series for yourself.

ISBN: 0-9759446-9-X
Retail Price: $19.95

www.madnorwegian.com

mad norwegian press

1150 46th St. Des Moines, IA 50311 madnorwegian@gmail.com

Out Now... In Whedonistas, a host of award-winning female writers and fans come together to celebrate the works of Joss Whedon (Buffy the Vampire Slayer, Angel, Firefly, Dollhouse, Doctor Horrible's Sing-Along Blog).

Contributors include Sharon Shinn ("Samaria" series), Emma Bull (Territory), Jeanne Stein (the Anna Strong Chronicles), Nancy Holder (October Rain), Elizabeth Bear (Chill), Seanan McGuire (October Daye series), Catherynne M. Valente (Palimpsest), Maria Lima (Blood Lines), Jackie Kessler (Black and White), Sarah Monette (Corambis), Mariah Huehner (IDW Comics) and Lyda Morehouse (AngeLINK Series). Also featured is an exclusive interview with television writer and producer Jane Espenson, and Juliet Landau ("Drusilla").

ISBN: 978-1935234104
MSRP: 14.95

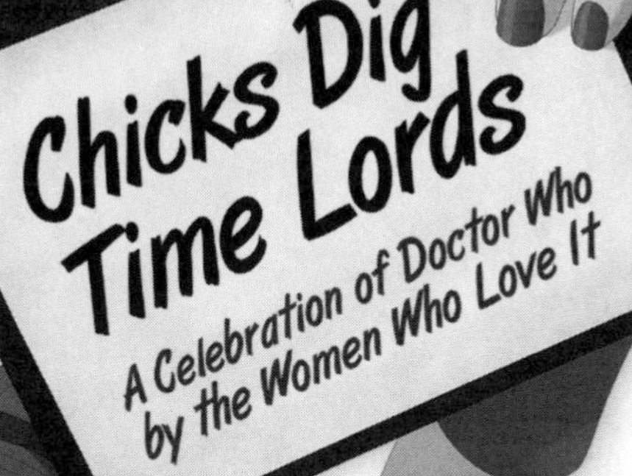

This book has ***three*** *settings!*

OUT NOW... In *Chicks Digs Time Lords*, a host of award-winning female novelists, academics and actresses come together to celebrate the phenomenon that is *Doctor Who*, discuss their inventive involvement with the show's fandom and examine why they adore the series.

These essays will delight male and female readers alike by delving into the extraordinary aspects of being a female *Doctor Who* enthusiast. Contributors include Carole Barrowman (*Anything Goes*), Elizabeth Bear (the Jenny Casey trilogy), Lisa Bowerman (Bernice Summerfield), Jackie Jenkins (*Doctor Who Magazine*), Mary Robinette Kowal (*Shades of Milk and Honey*), Jody Lynn Nye (Mythology series), Kate Orman (*Seeing I*), Lloyd Rose (*Camera Obscura*) and Catherynne M. Valente (*The Orphan's Tales*).

Also featured: a comic from the "Torchwood Babiez" creators, and interviews with *Doctor Who* companions India Fisher (Charley) and Sophie Aldred (Ace).

ISBN: 978-1935234043 **MSRP:** 14.95

www.madnorwegian.com

1150 46th St, Des Moines, IA 50311 . madnorwegian@gmail.com

Credits

Publisher / Editor-in-Chief
Lars Pearson

Design Manager / Senior Editor
Christa Dickson

Associate Editor
Joshua Wilson

Designer (Unravel)
Matt Dirkx

The publisher wishes to thank...
A deeply appreciated thank you to Deb and Liz, for the amount that they put themselves to the sword to make this book happen. Editors are inevitably on the front line in such undertakings, and their talent and commitment was evident through the whole process. Thanks also to Christa Dickson (my favorite chick who digs Gallifreyans); Katy Shuttleworth, whose covers are reliably awesome; Jeremy Bement; Matt Dirkx; Shawne Kleckner; Robert Smith?; Josh Wilson; and that nice lady who sends me newspaper articles.

1150 46th Street
Des Moines, Iowa 50311
madnorwegian@gmail.com
www.madnorwegian.com

And please join the Mad Norwegian Press group on Facebook!